Acclaim for *Hill Country*

"Hill Country is a book that will live forever in the mind and soul of everyone who reads it. It is a story of people who lived extraordinary lives in an extraordinary time in an extraordinary world called the hill country of Texas. Janice Woods Windle has told the story beautifully, artfully, deliciously."

—Jim Lehrer

"Hill Country is a love story, history, family drama, and chronicle of women's struggles. . . . It's a pleasure to read about a real woman who wouldn't let her gender keep her down."

—Jane Sumner, *The Dallas Morning News*

"Hill Country majestically spans about a century of Texas history, providing detailed political analysis along with the dramatic presentation of characters' lives."

—Paula Friedman, *Dayton Daily News*

"With detailed historical research and interviews with family and friends, Windle brings her grandmother's world to life, the world of Central Texas and the untamed Texas hill country. . . . The story is recorded in the history books, but Windle's page-turning, fiction-based-on-fact account of Laura's life adds drama to the story of Texas hill country and its peoples' roles in shaping America."

—Linda Heinzman, *Florida Times-Union*

"Windle delivers action, romance, suspense and political intrigue against an authentic historical backdrop."

—*The Tampa Tribune*

"History is at its best in *Hill Country,* the story of pioneers and politics in the Texas hill country. . . . [Windle] has turned the history of her own family into a historical novel that sheds new light on our nation."

—Ann Byle, *The Grand Rapids Press*

Hill Country

A NOVEL

JANICE WOODS WINDLE

SCRIBNER PAPERBACK FICTION
Published by Simon & Schuster
New York London Toronto Sydney Singapore

SCRIBNER PAPERBACK FICTION
Simon & Schuster, Inc.
Rockefeller Center
1230 Avenue of the Americas
New York, NY 10020

First Scribner Paperback Fiction edition 2000
Published by arrangement with Longstreet Press

Manufactured in the United States of America

10   9   8   7   6   5   4   3   2   1

Library of Congress Cataloging-in-Publication Data
Windle, Janice Woods.
Hill country : a novel / Janice Woods Windle.
p.   cm.
1. Woods, Laura Matilda Hoge, d. 1966—Fiction. 2. Texas Hill Country (Tex.)—Fiction. 3. Married women—Texas—Fiction. 4. Ranch life—Texas—Fiction. I. Title.
PS3573.I517 H55 2000
813'.54—dc21   99-088015

ISBN 0-684-86605-6

To all the children and descendants
of the Hoge, Woods, and Johnson families,
and to the good people of the Hill Country,
I dedicate this book.

"Good people will be remembered as a blessing . . ."
—Proverbs 10:7

Colonel-Doctor Peter Cavanaugh Woods
m. (1846)
Georgia Virginia Lawshe

William Pinckney
Sarah Cherokee
Carolina Davidson (Carrie)
Georgia Virginia (Little Sweet)

Peter Cavanaugh ————————————————————————
[m. Laura Matilda Hoge 1890]

Jeffersonia Ellen
Frank Lawshe
Mary Lois

Eugene Cavanaugh
Maxey Charles
Winifred Davis
Leonora (Nona)
Mattie King

Wilton George ————————————
[m. Virginia King Bergfeld 1936]

Peter Clifford

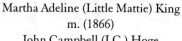

Martha Adeline (Little Mattie) King
m. (1866)
John Campbell (J.C.) Hoge

Charles Hugh
John Carlton
William Henry

Laura Matilda
[m. Peter Cavanaugh Woods 1890]

Lucy Sarah
Marguerite Jane
James Monroe
Ella Cyrene
Sidney Lee
Clay

Virginia King Bergfeld
[m. Wilton George Woods 1936]

Janice King Woods ———— Wayne Ellsworth Windle, Jr.
[m. Wayne Ellsworth Windle, Jr. 1958]   *[m. Janice King Woods 1958]*

The Texas

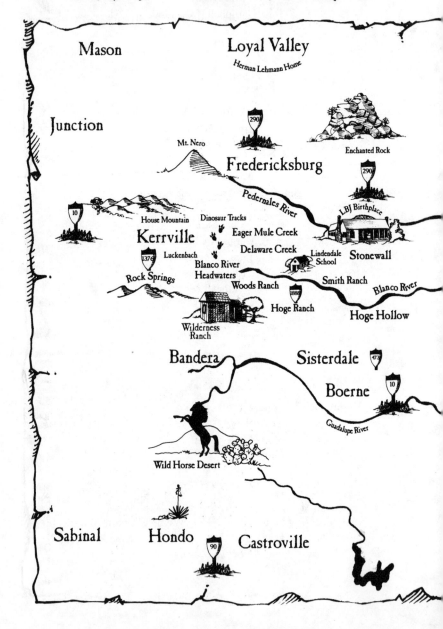

Mason

Loyal Valley

Herman Lehmann Home

Junction

290

Mt. Nero

Fredericksburg

Enchanted Rock

290

Pedernales River

10

LBJ Birthplace

House Mountain

Dinosaur Tracks

Eager Mule Creek

Kerrville

Delaware Creek

137

Luckenbach

Lindendale School

Stonewall

Blanco River Headwaters

Rock Springs

Woods Ranch

Smith Ranch

Blanco River

1888

Hoge Ranch

Hoge Hollow

Wilderness Ranch

Bandera

Sisterdale

473

Boerne

10

Guadalupe River

Wild Horse Desert

Sabinal

Hondo

90

Castroville

Hill Country

Llano

Marble Falls

Monument Hills

Buffalo Peak

Glasscock
Circus Camp

Johnson City

Johnson House

Hanging Tree Ranch

281

Mt. Bonnell

Woods House

Henley

290

Dripping
Springs

Austin

Little Blanco River

Mt. Lone Woman

Colorado River

35

Blanco

Baines House

Devil's
Backbone

Mt. Lone Man

32

281

12

Wimberley

Vogelsang
Hollow

32

City Cemetery

The Narrows

35

First Methodist
Church

Woods Mansion

San Antonio

New Braunfels

Landa Springs

San Marcos

10

Redbud Hills

The Alamo

Luling

10

Woods Home

Zion Hills

Seguin

Darst Oil
Field

Capote Peak

35

Gonzales

Contents

Hill
Country

FOREWORD ∞ THE SEARCH FOR THE STORY

IT WAS DISTANT, AT FIRST, LIKE THUNDER IN THE NEXT COUNTY. Not quite like an airplane. More loose and ungainly, like somebody slapping the air with lumber. It was like that, as I recall, a *whoopity whoopity,* the sound I heard above the elms and pecan trees towering above my family home in Seguin, Texas. It was June, just before my tenth birthday, and I remember the lawn was covered with peaches shaken from the tree by a thunderstorm the night before. A limb from an elm had been hit by lightning and was split and charred and I thought maybe the storm's thunder was returning for some reason beyond my comprehension, perhaps to complete the destruction of the tree. *Whoopity whoopity.* The strange sound grew louder and then I saw an amazing beast thundering over the trees and then pausing in the air above the house, its wings whirling and beating the tops of the trees and making the plants in my mother's rose garden dance. *Whoopity whoopity* was the sound it made.

Then from the beast came a voice speaking human words and I remember the voice to this day: "HELLO DOWN THERE GOOD PEOPLE! THIS IS LYNDON JOHNSON, YOUR CANDIDATE FOR THE UNITED STATES SENATE." Then, to my horror, the man in the grasp of the beast threw his Stetson hat out to the crowd gathered below and then the giant iron grasshopper settled down, down, down, into the vacant space between our house and the Guadalupe River bottoms. It had come, I knew, to carry us off to a place called the United States Senate, a kind of reform school, I supposed, for bad children. The monster's wings grew still and its mouth opened and the hatless man stepped out and began shaking hands and slapping people on the back with amazing intensity. I assumed he was celebrating his escape from the flying monster.

It all comes back to me with clarity and wonder. It was 1948 and I had just seen my first helicopter and it had hovered above the house and landed across the street. The man who threw his hat to the crowd was Lyndon Baines Johnson and the elderly woman who caught the Stetson, after running some distance and jostling children and neighbors, was my father's mother, my grandmother Laura Woods.

And when I think of her now, I remember her most vividly as she was on that day the helicopter landed across the street from our house and this tiny, birdlike, silver-haired lady came rushing from the crowd to catch Lyndon's Stetson like an outfielder might catch a fly ball.

Lyndon Johnson was running for the United States Senate and my father, Wilton Woods, was deeply involved in his campaign. Lyndon's political campaign consumed our lives in those days, a reality that would reach a quarter century into the future. Sometimes, to this day, when the telephone rings late at night, there is a moment when I think that it's Lyndon calling from Johnson City or Austin or from Washington to ask my father's opinion about political strategy or matters of conscience.

The helicopter was called the Johnson City Windmill. Each time the Johnson City Windmill prepared to land, Lyndon would throw his hat to the crowd and his advance man Jake Pickle would retrieve the hat by offering a dollar for its return. People always gave the hat back. My grandmother Laura Woods is probably the only one who did not. A photograph survives of my family standing before Lyndon's ungainly machine. My little brother, Woody, and I are frozen there as children and there, too, are Lyndon and my mother and father. And, of course, in the photograph, as in life, the composition seems to center on my grandmother Laura Woods. She had, in fact, just bamboozled Lyndon, and the pleasure of that is the expression we see caught forever on her face.

"If you wanted the hat back so badly," she told him, "you shouldn't have thrown it out of the helicopter. Lyndon, you've just got to take better care of your things."

And I remember to this day the look in Lyndon's eyes as he tried to reach around my grandmother's frail body in a mock attempt to recover his hat. Love was there, and enormous respect, an almost intimate light lingering between them, as if the two of them knew something no one else in the yard could know. I remember feeling the cold claw of jealousy.

On the day the helicopter landed, our yard was filled with milling registered voters and local Democratic candidates hoping to ride Lyndon's coattails into office. A western band called Lyndon's Hillbilly Boys was on a flatbed truck playing "Rose of San Antone," and the street out front was lined with cars decorated with crepe paper pendants and streamers and posters proclaiming the virtues of the Hill Country's favorite son. Mayor Roger Moore with his big flashy diamond ring was there, and Singing Sheriff Phil Medlin, in his white-on-white fancy shirt, was doing rope tricks for the children. Uncle Buck Bergfeld, the City Marshal, had parked his burgundy Cadillac out front and was moving through the throng kissing my mother's friends on the mouth. Towering over everybody but Uncle Buck was Lyndon Johnson, walking arm in arm with my father. And there was Laura Woods, passing out leaflets, moving fast, practically skating over the peaches the storm had shaken from the tree. This was Laura's world, the strange and bewildering comic opera of Hill Country politics.

Even though I was grown when she died, I mourned her with that special sense of betrayal a child feels when wounded by the death of someone loved. It is a wounding more severe than that suffered by adults who mourn with tears and flowers in dark rooms heavy with whispers and regret. I was angry with my grandmother for several weeks after she died. She was my ally and she had abandoned the only one in the family who understood that she was real and vulnerable and sometimes afraid. Only the child that I had been and the child she was becoming could feel the closeness we knew in those years before she died. At night, after saying goodnight to Jesus, I would cast my mind into that part of heaven where I imagined my grandmother was scolding angels and demanding the rules of death be changed so that she might set things right with her granddaughter, and I would ask her if death was all that bad. Sometimes she would say it was like sleeping and the lives of the living were her dreams. My life is the substance of my grandmother's dreaming and often, even now, I think that might well be so.

Some years before she died, Laura Woods decided to write a book about her life. It must have been when she was in her seventies and had purchased the blue Olivetti and taught herself to type. The early chapters were typed on the Olivetti. Later, chapters were in diary form or were recorded on bits of paper and written on envelopes and on the back of church programs or birthday cards or in the margins of newspapers. She had also collected boxes of photographs, articles clipped from Hill Country newspapers, campaign flyers, file after file of her correspondence, and packets of verse she had written to commemorate holidays, deaths, and the birthdays of her grandchildren. She wrote everything down: random thoughts, momentary furies, things she must do, things others should do, observed injustices, acknowledgment of the folly and error of those around her. The boxes also contained carbons and drafts of letters to American presidents from Teddy Roosevelt through Lyndon Johnson, and such notables as Gen. Douglas MacArthur, Amelia Earhart, Buffalo Bill Cody, Aimee Semple McPherson, Billy Sunday, and others of those she sought to advise over the years.

My father had saved all these things after Laura died, packing them away in a room at the back of the Seguin home that my brother, Woody, and I called the *real* LBJ Library, as opposed to the one in Austin. The walls of the room were filled with photographs of the days when Lyndon and my father were young and during their years in college and in the political wars. And here, in boxes carrying the faint aroma of jasmine and honeysuckle and the other exotic perfumes Laura Woods wore to attract butterflies, my grandmother's life was packed away.

I spent a month exploring this chaotic repository of ideas, dreams, convictions, and impressions that was to become the grist for Laura's life story. Little by little it became apparent that the boxes contained more than the woman of lighthearted eccentricity and meddlesome manner that filled family legend. I found a woman who had loved wildly, dreamed boldly, and suffered dimensions of pain and guilt and remorse few ever feel. I found a woman who was bright, outlandish, passionate, and in whom a Promethean fire burned as brightly as the Hill Country sun, without cease, for nearly a hundred years. And I found in her diaries and correspondence mysteries that only further research could solve, references to events both terrible and haunting.

Finishing the book my grandmother started was an idea that grew not unlike a child blossoms in the womb. I had all the materials in the "real LBJ Library" and I had the family's oral history, suspect though it was. But most of the people who knew Laura Woods best have passed away. She outlived nearly all her friends and would delight in the knowledge she survived her enemies, as well. My father is gone, and Lyndon, and his mother, Laura's great friend Rebekah Baines Johnson, and Col. Edward M. House, the mysterious millionaire who enticed my grandmother into the world of politics. All the freaks and acrobats at the old Glasscock Brothers Circus, where Laura spent so much time when she was a girl and where she suffered her first love, have long packed away their sequins and their secrets and rolled their wagons away.

However, there yet lived a few members of the family who had known Laura well, and who could help me tell her story. So one summer day I set out in my car to see if my kinfolks could help me find my grandmother, the woman beneath the myth.

The Woods mansion stood on a hill above the little Texas town of San Marcos like an old and elegant woman who had slept the night in her clothes. The great white columns slaves had carved were gray now and seemed less lofty, as if houses, like people, were diminished by the years. The once grand house was nearly in ruin. There were places where vines had torn away cornices and lattice. Warped, rotten pine siding revealed within the walls nests for sparrows and heavy hives of bees. The roof was patched with bandages of tar paper and rust-red tears wept from squarehead nails that almost held the house together. The fruit trees my great-grand-mother had planted were gone and the blue plumbago bushes that had once hidden the stone foundations had been beaten down and away by long seasons of rain falling from gutterless eaves. All that was left of the gardens were Confederate Lilies that had contin-ued to rise again, year after year, unlike their namesake cause. The balcony where I had known forever that my great-aunt Little Sweet had fired on the approaching Yankees seemed curiously askew, creating for the entire house sad and antigoglin perspec-tives. All the doors and windows were wide open and curtains, like tattered flags of surrender, yielded to the whim of the rising wind.

Although it was early afternoon, the day was growing dark. At first the air was the same color as the house and the edges of the old place grew insubstantial, like a time-exposure photograph taken by a startled photographer. Then, as the sky darkened and became that deep vibrant violet gray from which summer storms are born, the house emerged again from its dreamlike back-ground and I could imagine the four old women, my two great-aunts and second and third, even fourth cousins, wandering the rooms within. Could I find my grandmother here amid the secrets and fallen timbers of this house where she was never welcome?

For a long moment I stayed in the car. I suppose I was reluc-tant to see what had become of this place where so many family legends were born. As I watched the house, seeking to replace the image with how I knew the mansion looked in the days before the Yankees came, lightning tore a ragged seam through the day and thunder tumbled across the air, actually rolling and clatter-ing like a train within the cloud. The air grew cold and a few great dollops of rain fell with small heavy explosions in the dust of the yard. I still could not bring myself to approach the house. Then an arrow of lightning drew my eyes to the stable and I left the car and ran through the birthing storm to the place where the first killing had been done and where the horses were kept that led to the second killing years later.

The stable was half down, one end of the roof was actually

sagging to the ground. Although there had been no horses here
for years, I could almost hear their scuffling and nickering complaints and I could smell their hot, sour breath and the sweet hay
in the stalls and feel the pounding hearts of my great-grand-
mother Georgia's children as they waited, wondering if they
were capable of the thing they were about to do. I stood where I
imagined my great-aunt Cherokee had stood when the shots
were fired. Shots that would resonate years later in Laura's life.
As the rain began to pound on the ruined roof of the stable, and
the thunder rolled and rattled like cannonade, from the darkness a voice called my name.

The woman was the color of shadow or the breast of a dove,
dark, yet somehow pale, a dusky light gray. There was in her
cheekbones, her high wide forehead, and in her fine, almost
patrician nose, an echo of the beauty she had been. I was
reminded of Garbo in black and white stills, grown older. It
seemed she had been faded by the years; her hair, her smooth
skin, even her shawl, seemed, like the day, like the house, to have
renounced the gifts of the rainbow. Only her eyes escaped this
curious blending of smoke and shadow. Her eyes were vivid
blue, the same color as my own eyes, what my father's side of the
family calls Hawkins blue. Alice Benny Lawshe Brady was my
third cousin and a very old family friend. Her mother had been
a Woods family slave. She took me by the hand and told me she
could see the little girl in the woman I had become. We moved to
a part of the stable where the roof protected us from the storm.

"I got your letter," Alice Benny said. "You could have knocked
me over with a feather." The thunder was so loud we had to whisper to be heard, whisper somehow cutting more clearly through
heaven's timpani. "And Miss Laura. I think of her sometimes. She
was a caution. There was never in this world anybody anything
like Miss Laura." She paused. I could sense her fast-forwarding
through her memories of my grandmother, shaking her head all
the time, a smile parting her lips and lighting her blue eyes. "But
I'm surprised you'd come to this old tumbledown place."

"You knew her about as long as anybody. And you knew her
when she was young."

"She never lived here, you know. Not in this house. She wanted to something terrible. But she never did."

"So you don't think I'll learn anything here?"

"Oh, no, Miss Janice. Your grandmother didn't live here, that's a fact. But people's lives begin a long time before they're born. What happened here shaped Miss Laura's life just as sure as Jesus is in heaven."

As the storm wrestled around the old stable, Alice Benny told the story her mother had told her—a story that had been told and retold in the family through the years and that was as familiar to me as a Grimm's fairy tale. However, it always seemed about imaginary people and events in a faraway land. Here in the stable, with the storm battering the shingles, I could almost hear gunshots in the thunder.

"After that night Miss Georgia sent the family away to protect them from the Yankees. Little Sweet and Cherokee were taken to the old home place in Water Valley, Mississippi. Peter went with his older brother Pinckney to the head of the Blanco River. Only my mama and Miss Georgia stayed here on the hill."

"But Grandma wasn't even born then."

"That's true. But that night, when Miss Georgia sent her children away, she divided all her horses between them. Fine horses. A much better thing to have than money in those days. And I think it was those horses as much as Mr. Peter that made Miss Laura fall in love. And I think she fell in love with that big house up there, too. She was just a poor country girl and she sure was taken with the way Mr. Peter lived so fine."

"You mean she loved Grandpa for his wealth?"

"Oh, she loved the man for himself. I don't mean to say she didn't. But Miss Laura always dreamed of being something more or different than she was."

Outside, the storm began to move away. The sound of thunder was distant now and Alice Benny and I walked from the stable toward the mansion.

One of the old Woods women was watching us from an upstairs window. It was either Aunt Emma or Aunt Carrie or the strange, sad person called Cousin Flournoy. When Georgia

Woods died, Aunt Carrie was only one year old an.   Colonel-
Doctor married the young and beautiful Ella Rives Dupree
Ogletree. Aunt Emma was born from that union. Now even
pitiful Flournoy was old and Laura's in-laws had lived reclu-
sively in the old house ever since the Colonel-Doctor died.

"Don't be too surprised when you see in the house," Alice
Benny said, as we climbed the wide front stair. "I look after
them, but I don't have a say in how they live. They're like all you
Woods folks. You're going to do what you're going to do no matter what. Mostly those old women stay in bed or sit in their
rooms listening to radio. They don't tend to the house much."

It was like entering an ancient museum. Whole constellations of dust motes drifted through streaks of sunlight and
shadow and I was bathed in a thick, close aura of decay. There
was not much left of the original furnishings. I hadn't been in the
house since I was a child, but I recognized a pecan table and a
child's rocking chair crafted by the slave Ed Tom, Alice Benny's
father, and the floral wall coverings Georgia had installed after
the Yankees had marched away for good. Most of the furnishings
in the room combined the excesses of the Victorian Age with
reflections of a more primitive frontier life. Great gilded mirrors,
tapestries of gentlemen running to hounds or of portly nudes suffering the leers of gamboling satyrs hung next to mounted deer-
head trophies with great yellowing antlers. Dusty velvet draperies
were festooned above the windows and puddled in dreary heaps
on the floor. Weary sofas covered with horsehair fabric contrasted
with the room's profusion of lace and velvet, satin and damask,
everything fringed and swagged. A silent ormolu clock stood on
the mantel next to the Colonel-Doctor's silver spurs. All the furniture seemed fashioned for giants and the room was so crowded
with furnishings, great mounds of books and miscellany, that
pathways had been established to access one room from the next.
Displayed on the walls and on every possible surface were col-
lections of Blue Willow china and plates gathered from world's
fairs and various expositions. Piled on end tables, secretaries,
old radio consoles and even on the floor were newspapers saved
for some important reason long forgotten.

Alice Benny led me through the maze to the parlor where I was to await the entrance of my great-aunts and my cousin Flournoy. And there, in the parlor, in a huge glass case, was the storied butterfly collection assembled years ago by Cousin Flournoy. Somehow I hadn't expected this great marvel of my childhood to have survived the years. But there they were, pinned and labeled beneath the glass—mourning cloaks, monarchs, swallowtails, skippers, a southern dogface, even the *agrias amydon* that Cousin Flournoy had brought back from Brazil. The scientific names were beginning to fade, the wings of the butterflies were tattered like kites flown too long in the wind. I remembered how Laura Woods had once had a terrible row with Cousin Flournoy about the morality of catching and killing "God's most beautiful creations," a row that was inflamed when Laura poured all Cousin Flournoy's formaldehyde down the toilet.

Soon I heard them on the stairs. When I glanced up at the curving sweep of the grand staircase I was sure it sagged an inch or two beneath the accumulated weight of my descending kin. Aunt Emma came first, leading with her ample bosom, her head and shoulders held high and straight like soldiers of the palace guard. I had always remembered her as a woman of immense dignity. Even now, living on the thin edge of poverty, moving through the ruin of her home, there was something almost regal in her bearing.

Aunt Carrie followed her sister, as she had all her life, willing to let Aunt Emma test the waters of whatever encounters life offered. In contrast to her sister's austere expression, Aunt Carrie's cherubic face glowed with an almost aggressive goodwill, seemingly prepared to force happiness on even the most wretched of guests. And I could see, as she descended the stair, that the rumors of her uncommon habits of dress were true. Great Aunt Carrie wore all the clothes in her wardrobe simultaneously. The effect was startling. Her body, swaddled in layers of cloth, assumed the proportions of a minor planet, a billowing taffeta moon. She, too, moved through the canyons of collectibles in the parlor with more dignity than you would imagine from a woman wearing more than a dozen outfits at once.

Then came Flournoy. This distant relation, now grown old, was as tall and slim as Aunt Carrie was wide. When I was young, my aunt Nona explained to me that Flournoy was a hermaphrodite. For a long time I didn't know what that meant, except in a vague and unsettling way, and it was only years later in the Louvre that I actually saw, carved in marble, visual evidence of the creature my cousin Flournoy was whispered to be. Later, Alice Benny told me it was true that Flournoy had been born with the sexual organs of both male and female. But, as a child, I knew only my cousin wore men's clothing sometimes and women's clothes on other occasions and that Flournoy was the most knowledgeable and exotic person I had ever known. It was Flournoy who introduced me to the world of books, volumes that I loved first for their velvet, ivory, or leather covers, then for the magic they contained. Flournoy had traveled to all four corners of the earth, not merely to Paris or London or to the other stops on the Grand Tour, but to Timbuktu and to the headwaters of the Urubamba and to the temples of India and Tibet. There was nothing Cousin Flournoy didn't know, few places she hadn't been, and rare was the field of knowledge that didn't dwell somewhere in his bookcase or her mind.

Today, Cousin Flournoy was dressed as a man. She wore a pair of nondescript black trousers and a soft Byronesque shirt with an open collar. Her fine silver hair was cut short. Gently, Flournoy shouldered the two aunts aside and embraced me. Her eyes were as wide and innocent as a child's.

"Virginia," Flournoy said, her voice deep and wonderfully sincere.

"That's Janice," Aunt Carrie said.

"Virginia is her mother." This from Aunt Emma. "She just looks like her mother."

"Does not," Carrie rejoined, her merry eyes flashing. "She doesn't look anything like her mother, do you, dear?" She attempted to embrace me, but we were held apart by the closetful of woven goods she wore.

"She does, too, look like Virginia!"

"Does not!"

"Does too!"

"I say she favors Georgia Lawshe. Look at those Hawkins eyes."

Alice Benny cleared away places for us to sit in the parlor, and we talked away the afternoon. Or, I should say, it was they, the great-aunts and Cousin Flournoy who talked, bounding from one disagreement to another as was their helter-skelter fashion. They disagreed on the weather, the most expeditious way to get to Uvalde, Texas, the merits of vegetarianism, and a host of other subjects explored from the most oblique angles imaginable. I supposed the presence of a rare guest had unleashed this torrential and wayward debate, and I wondered if silence would again settle on the house with my departure.

The great-aunts and Flournoy argued about many things that afternoon, but their most ardent disagreement was centered on my grandmother Laura Hoge Woods.

"She was never really one of us, you know," Aunt Emma said. "She lacked a certain grace."

"She was very bright," Cousin Flournoy countered.

"For a country girl, I suppose."

"She wasn't a country girl long. Trouble was she was too sophisticated for her own good."

"How can one be too sophisticated?" Flournoy wanted to know.

"It's not proper for a lady to be that involved in politics," Aunt Emma said.

"How about Eleanor Roosevelt?"

"That's Washington. This is Texas."

"I think Laura did quite well for a child with her background," Flournoy said.

"She certainly married well," Aunt Emma said. "I always wondered where she came from. She was just suddenly there. This slip of a girl came and before you could say Jack Robinson she was the center of the family. I'm certain she married Peter for his position."

"She was on the rebound from that Indian at the circus. That white Apache!"

"I always thought she was sweet on that Colonel House, Woodrow Wilson's man," Aunt Carrie said.

"That's horrible to say!" Aunt Emma was shocked.

"I'll say what I please in my own home!"

"This is my home, too!"

"Laura loved Peter more than anything."

"Not more than Peter's horses."

"Not more than politics. Her children ran wild while she was out electioneering around the country."

"Those children were better off with her gone," Aunt Emma said. "Look what she did to poor Winifred. Her own daughter. Drove her right out of her mind."

An uneasy silence settled over the parlor as my ancient kin looked into the mist of the past. I had heard about the killing in the stable since I was a child, but only recently while researching in Blanco had I learned of the second killing on the road to San Antonio.

"Tell me, what happened?" I asked. The question intruded rudely on the silence.

"Promised not to," Carrie said. The others seemed to agree and the subject was dropped.

"Anyway, I pray Peter didn't know about Laura and Colonel House," Aunt Emma said. "Or the white Apache."

"Why are you so ugly?" Aunt Carrie wanted to know.

"I'm not being ugly."

"Yes, you are. You've taken on one of your evil spells."

"Socrates said the only real evil is ignorance," Flournoy said, warming, apparently, to a good philosophical debate.

As the great-aunts and distant cousin Flournoy explored the nature of good and evil, Alice Benny caught my eye and I followed her from the room. "You see how they are," she said. "I don't know what you can learn. Maybe it's worth listening and you can get something useful here and a tidbit there. Maybe I can fill in some spaces."

So I stayed at the old Woods house and I listened to my ancient kin and their strange contentious remembrances echo through the ruined rooms. And when they had retired to their beds and radios, Alice Benny and I remained in the parlor, surrounded by dead butterflies. We shared a decanter of sherry, trading tales of an uncommon woman whose ghost we felt at our shoulders and at the display case, seeking to free the swallowtails, the monarchs, the mourning cloaks, and all those other butterflies.

"She was a caution," Alice Benny said. "There was never in this world anybody anything like Miss Laura."

On my aunt Winifred's ninety-ninth birthday, I filled the car with balloons and a cake, my mind with questions I would ask about Laura, my father, Wilton, and Lyndon Johnson, and headed north from Austin on the interstate. At first I couldn't find the place where Winifred lived. I wheeled my rented Volvo off the highway at Georgetown and followed my penciled directions through town to the Sonic Barbecue and then turned left toward the Hillside Nursing Home. It was a surprisingly new building, a rambling structure of red brick rising bluntly from a cornfield.

I had not visited Winifred since I was a girl, and as I walked toward the entrance to the nursing home I felt the hot breath of panic I had felt on those childhood visits. Each time my father announced a trip to see Winifred, I would pray to be released from the chore somehow, that either I or Winifred would come down with some awful malady and the visit would be canceled. But my father was adamant. "Winifred is family," he would say. "We are all she has." And this made me dread the visit all the more. How terribly sad that I was apparently so important to Winifred and all I wanted was never to see her again. Once I pointed out to my father that Grandma Laura hardly ever visited Winifred. "That's not your concern," he said. Even after all these years I wondered what could have happened to drive a mother and daughter apart so completely.

In truth, I was afraid of Winifred, afraid of the fragile mortality she represented, the awareness that there could come a moment

when I would look in the mirror and I would see Winifred looking back. I thought old age and insanity were things I might
catch, like measles. I was also terribly afraid of Winifred's eyes.
They were night-dark and liquid like the Mayan sacred well I had
seen in a film at school and I was afraid I might fall in. All the stories of her violent past were locked in that compartment of my
child's mind where trolls and vampires lurked, and I was afraid
her eyes would release them and I'd be consumed.

The visits were always on a Sunday. In those days Winifred
was still in the insane asylum. My father would park the car and
fetch her from the foyer where she waited always in a pale blue
linen suit and a hat blooming with bright fabric flowers. A dark
veil, white gloves, a dark blue plastic purse, and high-laced black
shoes completed her outfit. My mother and aunts bought
dresses for her, but it was that one sorrowful ensemble that she
took out now and again to wear in her lonely room on birthdays
or anniversaries of half-forgotten events or when my father came
to take her to the Summer Haus Cafeteria.

I remember Winifred as she walked to the car, a slim, tall,
almost elegant lady with the posture and presence of a beauty
queen. At the curb she would bend and peer into the car to make
sure Laura was not there, for Winifred had long before insisted
that she never wanted to see her mother again for some
unknowable reason that fascinated my brother, Woody, and me
to no end. My father would open the door for her and she would
slide into the Chevrolet. "Hello, good people," she would say
and she would settle down beside me and Woody, her hands
clasped in her lap, her back straight as a gate. As the door
whooshed closed, there rose around us the aroma of dust and
Ivory soap.

We always arrived at the cafeteria just before the church
crowd, then moved down the line toward that treasury of aro-
mas that always lifted my spirits somewhat. I especially loved
the Summer Haus in those days because the plates were com-
partmentalized and the terrible anxiety of getting juice from the
green beans mixed with the mashed potatoes or getting gravy on
my Jell-O was greatly reduced. Winifred always filled her tray

with the same harvest: cherry pie, lime Jell-O with whipped cream, German chocolate cake, and a bowl of berries, or whatever was in season. I imagined that desserts were forbidden in the asylum for some dark reason, perhaps, I thought, because sweets incite lunacy.

Conversations were disjointed and halting, usually centering on Winifred's mild complaints about life in the asylum. It was not civilized to dine at five o'clock. Much too early. There was no one with whom she could carry on a conversation; the other residents were simply not of her class. And I remember one time when she capped her complaints about her fellow residents by revealing that "some of them have lost their marbles." Of course, Laura was never, never mentioned, and now it was just possible I could find out why.

I asked the attendant at the front desk for Winifred's room. Her fingers walked through the register.

"Winifred Caldwell?"

"Winifred Woods Caldwell."

"You're sure?"

"Certain."

"Could she go by another name? We don't seem to have a Winifred Caldwell."

A horrible thought flashed through my mind. Is it possible to lose an aunt? That she would somehow slip through the net, a victim of her decades of anonymity? Maybe, somewhere, in the great matrix of Texas nursing homes and asylums, my ninety-nine-year-old aunt was wandering, lost both in time and space.

"Are you sure she isn't at one of the other homes in town?"

I wasn't sure. For a brief moment I felt a sense of relief. I had tried to visit Winifred. I had tried to help her celebrate her near century of life on earth, but I had failed. As I watched the attendant dial one of the other Georgetown nursing homes, I felt my father had released me from my obligation.

"She's at Valley View," the woman said, hanging up the phone. She wrote down the address and drew a simple map.

Valley View was a horror. It was everything implied by the old notion of bedlam. Hollow halls filled with wheeled specters. A cloying aroma of excrement and bleach. But it was the sounds that almost defeated my resolve. Animal voices raised in anger and anguish and disbelief that such a time could come to pass. As I asked for Winifred, an ancient gentleman asked me if I had come to take him home. Another woman screamed a haunting and horrible accusation at her distant father: "No Daddy No Daddy No Daddy No Daddy." For how many years had she shouted that refrain? There was the sound of dishes clattering and of moans and the names of absent people called. "Winifred is at lunch now," the attending nurse said. "You can wait in her room or join her there."

Winifred's room was clean, even surprisingly cozy, a kind of refuge from the sound and fury of the halls. There were two beds, two small dressers and two tall metal cabinets. Above Winifred's bed was her college diploma, a master of arts degree from Southwestern University at Georgetown, Texas. There was nothing else on the wall. I looked in the cabinet and there was the pale blue suit and the floral hat and the shoes. The gloves weren't in sight. On the dresser was a small framed photograph of Winifred as a young woman. I had seen this photograph in a family album and it had haunted me through the years. Taken shortly after her marriage to Rob Caldwell, the photograph captured Winifred's astonishing beauty and also something of the melancholy that would fuel her madness. A second framed photograph hit me like a physical blow. It had been taken in San Marcos and all Winifred's family was gathered in front of Laura's old Model A car. Winifred stood next to her father, Peter, yet Laura's image had been cut completely away. The hole went all the way through the photograph and the backing of the frame.

The material accumulation of a century of living amounted to a college diploma, a self-portrait, a mutilated memory, and a pale blue linen suit. But in a way, those few possessions defined this extraordinary woman. Her intellect, her beauty, her hatred, and her elegance.

I walked back into the hall and was again assaulted by an avalanche of sound: the clattering of tin trays, the stern voices of attendants scolding misbehavior, the guttural complaints of human lives lived too long for grace. "No Daddy No Daddy No Daddy No Daddy." The tortured woman walked beside me down the hall, searching my face for something, imploring, demanding an understanding of her pain. A large man in a white uniform gently led her away.

Winifred's wheelchair was pulled up to a table where four other women sat. Winifred was terribly bent, her glorious posture taken away by time. Her white hair was thin, like wisps of poorly spun cotton candy. Always slender, she was now skeletal, her skin waxen and transparent. But there was something of the woman in the photograph that defied the passing of time. Winifred was still there. A curious composure seemed to surround her, an invisible wall protecting the fragile remnants of her person.

Winifred Woods Caldwell was the only one at the table who was feeding herself. The others were so feeble or so beset with tremors that they required assistance. One woman sitting across from Winifred was trying to eat unaided but she was trembling so the food spilled from her spoon before it reached her mouth. Patiently, time after time, she would try again with the same result. No one seemed to notice her struggle.

I walked up to Winifred, put my hand on her shoulder, bent down to catch her attention, and spoke her name, "Winifred?"

Slowly, she looked up from her plate. There were those black eyes that I had feared as a child. For a moment I felt a touch of vertigo, then the moist depths clouded over and I knew she didn't recognize me, or if she did it was only momentary and was gone now.

"It's Janice."

"Janice." Her voice was like old tough corduroy, as if she had not spoken for some time and her vocal chords had atrophied. Yet the sound was not a whisper. It had timbre and texture, two deep, ragged chords.

"How are you?"

"All right."

"It's good to see you."

"All right."

Her voice seemed somewhat stronger now. Beyond the room

a woman was sobbing. Another was shouting a rhythmic pattern of sounds, moans and gasps, not unlike the sounds of lovemaking. Winifred's expression was empty and old. I could see her aged teeth had yellowed. There were no chairs, so I stood next to Winifred as she picked at her food. I touched the back of her head where her hair was drawn up into a loose chignon. It was as soft as eiderdown.

"I've just come from Blanco."

"Blanco? There's some mighty good people in Blanco."

"Yes, a lot of good people in Blanco. How many years did you live there?"

"Oh, I don't know. I grew up there." There was a hint of embarrassment in her answer, a self-deprecating hesitation, a halting preamble to laughter.

"I grew up in Seguin."

"There's a lot of good people in Seguin."

"Were you married in Blanco? Who did you marry?"

"I think it was a man named Caldwell. It was a long time ago. Peter Woods was my father. Now, there was a good-looking man." Winifred seemed to drag the sentences from somewhere deep inside. The words were absolutely monotone and without expression. Her speech reminded me of talking toys, those dolls that speak when you pull a string and let it go.

"What about Rebekah Johnson?"

"Yes."

"And Lyndon."

"Yes."

"And Wilton Woods. My father was Wilton Woods. I'm Janice Woods."

"Yes. I'm Winifred Woods."

Then, for the first time, Winifred's mask softened into a smile. A sound like laughter emerged as she welcomed prodigal memories from the past. She looked up at me and the cloud was gone from her eyes. "Janice," she said, and then the mists returned and she looked back at her plate.

"Did you know today is your birthday?"

"No." The word was extended into a moan.

"When were you born?"

"I was born in eighteen hundred ninety-five."

"Do you know how old you are today?"

"No."

"You're ninety-nine years old. I brought a birthday cake."

"That's a long time ago." Winifred laid her spoon by the side of her plate and put both hands in her lap. "They burned my baby," she said. "That man Caldwell. Laura Woods." The words, absolutely devoid of passion, cut sharp as a blade of ice. *Was this the missing piece of Laura's life I had come to find?* Surely this was just a phrase torn from a ravaged mind. But something terrible must have happened. I wondered if she had dwelled on that distant tragedy all these years. *Had the loss of her baby consumed her mind for three-quarters of a century?* That would be like suffering the same event over and over for a lifetime. And apparently she blamed Laura for the death of her newborn child.

By now, the others at the table had been wheeled away. Winifred and I were alone. A silence grew and as I watched Winifred struggle to keep her memories from fleeing back into darkness, I felt an almost overwhelming sorrow. Here was a woman who had outlived everyone she had ever known or loved. The whole town of Blanco had long been beneath the ground. All that remained were two memories more powerful than the tyranny of time. The death of her child. And what seemed to be hatred of her mother, my grandmother, Laura Woods, the woman I had so loved as a child and whose memory I loved still.

I wheeled Winifred into her room. An attendant turned down her bed, lifted her from the wheelchair and slipped her under the bedcovers. The nurse was not a large woman and the task of lifting Winifred had seemed to require no effort at all. She appeared to be as light as a leaf. Almost immediately Winifred closed her eyes.

"Is she sleeping?" I asked the nurse.

"I think so. Sometimes they dream awake, I think. A sort of half sleep."

"Does she talk?"

"Sometimes. About Blanco. Her father. Her baby."

"Does she talk about her mother?"

"Not to me."

After a while I went out to the car to get the cake I had bought at Safeway. When I returned to the room I found to my horror that Winifred's roommate had returned. "No Daddy No Daddy No Daddy No Daddy." The awful refrain filled the room, the woman's alert, mad eyes followed my every move as I took the plastic cover from the cake and the box of candles from my purse. The nurse brought in a rollaway bedside table and gently stroked Winifred's wrist until her eyes opened and focused. She then fluffed an extra pillow and tucked it behind Winifred's head and shoulders.

"Seguin is a nice town," Winifred said. "There's some mighty good people in Seguin."

The nurse brought in two plates and two forks and cut thin slices of the chocolate cake. I had remembered Winifred's preference for Summer Haus German chocolate cake.

"I was born in eighteen ninety-five," Winifred said. "A mighty long time ago."

I hesitate to write what happened then because it sounds so terribly sad. I suppose it was the nurse who suggested we sing the happy birthday song. The nurse began singing and the cruel lament of "No Daddy No Daddy No Daddy" became counterpoint to the sappy, childlike refrain that wishes us happiness as we grow nearer to death.

After the cake had been taken away I sat with Winifred in silence. The roommate had succumbed to blessed sleep. I thought about Winifred's long life and about Laura and Peter, Wilton and Lyndon, Rebekah and Sam Johnson, and all those people Winifred had outlived. I thought about all the stories this family had woven through time, all the suffering and joy, death and madness. Somehow this old woman, this fragile reed clinging to life and to her retreating memories, symbolized so much of what we had been and, I suppose, what our children will be.

"It's time to go," I said and patted Winifred's hand. Her eyes met mine. Tears welled from the black depths, a drop or two, clinging to Winifred's lower lid, then sliding down her wrinkled cheek to her mouth. The pink tip of the old woman's tongue touched her gray lips and she seemed surprised to taste the salt. Then she lay back on the pillow and closed her eyes. I imagined she had returned to her wakeful dreaming.

I stayed for another hour, then moved to the bed and kissed Winifred on the forehead. As I was walking toward the door, she called my name.

"Janice." Again, tough old corduroy. I turned and bent low to hear her words.

"Janice," she said again. "Would you ask Mama to come?"

It is spring. Throughout the Hill Country the wildflowers are in riotous bloom. The chalky hills hold a collision of color, a landscape so dramatic, so compelling, that it has the power to slow automobiles and draw them from the road. From the cars people flow out into the fields to bathe in the Texas bluebonnets, Indian paintbrush, wild potato, winecup, buttercup, and black-eyed Susan as they would in a river or a sea.

This morning I walked out into a field of bluebonnets. I felt the vibrant, animate energy rising from the soil and breathed the divine ambrosial breath of the earth. Here, away from the highway, out beyond the sound of trucks passing by, was the world my grandmother Laura knew. She walked such fields as this one. Here in the meadows, in the violet peaks, beautiful limestone and oak solitudes of the Hill Country, was the setting for the mysteries and contradictions of my grandmother's life. Who was this woman who lived so very long, was a close friend of three American presidents, yet rarely left the primitive hills where she was born? Why was she so driven and so loved and so hated and so misunderstood? And what was the secret only she and Lyndon Johnson knew on that long ago day the helicopter landed in the yard of my mother's house?

Hill Country is the title Laura chose for her life story and this book is what she would have written had she not died.

1 ∞ THE STORY BEGINS

ONE JUNE EVENING, JUST AS THE FALLING SUN WAS BEGINNING to paint the Texas Hill Country with lavender halflight, Tom and Eliza Felps, having put their children to bed, were fishing for the fat little smallmouth bass that feed in the pools of Cypress Creek. Lightning bugs were beginning to scatter their minimal fire into the shadows. The night settled down like an old familiar comforter. Time lingered. A small wind breathed high in the cypress boughs. There must have been a moment of warning, a suspension of the cicada's song, a feeling of dread, an awareness beyond horror, for in a moment brief as a thought, Carnoviste, the rogue Comanche chief, came with his knife, and Tom and Eliza were disemboweled, their children taken away. A few miles to the north, Katherine Metzger was coming home from confirmation class when Apaches sent an arrow through her breast, then took her long yellow hair and her tongue. At Kickapoo Springs, while picking berries, Willie Stone and his little sister were captured by Apaches, thrown into the air again and again until they died, their bodies trampled and mangled by the horses. Then they were hung in a tree for the vultures. In Gillespie County, Henry Kensing and his pregnant wife, Johanne, were dragged from their home. He was killed and Johanne was tortured, the unborn baby ripped from her womb. In Sisterdale, Herman Rungie was scalped and mutilated by Apache raiders. Thirteen-year-old Anna Baumann was captured by Kiowa on the Pedernales River, her older sister tortured and killed. Within a day's ride from the Pedernales, Comanches came upon a group of Tonkawa preparing to eat the roasted leg of a captive. The Comanches, including Herman Lehmann, a white boy who had been captured and enslaved by the Indians eight years before, killed the Tonkawa, cut off their arms and legs and then burned all the body parts, including those of the living, in a bonfire.

The Kiowa, Arapaho, Apache, Comanche, the once great nations of the Great Plains were entering their final, dreadful hours. What had been a valiant defense of their land had become desperate banditry. Great chiefs, like Quanah Parker of the Comanche, who wanted an honorable peace, and Geronimo of the Apache, who sought a martyr's death, still maintained some influence over their people. But the bitter fury of the younger leaders, often rogues of uncommon brutality, held sway. The heart, the soul, of the tribes was splintered and the prodigal remnants of the nations fell on the families of the Texas Hill Country with all the terrible rage of the hopelessly lost.

In 1877, at Hoge Hollow, a few acres of rocky ranchland on a bend of the Blanco River, seven-year-old Laura Matilda Hoge and her brothers Charles and John Carlton Hoge were bathing in the shallow rock pools of the river near their home. Laura's big brother was twelve years old and very strong. She knew he would protect her should the Indians come. Even though her father had gone south for several days to hunt wild turkey so he could replenish the meat in the smokehouse, there was really nothing to fear: John Carlton was a match for the Indians and Laura's mother, Little Mattie Hoge, was just out of sight in the summer kitchen, baking a crab-apple pie.

Besides, Laura was not really sure there were such things as Indians. She had never actually seen one. But then, she had never seen God either, and when she told her father she did not believe there was a God, he switched her until she bled. So, on the subject of Indians, she kept her own counsel. Rarely did a day go by when she was not warned of Indians by her parents. Indians would carry her away, she was told, like they did poor little Herman Lehmann and Lewis Staeth and Emma Ahrens and Adolph Korn and some fifty or more other children from Hill Country families. In time, she began to see the Indians as the hand God might use to punish her for such mortal sins as sassing or whining or neglecting her chores. But since it was difficult for her to believe in God, it was also difficult to believe in

His avenging angels. Indians became, in her mind, somehow blended with other tales of horror children were told, of witches in dark forests who tried to cook and eat children and wolves who masqueraded as grandmas and trolls who lived beneath bridges and would eat you if you crossed. The Tonkawa certainly had no monopoly on the eating of children.

And so it was not surprising that Laura was unafraid when she saw Carnoviste, Black Cato, and Herman Lehmann come riding, like characters out of a myth, from the brush on the other side of the river.

It was apparent the Indians had not expected to find children in their way as they approached the Hoge place in search of horses. They paused, looked at each other, then back to where the children stood, frozen in a motionless tableau cut away from the flow of time, an interval of images alive with a clarity that would be etched in Laura's mind for the rest of her long, long life.

The man she would later know as Carnoviste was tall and powerfully built, his face painted with red, yellow, and black designs. He wore nothing above his waist and his skin glowed like a copper kettle. His hair, crowned by a fan of eagle feathers, was very black, his nose thin and fine, and Laura was surprised to see that he had no eyebrows above his calm and expressionless eyes. Carnoviste carried a bullhide shield painted with bright stars and a crescent moon, and across his shoulder he carried a short bow. The second of the riders was Black Cato. Later she would learn he was a former slave who had joined the Apache to fight his white masters. He, too, was a very large man. He wore a soldier's blue waistcoat pinned and stitched with a voluminous collection of medals and medallions. An army bugle hung from a lanyard around his neck.

The third rider, Herman Lehmann, was one of the most beautiful people Laura had ever seen. He reminded her of the pictures in her mother's Bible of David playing the harp for King Saul. His hair was golden and long and, in contrast to his two companions, his body seemed carved from ivory. Instead of a harp or a sling, he carried a shield, a rifle, and a bandolier of cartridges strapped across his back. As Laura watched the three strange riders, she was not afraid. Surely no harm could come from a boy so beautiful, even if his companions looked as fierce as any troll or witch in her brothers' fearsome stories.

Then, suddenly, time seemed to take her by the hand and mind and whirl her forward, the moments passing so quickly that one merged into the next in a constant and violent stream of sensation. She saw Charles thrashing through the water toward shore and felt John Carlton pulling her by the arm. The Indians' horses cast jeweled spray into the sunlight as they came flying through the shallows. Then when the horses reached the hole where the great-grandfather catfish lurked and where the flow was deep even in summer, the riders were slowed, holding high on the necks of their swimming mounts. Laura ran frantically, half carried along by her brothers, gaining distance from the Indians, flying across the bottomland, and she knew for an instant how the wolves must feel when pursued by her father and the hounds. She saw the contorted faces of her brothers and could taste the sharp, acrid, burning pain of their fear, now her own, a taste like blood in her throat. She heard the sound of an arrow whispering by and the howls of the Indians and the rau-cous ringing bleat of Black Cato's bugle. She felt the wind in her face and the sting of branches, like switches, the tall grass grasp-ing at her ankles. They dodged through the apple trees, run-ning, flying, screaming for their mother. Finally, she felt the inexpressible deliverance when they reached the yard, scattering chickens to the four directions, and then the blessed coolness of the house when they passed through the door with their lungs on fire. And she heard the thunder of Old Boomer, the ancient, ten-gauge, double-barreled, shotgun her mother kept loaded with number four lead shot to use when her father was away, and the howl of surprise and pain from the Indians who then retreated noisily to the safety of the edge of the yard.

Little Mattie Hoge bolted the doors, hurriedly closed and locked the shutters. While John Carlton reloaded Old Boomer, Little Mattie pushed apple barrels up against the doors. Laura's sister Baby Lucy, in spite of the noise, slept soundly in her cradle by the hearth. Laura felt betrayed by the golden-haired boy, by the world, and by the sunlit day that had given birth to evil and danger so quickly and unexpectedly. As she listened to the crisp, staccato talk between her mother and brothers, she decided she could never fully trust again.

"Only the three?"

"All we saw."

"It's Black Cato," Little Mattie said, rising by the window to her full height of four and a half feet. She watched the riders through a crack in the shutters. "And there's Carnoviste. Other one must be little Herman Lehmann all grown."

"Where are they?" John Carlton asked.

"By the well. Brazen as you please. Thinkin' things over. Tryin' to figure what kind of fight we'll make," Little Mattie said.

John Carlton handed Old Boomer back to Little Mattie, who was not much larger than the shotgun.

"Get the Colt, Charles," Little Mattie said, turning back to the window. Charles moved quickly to the pine cabinet that J. C. Hoge laughingly called the armory. When Laura's father was home, the Winchester was kept there, along with Old Boomer and the Army Colt he had used against the Yankees in the war. But now, with the Winchester gone, they had only what they called the poor folks' weapons. Charles loaded the Colt and moved next to his mother. Laura watched wide-eyed, her heart still pumping hard from the run and the fear she had seen in her brothers' eyes.

"They must know your papa's gone," Little Mattie said. "Musta seen him passin' on the trail. Wouldn't come around otherwise."

John Carlton called out. "One's leaving!"

"Which?" his mother asked.

"The white one."

"Herman Lehmann?"

"He's just riding on."

Laura moved to the window and looked through a crack in the shutters. Herman Lehmann was silhouetted against the misty distance, his hair flowing behind him like a golden cloak. The others called out words she could not understand, but Herman Lehmann rode on, never turning, until he disappeared from sight.

"Do you think they're all leaving?"

"I don't know," Little Mattie said. "I don't think so."

John Carlton asked, "What we gonna do?"

"Depends. Long as they're in sight, nothin'. Time to worry is when night comes. Likely they'll stay put 'til then."

"Then what'll we do?" It was John Carlton again. Laura was glad he was asking her questions.

"What we have to do," Little Mattie said. "Bring me that stool, John Carlton. Might as well be comfortable. It's a long spell before dark."

The afternoon passed slowly. That was fine with Laura. She wished she could slow it down more, maybe hold it by the coattails and drag it to a stop. As long as there was daylight, she felt relatively safe in the good, strong house her father had built of live oak and cypress and fine heart pine. And what really bad could happen with her mother there? Light from the window played in Little Mattie's dark hair. Laura was reminded that she had only recently come to the conclusion that her mother was not the most beautiful woman in the world. It had come as a shock, bringing a troublesome, uneasy guilt. She had compared Little Mattie to their neighbor, Mrs. Catherton, and Laura decided she would rather look like Mrs. Catherton when she grew up than like her mother. Little Mattie seemed dumpy next to their tall, graceful neighbor. But her mother was surely stronger, a better shot, and could tell wonderful stories. She had schooling and had a whole roomful of books, while Mrs. Catherton could not even read.

Occasionally, Little Mattie would notice that one of the Indians had moved from her line of sight. "John Carlton, look out back. Charles, Laura, get to the windows, peep out, but keep out of sight. We need to know where those rascals are."

The Indians stayed out of Old Boomer's range. They prowled out back, into the toolshed, the corn crib, and the henhouse. "What you reckon they want?" Charles asked. "There's not a thing out there worth much, even to an Indian. 'Cept the horses, and Papa took the best one."

"What they want is in here," Little Mattie said. For a moment Laura wondered what she meant. Little Mattie glanced at her daughter and then, seeming to reconsider, added: "Or maybe they're lookin' for a piece of that old crab-apple pie."

They waited. It was quiet outside. Baby Lucy awoke, fretting. Laura lifted her into her arms to pat her back to sleep. Little Mattie sighed and shifted her position at the window. "Did I ever tell you," she asked, "about the time I met President Abraham Lincoln?" A half smile creased Little Mattie's face, yet her dark eyes never left the crack in the shutter. "Might as well pass the time with some talk."

Laura loved to hear the oft-told tale, though she was not sure she could concentrate this time with the Indians outside. But when her mother's words began to flow and the image of the great, homely, sad face of President Lincoln came to her mind, she realized again her very own mother had known him. She embraced the story, projecting herself into Little Mattie's role and became the heroine of the tale, the good friend of Abraham Lincoln.

"You watch hard now, John Carlton," Little Mattie said, then began: "Well, I was about Laura's age. My daddy was a doctor and we were living way up there in Illinois, up where it snows in winter sometimes as deep as a child is tall. And old Abe Lincoln was running for the United States Senate. He was running against a man named Douglas. Stephen A. Douglas. And they saw opposite sides of just about every question of the day. If Mr. Lincoln said a thing was yellow, Mr. Douglas would say it was blue. If Mr. Douglas said a thing was big, Mr. Lincoln would say it would fit in a hat box. Well, the biggest thing those two disagreed about was slavery. And they traveled all around Illinois debating the right and wrong of the issue of slavery. One of their debates was in the town where we lived. And my daddy took me to hear. We got right up front. I could almost reach up and touch Mr. Lincoln's coattails."

Outside, a footstep?

Little Mattie tilted her head like dogs sometimes do listening. The sound did not repeat.

"Mr. Lincoln thought slavery was wrong. That a country couldn't be half slave, half free. Mr. Douglas disagreed and took the other side of the question. One would talk and then the other and what they said would change the world. It was like they were talking to me and I was a part of it, a witness to what was really important in the country.

"One night, after the debate, Mr. Lincoln came to our house. He knew my daddy because my daddy was trying to help Negroes go back home to Africa. And Lincoln wanted to know about his ideas and how the plan was working. So they talked long into the night and I listened to every word about what would be the right thing to do about slavery."

"And what did you ask him?" It was a question Laura always asked at this point in the story.

"I asked him if a girl could be president."

"And what'd he say?" This was the part Laura loved best.

"Well, he thought about it for a long time. Looked right at me and smiled. He wasn't the handsomest man I've seen, but his eyes were filled with a light that just kind of jumped out at you and made you feel warm and good."

"But what'd he say? About a girl being president?"

"He said she could."

The day faded. Baby Lucy awakened and began to cry. The sound was very loud and seemed to pierce the afternoon with all the volume of Black Cato's bugle. "Tend to Baby Lucy, Laura," Little Mattie said, her forehead creased with concern. "See that she's clean and dry." Little Mattie looked back toward the well and she could see Black Cato watching the house, the day's last sunlight flashing on his bugle. "Now," she said, "it's time to move. We're all gonna go down in the cellar. We're gonna hide down there and we're all gonna be quiet as mice. Not a breath. Not a peep."

"What about Baby Lucy?" Hunger had brought new and noisy complaints from the infant.

"Get that whiskey your papa bought for medicine," Little Mattie told Charles. When J. C. Hoge had bought the gallon of whiskey from a peddler, Little Mattie had laughed and said it was enough to get half of Texas three sheets to the wind. But it was a good price for medicinal whiskey that would probably last at least forever. Now their very lives depended on it. "Laura, take half a teaspoon of that whiskey and pour it into some of that honey over there. Mix it with a cup of water. When she gets fussy, feed her a sip. Maybe that whiskey'll keep Baby Lucy quiet." Little Mattie looked back through the shutters, then back at the children. "Then I want everybody in the cellar, except me and John Carlton. Take some blankets and make a nest 'cause you might be there a long time. And, Laura, you start feedin' that honey-whiskey to Baby Lucy."

"Where will you be?"

"Up here for a spell," Little Mattie answered. "Old Boomer and John Carlton with the Colt are gonna raise a terrible commotion. When it begins to get dark, we're gonna shoot from all the windows like we had an army in here. Then we'll come down into the cellar. Maybe those Indians will change their mind and go away. Maybe they won't. If they come in the house, well, let's just pray they don't. That's all we can do except hide and be as quiet as we can." Little Mattie looked back through the shutters, sighed, and said to her younger children: "Now come kiss your mama and then we'll see what's gonna happen."

When J. C. Hoge had built the house he had dug the cellar because of Little Mattie's fear of the tornadoes that so frequently thundered through her Illinois childhood. He had also provisioned the cellar as a place to hide in the event of an Indian attack, a much greater threat, he felt, than storm. He had cut the trapdoor to the storm cellar so precisely that the passageway was difficult to detect, and he had mounted the family bed on rollers so it could be rolled away from the wall for access to the trapdoor. The bed could be rolled back in place by pulling a rope from below. The trapdoor was hidden by deerskins and the many quilts that draped down from the bed.

Although Laura's brothers often played at hiding from Indians in the storm cellar, Laura had been there only once and had vowed she would never go there again. She was sure snakes and spiders lurked in the dark recesses, especially great, moving, shimmering, hairy, creeping, alien mounds of daddy longlegs, like those hideous writhing masses on the back wall of the tool-shed. To Laura the threat of daddy longlegs was more horrible than the thought of Indians.

Charles opened the trapdoor and a stale, cold breath of air was released from below. Laura shuddered as she watched her brother climb down the ladder, his lantern punching holes in the darkness. He set the lantern down and held out his arms for Baby Lucy. To avoid breathing the foul cellar air for as long as possible, Laura took a deep breath and held it all the way down the ladder. The lantern flame revealed clean-cut dirt walls, rough-hewn timbers overhead, a clapboard floor, and dark shadows harboring unthinkable menace. Laura willed her eyes not to penetrate into the awful gloom beyond the lanternlight. John Carlton dropped quilts down from above and, holding her squirming little sister under one arm, Laura spread the quilts into a pallet with her free hand. Baby Lucy was delighted with the shift in routine and was eager to explore. She sang out her sonorous unintelligible vocabulary of vowels while Laura strug-gled to hold her on the pallet. As she raised a spoonful of the whiskey mixture to her sister's lips, she wondered what she would do if Baby Lucy refused to taste, then decided she would hold her nose and pour it down, a thing her mother did when fighting children's fevers. But Baby Lucy loved her honeyed liquor and lapped it up in great, noisy, eager swallows.

How much time elapsed before the sound of gunfire filled the cellar, Laura couldn't tell. Baby Lucy was having difficulty keeping her eyes open. Even the roar of Old Boomer and the sharp and rapid report of the Colt couldn't stay her long, easy glide into slumber. The sound was deafening, seemingly ampli-fied by the hollow space of the cellar, and trembles sent swirls of dust down from the ceiling and even clods of dirt from the walls. The sound became a solid thing, a fist pounding the air and shaking the ground. Then there was silence. Footsteps. The trapdoor swung open, Old Boomer was handed down, Little Mattie and John Carlton descended, the family was together and the trapdoor was closed. Little Mattie pulled the rope that moved the bed back into position, hiding the trapdoor. John Carlton and Little Mattie reloaded the shotgun and the revolver. Laura held her sleeping baby sister. Little Mattie kissed each child again before blowing out the lantern. In the darkness, she began to pray. Her voice was a whisper, but Laura felt that whisper fill all the corners of her mind. "Dear Heavenly Father," Little Mattie prayed. "If it's your will, please look down on this family and keep us safe. In Jesus' name, Amen." Laura was sure she could see the words of the prayer rising through the darkness, through the floor and up toward heaven. Now that she had actually seen an Indian she decided she believed in God and told Him so. Then there was no sound at all in the cellar, or in the house or from the yard, and it was very, very dark.

First came the sound of windows shattering and the ring of flying glass. There was rifle fire and the pandemonium of lead striking kitchen pots and pans and shattering whatever lay behind the windows. Laura could tell what the bullets destroyed by the sound of the impact. For a long time, the firing continued. Then abruptly, it stopped and the night was again still as a graveyard.

Carnoviste and Black Cato came. It wasn't a sound they made, but a change in the air, a perception of the presence of evil. Laura could hear the sound of her blood flowing. She felt an uneasy, almost painful sensitivity in her skin, something like a cat's hair rubbed wrong. And there was an odor, like wet hounds on a hot day, or unbathed brothers. A sound. At the back, maybe the window. Clink. Then a clatter. For a few seconds a breathless silence, then suddenly a deafening explosion. "It's the front door," Little Mattie whispered, and Laura felt herself enfolded in her mother's arms. John Carlton and Charles moved closer. "They shot open the door," Charles mumbled.

Now the Indians were in the house. Laura could hear their footsteps as they searched the rooms. She could tell they wore moccasins. They moved stealthily, at first. As it became apparent the house was empty, their footsteps grew more bold and the sound of their deep voices, sounding not unlike Rev. Andrew Jackson Potter speaking in tongues, began to bound around the house. There was a shattering sound and a crash and Laura knew someone had kicked a chair, then a torrent of language that could only have been an oath. Chairs scraped on the floor, cabinets were forced open, drawers pulled out onto the floor. All this, Laura could see in her mind's eye as the Indians searched the house her father had built from cypress, stout live oak, and fine heart pine.

Silence, then a raucous explosion of laughter, another oath, a grunt and more laughter, the froglike bellow of a belch. More laughter, then what seemed a kind of chant from the deep voice, a song devoid of melody, then more laughter and several soft whispery sounds like liquid pouring. "They've found the whiskey," Little Mattie whispered in Laura's ear. Then Laura and her family listened to Carnoviste and Black Cato get cock-eyed drunk. As the night wore on, the intruders argued, shouted, sang, pounded the table, and once the rhythmic pounding of dancing boots shook dust down onto the pallet. Suddenly, one of the voices broke into phrases of English mixed with Indian language. Laura recognized the words "land of cotton" and was sure Black Cato was singing an Apache version of "Dixie." A deep voice cursed, there was a scuffling, and then silence. For a long time, the intruders were quiet. Laura imagined they were eating the crab-apple pie. Soft footsteps inches above their heads and then the heavy creaking of ropes, a groaning sigh, a torrent of low mumbling, and Laura knew the terrible Carnoviste was lying on the bed just over their heads above the trapdoor. She sensed her mother repositioning the great shotgun, the butt on the floor, the two massive barrels aimed at the now sleeping Apache.

The sound Laura next heard would haunt her dreams until the hour of her death. Rising from the silence was a clear, pure, sonorous wail, a sweet-flowing melody that filled the night. She felt tears in her eyes as the mellow sound moved like a sorrow through the house. Black Cato was playing taps on his army bugle. Laura thought it was a kind of prayer and wondered if even Black Cato had a soul and if the sorrow she heard dwelled in the Negro or in the horn. Then she began to feel the daddy longlegs moving on the pallet.

Even as the scream began to build, she knew she was killing her family. In one awful instant she realized the scream would give them away and they would die. But the spiders were moving up her leg, below her dress, and in her mind she saw them heaving and vibrating, crawling mindlessly over her body until she was buried and consumed. She fought against the emerging scream and began to tremble and slap at her legs, sobbing and making a low growling sound in her throat. Then she felt the footsteps of the spiders on her face and her eyes and a scream erupted like a death knell from the chambers of her gut.

The bugle fell silent. The earth stopped short on its journeys through the heavens. Every living thing held its breath. There was a creaking of ropes, a shout shattering the stillness, a guttural oath, booted footsteps overhead, dust wafting down, fear biting like hounds at their hearts. The air was filled with a profound and thunderous orchestra of sound, a great, bull-throated roar as Little Mattie let go one of Old Boomer's barrels, then the other, straight up through the floor. The trapdoor flew away like an injured vulture, the air filled with cordite and splinters, and Carnoviste's drunken cries of pain and surprise. Confused shouts, bootfalls, the sound of horses flying away, the bleating call of Black Cato's bugle, then blessed silence and a ringing in the ears as welcome as church bells. Carefully, quietly, the family climbed up from the cellar. The house was in shambles. It looked as if the tornadoes Little Mattie feared had come at last. The shotgun had blown two ragged holes in the floor and Little Mattie's bed was soaked with blood from Carnoviste's body. Laura's mother fell to her knees amid the devastation and motioned her family to kneel in prayer. As she thanked God for their deliverance, Little Mattie reloaded Old Boomer with number four shot just in case their prayers were premature.

∞

Laura could not stop crying. When the pearl and silver mists of morning came, she was still trembling and feeling so bad she wished she had never been born.

"What's the matter, Sweet Thing? It's all over now." Little Mattie sat on the edge of Laura's bed and with a moist rag washed away the stains of tears and black gunpowder from below Laura's eyes.

"I'm ashamed."

"You shouldn't be."

"I could have killed us. Even Baby Lucy behaved better than me."

"Baby Lucy was tipsy."

Laura smiled, then sobbed. Her stomach ached from her crying. "I couldn't help it. I just couldn't."

"I think you should be proud, Big Sister. Wouldn't surprise me if you saved our lives. There we were, hiding like cowards. You forced us to do somethin'. Gave us the gumption to fight back. And that's what we did. Old Carnoviste will be pickin' lead out of his backside for months."

Laura felt some better, especially thinking about Carnoviste's injury, but she knew, in spite of her mother's words, that she could have caused their deaths. She was fighting the possibility that her fear had apparently been greater than her love.

"Why are they so mean?" Laura asked. "Why would they want to kill us?"

"For the horses, for guns. Maybe something to eat."

"But they wouldn't have to kill us! I don't understand. What did we ever do to them?"

Little Mattie looked around at the destruction in the house and the trail of Carnoviste's blood leading out the front door. "Well, different things. They say buffalo hunters killed Carnoviste's wife and his children. Settlers took his land. He had a second family and they were killed when Rangers destroyed his village. I think that might make a man mean. And that meanness just goes round and round."

"Tell me about the white Indian that went away."

"Your papa says he's the worst one of them all. The Apache took him away when he was just a little boy. Over by Fredericksburg. Your papa says the only children that survive with the Indians are the meanest ones. That's how hard life is."

"But he's not an Indian."

"I suppose he is now. I guess we are what we do."

"Why did he leave?"

"I don't know, Sweet Thing. Maybe he's not as mean as your papa thinks."

"And the Negro? Did you hear him play that horn?"

"That was somethin'. Like bells. They say he was a bugler for the Yankees."

"But he's not an Indian. He's a Negro."

"We're all just people, Sweet One. We do what we have to. And we are what we do."

"Would you have killed them?" Laura asked.

"I meant to," Little Mattie said. Laura looked up at her mother's face and decided maybe she had been wrong about Mrs. Catherton being more beautiful. She felt so proud of her mother and what she had done. A woman less than five feet tall had chased away a band of murderous Indians, surely something more amazing than being president.

After all, how hard can that be?

2 ∞ WHITE APACHE

IN THE SUMMER OF 1885, SEVERAL YEARS AFTER BLACK CATO
and Carnoviste had been defeated in the Battle of Hoge Hollow,
Laura rode through her father's raggedy field of corn, cotton, and
sunflowers toward Eager Mule Creek. She rode Miss Ruth, an
ancient calico mare of saintly temperament that had been a
member of the family and companion to the Hoge children since
long before Laura could remember. It was the summer Laura
turned fourteen. She urged Miss Ruth over the low wall of stones
grubbed by her father from the fields, and she rode out through
the tall grass to islands of live oak where pink star and white rock
aster and rattlesnake flowers struggled out from beneath a counterpane of limestone. As she moved across the rocky soil, her
father was much on her mind, for she had been that day punished for sassing the old man when he had admonished her for
using bad language. At supper she had described crossing a
newly plowed field as being like "walking across the belly of the
earth." Her father had said a young woman just did not use
such language, especially at the table, and Laura had said the
sound of the word "belly" was musical and not like "stomach,"
which sounded like a melon falling off a wagon. Now her legs
were on fire, the saline sweat of Miss Ruth's bare back burning
into the fresh red welts from the switching J. C. Hoge had applied
with fury and willow.

Eager Mule Creek flowed from the limestone depths into a
series of pools within a canyon of shadow and fern. It was a
secret place that even the sun had difficulty finding. Beyond the
spring and the pools, the creek meandered toward the Blanco
River where imprinted in the stone were footprints great monsters or dragons had left as they passed this way in ancient days.

Two of the prints were here, in Laura's secret grotto, large as a wagon wheel in the stone. She often came to the clear pool at the head of Eager Mule Creek to find peace and sanctuary and freedom from her father's harsh dominion.

Laura slipped down from Miss Ruth and moved to the spring. She sat on a bench of moss, removed her boots and wide-brimmed hat, her skirt and shirt, liberated her hair from its single braid, and, wearing only her teddy, eased down into the cool water. It was no wonder, she thought, that people are healed and sins are washed away in streams like the Jordan River and the headwaters of Eager Mule Creek. The water soothed the hurt she felt in her legs, but she still hurt. She tried to forget her father, to become a part of the spring, a small piece of nature, no more or less than the frogs hiding beneath the skirts of the stream or the wind singing in the live oaks or the bluff daisies she could see leaning down from the crest of the canyon.

Laura had discovered her secret place along Eager Mule Creek the previous year, the year President Garfield was assassinated. It was also the year she nearly decided not to be president, despite what Lincoln promised her mother. She had lingered by the creek thinking about death and how Garfield had suffered for eighty days before he died. The most amazing thing about Garfield's life, Laura thought, was that he could write Greek with his right hand while simultaneously writing Latin with his left. It was a rare gift to bring to the presidency. Then, while on the way to a class reunion, he had been shot and he had died, and that is largely what he is remembered by.

Immersed in the crystal cool of the Eager Mule, Laura wondered if the ultimate purpose of life was to be remembered. There did seem to be a direct relationship between one's deeds in life and the size of one's memorial in death. Presidents had the most impressive tombs, as did pharaohs and certain philosophers. What, after all, were the headstones in the cemetery but the sad, feeble effort of the dead to be remembered? Those tombs crowned by an angel with widespread wings were remembered more than those with a simple granite slab. But there were few memorials to women, of any size. Only men were cast in bronze, with the possible exception of the statues of women who led the armies of the French Revolution and whose generous breasts were invariably bare. *What can I do with my life?* she wondered, as she watched Miss Ruth graze at the edge of the creek. She thought of all the world's forgotten dead from the beginning of time till now. "How can I be remembered?" she asked aloud, only slightly discomforted by the sound of her voice in the silence.

After a while she rose from the pool and moved to a place where a seat had been formed in the stone. It was smooth and perfectly sculpted to her body. From this natural chair she could look down and see her reflection in the mirror of the spring. She saw a face framed in luxuriant chestnut hair, a wide, high forehead above very blue, slightly almond eyes. She saw the half-smile that others said never left her face even when she was far from smiling. It was an affliction, she knew, that inspired her father's anger. But no matter how she tried she could no more make that smile go away than she could change the luminous blue of her eyes.

Laura knew she was pretty. When she examined each of her features separately she found them pleasing and without fault. But now, as she looked at her reflection, she wondered if every girl saw herself as beautiful even if she was not. Maybe we see ourselves as attractive because we have been companions of ourselves so long. We see our mothers as beautiful because they are so familiar and we love them. *There is a connection,* she thought, *between familiarity, love, and beauty.* She considered her father; small and hard: deep, mean, hooded eyes; leathery skin stretched tight across blade-thin cheekbones and bony brows. He was an ugly man, in looks and deed, and she was not at all sure that she loved him, and she felt guilt come down like a shade. After all, she did respect the man. He had become old and bent, his life drained away by his labors on behalf of his family. He had built their house by hand, dug the well, and built a rock bathhouse and a blacksmith shop where he made all his own tools. He had coaxed so many bees to his hives that he could sell five gallons of honey at a time. He raised rail and rock fences from the earth, and was skilled in the art of making home brew from crab apples.

He knew how to do everything, how to repair a wagon and skin bears. Laura respected her father, but now, in the sanctuary of the head of the Eager Mule, she knew in her heart that she did not love him. And this was a hard thing to admit, and it stained the perfection of the day.

Miss Ruth was the first to hear the sound, the crisp, quiet clatter of hooves on stone and the harsh whisper of someone passing through the brush. Laura heard her horse nickering, and she looked toward the place where she could see something moving along the creek bed. It was a horse and rider, more than half hidden by the trees, but there was something strangely familiar about the brief glimpses she caught of the rider coming her way. Something golden and dangerous.

The rider broke through the willows, and when he saw Laura he froze and remained entirely without motion for what seemed an eternity. Even his horse remained absolutely still. Laura felt adrift in time, and her mind filled with crystal sharp images of Carnoviste and Black Cato and the boy who now dismounted before her and led his horse to drink at one of the monster footprints in the creek bed. Although he did not speak, Herman Lehmann's eyes seemed never to leave her face. He was older than the image in Laura's mind, still slender, his hair golden, his eyes a blue very much like her own. He wore nothing but a loincloth. The welts of old scars marred the perfection of his bronzed body. Never removing his gaze, he stepped into the monster's footprint and drank the sweet springwater from cupped hands. Then he settled down in the pool, and they watched each other across the creek, across the years.

After a long silence, Herman Lehmann spoke. "Do you remember?" His voice was a woodwind, a softness almost indistinguishable from the wind and the song of the spring.

"Yes," she said.

"You've grown," he said, then he noticed the welts on her legs. "You've been beat."

Laura felt ashamed of the red marks the willow had made, and she tried to cover them with her hands.

"Me, too." Herman traced a long scar across his chest with his finger. Again, silence fell. Laura felt a kind of magnetism reaching out from the strange, beautiful boy. Her heart began to beat strangely, so loud she was sure he could hear the sound.

"Are you afraid?" he asked.

"I don't think so."

"You should be. It's dangerous to be out here alone. Indian might come and steal you away. Take you for his woman."

For the first time since he had entered the glen, Laura realized she was nearly naked. She felt more than terribly ill at ease. She knew the feeling from when she had heard coyotes near the house. It was a tightness near her heart, a lightness, a dryness in her mouth. But it abated somewhat when she remembered that Herman Lehmann had turned away from his companions, had apparently wished them no harm on that day so long ago. And now she bathed in the blue of Herman Lehmann's eyes.

"Do you know what made this footprint?" Herman asked.

Laura shrugged. "Not really."

"They say the Great Father made all the animals by breaking off pieces of his walking stick. The smaller pieces became the mouse and birds. Larger pieces became the deer and wolves and the bear. But the big end, the heavy part that he held in his hand, became the monster that made this print. It was so heavy and so strong that it made footprints even in this hard rock. But the animal became so strong that it challenged the Great Spirit, and so it was driven away and destroyed forever."

Herman paused, looked around at the silent glen, then back to where Laura sat in her chair of stone. "That's why you like to bathe in the footprints. Some of that power is still here. When you bathe in the water of the footprints, that power comes into your body and makes you strong."

"How do you know I like to bathe in the footprints?"

"Because I've seen you many times. This is my place, too."

Laura thought about the times she had removed her wet teddy before putting on dry clothes, and she felt herself blushing at the thought that he had been watching. She even felt a touch of anger that her secret place had been invaded. But what she felt most was something she could not name, a kind of warming not from the sun, an excitement that made all her senses seem particularly alive and acute.

"Come in the water," Herman said. He indicated the adjacent footprint, a shallow pool filled with the cooling waters of the Eager Mule. "Come get stronger."

Laura rose from the stone chair, covering herself the best she could from Herman's eyes. She felt that each step she took was leading from childhood to some unknowable adventure. There was something spellbinding about the beauty of the canyon and the almost magical feeling that the footprint in Eager Mule Creek might make her stronger. She was flattered that this beautiful boy would tell her the secret of the great animal that made the prints in the creek bed, and she was still trying to decide how she felt about the fact that he had seen her naked. They had shared the most vivid memory of her life once long ago. This was something else, profoundly personal, they shared.

Laura lowered herself into the footprint. She was several feet away from where Herman lay in the other footprint made by the monster's passing, yet she felt connected to the wild boy by the light that passed between their eyes.

"Why did you go away that time?" Laura asked.

Herman looked away, then when she had begun to miss his eyes terribly, he looked back. "When I was the age you were then, some Indians came to our place. My two sisters, Caroline and Gusta, and my brother, Willy, were out in the wheat field chasing birds away so they wouldn't eat the grain. We sat down in the field, and before long we were surrounded by Indians. They had paint on their faces. They caught Willy right where he sat, and the rest of us ran for the house, just like you and your brothers. They shot at Caroline and Gusta, and they fell. And Carnoviste told me they all was killed. Even my ma. So there was nothin' to come back to, and I never did. I became an Indian. When I saw you and your brothers running away, I remembered all that and that's why I went away."

"Would you have killed me?" Laura was astounded that she would ask such a question when she heard it coming from her lips.

"I was an Indian."

"What was that like?"

He told her about being tortured and beaten and starved, and how they kept him stark naked, and how he wished he was dead. "Carnoviste made me his slave. I had to do everything for him. Bathe his feet, pick lice out of his hair, take care of his horse. They burned holes in my ears and in my arms with red-hot irons." He showed Laura the scars. "I didn't want that to happen to you and your brothers. No tellin' what they'd of done to you."

"But you stayed with the Indians."

"To stay alive. There was an Indian that treated me good. A squaw named Laughing Eyes. I don't think I could have stayed alive if it wasn't for Laughing Eyes."

"Are you an Indian now?"

"I don't know what I am." Herman Lehmann rose from the monster's footprint and walked toward Laura, scattering pearls of water along the way. He stopped, sat down next to her, not touching, but very near. "Close your eyes and let the power come and make you strong."

Laura closed her eyes and waited. She was aware of Herman leaning close, and she thought how lonely he must be, suspended between two worlds. She waited. Then she felt herself slipping out of herself, lifting on invisible wings, courage and strength striking her like a soft arrow, somehow piercing her flesh without pain. She was aware of the moment the power touched her, or was that Herman's hand, rough, yet velvet.

How long she soared above the creek, she would never fully know. But soon the lightness was gone and she could feel the cool water on her thighs and the wild boy's hands holding her. "I should go," she said, and she wrenched away from the grip of his eyes and the touch of his hand. In confusion she rose, turned and quickly ran from the pool, pulled her clothes over her wet teddy and struggled into her boots.

Herman watched her dress. "I'm sorry," he said. "It's what Apache men do."

"Well, it's not what white girls do!"

"You're angry?"

"I don't know what I am," she said.

"Then we both don't know," Herman said, as Laura hiked up her skirt and swung astride Miss Ruth. "Will you be here tomorrow?"

"No!" she said, and she rode away from the troubling waters of the Eager Mule.

∞

For several weeks, Laura and Herman Lehmann met secretly at their Eager Mule hideaway. And each time they met Laura was sure she was falling deeper and deeper in love. What else could it be, she thought, but love, this need to be near him and hear his voice and know that when they were together they were the only two people on earth. She felt as Adam and Eve must have felt in the garden. She yearned to tell Little Mattie about her feelings and to ask her if it was a sin to feel so absolutely happy, but she did not dare. If her father would somehow find out she was seeing Herman Lehmann, it was possible the whole world might end. Often, over supper, J. C. Hoge would rail against the murderous bands of savages that still raided isolated homesteads. Once, when a neighbor had lost several fine horses, Laura's father had insisted that Herman Lehmann was the thief. "Nothin' I know is as contrary to God's plan as a white man turnin' Indian," he told Laura. "And if I see that filthy turncoat around here, he's gonna wish he was dead."

As the weeks continued to slide by, Laura and Herman Lehmann walked in the autumn meadows and explored the world along the Blanco River where the leaves were turning and casting their colors to the winds until they fell spinning, drifting, from persimmon and pecan and mulberry, to cover the bobcat and panther tracks on the path below.

Herman seemed to delight in telling her about the world as seen through Indian eyes, how the Sky was their father and the Earth was their mother and how the two were husband and wife, and how the Apaches emerged from a hole in the mountain, like children are born from their mother. Laura felt something moving inside her when she thought of Herman as her husband and the great mystery they would share. On the night Herman told her about the marriage of Sky and Earth, she blushed as she lay in bed, remembering how it felt when they walked together, and how it would be if he were next to her now. And it was hours before she could sleep, and even then her dreams took her breath away. In the morning, she felt ashamed of her dreams, but, after all, they were secret fantasies, and nobody could know.

On other days, Herman told Laura how the eagle is the messenger of the Great Spirit and the owl is sister to the moon. He told her how bears had the power to heal the sick, and he told her how to find food in winter and how to find the way home when lost. And he told her about the power of dreaming.

"I used to pray my mother would find me," Herman said. "But as time went by, I prayed less, then not at all. I decided God belonged to the white man. One night it began to storm. I went to a hill where they said you could hear spirits moving in the wind and in the thunder and rain. I stayed there all night. Listening. I stood very still and I became a part of the storm, of the night. Before long I could see all the world clearly, everything that had ever been since human beings were made. And I could see the end of the world."

"What did you see?"

"The moon grew dark. The sun changed color like a rainbow. There were showers of stars and then a blackness darker than the blackest night."

Laura shivered and he moved closer. She felt his heat. Laura loved to hear him talk, and she was not sure if it was the words she loved so completely or the strange, handsome boy. She wondered if he would kiss her, and when, and how it would feel. And she both feared and yearned for the moment to come. She was not at all sure if Indians kissed or if they rubbed noses like Eskimos.

Sometimes Laura wished they could be together like other boys and girls, without having to keep their friendship secret. She was terrified someone would see them together and tell her father. There was something exhilarating about her fear, like leaping across a deep creek in winter or climbing into the highest live oak or following a cougar track alone. But she was seldom alone during that golden autumn. Rarely did a day pass that she did not walk by Herman's side, exploring the wilderness along the Blanco, her hand in his, his heart in hers.

One Saturday, after riding along a particularly remote reach of the Blanco, they rested from their ride beneath a grove of live oak. The gnarled branches formed arches overhead. A spring flowed through a soft mat of grass, still green and inviting, and they settled down to enjoy the sounds and sensations of the Indian summer afternoon. Here and there, the sun slanted down through the live oak, and Laura raised the hem of her dress so she could feel the season's last sunlight warm her skin. After the intimacy of the ride, she felt closer to Herman than ever before. It was a sweet kind of sadness. They were quiet for a long time, lying side by side, holding hands. A vulture wheeled overhead and a cloud passed over the sun.

Out of the shadow Herman said, "I don't know what to do."

Laura saw a change in his eyes. "Do about what?"

"About where to go. Who to be. About being with you. I'm not an Indian and I'm not white. I'm nothing."

Laura squeezed his hand and turned toward him. "You're Herman Lehmann. My good friend."

"Herman Lehmann is dead. I don't know who I am. But I know I don't belong here."

"I love you," Laura said. The three words flowed as naturally as a spring from limestone. She was thrilled by their sound and terribly frightened.

"Then come with me," he said. "We can be together. Live free in the old way. We'll find Laughing Eyes and she'll teach you."

"You know I can't."

"Then what can we do?"

Laura looked into the liquid blue depths of his eyes. She traced the scar on his chest with the tip of her finger. He turned to her then and kissed her, and she could taste his tears. She was sure she would be swallowed whole by the love she felt, and the fire that raged softly at her center, and the terrible beauty of the moment. When at last their lips parted, she knew there was only one way they could be together forever.

"It's time to come home," she said softly, and she kissed the scar Carnoviste had cut across his chest. "It's the only way. If you love me, it's time for Herman Lehmann to come home."

3 ∾ THE MURDERS

FROM THE BLUFF ABOVE THE RIVER LAURA COULD SEE THE entire country spread before her from the Blanco below to the far horizon. The land rolled and twisted and folded like a blanket on a giant's unmade bed. Haze masked the distance and the afternoon light burned down through a white and cloudless sky. It was still unseasonably warm and would be till dusk. She rode along the bluff above the river, Miss Ruth's rope halter lying loose on her withers. Laura sat straight and tall, braiding her hair, guiding Miss Ruth with small pressures of her knees, trying to recall the feel, every precise nuance and subtlety of the glorious moments she and Herman had kissed.

The Blanco River curved through its white rock channel, cutting a canyon through stone and through time. The river ran low, thirsting for rain, and the roar that filled the air constantly in spring had diminished to a whisper now. She passed the other monster tracks along the Blanco. From the bluff she could look down on the prints and could see that the ancient creature had crossed the river and walked right across Hoge land on its journey toward the abyss. Maybe it had paused and slept on their place, its head near the house, its tail at the far stone wall of the cotton field.

Below was Hoge Hollow. Laura was proud that a whole place had been named for her family, their land reaching from the bluff south of the river, across the Blanco and far beyond. The Hoges were the only citizens of Hoge Hollow, and their log house the only home. Their fields of cotton and corn, their cow pen, their apple trees and hives of bees, a few hogs, comprised all there was of civilization for miles around. On school days, Miss Jeffie Woods, the teacher, and her pupils came to Hoge Hollow because Little Mattie had convinced Laura's father to donate a plot of their land for the little one-room country school. So far from the main road was Hoge Hollow that the only visitors were an occasional peddler or tinker or distant neighbor bringing mail from town.

Laura had once told her father she wished she had a different name. He had been furious and had told her that a name is all you have that cannot be taken away. Laura looked down at Hoge Hollow and wished it was called by another name, a far better name than Hoge, better even than Lehmann, the name she would have should she and Herman be married. She tried to envision Herman in a white man's suit and it made her smile. She would have to cut his hair. And then an image of her father's face, that dark, mean mask, intruded on her dreaming. It would take a miracle for him to allow Herman into their lives, even if he did give up his life as an Indian.

Laura rode on past Hoge Hollow into the long shadows of afternoon. She knew she would just have time to pick up the mail at Joe Harrison's place and still be home for supper. But she was not yet ready to face her father, his discipline, or the chores that would fill the evening. She thought of what Herman had said about the dangers of being alone in this country. Then she thought of Carnoviste and Black Cato and she found herself looking for movement in the shadowed stands of live oak. She wondered if she were less afraid of the Indians now that she was in love with one and now that she possessed the strength of the ancient monster.

Laura finished braiding her hair as she turned from the river along Towhead Creek, the small stream that led to the Catherton place. Nancy Catherton had said she could come pick as many peaches as she could carry. Now when her father asked her where she had been so late she could say the Cathertons and it would not be a lie. She left the path along Towhead Creek and then along Sandy Creek toward the Catherton place. The gnarled branches of the ubiquitous live oak arched over the Sandy and the vines of mustang grapes climbed into the heights, closing off sunlight, making the way along the creek as dark and mysterious as a cathedral. There was no sound, except the clapping of Miss Ruth's hooves on the stone creek bed and the wind. Suddenly Laura felt, and she was sure Miss Ruth knew, that they were not alone. Somebody was watching. The feeling was real, unmistakable, overpowering. With her legs she asked Miss Ruth to stop. It was still. She remembered what Herman had said about watching her and she wondered if he was following her now. But why? And besides, she felt there was something evil in the shadows, a dread menace that made her blood feel cold. She started forward again and remembered what her father had done when he found out his family had been attacked by Carnoviste and Black Cato. He and a posse had tracked them across country and trapped them in a box canyon near the narrows of the Little Blanco River. They left the horses and climbed along the canyon's rim to a place where they could fire down on the raiders. But the Indians had disappeared. When the posse returned to the mouth of the canyon, her father and the others found the Indians had slipped past them and had cut all the feet off their horses. Her father seemed to enjoy telling about how it looked when those poor horses tried to stand. Each time he told the story, Laura became sick, and now she wondered if all Indians, even Herman, were capable of such horrible things. She booted Miss Ruth in the ribs and they flew along the creek toward the Cathertons'.

The Catherton house stood on a rise before a field of limestone and dry brown corn. It was a stone house, solid and secure upon the earth. The sunlight bathed the white walls, and they seemed a beacon of safety after her breathless ride through the creek bed. Once she was out of the shadows of the live oaks, she began to feel sheepish about her fear. And there was Nancy Catherton, sitting on the porch, leaning against a porch column, nursing little Joshua, her newborn child. It was a scene out of one of Little Mattie's magazines, an image of domesticity. Laura rode closer. She waved. Nancy Catherton did not wave back.

The bullet had entered Nancy Catherton's eye and had carried away most of her head. The baby was covered with blood and was sucking at its mother's breast. Her husband, Judd Catherton, was lying in the doorway. The doorjamb was flecked with blood. Laura forced herself to feel for a pulse. He was dead, but still warm. Laura looked out toward Sandy Creek, then into the house, knowing the killer was near. She knew the killer or killers could not be Indians. Indians would have scalped the Cathertons and taken the baby. But, then, she could not be sure. The baby began to whimper. Laura lifted the child and to her horror, the blood that covered Little Joshua was still wet and the slippery wriggling baby nearly slipped from her grasp.

Wondering if she would hear the sound of the shot that would kill her, Laura scrambled into the house, slammed and bolted the heavy door and sank to the floor. She huddled against the door trying to make some order of her racing thoughts. She listened for a sound from outside, some movement. The killer knew she was there. Was that his step she heard, a light tread on the porch? Then, like a sob, the thought tore into her mind that she had locked herself in with the killer, that he was in the house, waiting in the shadows. She thought she heard him breathing. The smell of evil came like a cloud from the dark rooms. Laura closed her eyes, then willed herself to rise. The baby again began to fret. Laura gentled the child and holding it to her breast, she began to move from room to room, each step a massive effort of will, her fear like a knife of ice cutting and hacking at her heart. But the explosion and the pain she feared, the death she expected, did not come. The rooms were empty. She was alone in the house. She began to breathe again and, slumping down into a kitchen chair, she began to think of what must be done.

She knew she had to make a run for home. Outside, the sunset stained the west blood-red and the last light of day lingered in the pastures. If she left now she would be an easy target. She would have to wait until dark. The blood on the child began to thicken, became tacky and stuck to her skirt. From the darkness came the call of an owl. But was it an owl? Was Carnoviste out there? Was he waiting in the dark woods? She looked at Miss Ruth grazing nearby and she thought of horses without feet. No, not an Indian. It had to be a white man. But what white man would do such a horrible thing? Then came the most numbing thought of all and it made her feel sick with shame. Herman

Lehmann was a white man and her father said he was the cruelest of all. She hurled the thought from her mind.

A fire burned in the kitchen stove. Nancy Catherton must have been preparing supper when the killer came. Laura thought of heating water and washing the blood from the baby. But there was not time. She felt a powerful impatience to be gone from the Cathertons' dying place. On this most terrible day of his life, little Joshua laughed and cooed and sighed. Outside it was growing darker. Soon it would be time.

From an apron in the kitchen, Laura made a sling by knotting the lower ends around her neck. In this way, she could carry Joshua against her stomach and still have her hands free. Once the child was secure in its sling, Laura moved to Judd Catherton's body looking for a gun. But it appeared Catherton must have either been surprised or killed by someone he knew, for there was no weapon near the body. After a brief search, she found a holstered single-action Colt revolver hanging from a peg by the front door where Catherton could have reached it if he had felt the need. Laura spun the cylinder. The gun was loaded. She tried to strap the holster to her waist, but the belt was much too large. She considered putting the gun in the sling with Joshua, but what if the gun accidentally fired? Finally, she put the gun in a tow sack that she would hang from her saddle horn.

Now there was nothing to do but wait for the soot-black clouds to the north to come swallow the day. She had seen the clouds coming, like the prodigal black sheep of heaven, herded by the northerly wind. Joshua was asleep. She could feel his warmth against her stomach and it reminded her of her punishment for uttering such an evil word as belly. She had to smile when she considered how furious her father would be if she got herself killed. He would be fit to be tied, for sure. It would be worse than neglecting chores or being late for supper.

The fields and woodlands around the Catherton place were swept by shadows of the darkest possible lavender, then a kind of liquid blackness spilled onto the land and into the trees until the world along the Blanco disappeared from view. It was dark as the eve of the first day of Creation.

For a moment more Laura listened to the night. The wind was a French harp in the trees. In the distance, down by the creek, she could have heard a horse whinny, but was not sure. *No matter. There's nothing to do now but ride.* It was full dark and time to go.

Laura whistled softly and Miss Ruth appeared out of the darkness. Carefully, she climbed from the porch onto the horse, checked to see that Joshua was tucked firmly beneath her breast, turned toward the mountains and the long way home, then was swallowed by the same darkness that swallowed the day.

For a while, as she rode toward Hoge Hollow, Laura tried not to think about anything beyond the horse's next step along the path. She wanted to recall the feel of Herman's kiss, but it had gone away, like it had happened a hundred years ago. Perhaps if she closed her mind to the idea she was being followed, the possibility would cease to exist.

She rode on, down off the bluff to the river bottom into Hoge Hollow and across the Blanco. Even in the darkness the landscape was familiar and she knew she would soon be home. Somewhere toward the head of the Blanco the dark clouds must have brought rain, for the river was running fuller now, nearly stirrup high. As she urged the horse up the far bank and entered the small apple orchard her father had planted when she was Joshua's age, a powerful human presence struck her like a club. Someone was there. Her heart thundered in her ears and she felt a silent scream borning in her abdomen. Instinctively, she reigned in hard and whirled the horse back toward the river. But when she reached the water, she realized that safety lay the other way, toward home, not out into the terrible darkness. So she turned again, reached into the tow sack and yanked out the revolver. A shadow moved in the gloom beneath the apple trees. It was a shape, a shade, a form of enormous dimension, wearing the dead of night like a cloak. The form stood between Laura and home and she knew there was only one thing to do. She raised the pistol and charged her fear, firing again and again. The world was a storm of sound and motion and terror. She heard the explosions of the gunfire and then an explosion that seemed to be within her head. She felt herself falling and then felt nothing at all.

"First you should'a come home for supper," J. C. Hoge scolded. "That's the first thing. Second thing is, you shouldn'ta shot at your pa. And the third thing is, a girl that's fourteen years old oughta know how to shoot better."

"Let her be, J.C.," Little Mattie Hoge said. She was holding Joshua, and Laura could tell by the look in her mother's eyes that she had a new baby brother. There was love enough in Little Mattie Hoge's heart for all the orphans in Texas.

Laura was safe in the lap of her family, listening to the familiar humorless railing of her father, the great blue knot on her head throbbing in cadence with her pulse. It was little more than an hour since Laura had been swept off her horse by the limb of an apple tree while firing a salvo at her father, and she could tell by the expressions on her brothers' faces that they were memorizing every detail of the moment. Her brothers regarded her with a respect they rarely showed, and sister Lucy waited on her hand and foot, serving the warmed supper of venison stew and biscuits she had missed by coming home so late.

"I know this for certain," J. C. Hoge said. "From what you described, it weren't no Indians. And I know who done it. It was that Herman Lehmann."

Laura felt something like a sob beneath her heart. She looked up at her father's face and saw the hate in his eyes and in the pinched slash of his mouth.

"I don't think it was," she said. It was a kind of reflex.

Her father's eyes narrowed. Laura wished she had not spoken.

"What makes you so expert on Herman Lehmann?"

Laura kept her eyes on her plate. She had never been good at lying. It always seemed her lies became more and more unbelievable with the telling. Now she was afraid any denial would merely reveal what she wished to deny.

"It was somebody Mr. Catherton knew well enough to leave himself unarmed. I don't think he knew Herman. He would have . . ."

J. C. Hoge interrupted, obviously not interested in his daughter's theories. "It was Herman Lehmann! And when I catch that filthy turncoat I'm gonna do to him what he did to my horse once."

"What's that, Papa?" John Carlton asked, eager to hear the grisly details.

"I'm gonna cut off his feet." The statement was made without emotion, in the dispassionate tone of a man commenting on the weather. Laura looked up at her father, horrified, her mouth open, her eyes round and pained. Her heart was beating faster than it had when she thought she would die at the Cathertons'. She knew if anything happened to Herman, especially at the hands of her own father, she might as well be dead. For a moment, Laura did not even care if the tears welling in her eyes gave her away.

Then her father smiled. The tracery of deep creases in his leathery face shifting hideously. "Well, now," he said. "Looks like we've got an Indian lover in the family."

"Herman ain't an Indian," John Carlton said.

"You be quiet, boy! Don't dispute your pa!" J.C. turned back to Laura. "And you, little Miss Indian lover, when I'm through with him you can have him. All I want is his feet to stuff and put on the mantel. You can have the rest of him."

"It was Indians," Laura managed to whisper.

"You said it wasn't."

"It was."

Now J.C. was laughing, looking at his daughter and howling with laughter, as if the whole thing was a joke. But Laura knew he would do what he said. It was the way he was, right or wrong, he would always do what he said. She wondered if somehow he had guessed the truth, but decided if he had she would already be near dead from beatings.

"You feel like you can ride?" J.C. asked Laura.

Laura said she could, but dreaded the thought of getting on a horse and riding back into the night. She hated the thought of going back. Even more, she hated the idea of them being gone and staying home alone, wondering where Herman was, wondering if he was capable of doing what was done to the Cathertons. Wondering.

"Can't we wait till morning?" She pushed away her plate of stew and watched her father reload the family's arsenal and her mother gather the things they would need at the Cathertons'.

"Need to get a move on. Can't leave those folks out there like that. Sooner they're tended to the better. Sooner we get after that white Apache, the easier he'll be to catch."

"What if he's still there?" Lucy asked.

"Won't be," J.C. said. "He'll hole up somewhere else. But I'll ride out there with you before I head into town just in case."

"What if there's more than one?" Lucy asked. "How do we know they didn't kill a lot of people? Maybe there's more dead than Laura saw?" Lucy asked the questions that crowded Laura's mind.

"What if you just hush up, little lady. It's time we did what's got to be done," J.C. scolded.

The night was still dark. Laura was almost thankful for the pain in her forehead for it kept her mind off the killer whose presence she could feel filling the darkness. If it wasn't Indians and it wasn't Herman, who could it be? She wondered if he would follow her the rest of her days, a shadow disturbing her peace forever. It seemed so terribly unfair that she should be out again among the dark fears she had so recently escaped. She wished she was safely in bed, waking to the realization the whole night had been a terrible dream. Or was the night a waking from a dream. The horses' hooves drummed in the night. She rode close to her father. A full moon slipped now and then from behind the clouds to light their way to the Cathertons', and vultures wheeled against its light.

Judd and Nancy Catherton lay in grotesque repose. Laura

had hoped they had somehow been swept into Heaven or that she had dreamed their death or had missed their pulse and they had survived. But they were there where she had left them, the moon reflecting in their sightless eyes. Little Mattie helped J.C. lift the bodies and carry them into the house. There was no room to lay them out on the dining table, so they were laid upon their bed.

"I'll take a good look around," J.C. said, "then I'm goin' on into town. We'll have a posse made by morning. The boys'll stop along the way and tell folks what's been done." For a long while he gazed out the window and stood as if listening for sounds in the night. "He's a long piece away by now," he said, "but bolt the door and keep a good watch all the same." Then he and the boys were gone.

Little Mattie undressed Judd Catherton while Laura struggled with his wife's stiffened clothing. It was only when they began removing their clothes that the terrible knife wounds were visible. The bodies had been slashed and the wounds lay open like the mouths of beasts, closing on the cloth that had to be torn from the flesh and dried blood. With warm, soapy water, Laura washed away the blood, but there was too much and the wash water and bedclothes were stained crimson. When Laura pulled the stained sheets from under the bodies, she felt a weight of a profound sorrow settle down upon her shoulders and her mind. The Cathertons lay like lovers sleeping away the night on the bed they had shared for so many years in life. Laura wondered about death and if it was like a long night without dreaming. Little Mattie searched for clothes the Cathertons could wear into the ground. Then she began to dress the stiffening and unyielding bodies, like some awful play with badly damaged dolls.

Laura was weary to the very center of her being. Weary of being afraid. Weary of knowing such evil could be done to people who had done no harm and deserved better than a madman at their door. Laura considered the heart of the man who had ended the Cathertons' lives. Had he known his act was evil? Or did he justify what he was doing in some curious and demented fashion? And why did he keep killing them with a knife after he had killed them with the gun? Laura was weary of thinking and she tried to stop. She felt Little Mattie's hand on her shoulder.

"That's all we can do," Mattie said. She pulled a quilt up over the Cathertons' faces. "Why don't you rest now, Little Sister." There was another bed in the room, probably where children had slept when still at home. Little Mattie led Laura to the bed and tucked her in and sat with her for awhile, her hand pushing a lock of hair away from the bruise on her forehead. "Close your eyes. Soon we'll all be back home and this will be over."

Laura was sure she was too exhausted to sleep. She prayed to the Lord Jesus that Herman would ride, ride, swift and far and safe from her father's knife. Then she was gone, dreaming that Judd and Nancy Catherton were alive and whole. Little Mattie stood watch, her rifle within reach. Beyond the window, evil rode beneath the moon.

J. C. Hoge returned in late afternoon the following day. *Too soon,* Laura thought, *too soon.* If Herman had escaped, the posse would still be searching. J.C. would not be out there now, a rider in the distance, coming this way, unhurried. Laura felt the crushing weight of dread pressing her down, unbearable, pressing the breath from her lungs. She watched her father come and tried not to think or hope. "Dear Jesus," she whispered, "let him be safe."

J. C. Hoge dismounted and he walked forward with that slouching swagger Laura despised. His face was expressionless, an empty, wrinkled slate. He walked up to where Little Mattie and Laura waited and he spat brown in the dust.

"Well, we got him."

Laura turned away, certain her world had ended, hating Jesus for what He did not do. She felt dizzy and sick. She just wanted to lie down in the dirt and die.

"Damndest thing," J.C. said. "Man's name was Lackey. He apparently went loco. He just started doin' bloody murder, like he was killin' hogs or chickens. First his own kin, including his wife and family. Then the old Stokes couple and the Cathertons.

Just started shootin' and then cuttin' them up with his knife. Killed six in all. Cut 'em up into pieces like a butcher cuts meat. When the killin' started, Miz Lackey ran and hid in some bushes and she saw old man Lackey take a knife to his own neck. Started sawin' away like he was gonna kill hisself but then got scared to." J.C. spat again and shook his head. "Damndest thing. Like I said it was a white man."

"You said it was Herman Lehmann." Laura could not look at her father, afraid he would see the sudden joy, the glorious relief she felt.

"Well, he's done just as bad. Coulda just as well been him."

Later J. C. Hoge told Little Mattie and Laura that they had come upon an encampment of Indians in the willows of Nameless Creek. Thinking that Herman Lehmann was among the Indians they had swept in and during the melee the Indians got themselves killed. But Herman was not there. The posse, which included just about every man and boy in town who could be gathered quickly, then learned that it was not Lehmann but Al Lackey who had done the killings. The posse found Lackey so easily that most of the riders felt cheated somehow. It was not often they were able to pursue such unambiguous evil. Lackey gave up without a fight and was led to jail unrepentant, cursing his captors all the way.

By evening, the Cathertons were laid to rest beneath an oak in Sandy Cemetery on Double House Road. A small gathering of friends and neighbors stood at the graveside. Rev. Andrew Jackson Potter said a prayer and the bodies were covered over. J. C. Hoge drove two wooden crosses into the ground with a shovel, then straightened up and said, "Let's go home."

4 ∞ THE HANGING TREE

THREE DAYS AFTER THE KILLINGS, J. C. HOGE DROVE HIS FAMILY into town. "I want to see what the mood is," he said. "Trial supposed to start while we're there, but I don't reckon there'll be one."

"Why no trial?" Laura asked as they hitched the wagon to the team.

"A lynchin'?" Charles asked.

"Ol' Man Lackey gonna be decoratin' a live oak. Gonna be human fruit."

Little Mattie lifted baby Maggie up to Laura, then with the Cathertons' Joshua cradled in her left arm, she swung up into the wagon. "Let's not be talking about hanging, John. Not on a beautiful morning like this."

"Hangin's just part of livin'. The way things is. He took the Cathertons, now it's his turn to be took. He mighta took our Laura! I mean the blood was still wet and warm when she was there. It's just plum dumb luck he didn't kill Little Sister!"

"But he didn't."

"But he woulda if he coulda. He mighta. So he deserves what he gets. The way things is. So they're gonna haul him out of jail and up a tree. Trial or no trial it amounts to the same."

"Pa, can we go?" It was brother Charles that asked.

"To the hanging?"

"Please, Pa."

"No, you can't go!" Little Mattie said.

"If there's a lynchin' while we're in town, I believe we all oughta go," J.C. said. "Be a lesson for the chil'ren. Teach 'em right from wrong."

The day was unusually warm for October, as if the sun could not sleep and had awakened early to chase away the chill. The mules moved in near perfect unison, like a single beast, along the river road toward Blanco.

Laura had mixed feelings about Al Lackey's fate. She was both curious and repulsed by the images a hanging impressed on her mind. She was relatively sure her father had planned this trip into town for a reason other than obtaining supplies and a new hickory handle for his ax.

As the miles crept by, Laura felt liberated from the normal routine of the day. *If old Al Lackey was not facing the prospect of hanging, I would be home helping mother plant a second crop of black-eyed peas, or weeding potatoes, or cutting or bundling hay.* In the last few days, the cotton bolls had begun to open and soon her father would lead his children out into the dawn fields to pull the lint from the sharp dry bolls and they would stuff the cotton into the bags they dragged behind them between the rows. Lucy, even little sister Maggie, would move among them with gourds of water, and she and her brothers would pick cotton until dark, and then come home with their backs on fire and their fingers raw and bleeding. In some ways Laura loved those summer days upon the land, and it was only thinking about it from a distance that made her life seem so hard.

Not far from Blanco, on the south bank of the river, the road passed a great mansion built by a very wealthy man named Lawrence Hall. Facing the river, the home rose two stories high and was fronted by a wide balcony from which you could see nearly all the known world. Whenever Laura passed, she tried to imagine what it would be like inside and what it would be like to be rich. She imagined there was a square rosewood piano in the music room and a library heavy with books: literature, philosophy, the great classics of the ages. She imagined herself mistress of the mansion, overseeing the tenant farmers who worked the fields and cared for the animals in the pastures. She wondered if wealth removed a person from the earth. Surely the Hall children did not pick cotton or clean weeds from around the cistern or haul heavy buckets of water from the spring. In fact, one of the great marvels of the Hall mansion was a hydraulic pump that automatically lifted water from the Blanco into a cistern. Even her father could not explain how it worked. Surely the Hall children bathed with store-bought soap, while the Hoge children washed with soap made from mixing ground limestone with bacon grease. While Laura's family had supper on stools around a rough pine table, she was sure the Halls dined around an elegantly carved mahogany table, sitting on chairs upholstered in velvet. Little Mattie Hoge served her meals with spoons made from gourds, while the Halls were certainly served by servants with silver. Sometimes Laura wondered why some people were born rich and others born poor. She wished to be mistress of a home with chandeliers of brass and crystal prisms, and damask drapes and a square rosewood piano instead of a home of hewn logs with clapboard walls. But then there were times, like those times she bathed alone in Eager Mule Creek, or when she rested close to Herman on a couch of moss watching an eagle's flight, when she wondered if the Hall children were not the ones to be pitied. *They were surely strangers to the sun, the moon, the evening star. And certainly they could not know the love of nature she shared with Herman. Some people were born to be rich and some were born to be poor. And some, like Al Lackey, were born to be hanged.*

The town of Blanco seemed to rise reluctantly from the banks of the river. It hugged the earth, with no building, not even the new courthouse in the town square, being much higher than the tallest Spanish oak. The courthouse dominated the stone and frame buildings lining the square, like a great stone hen surrounded by her chicks. They passed the saloon where old men sat reminiscing in the shade of its wooden porch. They passed the blacksmith shop, the Blanco Hotel, the stationers, and the carpenter shop of L. H. Wall, whose gifted hands had made most of the wagons in town. These wagons, hacks, and buggies filled the square and the streets, especially in front of the courthouse, where a crowd had begun to gather, seeking the latest news of Al Lackey's trial set for tomorrow.

J. C. Hoge tied the mules to the hitching rail. The brothers headed for the jail to see if they could catch a glimpse of the condemned man. J. C. Hoge joined the group watching the day go by from the gallery of Alexander & Spear's Drugstore. As Laura, her mother, her sisters, and Baby Joshua moved toward the marvels of the market, Laura noticed people seemed to be staring at her, pointing and whispering behind their hands. At first she thought she imagined the attention, then she heard a voice announce: "That's her. Laura Hoge. The one that found the bodies." A man stepped into their path, bowed, and introduced himself as William Wright, publisher of the *Blanco News*. He was a large man with a round, kind face. His hair was the color of a summer cloud.

"And you must be Miss Laura," he said. "I understand you found the Cathertons. Saved their little boy. Is this little boy the one?" He indicated Baby Joshua.

Laura said it was.

"I must say, that was quite a heroic thing to do."

Laura was mildly surprised, yet pleased at Mr. Wright's attention. She had not considered herself a heroine. In fact, she was ashamed of the terrible fear she had felt. And she had very nearly shot her father.

"I'm finishing a story about the killings for the *News*. I'd be obliged if you would tell me what happened. What you saw and heard."

Laura looked from the editor to her mother. "She's been through a lot," Little Mattie said. "The facts are known."

"But there are many versions of the facts, Mrs. Hoge. Emotions in this town are stirred up. I'd like to be sure my story is accurate, not based on rumor and supposition."

"You might find the truth will stir people up more than rumor. But Laura, it's up to you."

William Wright led Laura to the little clapboard print shop where the *Blanco News* was published. And there, surrounded by complex and graceful machinery of the printer's mysterious art, she told what she had seen and heard the day and the night the Cathertons were killed. At first, she thought the telling would bring back the fear, but she found she was strangely exhilarated. She felt important. There was something exciting about knowing her words would not just disappear into the air but would be captured in print and would last until the paper turned to dust. She looked over at the old single-cylinder Campbell press that would soon clatter out her story at several hundred sheets an hour. It was like talking to hundreds of people at one time. Wright asked an occasional question, jotting notes on a pad. As she told the story, she was reminded of details, subtleties she had been frightened to consider at the time. She even remembered the smell of biscuits baked just before the intruder came and the amazing fact that Baby Joshua did not cry once during the long and horrible ordeal.

"Do you think the killer was near?" Wright asked. "Maybe outside the house. You say the bodies were warm. He must have been near."

"I had the feeling he was all around. Everywhere. I felt surrounded."

"But you didn't actually see Mr. Lackey?"

"No, sir."

"And how did you feel when you heard the killer had been caught?"

"I'm not sure I know." Laura could not bring herself to say what she had felt, how relieved she had been that it had not been Herman.

William Wright folded his notes. "Well, you're a very brave young lady and I appreciate your help." He rose and offered his hand.

"How'll the story end?" Laura asked as she rose.

"I'm afraid with a lynching."

"Shouldn't he get a trial? I thought everybody was supposed to get a fair trial before a jury."

"Sure. Theoretically. But there were witnesses. People who saw it happen. Al Lackey is guilty as they come."

"I thought that was for a jury to decide."

"Where are you going to find a jury this time of year? Cotton's coming in this very week. There's hardly a man, woman, or child in the county who won't be pickin' cotton from dawn till dark. It may not make justice, but it makes sense."

"I think it's wrong," Laura said.

The editor sighed and looked again at his notes. "What do you think I should write?"

"That every person has a right to a fair trial. It's in the Constitution. Maybe you should write that the posse killed a family of Indians before they found Mr. Lackey. That's wrong, too. You could write about that!"

Again, the editor sighed. He looked at Laura for a long moment.

"You're a smart girl, Laura. Most young people don't think so deeply about the right and wrong of things. What are your plans? What do you want to be?"

Laura told Mr. Wright what she had been thinking ever since the Cathertons were killed. "I'd like to help people stop hating each other. I'd like to change the way things are. All this hate and killing." She thought of Herman and her father and horses without feet and the Cathertons sleeping deep in the earth and the crowd gathering for Lackey's hanging. "Maybe politics."

William Wright smiled. "Not exactly woman's work. What makes you think you could be a politician?"

"My mother knew Abraham Lincoln. He told her a woman could even be president one day."

The editor smiled again and then his face grew sad. "My dear girl," he said. "You are too bright to waste your life on empty dreams. You cannot be president. You cannot be governor or have any political office. *You can't even vote.* It just can't be. Politics is a man's profession. A woman's . . ."

". . . place is in the home."

"I didn't say that, Laura. Not at all. Maybe you can't be in politics, but you can write about it. There are fine women journalists. A journalist can change things with the written word. A journalist can be the conscience of the people."

"And not write about how wrong it is to hang a man without a trial?" Laura saw the editor close his eyes and look away, embarrassed. She felt bad she had offended such a kind man. "I'm sorry, Mr. Wright. I . . ."

The editor interrupted, holding up his hand. "No, Laura, I'm the one that's sorry." William Wright led Laura to the door and she hurried back through the stares and whispers to the wagon where her father scolded her for not staying put.

J. C. Hoge continued to scold his daughter all the way to the jail where he had been invited to supper with leaders of the posse that had captured Lackey. In the interest of his children's education, and against Little Mattie's objections, J.C. had demanded the three oldest children join the group for supper.

"Don't worry," J. C. Hoge told Little Mattie. "If we hang him it won't be until later. Wouldn't want to spoil a good supper."

The prelynching supper was served on the grounds of the Blanco County jail. Wagon beds arranged beneath great spreading pecan trees served as tables. A barred window faced the wagon beds and Laura could see a shadowed form passing back and forth, probably Lackey pacing away the minutes he had left in this world. Apparently, J.C. was the only man there teaching his children the difference between right and wrong, for there were no other young people among those at the supper. Laura noticed the sheriff was nowhere to be seen. Although he and the deputies had set up the tables and their wives had provided the spread of beans and barbecued beef, the officers of the law had disappeared before the blessings. Laura counted eighteen men at the table. Most of them she recognized, some from church, others the parents of her schoolmates. These were good people. How could they do what they were setting out to do? She was embarrassed and ashamed to be a part of the meal, especially when the blessings were said. *How can these men who say grace before eating do something so evil?* If she were a journalist like Mr. Wright, or a politician, she would show people that lynching was wrong and should be ended forever.

"Where they going to hang him?" John Carlton asked Mr. Sawyer, the postmaster.

"They was going to hang him in the town square," the postmaster said, pointing at the nearby gallows tree with his fork. "But the Widow Harnsworth's window is right next to the tree. She's real sick and we was afraid the commotion would disturb her rest. So we thought we'd better do it out from town."

"Where's the sheriff?" Laura asked her father.

"Don't worry, he's left the keys to Lackey's cell where we can find them easy." Alex Waldron, John Higgins, and a few of the others laughed. "This ain't his business now anyhow," J.C. added.

"Why not?" Laura asked. She knew she was treading on thin ice but she could not help the anger she felt, the sense of being a part of something terribly wrong.

"You just hush up, young lady." J.C. glowered at his daughter and then turned back to the others when he heard the hated name of Herman Lehmann.

"Sure wish Herman woulda been with them Indians over on Nameless Creek." Laura saw it was Sam Wilkinson who spoke, the father of Alice Wilkinson, her friend. "We coulda strung up two for the price of one."

Laura knew she should hold her tongue. But Mr. Wilkinson had hung swings for Alice when they were small. He had swung them high and told them stories when she stayed at their house. "That's awful," she said, softly, indignantly, not expecting to be heard. But the words filled a void in the conversation and they rang out clearly like clarion. She could feel the eyes of the hang-men like stones thrown.

"Herman Lehmann didn't do anything," she said weakly, unwisely, and then she felt an explosion against her face and scarlet streaks of fire behind her eyes. She felt her father grasp her by the shoulders and shake her violently and he was still shaking her when Laura opened her eyes and saw his hard, mean face weaken as he became aware everyone at the table was looking at this man who had struck his near-grown daughter in public. Laura could tell her father felt the censure of his fellow hangmen, for this was something simply not done in decent society. Her face burned with pain and shame and confusion. Laura tore away from her father's hands and ran from the jail-house feast back to her mother who was waiting by the wagon.

∞

It was providential that the place on the Blanco River bank J. C. Hoge selected for their camp was only a half mile or so from the live oak on which the townspeople decided to hang Mr. Lackey. Laura had expected a mob, a lynch mob, spontaneous eruption of passion, shouts of outrage. But the parade from town was orderly.

After all, Laura thought bitterly, they had waited until after a leisurely supper before they had found the hidden keys, then bound and lifted Mr. Lackey onto a wagon for his ride to the newly selected hanging tree. It was not passion that was hanging Al Lackey, it was convenience. The crowd increased in number as it moved beyond town, yet was never really large. When the procession passed the Hoge camp, Laura thought they might just as well be going to hear a fire-and-brimstone sermon or to a performance of one of the more dangerous high-wire acts at the Glasscock Circus. There was the same quiet awe flowing through the crowd. J. C. Hoge gathered his children and joined the townspeople following the hangman's wagon.

It was growing dark as they reached the hanging tree. Laura watched the men cast a heavy rope over a low limb, the hangman's naked noose swinging obscenely as they adjusted it to the proper height and secured the bitter end. They backed the wagon under the noose. Somehow Laura had expected a ritual with speeches and posturing and warnings about the wages of sin, but even with the wagon in position, the crowd stayed strangely quiet. Once the noose was so fearsomely displayed before the crowd, the people grew restive. They shuffled their feet, slapped at mosquitoes, and kept their eyes cast down or lifted them up to look into the trees. Laura felt their unease and wondered if the hangmen and the crowd might change their minds. Clearly, nobody wanted to take the first step. Laura thought it must be humiliating to be hanged by a crowd so lacking in passion.

"That limb's too damn low, anyway," Lackey said from his place on the wagon. His words had the opposite effect from what he had apparently intended. His voice galvanized the hangmen. Someone shouted, "Let's get it done!" Other voices rose and joined in a guttural chorus. Laura felt death coming. She saw her father and the others yank Lackey into a standing position and place the rope around his neck. She could feel the rough hemp and she winced as she saw the rope scrape his wound. Someone in the crowd shouted, "Shoot him!" There was a momentary pause as the option was discussed, then a new tension began to build with the crowd's desire to see the hanging done and over.

Laura heard Mr. Waldron suggest to Lackey that he jump high into the air from the wagon so the fall would break his neck and he would die quickly. Lackey nodded his head. The thing Laura feared most was the sound of Lackey's neck breaking.

J. C. Hoge asked if Lackey had any last words. Lackey said he did. "It don't matter if I say I didn't do it. So I'll just say you should let me go so's I can dig those fools up and kill 'em all over again!"

The voice of the crowd rose angrily into the night. Laura felt the hatred flowing like a dark cloud through the trees. "Hang him! Hang him!" The phrase became a chanted liturgy.

In those last moments, Laura put herself in Lackey's position. If she were to jump from the wagon in order to die quickly she would be denying the possibility of a miracle. Maybe some kind of hellhound would have leaped from beneath the earth to carry her away, or lightning would have hit the hanging tree, or Herman Lehmann would come to sever the rope with an arrow. She imagined she would have made the same choice Mr. Lackey made when they whipped the mule and the wagon was driven away.

Al Lackey did not jump and he was right about the limb being too low. When the wagon moved out from under him, Lackey was dragged from the wagon by the noose into the air. There was no jarring fall to break his neck and Laura was spared the sound. His weight bent the tree limb down to where his toes just barely touched the earth, and then the limb took him skyward again. Laura watched the gruesome dance, fascinated, as first his toes touched, taking the weight off the noose, then he was hefted up again, the noose tightening. He made no sound. Laura heard her father say he thought Lackey's vocal chords were crushed. Lackey's eyes remained open and staring, sometimes looking up as if to implore the heavens for release, at times sweeping the crowd with an accusing gaze Laura would never forget.

Lackey would not die. He was suspended half between this life and hell, his arms and feet bound, the noose cutting deep into the wound on his neck. In the torchlight, his face was the color of rotting plums, his eyes cast curses at the fading day. The crowd gathered close, only a few feet from the hanging man, transfixed by his pendulum motion. J.C. suggested they cut Lackey down and start the hanging over from a taller tree. Someone else said Lackey was nearly dead now and to hang him twice for the same crime would be against the law. Mr. Wilkinson argued they should shoot him to put him out of his misery and someone else recalled how vicious and evil his crimes had been and he deserved all the suffering he could get. Laura could swear Lackey's unrepentant eyes followed the debate. She felt sick and had to look away. In the end, the hangmen left him there, dancing slowly beneath the live oak, and they turned one by one to follow the wagon back into town.

Later that night, as Laura lay on a blanket beneath the stars, brother Charles touched her shoulder.

"You think he's dead?"

"I suppose."

"What if he's not?"

"Then he's not." Laura really did not want to think about it any more. After all, it was all she had been thinking of since she had made her pallet on the riverbank.

"I think we should go see." Charles looked under the wagon where their father was noisily sleeping, then said, "Come on."

The night was filled with a bedazzling display of starlight. The constellations seemed close enough to touch and the Milky Way looked exactly as it must have looked when named, a fluid stream of light, as if God were pouring it across the heavens. They walked along the Little Blanco for awhile, then cut north along the road to Johnson City. "What're you gonna do?" She had to take large strides to keep up with her brother.

"Depends."

They approached the hanging tree carefully, crouched down, moving from shadow to shadow. The starlight revealed the large form still hanging from the live oak. Mr. Lackey was moving slightly and slowly up and down, his toes touching the ground, then lifting off again, as the wind moved the branches of the tree.

Laura wondered how long he must have danced till he died, keeping alive by tiptoe.

They moved closer. Charles asked Laura what she thought.

"He must be dead."

"He's moving."

"It's the wind."

"We oughta go see."

The wind turned the body until the ghastly face was staring their way. The head looked immense, canted at an inhuman angle, the face so dark the starlight was absorbed in its blackness. Only Lackey's long tongue and his eyes reflected light. As the hanging man turned, a low moan came across to where Laura crouched and a terrible chill engulfed her heart. "He's alive!"

"It was the rope makin' that noise!"

Laura stood and moved from the shadows into the presence of the hanging man. Charles followed.

"I think we should cut him down," Laura said.

Charles was horrified. "Why?"

"Why not? This whole thing's wrong. He's dead enough."

Charles and Laura stood together before the horrible bulk of Al Lackey. A shooting star hurled itself across the sky. The body swayed in the rising wind. Suddenly, a gust tugged at the live oak and the rope slipped and Al Lackey dropped to his knees and a great moaning sigh escaped from within the hanged man. Laura and Charles backed away from those staring eyes and then wheeled and fled. When they reached the road, Laura turned to see a shadow cloaked in starlight move to where Lackey kneeled. A blade flashed and she was sure Herman Lehmann had come to cut the hanged man down. She would have called out to him, have gone to him, but her brother was watching and she was not entirely sure what she had seen in the darkness. Then they ran and ran as though pursued by the devil and all his hordes. They ran until they reached camp and then lay sleepless, eyes wide, through the night.

In the morning, on the way home, the family made a detour past the hanging tree. Al Lackey was gone. In town, nobody seemed to care who buried him or where.

5 ∞ THE GLASSCOCK CIRCUS

LAURA HEARD THE CIRCUS COMING WHEN IT WAS STILL A MILE from town, a distant trumpeting tugging at the stillness of the Hill Country dawn. At first she had a fleeting thought of Black Cato's horn and that he had come at last to avenge Carnoviste's wounded backside, but the sound was too wild and animal, not at all as musical and sad as the trumpet of Black Cato had been. Then she saw the elephants, like great drifting gray barns, trumpeting along the road, following wagons the color of late summer sumac and green apples to the field next to the Blanco River where the Glasscock Brothers Traveling Circus made its camp for the winter.

The sun was beginning to burn off the mist when the roustabouts and riggers and canvasmen began to raise the tents. It was like watching a ballet. Each action, each movement of the strangers carefully choreographed. The kitchen tent rose first, then the dressing tents and the tent covering the animal cages where great captive cats screamed and roared. Laura had come to help Charles sell a load of hay to the animal keepers. But her attention was swept away by the sight of elephants lifting the huge center poles of the Big Top and the vast pastures of canvas that rose to cover the entire sky.

All morning and into the afternoon, Laura watched the compelling metamorphosis of the circus. It seemed to bloom upon the earth like an exotic flower. Among the circus people she recognized performers she had seen the year before. The family of high-wire acrobats, the beautiful bareback riders, the gypsies, a midget, the Fat Lady, and the clowns all moved on their mysterious errands. A lovely dark-eyed gypsy woman and a clown passed by. They were holding hands. As Laura watched, the couple paused and kissed. When the clown touched the woman intimately, Laura looked away and the thought of Herman came as a sweet, sharp ache. Because she was afraid what her father would do if he found them together, she and Herman met only rarely, and briefly, in their hideaway on the Eager Mule.

Watching the clown and the gypsy made her miss Herman terribly. And that was part of the reason she felt strangely sad as the circus set up its annual winter camp. The strangers seemed so free. But she was locked away on a tiny crossroads in the wilderness, in love with a man she could not be with, held captive by a cruel father and facing a life without a future.

That night Laura helped Little Mattie bake a crab-apple pie. It was late, as Little Mattie's workdays often were, and they were alone in the kitchen. Laura told her mother about the circus camp and all the wonderfully strange people she had seen and about the exciting life they seemed to lead.

"Mama," she asked, after a silence, as her mother sliced the small, bitter fruit, "what will my life be like?"

Little Mattie looked up and sensed her daughter's mood. "Nobody can know that, Little Sister. We just have to be ready for what comes."

"Sometimes I think I can see it. Years from now I'll be right here where I've always been. Doing what I've always done. Cleaning, chopping cotton, having children, getting old. And life will be gone and no one will really know I was here."

Little Mattie put the crab apples in a bowl and wiped her hands on her apron. "So you want adventure. Like the people in the circus." Then she leaned back against the kitchen table and riveted Laura with that disapproving look that she generally reserved for her husband. "There are some who'd give their eye-teeth to have what you don't want. To have a place of their own. To have a family. You may not know it, but that life you seem so all-fired anxious to escape is *my* life. And you should pray you're as lucky!"

"I'm sorry, Mama. I didn't mean . . ."

"And as for adventure," she continued, "what do you call this life of ours if not adventure? How many of those circus people have fought off Comanches? Or have had to make do in the wilderness. By the way, the panthers and bears around here aren't in cages! They're right outside, loose in the night, in our lives. Why, you've lived more adventure in your few young years than anybody in that circus. Your adventure is real. Theirs is fake as a freak show."

"I didn't mean to get you all upset."

"Don't you think I've had those same feelings? Don't you think I've wondered what I might have been or done if the world had been different? Don't you think I've sometimes felt trapped? When I was your age, my father was a physician, a highly respected man, Abraham Lincoln's doctor. Just imagine! A man who would become the president of the United States was in our house. Just imagine the dreams those visits inspired. In those days I wanted to be a doctor. My teacher said every boy in America could grow up to be president. But a girl couldn't even grow up to be a doctor! My papa scolded me for having unrealistic dreams."

"But President Lincoln said . . ."

"That's just a story."

"You mean it didn't happen?"

"Oh, it happened."

"What *exactly* did he say?"

"The point is that some things are possible, but not very probable. It's possible there's people living on the moon. But don't bet your life on it."

"What can I bet my life on?"

"Not on the circus," Little Mattie said. She turned away from Laura with a quick, deep sigh. They stood for awhile saying nothing. Laura could hear her father, out by the barn, hammering on something iron, working away his rage. Laura felt tears forming and she knew something was happening between her mother and her that was important and irreversible. She wanted desperately to tell her about Herman and how she loved him so and how she could not imagine why Little Mattie would have married a man so hateful and cruel as her father. But she knew that to talk of these things with her mother would be, in itself, a cruelty. What could her mother do or say? She had lived with her man for an entire lifetime. They had endured pain and created life, and maybe that was greater than love. She could feel the space between her and her mother trembling, flowing, seeking some acceptable equilibrium.

Little Mattie wiped away tears with her apron and turned back to her pie. It was the first time Laura had ever seen her mother cry.

"So here I am," Little Mattie said. "Baking a crab-apple pie. But I'll tell you this, Little Sister. It's going to be the best crab-apple pie in the county!"

Laura folded Little Mattie in her arms. It reminded her of how tiny her mother was. For a while they embraced, listening to the ringing of J. C. Hoge's hammer, then Little Mattie dropped her arms and once again wiping away tears she said, "Go on and dream your dreams, Little Sister. But remember this. There are some things that are dreams and some things that are real. One is one thing and one is another. And those who can't tell the difference are in the lunatic asylums."

Little Mattie wiped her eyes, then smiled up at Laura. "Well, well. Aren't we something. So serious." She touched her hand to her forehead as if seeking to remember where she was in the process of making the pie. "Sugar," she said, pointing to the crock on the corner shelf. Laura walked to the shelf, wondering if she had the will to tell the difference between what was and what she wished. It was only as she turned away from the corner with the sugar that she heard the dread and unmistakable salutation of the rattlesnake.

The rattle was louder than the snare drums of the Glasscock Circus band and Laura's heart stopped. She could only stare at the huge snake which seemed to grow larger and larger there in the corner of the kitchen as it poised to strike. Laura knew she could not move in time and so she did the best she could do. She threw the crock of sugar with all her might. It exploded in shards of glass and white cloud. Then Little Mattie's iron skillet rang and rang again, like damaged carillons, and the rattler's blood began to stain the pure white sugar on the counter crimson.

Laura and her mother stood motionless, watching the terrible mess they had made.

"So you want more excitement in your life?" Little Mattie asked, and there was just the ghost of a smile in her eyes.

In the weeks that followed the hanging of Al Lackey, Hill Country farms continued to lose livestock to the few wandering bands of Indians remaining in the territory. It was generally thought that Herman Lehmann was among the raiders, even though he was rarely seen. One Saturday, after she had finished her chores, Laura rode Miss Ruth out to the Eager Mule. Herman was waiting. He had spread a bearskin to keep away the autumn chill. They sat close, holding hands, listening to the melody of the stream.

"Why do they tell all those lies about you?" Laura asked.

"What lies?"

"About stealing cattle."

Herman looked at her and smiled. "What they say is true. I have to eat. There are women and children who would starve without that meat."

"I thought Indians hunted deer and wild animals."

"But the land is owned by the white man. They won't allow us to hunt on their land. And we will not be farmers."

Laura wondered if it was time to ask the question she had come to ask. She pulled the bearskin up to her chin and glanced at Herman to see if she could read his mood. He seemed to be dreaming, lost in that faraway province where she seemed unable to follow. Often he let her accompany him a little way into that world, but there was always a point where he lifted an invisible gate to bar her passing.

"Have you thought any more about going home to your family?"

"That's all I think about."

"We could talk about it if you want."

"Sometimes I think they don't really want me."

"You know they do. Your mother prays for it. For you to come back."

"My father's dead. My ma remarried. A man named Buchmeyer. Who knows what my new father wants. Probably not an Indian son. For all I know he hates Indians just like everybody else."

Herman put his arm around her and held her under the bearskin. She leaned her head on his shoulder. She waited for him to continue. She suspected he was afraid to come home but knew he would never admit it. "If it's the only way we can be together, I'll do it. I'll give myself up."

"But not here," Laura said. "It would be too dangerous. Why not to the soldiers at Fort Sill. Tell them you've decided to come home to your mother and your family. If you come back under the protection of the army you'll be safe from people like my father."

"When most children are recaptured from the Indians, they return as heroes. Maybe it will be the same with me. I'm older, but maybe that's all right. The hard thing would be my mother. I know she'll never understand. I could have escaped. But after awhile I didn't want to. I was where I wanted to be. How would I explain why I didn't want to see her all those years? What would I say? How would I act?"

"You just have to love her."

"I don't even know her."

"You have to give it time."

"Then you will be my woman?"

"I'm your woman now."

"Not in the Indian way." Herman lifted her face and kissed her.

"You have to give it time," Laura said when their lips parted, not absolutely sure she knew precisely what they were talking about.

∞

One day, in the fall of 1883, as Laura was gathering eggs in the chicken house, being careful to look for snakes before reaching into the nests, she heard her father come home from town in a rage. "They're bringin' that heathen Herman Lehmann home!" He spit the words like tobacco juice out onto the ground. "Next thing you know they'll be askin' Sitting Bull to preach the Sunday sermon." J. C. Hoge unhitched the wagon and, still fuming, went into the house for supper.

It had been years since Black Cato, Carnoviste, and Herman Lehmann had been driven away by Little Mattie and Old Boomer. Laura had heard rumors that Carnoviste was dead, killed by Rangers, and Black Cato had ranged down into Mexico. She knew Herman Lehmann had become something of a legend in the Hill Country, a symbol for all that was wild and murderous in the human heart. There were some, however, including her father, who did not believe anything Indian was human, especially a converted white boy like Herman Lehmann. "How his ma can take him back is beyond me," J. C. Hoge said over cabbage that had been cooked outside because Little Mattie believed its aroma attracted flies. "I'd as soon take in a rattlesnake. It would be a kindness to bring that white Apache home dead."

Little Mattie gave her husband a look of disapproval, that expression she wore frequently in his presence, the one he never seemed to recognize. "He's just a boy, J.C."

"That boy's a man. Must be nearly twenty now. And he'd as soon cut out your liver as blink an eye. I can't count the number of scalps that white Indian took. Enough to fill a washtub."

As the days passed, the people of San Marcos, Blanco, New Braunfels, Stonewall, Comfort, Twin Sisters, Loyal Valley, Luckenbach, and other Hill Country towns became obsessed with the restoration of Herman Lehmann to the civilized world. Everywhere Laura went there was little conversation that did not center on Herman Lehmann's return. Outside churches and the livery stables or at quilting bees or in the home people wondered how he would look, or act, whether he would speak Texan or his heathen tongue, and how he would be accepted by the men who had been so eager to see him dead. Once, while hunting the nests of stray turkey hens, Laura heard her brothers and their friends making wagers on how long Herman Lehmann could stay alive.

The whole community sympathized with Herman's mother, a woman who for nine years had prayed for her little boy's return. Most were skeptical that the reunion would cause her anything but pain. Little Mattie and others who believed that a person could be changed by faith, prayed for the Lord to touch this wayward child and drive out the demons that had come to dwell in his heart. Laura simply prayed for his safety and for a miracle to strike her father, if not dead, at least reformed.

A great feast had been prepared to celebrate Herman's restoration to the bosom of the community. The women of Loyal Valley persuaded their husbands to barbecue beef, ham, and sausage, and as they took turns watching the fires all night, Laura thought she sensed their anger about Herman's return was lessening and she allowed herself to think that maybe things might be all right after all. Even her father seemed to be less belligerent than usual, his anticipation of a rare feast day greater than his anger. Laura read in William Wright's *Blanco News* that people were coming from all the surrounding counties, some invited, some not.

On the morning of the feast, the people began to arrive in Loyal Valley. They came by horse, by carriage, by wagon, and by foot. Each family brought fruit, bread, pies and covered dishes. All the talk was about the joyous reunion between Herman and his mother. Laura could hardly contain the excitement she felt on one hand, and her anxiety on the other. Maybe it had been a mistake to make Herman's return so public. But the feast had simply happened spontaneously, the excitement of celebration kindled by the generous heart of every woman who had ever had a son.

Herman's mother was an attractive woman with a shy, yet pleasant manner. There were streaks of yellow beneath her gray hair and Laura could see something of the son in the silver-blue eyes of the mother. Mrs. Buchmeyer wore an uncertain, tentative expression and she seemed overwhelmed by the attention and gifts of food she received from neighbors and strangers. Laura could see the pain in her eyes, the years of waiting and wondering if her son was alive, and then that different, yet very real, agony of knowing he was. As Little Mattie and Laura approached Mrs. Buchmeyer to pay their respects and deliver a loaf of fresh-baked bread, Herman's mother was being interviewed by William Wright.

"What was that moment like when you first saw Herman after all those years? It must have been a wonderful moment."

"It wasn't." Mrs. Buchmeyer wiped her hands on her apron and looked down at her feet. "The soldiers brought him in. And he was there. It was dark." She paused and her eyes pooled with tears. "I didn't know what to do. He didn't look . . ."

"You mean you didn't recognize him?"

"I wanted to. With all my soul I wanted to. I looked for some sign, I prayed for some sign that this was my boy. But I didn't think it was. I was afraid." Mrs. Buchmeyer turned away from the newspaperman. Mr. Wright followed, his pen poised.

"But it *was* your boy."

"I know that now." There was an edge to her voice. Laura was certain Mrs. Buchmeyer was ashamed that she had not recognized her own son.

"So when did you first know?"

Mrs. Buchmeyer put her arm around a young boy by her side. "Little Willy knew it was his brother."

"I seen the scar," he said, proudly. "I seen the scar where I cut him with a toy hatchet a long time back."

"So then I knew my baby boy was back home," Mrs. Buchmeyer said, "and I rejoice and praise God for His goodness and mercy."

"And Mr. Buchmeyer? He's here?"

"No. He was detained." She wiped her eyes and turned away. When Mr. Wright stepped around to face her, she turned away again. Laura wished the editor would leave Mrs. Buchmeyer alone. After all, it was obvious to her why Herman's stepfather had not accompanied his wife to the most important day of her life. Herman was probably right. His new father was no different from his old one.

Little Mattie, J.C., and Laura joined the guests seated at long tables and on blankets spread beneath the trees. A group of fiddlers was playing and there was a sense of high expectation in the air. Laura, too, could hardly wait for the appearance of the guest of honor. Her heart was rocking around behind her ribs and she felt slightly feverish. She glanced at her father fearing he would notice she was flushed.

There was a murmuring in the crowd, like bees disturbed, or the sound the Blanco River makes rising in a rainstorm. All eyes were drawn to a small group of people preparing to take their place at the head table. Among them was Mrs. Buchmeyer walking on the arm of her son.

Laura was shocked when she saw Herman. This was not the wild warrior who had terrorized her childhood or the secret love she had found at the Eager Mule. Rather, a slight, awkward boy took his place at the table. His golden hair had been shorn and there was a cowlick now where his flowing mane had been. He was dressed in a stiff new suit, with high-top shoes and a red tie. Herman Lehmann appeared to be the most ordinary young man at the celebration. Only his silver-blue eyes seemed the same as the image she carried and so carefully guarded in her mind. Surely this was not the savage killer whose freedom so enraged her father. The boy's eyes were sweeping the crowd. Laura eased down on the blanket, hiding from the stranger masquerading as the boy she loved. Finally, their eyes met and he smiled and all her love came flooding back. Herman seemed to grow taller. Clearly her presence had given him strength. In spite of her father's ominous presence, it was all Laura could do to hold back her tears of happiness. Or was it some kind of fear or sorrow she felt? She knew events were gaining a momentum of their own, and she and Herman were being swept along like driftwood in a Blanco River flood.

Rev. Andrew Jackson Potter, one of the great evangelists and orators of the time, rose to offer a prayer for the prodigal son. His deep voice was like the tolling of bells. "What man of you, having a hundred sheep, if he lose one of them, doth not leave the ninety and nine in the wilderness and go after that which is lost until he find it."

The reverend was in fine form, Laura thought, and she was proud that such a great man had been chosen to welcome Herman home. She knew her father admired Andrew Jackson Potter. If a man of God could accept Herman, maybe her father could learn to accept him, too.

"And when he cometh home, he calleth together his friends and neighbors, saying unto them, Rejoice with me; for I have found my sheep which was lost."

As Rev. Andrew Jackson Potter continued with the parable, Laura prayed that Herman could find the strength to face what must be a terrible moment in his life. Suddenly she saw him as a wild animal being led into a cage, and for the first time she wondered if they were doing the right thing. Had she asked him for more than he had the strength to give? Again, their eyes met and she saw more panic there than love.

When Reverend Potter concluded his invocation, and Mrs. Buchmeyer had thanked everyone for coming and sharing her happiness, Laura was aware of a curious pause, an uncomfortable interval in the ceremony. Appalled, she suddenly realized the hundreds of guests expected Herman Lehmann to speak, to acknowledge the crowd, make a prepared statement about his absence and his return, and then offer some meaning to the whole bizarre scenario that had been his life. She felt caught up in the same expectation, hoping against hope that he would find the strength and the words, terrified that he would not.

Urged by Reverend Potter, Herman rose. From the throat of the crowd there escaped a breathy exclamation. Laura thought such a sound must have been heard from those who saw Lazarus rise from the dead. Everyone watching, including Laura, was expecting some kind of miracle.

For at least half a minute, Herman Lehmann stood gazing at the crowd, then up into the pecan trees, then back to where the multitudes waited for the words that they were prepared to memorize for retelling through the years. Laura wondered if Herman had prepared for this moment. She remembered the marvelous stories he told her of Sun, Moon, and Morning Star, eloquent in their simplicity, told with warmth and flair. She began to feel that the words would be there when he reached for them. But then why were his eyes growing so wide? To Laura's absolute despair, Herman opened his mouth and began to howl.

The sound rose high and awful into the trees, a long, wavering contralto yowl. Then, barking and yelping, he kicked over the head table, scattering the banquet onto the ground. As the crowd watched in horror, he tore away his red tie and rushed from the grounds hollering his hatred of what he had been asked to become.

That night, after supper, Laura slipped from the house, whistled softly for Miss Ruth, and hurried to the Eager Mule. Herman was there waiting in the shadows. She rushed to him and held him close. She put her hand on the back of his head to pull his lips down to hers and his short brush of hair was a surprise. Herman pulled away as if embarrassed about his hair, his white man's clothes, ashamed of what he had been unable to do.

"I just couldn't do it, Laura. I just couldn't. I looked out at all those faces and I couldn't."

"I know," Laura whispered, and she placed a finger to his lips to silence him. When he was quiet, she replaced her finger with her lips. "It's all right. It's my fault. It was too much to ask."

Laura did not return until late that night and her father beat her with a strap of leather when she got home. She thought the pain was nothing compared to what Herman felt.

Other than their hideaway, the only place Laura and Herman felt safe together was at the nearby circus camp. They were drawn to the place by their loneliness and the need to feel the presence of other people. At first they watched the circus folk from a distance, but gradually they gathered the courage to move closer, under the fringe of the great, faded canvas Big Top to watch the performers practice their exotic arts. All the people who seemed so extraordinary during performances now seemed accessible and very human. They were busy repainting sections of grandstand in gaudy colors, exploring new ways to balance precariously on the high wire, patching the places where the canvas tent had been torn, teaching the great cats and horses new tricks, repairing the bright gold, green, and red spangled

costumes of the beautiful bareback rider. Laura and Herman felt
at home among the outcasts.

After a time, they were accepted by the circus people, especially the huge Indian named Ball Coon who trained the elephants. He was quick to recognize that Herman was caught
suspended between two worlds and that the young couple
needed friends to share their secret life together. He offered Herman a job helping with the animals.

"It's a good life," he said. "In the spring we start touring the
country. Circus people are good people. Outsiders leave you
alone."

Laura was delighted. "Oh, Herman, it's perfect."

Herman was not sure. "But what about you?"

"There's always work for a strong country girl like Laura,"
Ball Coon said. "Room for you both. There's a lot of married
couples travel with us. They raise their families along the way."

Laura blushed at the thought. It was a preposterous notion,
of course, an absolute insanity, but wouldn't it be fine just the
same? She tried to picture her father's face when he discovered
she had run away with the circus in the company of the hated
white Apache. He would be fit to be tied. She thought of the
leather strap and her beatings and how it would be heavenly to
be free of his tyranny.

When Ball Coon learned of their situation, he said that the
circus was the only place on earth where they had a future
together. "I was where you are now, Herman," he said. "Wasn't
accepted by whites or Indians. But I'm accepted here. Here they
don't care about the color of your skin or if you are only two feet
high or are big as a barn. Everybody is accepted for who they are
and what they can do."

It was clear the circus people applauded the audacity of the
strange young couple. One Saturday, they were asked to lunch
in the cook tent and they squeezed between the Fat Lady and
the Mighty Midget. Later they laughed about the disparity
between the servings of the enormous woman and the tiny man.
It became more and more apparent Herman belonged and she
was proud that he had been accepted by the performers and

roustabouts of the Glasscock Brothers Circus. Here among the freaks and sword swallowers and human pincushions, loving a lost warrior did not seem so outlandish.

One day, Laura noticed Ball Coon helping Herman up onto one of the huge trumpeting beasts. It was a warm autumn day and Herman was wearing only a loincloth and he reminded her of the wild boy she once saw riding across the Blanco at Hoge Hollow. Then, Ball Coon motioned to Laura.

"Come ride," he said, and he led the elephant to where Laura was standing. Before she could protest, Ball Coon grasped Laura by the waist and in one fluid motion swung her high and pivoted her around until she was standing on his shoulders, leaning on the elephant's side. Herman reached down, grasped Laura's arms, and lifted her up behind him onto the elephant's back. "Hold on," Ball Coon called, and Laura was forced to either wrap her arms around Herman's waist or risk a fall. It was not an easy decision and the only place she could hold Herman that was not bare skin was worse. "Best hold on," he said, and her arms encircled his hard, warm waist and she was glad Herman could not see her face, for she was sure she blushed crimson as the cap of a clown.

The elephant seemed to fly across the field, twice scattering coveys of quail. Laura could feel the boy's heart beating beneath her hands. As Ball Coon rushed ahead, holding a long tether, the great animal rocked and thundered through the brush, faster than Laura imagined such a large beast could run. They raced through the field, then along a creek bed, through fern, maiden hair, willow, and grape, Herman holding on to the elephant's ears, Laura holding on to Herman. She was certain she had never seen the world from such a magnificent viewpoint. How different things seemed when flying so high above the earth on a wild elephant with a wild boy. Once Herman looked back at her, his eyes and his smile wide with wonder and exhilaration, and she could almost feel his joy flowing into her through the fingers of her hands. When the elephant raised its head and its trunk to trumpet, Herman yelped and Laura laughed so long and hard she was afraid of losing her grip and falling, but she held on and closed her eyes and wished the ride would last forever.

After the intimacy of their ride, they moved to the barn where food for the animals was kept. They lay down together on a blanket spread upon the hay. Laura knew this was where Herman slept ever since he had been hired by Ball Coon. It suddenly came to her that she was lying in the bed of the man she loved. It was a beautiful, terrifying thought. She knew at that moment that she would stay with him this night, no matter what the consequence. She would be what he wished, do whatever he wanted her to do. If only there had been time and an opportunity to ask Laughing Eyes about what was expected. Laura even decided if Herman were too shy, or too afraid of offending her, she would guide his hands to where she had only dreamed his hands before. She wondered if she would be the same person tomorrow or if she would be made new and emerge like a butterfly from the person she was.

When it grew dark, they lay on the blanket for a very long time, not speaking. She could hear Herman breathing and the deep, resonant growling of a lion off in a cage somewhere, and the liquid babble of foreign tongues. Here and there, workers gathered by cookfires, talking low, roasting bits of highly seasoned meat on sticks, laughing about something beyond Laura's understanding. It was almost a domestic scene, yet there was a certain sense of danger, of mystery, of otherworldly sorrows and joys.

From where she lay, Laura could see the moon and she was surprised to see the silhouette of the hanging tree where Al Lackey had died. She had forgotten the tree was so close by and she felt a thousand years had passed since that awful night when she had seen—had seen what? She wondered why she and Herman had never talked of that night.

"Herman?"

"Um," he said.

"Was that you I saw cutting Al Lackey down?"

He did not answer for a while and Laura turned to see his face. "Was it you?"

"Yes."

"Did you bury him?"

"No. I just cut him down. It was wrong to leave him hanging there."

"But he had done such awful things."

"No worse than others."

Laura looked out at the hanging tree, then back. To their dark space there came the sour smell of animals, of sawdust and curry. An elephant trumpeted, and Laura could hear the chinking of its chains. The moonlight found Herman's eyes. They were sad and distant.

"What do you mean?"

"I cut him down because that could have been me hanging there. Because of what I've done."

"So you stole some cows. What else? What could be so bad?"

Herman's eyes found the far distance. "If you knew you'd hate me."

"I couldn't ever."

"You don't want to know."

"I do, Herman. We shouldn't have secrets. Especially tonight."

Then Herman looked into her eyes for a full minute. He sighed, took a deep breath, and began talking. He spoke hurriedly, his voice a soft monotone. He told her again how he had accepted the Indian ways and how he had been forced to do things that white people would not understand. Things he would have never done if he had not been forced.

"I understand," Laura said, certain that she did.

Herman continued. His voice remained soft, without passion. "One day we found this wagon," he said. "There was a man, a woman with a baby, and two older children. It happened fast. We took them most before they knew we was there. Killed and scalped the man and the woman and the baby."

"Don't tell me this," she said, thinking of the baby, something heavy suddenly pressing down on her heart.

"I have to. It's like poison in me. If I don't get it out I'll die." Looking at his hands, he continued. "We took the two other children but killed them about four days later."

Laura covered her ears. "I don't want to hear." She felt she had been dropped into a nightmare. There were demons in the dark.

"I don't know if I killed 'em or not. I could have. I know I didn't cut their heads. That came later when Carnoviste had captured this Mexican. Carnoviste told me to kill him. So I did. I shot him through the heart with an arrow. Carnoviste told me to scalp him. But I didn't want to. He said he'd kill me if I didn't. So I did. I took my knife and cut all around the top of his head. I got a handful of his hair and jerked backwards and the scalp came off with a kind of popping sound. I can still hear that pop of his scalp comin' off."

Laura felt as if ants were crawling up the back of her neck. She shivered and tried to wish the images of death away. Herman Lehmann began to cry. The tears came streaming down his face and ran down his chest in rivulets. There was little sound to his crying, but his shoulders convulsed and pulled inward as if to cover his heart. "What can I do," he cried, "after what I done?" She wanted to reach out to him, to hold his hand, but then she thought of what those hands had done and she could not. She wanted to say something comforting, some phrase of forgiveness, but the words got lost somewhere between her heart and her lips. She wanted to tell him she understood his pain, but she did not understand, and she did not speak. She wanted to tell him she loved him, but the very thought of actually expressing the words was terrifying now and she was not really sure anymore that it was true. Herman Lehmann lay weeping against her. She yearned to gather him up into her arms but the images of the dead children were too vivid in her mind and it seemed her horror was greater by far than her love. She sat there, her hands at her side. Herman Lehmann's tears ran in rivulets down her shoulders and onto her breast and they were cold.

6 ∞ THE TREES OF EDEN

(From Laura's unpublished autobiography)

As I grow older I begin to suspect that God is using this world to round off the rough edges and sharp corners of His creation in preparation for His next illusion, a more perfect world, especially in regard to the souls he distributes with such surprising and consistent unsuitability. I imagine He possesses a great trunk, wooden, leather-bound and old, fashioned from the trees of Eden, filled with the souls of the departed and the unborn. From His throne above the clouds, He contemplates this teeming trunk of souls, the distribution of which is a daunting chore for even the Lord of Hosts. Further, I imagine He puts off the task, submitting to divine procrastination, knowing that pairing these souls, man and woman, is an imperfect art, at best, and so the Lord simply tips the souls out onto the clouds and they fall randomly down to earth where the final distribution is the responsibility of mischievous angels. What other possible explanation could there be that the soul of Herman Lehmann and my own would be brought together, entwined, only to be bruised so badly.

Even now, after nearly fifty years, when I think of Herman, I feel something coiling in my heart. When I try to identify that feeling, to hold it still and wrap it with words, it squirms away like an animal too tightly held. I'm sure what I feel is love, for I think I even love him now, and the key that winds the coil in my heart is regret that I let him go, that I drove him away. And I feel shame, as well, a deep abiding shame that I had not the strength to forgive him for being what the world made of him. Why did I let him go? Was I afraid of the wildness of him, the wildness he stirred within me? Was I afraid of love itself, both the sentiment and the act? I was standing that last night at the door of a love that would have hurled us forever out into the wild. And I wonder if all my life since hasn't been a fight to scramble back from that wildness to a more orderly, stable, humane and predictable place to stand. But something hard, all sinews and elbows, is writhing in my breast and I need and I wish . . .

The woman I became scoffs at such wanton thoughts, such nonsense, let it go, it's done. But I can't help but wonder what our life together would have been. The woman I am now finds it difficult to even contemplate how absolute the difference between that lost life and this one I found later would be. Dangerous? Certainly. Turbulent? Terribly. Tragic? Probably. But I can still feel his touch. I can see into his dreams when I'm sleeping. Something hard, all elbows, is writhing, coiling in my breast and I need and I wish . . .

The woman I became would not have fallen in love with Herman Lehmann. But she would have forgiven him, possibly become his friend. She would have fought for him and assailed those who would hurt him. But the hearts of children are hard. Only with bruising do they grow softer.

When I think about driving Herman away because of what he did and because I couldn't bear the touch of hands that had caused such violent death, the irony of that choice is apparent, especially as things turned out. As a child I fled from Herman's savagery, only to marry a man who had killed as a boy and again, in anger, as a man. I slept in those arms for half a century. Both my loves carried crimson blades. Mine was a blade of ice, for I also killed, but I'll come to that in time. The woman I have become is shocked by the sins of the woman I was.

The two words that are most liberally used by the writers of the Scriptures are the words *sin* and *love*. This I am told by my daughter Winifred, who counted them, and so I'm sure it's true. I would suppose this is evidence of the importance with which the Lord holds these opposing concepts, one to be avoided and the other to be pursued. When I think back on my life I find it difficult to divide the notions of sin and love because they are all too often of the same cloth. They hold the same electricity, touch the same nerve ends, have the same power to summon sorrow from the dark cells in our heart. My love of Herman Lehmann was a sin, or certainly would have been before that last night ended in horror and bitterness. Saint Paul has said the greatest of all gifts is not faith nor hope, but charity, love of others. My own view is that forgiveness is a far greater gift than these. For love is an ally of sin. Forgiveness is sin's bitter enemy.

When I look back on my life I find so much need of forgiveness. Forgiveness of Herman for his cruelty, of my father for his bigotry, of poor Al Lackey for his hating heart. Forgiveness even for dear Peter who was my lover, my husband, my companion, yet warder unaware who kept me captive to the earth and to the hearth for so many years. Did I make the right choice? One wild and free, the other a life contesting against the cage. Before I die, will I be able to forgive all those I've loved and especially the woman I was and the woman I became?

7 ∞ THE CANYON WALLS

JUST TO THE EAST OF HOGE HOLLOW, WHERE THE BLANCO takes a wide turn to the south, Peter Cavanaugh Woods owned a large horse ranch. Often when riding Miss Ruth along the ridge above the river, Laura could look down onto Peter's land and watch his horses running through the grass like something from an Arabian legend. Just to watch these magnificent animals made Laura want to apologize to Miss Ruth for the envy the old mare must surely have felt. Sometimes she would see Peter riding among his horses, tall and lithe, a kind of poetry made flesh. It was said Peter Woods had more horses than the Sultan, gifts from his mother, Georgia Lawshe Woods, of San Marcos, a beautiful and mysterious woman who came to Texas, it was said, with Peter's father, the Colonel-Doctor Woods, a hundred slaves and a golden coach filled with silver ingots. Peter had moved from the Woods mansion in San Marcos to establish his ranch a few years after the Civil War and had become one of the area's most respected citizens. One of Peter's many sisters, Miss Jeffersonia Woods, had followed Peter to the Blanco to teach at Laura's little Lindendale school.

Stories told about the Woods family were legend. Yet what fascinated Laura most about Miss Jeffie's celebrated family were the stories not told—vague whispered references to dark secrets that threatened to tear the family apart like the pendulum in the Edgar Allan Poe story. There were rumors of a killing in their great white house in San Marcos, stories of blockade-running and smuggling, even speculations that Georgia Lawshe Woods had been descended from a Cherokee princess. What girl of fifteen could fail to be fascinated by a tall, handsome, wealthy smuggler who rode his horse in the meadows by the Blanco with all the dash and grace of a cavalier?

One day, as Laura and Miss Ruth were watching Peter working with his horses, she suddenly realized he was looking at her, his hand shielding his eyes from the sun. Then he was riding her way, crossing the river, and in a heartbeat he was at her side, his horse dancing in place.

"Miss Laura?" It seemed both a question and a greeting. Laura was surprised he knew her name, then realized Miss Jeffie must have spoken about her.

"Mr. Woods." She busied herself untangling Miss Ruth's mane.

"Call me Peter. After all we're neighbors."

"Peter."

"Jeffie says you love horses."

Laura nodded. She wondered how old Peter was. *Maybe in his thirties,* she thought. Nearly as old as her father. But he was so unbelievably handsome. Bronzed by the sun, his jaw square, his eyes spaced wide like Miss Jeffie's, bright blue and kind. He had obviously seen much of the world and he wore that experience in the lines at the corners of his eyes. His eyebrows were arched in a way that made Laura think he was always on the verge of asking a question. His entire manner seemed to draw her in, to invite her to be comfortable in his presence.

"Well, then. I wonder if you could help me out, Laura. I'm training some foals and it's a little more than I can handle by myself." His voice was deep and she could hear his schooling in the way he pronounced both ends of words, not like her father who spoke just the middles. "Thought you might ask your papa if you could help me out. Consider it a job. We can work out pay with your pa."

Laura felt herself flowing into Peter Woods's eyes. "Why me?" she asked. "Why not my brothers?"

Peter laughed. "I've seen you ride. I've seen your brothers ride. I think I made the right choice."

J. C. Hoge readily agreed to the arrangement and for the next several weeks Laura rose each morning before light and she and Miss Ruth raced the sun to Peter's place on the Blanco. There was about those morning rides an almost overwhelming exhilaration, a powerful sense of future, as if her life was waiting, calling to her, urging her to hurry. And when she arrived and began to work with the foals, she still felt this need to rush forward through the day.

Laura could not understand her feelings toward this older man. Sometimes she thought it might be love. Or was it really his life she loved and not the man? She knew her feelings were not the same as those she had for Herman Lehmann. A thousand years could pass and she would never question that love. It would be with her the rest of her life. But she was attracted to Peter and she could not help picturing how life with him would be. She respected him enormously. He was a leader in the community and her father had said he was chairman of the Blanco County Democratic Party and maybe even had a future in politics. He was even chairman of her school board. Surely, in time, she could learn to love this good, gentle man. Anyway, she thought, it will not hurt to see where things might lead.

"Slowly and gently," Peter said when they began working with the horses. "You can't expect a horse to progress too rapidly. Don't ask too much too soon." Laura thought that might be good advice for her to follow in her pursuit of Peter.

Peter showed Laura how to teach the young horses to accept the halter and to lead. "The first secret is to begin early, before the horse is weaned, when it's still easy to handle. The second secret is love. To gentle the horse, rub the foal all over its body. Not only does it let the horse know you're no threat, but it gets the foal accustomed to grooming. You've got to be gentle. Anybody can beat a horse, but not everybody can train one."

Once they had taught the foals to lead properly, they worked them in Peter's round corral. Soon Laura could get them to walk or trot or canter with simple word commands. Peter held a whip, but never used it, except to lightly tap the horse from behind. He showed Laura how to get the older weaned horses to stand quietly and accept the weight of the saddle. He taught her how to tie the proper knots for restraining a horse, how to bridle, saddle and mount a horse and how to avoid kicks. "Always let the horse know where you are. Run your hand along his side. Sometimes you can't avoid kicks," Peter told Laura, "what you can do is always stay right up against the horse. Then if he kicks, he can't generate as much power and you won't get the full impact. But the best way to avoid kicks is to be calm and confident. A nervous trainer will have a nervous, unpredictable horse."

The days flew by and Laura fell absolutely in love with the life she was leading. She was surprised to find that adventure could be found so close to her backdoor. Peter Woods was a magician, a sorcerer, a man who had a gift for taming what he called the "sons and daughters of the wind." And little by little, she was beginning to adore this strong, good man who could speak to horses with his eyes or with a touch of his hand. Maybe the greatest adventure of her life was right here where, at least this summer, she found the center of the world to be. Little by little, the dull ache that seemed to press on her heart when she thought of Herman began to diminish. She thought less of the circus and Ball Coon and the beautiful gypsy bareback riders.

Once she asked Peter about Karl Benz and the horseless carriage he had invented in Germany. "Maybe people won't need horses anymore."

"Can that horseless carriage plow a field?" Peter asked in return. "Can it leap a fence? Charge the enemy? Swim rivers? Can it work cattle? Can it bear young? Can it love you back? I'll bank my future on what God created with flesh and blood and spirit, not on what man made with wire and tin."

They worked well together, established a kind of rhythm, and the days passed, sometimes without speaking more than a word or two. But Laura felt there was something more powerful than mere words passing between them. They shared a love of horses, and she knew he respected how she had learned so quickly and how she seemed to sense what each situation demanded without being told. "You're a marvel," Peter said one day when she mounted a horse that had never been ridden and walked it around the corral with cautious calm.

Only once did Laura venture to look into the personal life of Peter Woods. One day, when their work was done and she had lingered, listening to Peter talk about his dream of having the finest breeding and training operation in Texas, she mounted Miss Ruth for the ride back to Hoge Hollow. Peter was offering Miss Ruth a handful of wild oats and thanking the old mare for waiting all day so patiently for her mistress. Laura looked down at Peter and realized he would now spend the rest of the evening and the night alone. "Don't you ever get lonesome?" she asked.

He looked at her a moment with those quizzical eyes. "Yes," he said, "I suppose I do." Then he smiled, patted Miss Ruth's neck, turned and walked back toward his cabin beyond the remuda.

One afternoon, when their work was done, yet it was still too early to go home, Laura went for a long walk through the pasture and down by the river. She lingered for awhile, wading in the shallows, looking for the tracks of any monsters that might have wandered by. She thought of Herman, her mind toying with fragments of their times together, and the hours and the day slipped away. She heard hoofbeats drumming, then Peter's voice called that it was late and time to go.

Peter reached for her hand and swung her up onto the back of his horse. They raced away over the pasture and she recalled her elephant ride with Herman. Unlike that wild ride, she and Peter seemed to flow through the wind, easy and fluid and in perfect control. Peter was absolute master of their motion and the moments through which their motion passed. As they flew across Peter's land, she decided the two men she had known appealed to opposite aspects of her nature. Herman had made her feel somehow deliciously imperiled, like the lion tamers must feel in the lion's cage at the Glasscock Brothers Circus. On the other hand, Peter made her feel safe. Herman was a passionate wanderer, lost and disconnected, and life with him would have been a wild elephant ride. Life with Peter would be a ride on a thoroughbred, still thrilling, maybe faster, but civil and restrained and comfortable.

As Laura and Miss Ruth hurried home for supper, she thought about what her life might be like if she were Laura Woods. *What would it be like to share his bed, his dreams, and bear his children? What if Peter ran for office? Maybe I can't be presi-*

dent, but Peter could! He's wealthy, handsome, from a prominent family! That night, before sleep came, she saw herself in a white gown on the lawn of the White House, and she could not help but smile when she thought how terribly distant that image was from an elephant ride with Herman.

As the summer passed, Laura sometimes wondered if she was taking unfair advantage of Peter. He was a lonely, older man and she was young and pretty, and she could sense the power over him she possessed. *What if it isn't love I feel?* But something else?

Laura talked with Little Mattie about her feelings. "One of the problems with being a woman," Little Mattie said, "is that there's no training for beginners. When men decide to be lawyers or doctors or preachers, there's all kinds of schools with good teachers and libraries full of books where men spend as much as ten years of their life getting ready to do what they do. Now, woman's profession, being a mother and a wife, is just as complicated as anything a man does. Lots more, generally. It includes taking care and nursing babies and children, healing their bodies and training their minds. A woman is the manager of the household. Her responsibilities include doctoring, lawyering, and teaching children morals just like a preacher does. She's a teacher, a bookkeeper, seamstress, gardener, and cook. The duties of a woman are as sacred and important as any duties a man does, yet there's no school in the world where these things are taught."

One early morning as Laura and her mother were preparing a new green-grape pie for Sunday dinner, Laura asked how Little Mattie could have lived so long with a man and not fought like brothers and sisters do. "I mean, I love my brothers, but sometimes they drive me crazy. They have these little habits that I can't stand, that make me angry. But I never see you and Papa fight."

"We disagree. But I decided a long time ago that he's he and I'm me. We're different people. Bound to have different ideas about things. A good marriage doesn't just happen. It requires work and commitment and a real good understanding between a husband and a wife. In the Bible it says that a man's body belongs to the wife and the woman's body belongs to the husband. We are dependent on each other. Equal under God."

"I think sometimes the woman is less equal than the man," Laura said, and Little Mattie's laughter filled the kitchen.

"If you make the right choice in a husband, if you choose a man like your father, he's going to take care of you and the children you have together. He'll farm the land, or manage the store, or treat his patients, and his earnings will pay for the roof over your head and the food on the table. This is his role. It's been his role since time began. But in return, there is something you must do. You must support this man, make him happy in every way. Keep the home clean and straight and keep the children loved and clean and fed."

Laura wondered if her mother's ideas were a little old-fashioned. "You make it sound like the woman is nothing without the man," Laura said.

"It's true. Where would we be without your father? There would be no family. How could I feed us all? We'd be in the poorhouse. Or you children would be divided up and placed with neighbors. Probably have to work for your keep like indentured servants. I'd be nothing without your father. And so it's my choice to make him as happy as I can."

"I've seen that look you give him sometimes. It doesn't look like a happy look to me."

"Of course there are times when he gets out of sorts with me. And days I get under his skin. But those are such silly things. Of no importance. Life is hard and I guess God planned it so a man and a woman have to work and struggle together to keep a family going. He gave women the privilege of bearing and raising children. He gave men the responsibility of providing. Maybe you think that sounds unequal. But I don't think so. It's just the way it is."

All that summer, Laura worked with Peter and the horses during the day and attended the Little Mattie Hoge Female Institute at night. In the laboratory of the kitchen, the parlor, the bedroom and the great outdoors she was exposed to a bewildering range of information including such diverse courses of study as how to sweat a fever; how to budget the family income; what kind of wood is best for the kitchen fire; how to worm a hound; how to deal with a child who tells a lie; how to make good butter; how to weave rope from the hairs of a horse's tail; how to heal a burn with creosote, wood soot, or flour; how to graft a rose; how to love unpleasant people; how to motivate a lazy child; how to let a man know what you really mean; how to make candles, care for lamps, trim wicks; how to prepare at least one hundred meals without repetition; how to trick a child into chewing its food; how and when to breed swine; the care and maintenance of the earth closet and the privy; how to overstitch, hem, backstitch, chain stitch, darn, gather, and whip; how to prepare remedies for colds, cuts, bruises, aches, nosebleed, nausea, spider bite, and boredom; how to prepare a proper sickroom; how to deliver a baby and wash the dead.

By midsummer, Laura was well on her way toward graduation from the Little Mattie Hoge Female Institute, approaching her advanced degree in being a woman, a wife, and a mother. She was also struggling with her feelings toward her friend, neighbor, and employer, Peter Cavanaugh Woods. She pictured their life as one of position and privilege, filled with exciting people and unlimited possibility, each hour a magical basket to be filled with adventures of her choosing. Sometimes she thought of the alternative. A life like her mother's, the years rolling slowly by, full of drudgery and toil, a life seemingly without meaning. Surely there had to be more to life than was revealed in her mother's philosophy. Sometimes Laura would look out at the world around her and nearly all the people she saw were letting their lives slip away, like coins through their fingers. They tilled their fields, tended their children, walked the same roads each and every day, and it seemed their lives had no more importance to the world than a prickly pear or a stone.

By July, she had made her decision. She would pursue Peter with all her might and come what may she would love him the very best she could.

∞

The great Confederate Reunion of July 1886 was like a page turning in Texas history. Robert E. Lee was long dead; he had not even been alive during Laura's lifetime. Lincoln was no more. Jefferson Davis was an old and feeble survivor. There was no evidence of war in the fields or in the streets of the towns, and cotton still grew in the rich, dark soil of the valleys. The mansion of Peter's father, Colonel-Doctor Woods, still commanded the highest hill above the town of San Marcos.

Most of the veterans who came to the reunion had served under Colonel-Doctor Woods in the Thirty-Second Texas Cavalry. They were men who had fought in the service of a country that no longer existed, that was now a part of a larger nation, and whose loyalty to a lost cause bound them into a fellowship that would endure as long as they lived.

Laura watched the trains pull into San Marcos coughing smoke and decibels into the clear Texas air. A brass band and a company of the Chautauqua Rifles and a deputation of leading citizens, including Colonel-Doctor Woods, met the passengers as they disembarked, many in the gray uniforms they had worn more than twenty years before. The Colonel-Doctor greeted the veterans warmly, embracing each one. The band played the funeral march of Robert E. Lee and the old soldiers' eyes grew moist and many wept openly as they embraced their comrades. Laura felt the town was suspended between deep sorrow and celebration. It was not difficult to understand the sorrow. But what were they celebrating?

Laura decided they were at last celebrating the end of the war. Now there was an entire generation of people like Laura who had never heard the cannonades or seen the mounds of the dead or smelled the smoke of burning homes or had known the humiliation of defeat. It was an ending of the old and a beginning of the new. So the old soldiers were formed up in ranks and once more they marched through the streets of San Marcos as they had done so very long ago. Following the Stars and Bars and marching to the music of the old Confederate brass band, they marched to McGehee's Grove where nearly five thousand people were assembled.

In the crowd of mourners and celebrants, Old Colonel-Doctor Woods stood with his sons Pinckney and Peter. Laura watched Peter move gracefully through the crowd, almost as if he, not his father, had commanded these men. He was so dear and familiar to her. She knew every line of his face, the way he walked with a kind of roll on the balls of his feet. She could anticipate his every gesture. She even knew what he dreamed. She caught his eye and he smiled and she knew for certain in that instant that she had made the right decision and she would marry Peter Woods and they would raise the most beautiful horses and children in the world. She would become the woman behind Peter's climb and she hoped it was to the governor's mansion or even the White House.

The Colonel-Doctor moved to a platform and the crowd grew still. Then he spoke and in the absolute silence, broken only by the wind in the old oak of the grove, his voice was strong and clear. "I am gratified," he began, "that relentless time has spared so many of you to participate in this reunion. As I look over you I see the youth of twenty years ago, now in many cases with silvered head, shoulders heavy with the weight of years." He paused then and for a long moment looked out over the grove as if seeing these same men as they had been when they first embarked on their tragic cause. "I, too, feel the passage of time and am admonished that the suns of summer and the frosts of winter since we bivouacked and marched together have left their impact on me. I feel that the sere and yellow leaf of life is imminent, but today I am thrilled by the recollection of our army association. And as I step with a firmer tread I feel an extra heartbeat and I stand a proud man in your presence as I recall the service we jointly rendered. No body of men who tendered their services to the Confederacy were of nobler hearts or more soldierly material than the officers and men I had the honor to command." A great cheer from the veterans filled the grove as the Colonel-Doctor removed his glasses to wipe away his tears.

The Colonel-Doctor began to call the roll of the Thirty-Second Texas. He called the names of Lt. Nat Benton and Capt. Corolin and Capt. I. K. Stevens. Sergeant Major Swant, Ed

Stevens, Theodore Podewils, Philip and William Bitter, Calvin Turner, Max Starcke. "Porterville, Sherwood and others whose names I do not recall but whose lives and hearts and graves are green in my memory."

At this point, Colonel-Doctor Woods was unable to continue. He simply stood before the crowd, motionless, his eyes fixed on a point in the distance only he could see, as tears ran down his face. He no longer bothered to wipe them away. Sorrow flowed through the grove like a sweet, dark wind. People embraced and they looked down at the earth, embarrassed at the emotion memories had stirred. Laura moved to Peter's side and on an impulse she took his hand. Peter looked down in surprise, then smiled and looked back where his father was struggling to continue his address. Peter did not remove his hand from hers and Laura was sure his fingers tightened on her own.

"I would be derelict in my duty," Colonel-Doctor Woods continued, "did I fail to give word of welcome and of thanks to you noble women who grace this occasion. You sustained us by your industry and unfaltering love and you are worthy of a badge not less honorable than is worn by us. Your fidelity encourages us and if we had heroes in the field, we also had heroines at home." Colonel-Doctor Woods paused, and there was polite applause.

Then he continued. "It is proper, too, my friends, to pay tribute to that man, the grand and central figure of our struggle, who is today worn by age and the trials of a most eventful life. However he may have erred in judgment in the conduct of the war, no question can be raised as to his faithfulness to his people, and though old and enfeebled he stands unsullied in honor and peerless as a representative of the cause he upheld. Let us send our greetings to Mr. Jefferson Davis."

Once again the crowd broke into applause and Laura noticed it was not nearly so restrained as the applause for the noble women. The Confederate band struck up "Dixie," and the men of the Thirty-Second Texas Cavalry were formed up and formally dismissed to mount an assault on the seventy-five barbecued beeves, hogs and muttons the people of San Marcos had provided for the celebration.

There were few gatherings in the Texas of these days that were not essentially political conventions. Not only was the Confederate Reunion an occasion to renew old friendships and loyalties, it was a forum for spirited political discussion. Politicians moved through the crowd, shaking hands, seeking votes. After the band had played, speakers rose to urge control of the railroads and to stop New York bankers. Others passionately denounced alien land ownership, demanded labor reform, an end to currency inflation, and increased wages for ranch workers. Laura had always known politics as a process that directly influenced peoples' lives. But this was both direct and personal. Here was a man seeking to raise the wages she was paid working on Peter Woods's ranch.

In the interval between speeches, the politicians moved from family to family, quietly paying their respects, asking about children and relatives and old friends. Laura walked among the men, fascinated. She noticed that all the politicians found their way to where Peter stood, vying for his attention, and he was often surrounded by candidates Laura had seen earlier giving speeches. She watched the politicians working the crowd, listened to the rhetoric ringing in the heavy summer shade, and she felt beautifully connected to it all. She felt included.

It had long been dark when Peter found his way to where Laura stood beneath the shadowed trees of McGehee's Grove. All the fried chicken, pickled peaches, and butter beans were gone and only the candidates remained, probably looking for the last of the day's hands to shake. "Well," Peter said, when he was at her side. "You've heard all the speeches. Who's your man?"

"You are."

She could tell Peter was blushing.

"I mean the candidates."

"I like the one that's promising better wages for ranch hands." Laura looked into his eyes and smiled and she willed him to take her hand and then walk her back. The moon accompanied them all the way.

∞

Peter and Laura became inseparable. They worked each day with the horses, and when work was done Peter would often accompany Laura and Miss Ruth back to Hoge Hollow where Little Mattie would prepare a supper for their neighbor, her daughter's employer, and her prospective son-in-law. On weekends, Laura and Peter rode out over the hills with picnic lunches or hosted barbecues for Peter's friends at his ranch. Peter had built a small stone bungalow on the place and on those weekends Peter entertained, she imagined she was married and the rude bungalow was the celebrated Woods family home in San Marcos. Laura was certain she and Peter would have servants and they would live in the white house high on the hill, the toast of San Marcos society.

Once Peter and Laura rode over to visit Laura's friends at the Glasscock Brothers Circus, recently arrived from the summer's touring and settling with weary relief into their long winter encampment. Contemplating the visit beforehand had made Laura uneasy, consumed by a feeling of disloyalty. But she was not quite sure if she was being disloyal to Peter or to the memory of Herman. She introduced Peter to Ball Coon and asked about Herman Lehmann. "Not a sign," Ball Coon said. "That fella just slipped off the face of the world."

"Who's Herman?" Peter asked when Ball Coon had left.

"Just a boy."

"You mean Herman Lehmann? That Indian captive?"

Laura's heart galloped in place. "He worked here with Ball Coon for awhile." She felt cleansed by a torrent of relief. That's that, she thought, the name is out. And if it comes up again in Peter's presence, I won't have to explain.

They had lunch in the cook tent with the Fat Lady, the midget, and Captain Blood, the aerialist. As they ate, Laura was struck by the thought of how close she had come to sharing the lives of these people.

"Once I thought about running away with the circus," she said to Peter as they rode back to the ranch.

"That's every young man's dream."

"Well, this girl had it, too."

During that summer, Peter and Laura met at another kind of encampment on the Blanco River. Laura and her family had rented a tent at the Chautauqua that was held each year at the head of the Blanco, far to the northwest of Hoge Hollow. Laura loved these pilgrimages out into nature where you could hear lectures on such subjects as "Aristotle and the Free State," or "Whether Girls of Well-to-Do Parents Should Enter Business Life," or "The Harp of the Senses; the Secret of Character Building." From a platform built beneath the trees, lectures were presented on art, music, philosophy, religion, and any number of subjects designed to uplift morals and nourish the spirit. Peter attended primarily to hear the sermons of the Rev. Andrew Jackson Potter and other preachers, including George Waverly Briggs, whose lecture, "The Humors and Heroisms of the Pulpit," was a favorite at the Blanco River Chautauqua. Here in a rough and tumble country, people tried to distance themselves from the reality of their everyday lives. How alien, for instance, were Mrs. Jean Sherwood's lectures on the Louvre and the early French painters to the hard life of the Hill Country? Laura marveled at the mysterious and apparently universal human impulse to perfect the gifts of mind and spirit.

Of course, the main reason Laura liked this year's Chautauqua was the opportunity to be with Peter alone after dark. After eluding sisters Maggie and Lucy, Peter and Laura would meet, late beneath the moon, when the encampment was still, and they would sit under an umbrella of cypress trees by a small stream. Here it was Laura and Peter first kissed. It was, this kiss, a religious experience, and long into the night she and Peter were eager, fervent pilgrims.

One Saturday, as the summer was drawing to a close and the leaves of the sumac were turning the color of a cardinal's wing, Peter and Laura rode out to the Narrows, a canyon where the Little Blanco River slipped into a crease in the limestone hills. There had been unseasonable rains and the river was flowing at nearly springtime levels, easing over sculpted stone boulders into azure pools of liquid crystal. The Narrows was to Laura one of nature's most elegant surprises. It was just suddenly there, a cool, mystical world, hidden in the midst of a harsh, almost bitter landscape, an oasis in the desert. Sometimes, like now, as she and Peter climbed down into its shade, she thought the Narrows might even be a mirage. But Peter was holding her, lifting her down over the smooth boulders, down to a wide bench almost hidden from the burning sky, and his touch was very real. The moving water had carved strange shapes in the limestone—some like animals or mythical creatures frozen in time. Others were like the houses of a fairy city built by a forgotten race of elves long gone away. The pools were clear, and they sat on the warm stone and watched the quick silver motion of fish beneath the surface.

"When we were boys, we used to swim through the tunnels down there," Peter said. "The pools are joined beneath the ground. If you take a deep breath you can make it. But just barely. The worst thing that could happen was to be afraid to do it. It could wreck your whole life, we thought, if you were scared."

Laura could see the mouth of the tunnel just below them. It opened into deep, shifting, blue shadows. "Do you remember the first time?"

"I was twelve. There were about five of us. And we dived off this very place. Into that pool. Have you been down there?"

"No."

"It doesn't look deep, the water's so clear. But it is. Maybe twelve feet. Then it goes back under the rock for maybe, I don't know, twenty feet or so. I know it seems endless. Goes on forever. And everybody knew there were false passages. The tunnel divided and some of the passages were dead ends and you could get sucked into these dead ends by the current. Of course that wasn't true, but it was always in your mind that it might be. The other boys were older and I could see they were taking my measure. It was an unspoken challenge. There were two kinds of boys in the Hill Country. Those who had been through the tunnels in the Narrows and those who hadn't. I knew before the day was over I'd have to swim the tunnel. It was a rite of passage."

"So you did."

"So I did. And when I came up over there on the other side,

nobody said a thing. It wasn't like an initiation where everybody congratulates you on your achievement. They just ignored it. It was terrible if you didn't do it, but no big thing if you did."

Laura looked down into the blue water. "Come swim with me," she said. "Turn away." She removed her outer garments and climbed down closer to the water, then jumped. The water closed around her and she rose to the surface just as Peter plunged past in a rush of silver bubbles. They swam to a place where the little river flowed over a lip of stone and they stood beneath the waterfall, his arm around her beneath the water. Laura was very conscious of his body. It was hot in contrast to the cold water and she turned and put her face against his chest. Through the waterfall she could see the entrance to the tunnel, like a dark corridor into the heart of mystery.

"I'm going through the tunnel," she said. The sound of the waterfall drowned her voice.

"What?"

She stood on her tiptoes, pulled herself up against him and spoke into his ear. "The tunnel. I'm going through." She found herself suddenly very excited, her heart beating so rapidly she was sure he could feel it against his chest. While still on tiptoes, she kissed him. He closed around her and they kissed beneath the waterfall for a long time until she could feel the strangeness of him growing hard against her. Laura broke away and swam to the bank and climbed up to the spot where Peter said the boys had launched themselves into the water. She stood looking down. The air was still, the wind blocked by the canyon walls, the sun just cutting through the narrow gap above her head. She could still feel Peter against her, a physical echo, and he called: "Laura, wait! We'll do it together." He climbed up beside her.

"You're sure . . ."

"I'm sure."

"No girl ever has."

"All the better."

Peter looked into her eyes. Laura saw her reflection smiling back at him, then she looked back to where the shadows loomed beneath the surface at the far end of the pool. "Do you see down there, beyond the sunlight? And that orange stone to the left. That's where to aim. Just follow me."

Peter was still taking his stance when Laura took a deep breath, left the earth, felt her weightless, breathless passage through the light and shadow and then the cold shock of the pool. She swam down and down. Peter was gone and she was absolutely alone in a world as silent as any she had ever encountered. She swam on and the light diminished into a sort of blue twilight. She listened to the silence and found it filled with a strange treble melody, like ice in crystal or tuned glass bells. She wondered if the sounds were coming from within her or from the shadows at the edge of the passageways. Thoughts of the false passageways touched her mind and she brushed them away, but they came back again, like cobwebs, and stayed. It grew darker and she could hear the sound her muscles made as she swam harder now, desperate for the dark to become lighter so she would know she was halfway through. She heard a groaning sound and a sighing, highly amplified, and realized it was caused by her own struggles through the water. The melody of bells she had heard now became a thunderous bass and she thought of Peter and almost turned to see if he was following, but then swam on. Now it was all dark and her lungs began to burn. She began to lose confidence in her sense of direction. Am I swimming straight? She could not see the stone sides of the tunnel. Was it so wide here that I might circle back? And what if I brushed against the sides and there were awful ancient things living there? She thought of spiders and she heard the distant call of Black Cato's trumpet and she struggled against the panic that had nearly killed her so long ago. Then, she saw the light. And it was like God there to guide her toward the gates of Paradise.

She and Peter broke the surface of the water at the same time, their laughter and whoops of joy echoing through the canyon. She reached for him and they embraced, dragging each other down again, then releasing and surfacing noisily once more. Peter pulled her to the shore and they climbed up on the warm stone and lay back, exhausted and alive. Laura felt immortal. *This is how the gods must feel on Olympus,* she thought.

"That was wonderful," she said, reaching for his hand.

"You're amazing," Peter said.

"I know."

"I'm not sure I can keep up with you."

Laura watched Peter's chest rise and fall and she felt a yearning so strong it was almost sorrow. Although they had completed the swim some minutes ago, her heart was beating as fast now as it ever had.

"When you swam the tunnel, what did you boys wear?"

"Nothing. Naked as the day we were born."

"Let's wear that now."

"Laura!"

She rolled toward him and touched his face. "Peter, there's no one here. I want to be close with you. I love you so much, Peter Woods." She was amazed when she heard the words tumbling out and astonished that there was no immediate reply. She turned to see if his eyes said what his lips had not. He was looking at the sky.

"Peter?"

"Think what you're saying," he said. "They're more than words, Laura. They have to do with the rest of our lives. I'm not sure."

"Not sure you love me?"

"Not sure I know what love is."

They lay on their backs, on the hard stone, looking at the melon slice of sky above the canyon walls. They were not touching, but Laura could feel him there. For a long time neither spoke. She thought about the afternoons with Herman Lehmann when they had told each other the secrets hiding in the corners of their minds and hearts. "Have you ever been with a girl? A woman? I mean have you ever, you know."

"Laura, please. I wish you wouldn't . . ."

"I don't want us to have secrets. Anyway, I haven't been with a boy. Not really, you know. I wanted to once and would have, but didn't." She told him then about Herman Lehmann and how he had wanted her to go away with him and live off the land. She told Peter how she had refused and how Herman had gone away without a friend in the world. "I've told you my only secret. Now it's your turn."

Peter said nothing.

"There's nothing sinister I should know? Like you're some kind of monster?"

"No. I guess I'm not that interesting."

Laura sat up and looked down at Peter's face. "I want you to love me, Peter. If you really love me you'll love me. Right now."

"There's time, Laura."

"What do you mean, there's time?"

"We have all the time in the world ahead of us. I want to do this right."

"Do what right? Looks to me like you're doing nothing. And that's wrong."

"Look, Laura." There was an edge to his voice. "I had this all planned. And this isn't the way I wanted it to happen."

"What plan? What to happen?"

"A proper engagement and wedding ceremony, Miss Hoge! A wedding cake! Flowers and music!" He was laughing now. "I was going to ask you to marry me, but you won't give me a chance! I wanted to tell you how much I love you and I was going to give you a ring later, when we were dressed. You can't give an engagement ring to a naked woman!"

Laura threw herself on Peter and covered him with kisses.

"Laura! Give me a chance to do it right." Peter grasped both her arms and forced her away. "Now just lie there and listen. And don't speak until spoken to."

"Peter, you are so absolutely conventional."

"I hope so. Now listen. I love you more than the world and I want to spend my life with you. Will you be my wife, Laura?"

"May I answer now?"

"You may."

"Thank you. The answer is yes. May I kiss you now?"

"No. I will kiss you. You may kiss me back if you care to."

And so they did. But there was time.

8 ∞ THE WOODS MANSION

WAKING ON HER WEDDING DAY, LAURA TRIED TO REMEMBER LAST night's dream. She felt a small disquietude, a subtle apprehension, and hoped that the feeling came from a lingering dream rather than a foreshadowing of something yet to come. She lay in bed listening to the flamboyant repertoire of a mockingbird outside her window, feeling that things were not quite right. Although there were a thousand things to do, she was reluctant to leave her bed. After all, it might be the last time in this life she would sleep alone. Never again would she have the first moments of each day entirely to herself. Maybe this is what troubled her, the loss of the private treasure of the dawn.

"There are three great events in your life," Little Mattie had said, once her father had given Peter Laura's hand. "There is birth, death, and marriage. A woman can't control her birth and death. All she can control is the decision to marry. So choose carefully." Laura often wondered why, given free choice, any woman in her right mind would have chosen her father to marry. She had thought to ask Little Mattie, but never had. *Maybe this explains my apprehension about today,* she thought. *I'm ashamed of my father and the impression he'll make in front of Peter's family.*

For the first time Laura could remember, she had managed to make J. C. Hoge happy. His hard, mean face occasionally now held a smile, a cadaverous mask which Laura found grotesque. He was, of course, delighted that his family would be allied with the important Woods family of San Marcos. In the past, he had cursed the Colonel-Doctor for his ostentatious wealth, but now he had nothing but praise for the famous Woodses, especially Peter. Laura knew it was because in the few years since Peter's mother had divided her horses among her children, his ranch adjoining Hoge Hollow had grown to rival his father's property.

J. C. Hoge had insisted that Laura and Peter be married in the Blanco United Methodist Church and that he, father of the bride, host the Woods entourage at a reception in Hoge Hollow. This is part of what troubled Laura as she lay in bed on the morning of her wedding day. *How could a man who possessed all the social graces of an anvil possibly hope to entertain the most glamorous and sophisticated family in the Hill Country?* She covered her head with her Texas Star quilt and would have gone back to sleep if it had not been for the melodic racket of the mockingbird.

Laura dozed, then felt Little Mattie's weight on the edge of her bed and then her hand brushing back a wayward lock of her hair. When Laura opened her eyes Little Mattie said, "I'll miss you, Little One." Then she rose and busied herself about the room and Laura knew her mother was fighting back tears.

"I'm just going next door, Mama."

"That's a very long way."

"Not more than four miles as the crow flies."

"I'm not talking about miles, Little One."

While J. C. Hoge watched over the fires on which hams and beeves were roasting for the reception barbecue at Hoge Hollow, Little Mattie helped Laura try on her wedding dress. Little Mattie inspected the gown she had made of sky-blue silk and navy blue lace given by Peter's sister Jeffie. She stood for a moment to survey her work.

"I wish it was white," Laura said.

"Nonsense," Little Mattie replied, pins held tightly in her lips. "You've got to wear this dress for years. White won't do. I'll make a wreath of white clematis blossoms for your hair," she said.

"I'll look like a flag," Laura said, turning in front of the dresser mirror. "Red hair, white clematis, blue dress. Old Glory."

"You'll look beautiful!"

After a moment Laura asked, "Do you think they'll like me?" And this was the other part of what troubled Laura on the morning of her wedding day.

"Who?"

"Peter's family. His father. All those sisters."

"Of course they will. They'll adore you."

"What if they don't? I mean I'm so much younger than he is. And, compared to them, we're scrub-ranch poor. What if they think I'm only marrying Peter because . . ."

"Pshaw," Little Mattie interrupted. "In the first place, it doesn't matter one fig what they think. It only matters what you think. You're not marrying Peter's family, you're marrying Peter. And in the second place, when they see you in this dress, walking down the aisle, they will be absolutely swept away."

The evidence in the mirror was incontrovertible and the apprehension she had felt all morning began to fade, like ground fog before the sun. In the glass, she saw a beautiful young woman who was about to embark on an adventure with a good and handsome man. A warm wind carried the rich aroma of burning mesquite into the house. Little Mattie hummed a tuneless melody through the pins she held in her lips. The air seemed to vibrate as it does before a storm and Laura felt happiness and an almost giddy excitement rising around and flowing through. She wished she were at the altar right now.

The wedding was scheduled for three o'clock in the afternoon. Shortly before noon, J. C. Hoge brought the mule team around and hitched the wagon. Laura and her family climbed aboard and they began the long trip into town. As the miles crept by, the day seemed to grow hotter, the air so heavy in the river bottom it was difficult to breathe. Laura was torn between wishing the mules would hurry faster toward Blanco and that the ride would go on forever. She found herself saying good-bye to things: the mules, the wagon, her siblings. They passed the place where she and her brothers and sisters had been swimming when Carnoviste, Herman, and Black Cato had come riding into their lives about a million years ago. They passed close by the Eager Mule and Laura whispered a good-bye to the monster's footprints and to first love.

Before taking Laura to the parsonage where she would dress for the wedding, the family stopped by the church. As they approached the stately stone chapel with its narrow arched windows and tall wooden bell tower, Laura heard someone playing the foot organ that stood at the side of the pulpit. It reminded her of the windblown brassy music of the Glasscock Brothers Circus and she imagined white horses circling and prancing among the pews.

The Blanco United Methodist Church was as plain and unadorned on the inside as any structure could be. There was a plank board floor, rough board benches, and wood lath walls and ceilings imperfectly plastered. A simple wooden pulpit stood on a raised platform at the west end of the building. Laura had always thought the gloomy church was more appropriate for funerals than weddings.

Old Man Roon, the caretaker, with his white hair and vacant eyes, was sweeping, his broom banging woodenly against the benches. Several ladies of the church were placing flowers on tables behind the pulpit. Noticing Laura's dismay, Little Mattie said, "Don't you worry, by the time you and Peter stand here, this old church will be as pretty as you please. We'll have flowers everywhere. And a white ribbon to mark off where the bride's family sits and another to circle the Woods folks. You'll see. Or maybe you won't. You'll probably only have eyes for your man."

Laura remembered how handsome Peter always looked; tall and distinguished in his vested gray pinstripe suit. She looked to the front of the church where the Woods family would occupy four rows of benches, and she wondered what wondrous gowns Peter's sisters would wear. Something like butterfly wings beat in her breast as she thought of the Woods family. She imagined them turning in unison to watch her coming down the aisle. What would she see in those eyes?

The few hours before the ceremony passed in a blur of activity and anxiety and concern for things forgotten. Laura's hair would not stay pinned and the dress that had been so carefully hemmed threatened to creep under her heel when she walked. Would her father still fit into his heavy wool suit, the only one he owned, not worn since his own wedding? Dressed before everyone else, J. C. Hoge was sweating profusely and complaining

profanely. Little Mattie was everywhere at once, ever the calm
soldier among troops verging on undisciplined flight. Lunch
was offered to Laura, but she had no appetite. Brother Shaw, the
Methodist pastor who would marry the couple, occasionally
emerged from his study to reassure the bride and calm the family. Noon danced by. The butterfly in Laura's breast metamor-
phosed into a starling with leather wings.

The wedding party walked from the parsonage to the church.
Laura held up her skirts so they would not sweep through the
summer dust of the road. The wind assaulted her hair. Memories and a new rush of apprehension filled her mind.

"Something's wrong!" Laura said to her mother, panic rising,
flooding, flowing.

Little Mattie patted her daughter's hand. "Everything is
fine." There was an edge to her voice, and Laura realized she
had felt the sharpness of that edge all of her life. "Get hold of
yourself" was what her mother meant without saying it. "We are
strong. We are not women who panic."

They walked on through the dust and warm June air. At the
church door there was a flurry of flattery and bright smiles, and
Laura felt a surprising fondness for her father when he came forward and took her hand. "You sure are something to see," J. C.
Hoge said, as close to a compliment as he would ever give to this
daughter. Laura reached on tiptoe to kiss her father's cheek. She
was astonished that she had done such a thing and that he had
not wiped her kiss away. She wondered if she might have loved
him given more time. Then the little organ with its breathy,
brassy voice was calling them down the aisle.

Laura would later wonder which she saw first: Peter before the
altar or the vast wasteland of empty benches where the Woods
family was supposed to be. The starling in her breast fell dead,
bludgeoned, already beginning to rot in the bitter acid of Laura's
hurt. She was pulled forward by her father's arm as she searched
for her mother's eyes in the sea of faces. When she found them
they said, "Be strong. We are not women who panic." But it was
not panic that was locking Laura in a struggle of epic proportion.
It was laughter. All that terrible worry of what the Woodses

would think of her as she walked down the aisle was for nothing. Their absence spoke volumes. Laura's only fear was that she would begin laughing and would be unable to stop.

After the wedding reception, Laura and Peter talked for a long time. They listened to the wind move in the highwood and to the coyotes howling in the darkness outside their ranch house. Laura's dress was folded neatly on a chair by the bed. Peter did not apologize for the cruel absence of his family. "It's their loss," he said. "What a beautiful thing they missed."

"But why?"

"It's because you outshine them. You are the sun and my sisters are but minor planets. They aren't angry at you. They're angry at me for having all this youth and beauty to myself."

"But your father?"

"He's old now. He does what his daughters wish."

Laura sighed and turned to look into Peter's eyes and she knew he loved her no matter what his silly family thought.

Laura had been to Peter's little house many times before. *Now it is my house, too,* she thought.

Peter blew out the lantern by the bed and the room filled with a dark so pure and fine it was like a soft cloak she could feel against her skin. Peter undressed her then and she felt a flush of embarrassment, not that his hands were touching and lingering on her face and shoulders and breasts, but that it seemed she was outside herself, watching this man and this woman make love. It was a surprisingly beautiful thing to see and feel and as the moments passed she began to realize just how marvelous and mysterious were the creatures God made on the day before He rested.

When Laura's heartbeat had returned to something near normal and the strange sweet pain began to depart, she began to be aware of Peter's weight and his breath in her hair. She was certain they were now a single creature, joined by both flesh and soul. He stirred and rolled to her side and they parted. But to her surprise she still felt him inside her and all around her and she knew that he was so much a part of her that they would never really be apart for the rest of their lives. She tried to think of a way to tell him so but it was too complex. Instead, she climbed on top of him and pressed herself to him, trying to make as much of the surface of their bodies touch as possible. She was so happy she cried and her tears fell down into his eyes.

Near midnight, there was a startling sound outside, an alien iron clatter and whispers. From where Peter lay, he reached beneath the mattress and, to Laura's amazement, he withdrew a revolver. It seemed huge and terrible in the moonlight and for a brief instant Laura was not sure whether to be afraid or amused at the sight of a naked armed man. Without a word, Peter pulled on his trousers and moved stealthily to the window. Suddenly, the night exploded with a ringing, rattling, avalanche of sound. There were howls of laughter and shouts from the darkness as it became apparent that she and Peter were victims of a shivaree. Peter's friends were playing the traditional wedding night prank of terrorizing the bride and groom.

Peter was not amused. He ordered his friends away with such authority that they departed in confused haste, trailing apologies into the night. Peter stood at the window, breathing hard, the revolver still in his hand. "It was only a prank," Laura said. "Come back to bed." Peter did not move from the window. Laura wrapped her gown about her and moved to where he stood watching shadows cast by the moon. "What is it, Peter? What's wrong?"

"Nothing," Peter said, with a small gesture of his hand. He moved back to the bed and returned the revolver beneath the mattress. "It's not important." He touched her lips with his fingertips. His hand smelled like iron. "What's important is I love you."

Laura did not sleep until daybreak. She was confused by Peter's silence. *What kind of man,* she wondered, *would take a revolver to bed on his wedding night?* She remained awake all night watching Peter's face, profoundly aware, like the princess in the fairy tale, of something hard beneath the mattress.

And now Peter was gone. For three days and nights they had been so absolutely inseparable that, in his absence, she was more alone than she had ever been in her life. When Peter had announced his trip to Austin to buy horses, Laura had wanted to go with him. Maybe they could have a brief honeymoon in a fancy Austin hotel. But Peter said there was ranch work to do, for him on the road, and for her at home. She knew Peter would have to make these trips away from the ranch, but somehow she had pictured herself going along. Now, as she stood by the front door of her new home, looking out at her husband's ranch, she began to realize just how much work there was to be done. What had seemed such a romantic place when she first fell in love with Peter Cavanaugh Woods, she now saw with new, more realistic eyes.

The vast pastures where she had first seen him riding like a prince among his enchanted horses was, in reality, a great sprawling wilderness of rock and oak and brush. Peter said it was so thick even rattlesnakes had to back out once they entered because there was no room for them to turn around. Thriving around their little frame, two-room ranch house was a miscellany of persimmon, crab apple, dewberries, and wild plum, and Laura wondered if it would be her duty to harvest these trees forever, filling jars and pies, jellies and preserves with their bounty. *Will it be my destiny to fill these wide-mouthed jars until I'm as old and small and weary as Little Mattie? Maybe that is the price one pays for a good man and a few moments of ecstasy.*

Each morning during Peter's absence, before the sun became an enemy, Laura spent an easy hour working and thinking in the garden she had started in the spring when she had been Peter's ranch hand. She had planted both flowers and vegetables as if uncertain whether the garden's harvest should be salad or a bouquet. Along the garden wall and sometimes among the rows of vegetables, she had welcomed sneezeweed and firewheel, yellow daisy and Mexican hat and now as she sat upon the warming earth with the soil beneath her fingernails, it came to her that she was a woman blessed. She was sure she loved Peter. When she thought of him, it actually brought a physical thrill and made her breath come faster and she had to clasp her hands together because they felt so empty with Peter gone away. She wondered if the process of analyzing her feelings toward Peter was an act of disloyalty. And were her occasional thoughts of Herman when she and Peter were making love an act of infidelity? But she decided she was perfectly free to think anything she wished. It was only her body and her labor she had traded for a good man and those occasional moments of ecstasy. Her mind was her own.

As the days passed and her loneliness diminished, she discovered that Peter's ranch was not so godforsaken after all. As she rode out into the pasture with the horses and watched the newborn colts cavort around their mothers, she began to find God everywhere she looked. In cleaning and reordering the little ranch house, she realized that being mistress of a tiny house of your own was nearly as good, or better, than being mistress of someone else's mansion. And she saw God in the quiet corners of the little house with its roughhewn beams and thick board walls whitewashed bright as the corners of a child's eye. She saw God in her mule-eared chairs and unadorned cabinets and in the pine daybed that served as sofa and in the other hand-me-downs that had spilled from her dowry chest. She saw God in the huge spool bed with its fine floral quilt where she and Peter spent so many hours in passion and repose.

Then he was back, riding fast through the hurled lightning bolts of a sudden summer thunderstorm. Laura rushed out into the rain to welcome him home and soon they had removed their drenched clothing and had settled into the warm privacy of their four-poster. The wind came storming from the north and the oaks thrashed and the windows rattled with each salvo of thunder. As they held each other and moved together, accompanied by the fury of the storm, Laura felt she and Peter were drifting through time. It was as if they lived many thousands of years before and they were safe in their cave from the storm and from the beasts that prowled the dark. Maybe they were the only man and woman on earth.

When the storm had passed and they lay side by side on their backs listening to the distant thunder, Peter told Laura about his trip and the horses he had arranged to purchase. He had brought home a little Tobiano Paint mare, a Palomino stallion, and a handsome roan with a white star blaze on its face. Laura was amused that this noted authority on fine horses seemed most pleased with his purchase of a pair of mules.

"Don't scoff at my mules," Peter said. "The American Jack is one of the smartest animals known to man. It's steady, courageous, and as surefooted as a mountain goat. And these I bought are descended from the stock George Washington was given by the King of Spain."

"So these are royal mules?"

"Exactly. You must show proper respect. Love me, love my mules."

Then he told her about the party his family had planned in San Marcos. "It's a wedding party in your honor. All my family and their friends will be there to meet my beautiful bride. Even the governor."

Laura felt a cold current of air, perhaps left behind by the storm. "When was this all decided?"

"While I was in San Marcos."

"I thought you were in Austin."

"I rode down to see my family."

"I was alone, Peter. I wish you would have come home instead."

Peter turned on his side, reached for her, and kissed her. "I'm sorry. I thought you wouldn't mind. I wanted to surprise you with the party."

Laura looked up into Peter's eyes. They seemed so innocent. Did Peter know how badly she had been hurt by his family's refusal to come to the wedding? She could not believe he would be so insensitive to her feelings.

"Are you angry?" he asked.

"No," she answered. "I'm not angry."

For an instant she felt as if a stranger had taken her husband's place in bed. She thought she knew everything about Peter, every inch of his body and his mind. But he should have known the depth of her hurt. There was a revolver beneath the mattress. *Maybe you can never really know another person,* she thought.

∞

Peter drove Laura and her parents slowly up the hill toward the great white house Peter's mother, Georgia Lawshe Woods, had given the Colonel-Doctor when he came home from the war. The house commanded the highest hill in town, and from the perspective of the land leading up the rise, its milk-white columns seemed to reach into the sky itself. It reminded Laura of the grand and imposing house on the Blanco River road.

"Damn," J. C. Hoge exclaimed when the house came into view. "Lord Almighty hisself'd get lost in them rooms." He was wearing the same black woolen suit he had worn to the wedding, and Laura prayed that her father would behave and would not do anything to add to the embarrassment his appearance already made her feel. Long before they got to town, Little Mattie had warned J.C. to mind his manners. Laura heard him say that he had just as many manners as anybody else. "They're just folks like us," he said. "No better, just richer."

Other buggies and carriages were climbing the hill above San Marcos like a caravan of celebrities. Peter pointed out Gov. John Ireland's carriage, followed by that of George McGehee and Peter's sister Cherokee McGehee. Beyond was the buggy of Peter's sister Little Sweet and her husband, Charles Montgomery. Laura looked up at the Woods mansion to the tall double porches on the second level and imagined Little Sweet Woods firing down at the Army of Occupation troops. Peter pointed out the upstairs porch to her parents. "That's where my sister fired on the Yanks. Trouble is the war was over. Little Sweet saw them coming up the lane, and she saw Martha Benny running alongside shrieking at the soldiers, 'You white-trash Yankees!' When the lead man pulled his whip and started lashing Martha Benny, Little Sweet wanted to stop him. She grabbed up a rifle and started firing down on them. I'm sure she'd do the same thing today if she had half a chance."

Perhaps the most impressive arrival was the lavishly appointed carriage of Capt. Lewis Lawshe, Peter's ninety-year-old grandfather. The carriage was driven by an enormous Negro with hair the color of a soft white cloud. "That's old Ed Tom Lawshe,"

Peter said. "Used to be a slave. He and my mother grew up together. I've known him all my life."

Soon their buggies drew in front of the mansion, and Peter led Laura and her family into the house. As they moved into the parlor, Laura was sure she had never seen such elegance of manner or dress. She was amused by the return to fashion of the ridiculous bustle which enlarged and sometimes added as much as ten pounds to the afterparts of gowns. She wondered why the men designers of Paris and New York, whose works were displayed in her mother's *Harpers* and *Godey's Lady's Book,* seemed intent on making a woman look like a hippopotamus. But the gowns themselves were gorgeous. In contrast to her own simple homemade dress, she saw gowns of apple-green French faille, richly embroidered cream satin fringed with gold, and silk panels decorated with loops of Venetian pearl beads. Peter's oldest sister, Cherokee, was wearing a cream-white brocade with woven bouquets of flowers so real and natural that Laura felt she could pick the blossoms and put them into a vase.

The unsettling thing about all these wondrous gowns was that so many of them were filled with Peter's sisters. No sooner had Laura entered the parlor than they descended on Peter and the guests. Laura calmed herself by considering how very much they resembled hippopotamuses.

"My word, Peter," Cherokee said. "I've nearly forgotten what a lovely little thing she is."

"Like a little bird. A baby robin." This from Little Sweet who had joined her sister to greet the guest of honor. It seemed to Laura they were talking about her as if she were not there, examining her as she had seen Peter examine a mule he considered buying. What next? Would they examine her teeth?

"I just think it's so romantic about you and Peter," Cherokee simpered. "What an absolutely delicious novel it would make. The gentleman marries his former stable girl. How fortunate we are to live in a land where marrying up is so refreshingly possible."

Cherokee grasped Peter's arm and led him away. Laura felt more angry than insulted, a rush of anger that quickly cooled when she realized she could cut Cherokee to the quick if she cared to. Cherokee might have been a beauty when she was young, but that had been a few years and a few pounds ago, and Laura knew, even in her simple dress, she was ravishing compared to Peter's sisters.

Peter's sister Jeffie, who had been Laura's teacher, came to her rescue. When she heard the remark about the stable girl she apologized for her sisters. "It's just that they have seen how Peter looks at you," she said. "And they just think you're awfully young. They don't know you like I do. Give them time. They'll come around."

Jeffie led Laura to the old Colonel-Doctor who wore his advanced years with elegant grace. He was kind, if distant, and he regarded Laura with what seemed amused curiosity. Laura knew for certain that the Colonel-Doctor did not disapprove of the difference in her age and Peter's. The Colonel-Doctor's second wife, Ella Ogletree Woods, had also been called a child bride.

Peter returned to introduce Laura to his friends. As they moved through the rooms and she was presented to the guests one after another, including Governor and Mrs. Ireland, Laura felt like a beautiful, mysterious stranger in an exotic foreign land. She began to feel more than a match for Peter's considerable sisters. She was proud that her husband seemed on such intimate terms with Governor Ireland and other luminaries, some of whom had come from as far away as Austin. She was especially aware that Peter seemed so proud of her.

Occasionally, she caught a glimpse of her mother and father on the edge of things, quietly observing from the sidelines. Though Little Mattie could be an engaging and lively conversationalist, she was dutifully staying by her husband's side, probably to make sure he behaved. J. C. Hoge was simply not the kind of man who drew strangers to him and there was no telling when he might grow angry about some real or imagined slight. Laura watched her father standing stiffly in his ill-fitting wool suit, his great hands hanging below his cuffs, his dark eyes filled with misery, and she knew he must be hating every minute of the party. For a moment, she felt almost sorry for him and would have gone to keep him company had not Miss Ella Woods moved to her side and asked her to see the rest of the house. "Come along," she said, "I'll give you a tour."

Miss Ella, the second Mrs. Woods, was a brunette, with dark eyebrows. She was slim and graceful. Her smile was genuine and warm and Laura felt immediately comfortable in her presence. Miss Ella took Laura's hand and led her away from the crowd. Going from room to room, Laura decided the Woods must surely be the most well-to-do people on earth. Every inch of floor space was filled with chests, chairs, desks and settees, massive pieces of mahogany, rosewood and pine that Peter's mother had ordered from the gifted master craftsman John Ullman, of Washington County, Texas. In the music room there was an elaborately carved piano bearing the sheet music to the rebel songs "God Save the South" and "The Drummer Boy of Shiloh."

But of all she found in the Woods mansion, her favorite discovery was Miss Ella. Laura felt she had found a kindred soul. She could imagine what kind of treatment Ella had received from Peter's sisters when the Colonel-Doctor announced he was marrying a girl about the same age as his daughters.

"What a magnificent house," Laura said, as they walked up the curved staircase to the second floor. "If it could only speak, what stories it could tell. Is it true this house was built as a gift to the Colonel-Doctor from Peter's mother?"

"Yes, that is true. Georgia was a very smart lady. She learned from her papa how to make money. All the folks adored her. Sometimes, I feel she's still alive, watching me. It's very hard to measure up to a ghost."

"What was she like?"

"Very beautiful. Very determined. She died young. Only forty-two. In a way, the family still mourns her death."

They entered a lovely room with tall draped windows that afforded only meager light to pass. Laura felt an oppressive stillness. Although the room was elegantly furnished and had been recently dusted, there was a sense of abandonment. "This is her bedroom. Georgia's. Exactly as it was. This is where she died. The Colonel-Doctor wouldn't let me change a thing."

They walked from the room to an upstairs porch. Below, servants moved among the guests. The ring of crystal and silver and an occasional fragment of laughter punctuated the chorus of conversation. "You must love this place," Laura said.

"I wish it were mine," Miss Ella said. "But it's her house in every way. Every piece of furniture. The silver. Her land, her horses, her family."

Laura could feel the woman's pain. She wondered if Miss Ella had fought against the intrusion of Georgia into her life before she had surrendered to the woman's ghost. *I'll never let a dead woman control me,* she thought. *Not my life or Peter's either. Georgia Lawshe Woods might be a powerful adversary, but her day is done and now it's time for the living.*

Miss Ella and Laura returned downstairs and then out onto the lawn. Miss Ella took Laura's hand again and led her to a marble bench hidden among the Confederate lilies. Laura was suddenly worried by her expression. Tears seemed very near the surface.

"What's wrong?"

"Nothing's wrong."

"Something about Peter?"

"In a way. About you and Peter."

"You don't approve?"

"Of course I do! It's wonderful. Peter's not only my stepson, he's a dear man. It's just that you remind me of that time when the Colonel-Doctor brought me into the family."

"Tell me."

"Well, this is a strange family, Laura. And your Peter is a complicated man."

"Miss Ella, what are you trying to say?"

Ella Woods looked away. For a long moment she was silent. Laura could hear the sounds of the party drifting lazily on the wind. To the west, smoky clouds had gathered. It grew cool as the clouds passed beneath the sun. Laura let Miss Ella's silence lengthen, then became impatient.

"Tell me."

"Something bad happened at this house, Laura. There was a

death. A man was killed. Peter was involved. So was Cherokee. And Sweet. It's unspoken in the family. And I have a feeling it might not be over. Sometimes I think something terrible is going to happen again."

Laura shivered, remembering the revolver beneath their mattress. She had expected a warning about Georgia Lawshe Woods's powerful influence on her son. But not this.

"You mean Peter's in danger? Who? What could happen after all these years?"

"I don't know. They won't say. I came into the family a few years after it all happened. But I know the Colonel-Doctor and Peter feel there is still danger."

"Why do you tell me this?"

"Because Peter probably won't. There'll be times in your life together when he will seem secretive and distant. Now you know why. It won't be because of you. But because of the other. The thing they did."

"This is hardly fair, Miss Ella! You tell me something terrible might happen! And then that's all? End of conversation?"

Miss Ella sighed, seemed to grow smaller. Laura saw there were tears in her eyes. "Don't be angry with me, Laura. That's all I know. They won't tell me either. Maybe I shouldn't have spoken to you about it. Maybe it's none of my business. I just thought you ought to know. It might make a difference later."

"And Peter's sisters? They know?"

"I think what happened explains them in a way. There must have been a great deal of pain."

Laura and Miss Ella sat together silently on the garden bench. A few great dollops of rain fell with small heavy explosions in the dust of the yard. There were shafts of sunlight slanting through the clouds.

"The war. Georgia. What happened here. Those are things you and I can never speak a word about. Not with the Colonel-Doctor. Not with Captain Lawshe. Not with Peter. Not anyone."

Laura remembered Cherokee's remark about the stable girl. "So we are to be ignorant hired hands. Hired to have their babies and run their houses. I don't think so, Miss Ella. Not in this life."

Laura looked out over San Marcos. She felt strong. A summer shower was moving their way through the late sunlight. "There'll probably be a rainbow," Laura said, and they moved into the house.

∞

The table was covered with great expanses of linen and Georgia Lawshe Woods's elegant old coin silver somehow saved from the Yankees. Laura was seated between Governor Ireland and old Captain Lawshe. Peter was seated between Cherokee and Little Sweet, directly across the table. The servants moved swiftly and silently serving okra gumbo, guinea fowl, quarter of lamb, and later, meringue light as a cloud. Shortly after they were seated, Laura heard the governor insist that Peter run for political office.

"Texas needs men like you, Peter," the governor said. "I certainly am in sympathy with most populist notions. It's not the message, it's the messengers. They are passionate and on the side of the angels in most cases, but generally a rough sort. I believe you can be for the common people without being a common person."

Laughter rippled around the table. Laura glanced down the table to where her father glowered. She recalled that political discussions often ignited her father's rages. She prayed they would change the subject. But she was fascinated by this new idea of Peter in public office. She looked across the table at her husband and then glanced sideways at the governor. Peter looked every bit as distinguished as Governor Ireland. Laura regarded Mrs. Ireland picking daintily at her fowl and she imagined herself by Peter's side as he accepted the people's nomination for the office of governor of Texas, an office her father claimed was more desirable than that of president of the United States.

"I think James Steven Hogg is a good man," Governor Ireland said of the state's most vocal populist politician. "I'm for anyone who stands for reform. But he is like a diamond in the rough, without the grace a leader requires. On the other hand,

Peter is polished to a fine sheen. His facets cast light, not fury, like James Hogg. Maybe we should look for a new fella to run. I would be proud to pass the reins of government to a new man like our friend here Peter Woods."

Then Laura heard the sound she had dreaded ever since the meal began. From down the table came the harsh, deep voice of J. C. Hoge. "Reason why Hogg is for working folks is because there's more of them than any other kind. Just makes good sense. There's only a few like them that's here."

There would have been a longer silence, except J.C. noticed everyone at the table was looking at him. Laura knew he would interpret this as interest in his political theories. She actually shuddered.

"I'll tell you why I'm for Hogg," J.C. said into the interval of profound silence. "'Cause he's against the railroads and the big city banks and all them robbers and no-good thieves that have been takin' what rightfully belongs to the farmers like me. If you want to fight the rich, you got to elect a working man. And that's what Hogg is. If you want to fight for what's right you need to elect a fighter. And that's what Hogg is, too."

"There are fighters at this table, Mr. Hoge," Cherokee said. "My papa is one of the great heroes of the Confederacy."

"We had a noble cause," the Colonel-Doctor said.

"I certainly had a noble cause," Captain Lawshe said. "The Yanks burned my place to the ground. I went to bed one night worth $250,000 and the next morning my place wasn't worth twenty-five Confederate cents! Some things just make a fella mad. And burning his house down is one."

"It seems," Cherokee said, without looking up from her china dinner plate, "that people have been fighting for you farmers for some time now, Mr. Hoge. Several of them here at this table."

Laura glanced at her father. His dark, hooded eyes were bright with fury. It was an expression she had often seen when he began removing his leather belt before making her bend over for a beating. But she sensed a basic unfairness, an unnecessary baiting on the part of Cherokee. Her poor father was no match for this crowd. *Where were the storied manners of the privileged class?* Suddenly Laura knew she had to come to her father's defense, even if it meant crossing Peter's older sister. Whatever she would say would be far less inflammatory than whatever J.C. seemed on the verge of saying.

"No one fought harder or longer against the Yankees than my father," Laura said. "He fought under General Shelby for three years."

"Still, your family does have a *northern man*. No use denying that is there, Mr. Hoge?"

"Well, ma'm, my brother had a mind of his own."

"My, my," Cherokee said. "So it is true. You do have a traitor in the family."

Laura could tell her father was silent only because he was shocked that any woman, highborn or not, would speak so rudely to a guest.

"We're not ashamed," Laura said. "It's true Uncle Joe fought for the Union. A sergeant. Fourteenth Regiment, Kansas Cavalry. And yes, he was the *northern man*. He fought bravely and was no traitor to his cause." Laura felt her anger begin to slide out of control. "At least the Hoge family didn't get rich off the war. We didn't run cotton to Mexico and get paid in British gold while the rest of Texas starved to death on Confederate money!" As soon as the words were spoken she regretted them.

The Colonel-Doctor's voice was gentle, yet firm. "Too much has been said already. I apologize for my daughter, Mr. Hoge. Her words were unwarranted. And I'm sure Peter apologizes for his lovely bride."

Laura was about to insist that she was quite capable of speaking for herself and that she would certainly not apologize for speaking the truth but she saw the silent entreaty in Peter's eyes. He was angry and obviously embarrassed for his sister and his wife. Down at the end of the table Laura's father was fighting his own fury, assisted by Little Mattie who was holding one of his hands in both of hers. Cherokee's face was crimson with some roiling emotion emerging from beneath her powder. Laura could feel the tension suspended in the room and she could tell everyone at the table was waiting to see what she would say. And what she said was, "I'm terribly sorry. Please forgive me." She knew if she was to be the wife of a future governor of Texas she would have to learn when to hold her tongue and when to speak her mind.

9 ∞ THE FINEST HORSE RANCH

IN THE WEEKS FOLLOWING THEIR RETURN FROM SAN MARCOS, Peter remained near the ranch. Laura was certain he was foregoing trips away to make amends for the rudeness of his sisters. She had let him know, with small gestures and little ghost moods of disapproval that she disliked the prospect of the frequent journeys he would take away from the ranch to buy horses. She knew these journeys to the livestock auctions in Austin and San Antonio were necessary if the ranch were to prosper, but for now, just a while longer, she wanted her husband all to herself. She gloried in his presence and found, to her utter surprise, that she received great pleasure in preparing meals she knew he would enjoy, keeping his house clean and comfortable, and making their nights together in the four-poster odysseys so magical that any other journey would be for awhile driven from Peter's mind.

Often, during those early weeks, Laura hurried through her kitchen chores after supper so they could walk out on the land to watch the horses play in the soft lavender light of evening. Peter would talk about the land he loved and the natural cycles of the seasons and it would remind her of poor Herman Lehmann. *How strange that two such different men would love the same woman and the same natural world, the one man so wild, the other so refined.* She and Peter would sit on the broad top rail of the corral, watching the mares and their foals silhouetted against the sunset while Peter told about the origin of the beautiful animals that posed and cavorted in their pasture.

"My brother and I and some cowhands used to ride down into the Wild Horse Desert. My mother sent us down there for the horses that roamed free by the thousands. Like deer or antelope."

"Surely they belonged to someone."

"Nobody. They were descended from the Arabian horses Cortez brought to Mexico. And over time they just went wild. They belonged to whoever would go down there and drive them back."

"Seems like the place would be crowded with people after free horses."

"It wasn't that easy. That was wild country. There were bandits down there and Mexican revolutionaries. Poisonous snakes and poisonous people. It took some doing to get there, much less survive when you got there."

"So our horses have Arabian blood?"

"Some have bloodlines going back thirty-five hundred years. Their ancestors pulled the chariots of the Egyptians and carried Alexander the Great into battle."

Laura watched the horses, graceful shadows now in the twilight. The world seemed to open before her mind, the Blanco flowing into the Nile. She listened for the rumble of chariots. The fallen sun had brought a cooling breeze. It carried the scent of clover and of manure and a blending of other earthy scents Laura found heavenly. "How did you get them back from the Wild Horse Desert?"

"We had to catch them first. We'd pick out the best and run those mustangs down, the cowboys working in relays so there'd always be fresh mounts for the chase. Sometimes all day and all night those little horses would keep running. But then they'd wear down, get so tired we could either rope them or drive them back into a corral. Then we'd break them and gentle them like you and I did last summer. And we'd bring them home."

"And that was the beginning of your herd."

"That was half of it. My mama raised fine horses. It was my idea to combine the best qualities of the thoroughbred with the best qualities of the mustang. To combine the speed of the thoroughbred with the toughness, endurance, and courage of the mustang. I mean the mustang was so tough it survived down there in the Wild Horse Desert for four hundred years. That's the Arabian in its blood. It can go for days without water. It'll even eat the bark off cottonwood limbs. So the idea was to blend that toughness and endurance with the size and speed of the thoroughbred. If we could do that, we'd come close to the perfect horse."

"Like those out there?" Laura pointed to several two-year-olds standing next to their mothers. The colts had the small heads of the Arabian and the sleek bodies of thoroughbreds.

"In time. If we just keep working at it. Find the right combination."

"The perfect horse," Laura mused. "It's like being a sculptor, yet the thing you're shaping is alive."

"And to do that we need land. The land is the basis for everything. That's why we have to live out here so far from town. We need space for the horses."

That evening as they lay together listening to the night sounds, Laura wondered, for the first time, what their children would be like. She moved her hand across her stomach thinking that a child might at this very moment be emerging from wherever children are before they are conceived. She wondered what kind of mother she would be and if she would have the influence on them that Peter's mother, Georgia, had on her children.

She turned to face Peter. "Tell me about your mother."

Peter was silent for a moment. "What do you want to know?"

"About the horses."

"After the war, the Yankees took over our place. Made it their headquarters. They took everything we couldn't hide. And it just got worse and worse. Confederate money wasn't worth anything and the silver was buried to keep it from the Yankees. The only thing of value we had was the horses and our lives. But those were dangerous times and it looked like we might lose both. So one night, my mama divided the horses between me and my brothers and sisters and she sent us away. All in different directions. I came to this place on the Blanco. It was family land."

"She stayed in San Marcos?"

"She refused to leave. Said she'd rather die. And she did."

"Peter, how?"

"The house became a hospital. She treated soldiers coming

home from the war. She caught something. Consumption. And she just died. She was younger than I am now."

Laura longed to hold Peter close in the darkness and kiss away the perspiration she saw glistening on his forehead. But she felt the presence of her dead mother-in-law flowing like substance in the room, looking down, judging her.

"We were all there. Watching her whither away. I was just a boy and for a long time I thought I dreamed she died. Each day I waited for her to come into my room and throw open the window and wish me good morning. She never came. Not then. But now sometimes . . . sometimes I think she does."

"In a dream?"

"No."

"Then?"

"Laura, I don't know. But it seems she's actually there." He paused, then took a deep breath. "But she's dead. The horses are all I have left of her."

Laura pulled the sheet up over her body. "Go away," she whispered in her mind to Georgia Lawshe Woods.

As the summer waned, word of Peter's way with horses began to spread and the ranch became known as a place where fine, highly trained mounts and teams could be obtained. Important people from throughout Texas began to come by, not only to buy fine horses but to discuss local news and the political issues of the day. Many of the buyers were from the great cattle ranches to the west, ranchers who mourned the passing of the open range. The introduction of barbed wire had closed the range forever and speculators had brought settlers onto lands that had traditionally been vast open spaces. To Laura it seemed the ranchers brought their problems to Peter believing he had the power or the wisdom to resolve them. After conducting their business they stayed in the horse barns talking with Peter and asking for his opinion about the recent drought and the farmer's alliance, barbed wire, or temperance. Laura recalled Governor Ireland's insistence that Peter should run for political office. She watched the deference the visitors paid Peter as he talked with them about politics and horses and she knew he could win any election he entered. In truth, Laura saw that he would be a perfect candidate. He was now known by all the right people. *Maybe it can be,* she thought. *It just might happen.*

In the meantime, Peter continued his efforts to breed the perfect horse. Among his stallions was an Arabian named Sultan, and Peter's quest entailed breeding Sultan to Willow, a young maiden thoroughbred mare named after the little Hill Country community of Willow City.

One day when Peter was certain Willow was ready, Laura and Peter hobbled the mare to keep her from kicking and carefully washed the genitalia of both horses with a mild soap and water. As Laura held Willow, Peter led Sultan into the paddock where he was at last allowed to mount the mare. The union proved successful.

Peter and Laura awaited the foal as if it were their own child. When her expected foaling date approached, they brought Willow into a small, clean stall and took turns waiting there, spending more time in the barn than in the house.

Willow's water broke about midnight. Laura rushed inside to get Peter and when they returned the mare was down. She was covered with sweat and rolling, kicking at her belly. Time struggled by, hour after hour. It was obvious Willow was in labor, but the foal did not emerge. After what seemed an eternity, one foreleg appeared, then another, but no head.

"She's in trouble!" Peter said. The words were like hammer blows.

By day's first light, the foal lay motionless in the straw.

"He's not breathing," Laura whispered.

"Rub his body! Hard! The ribcage!" Peter removed the placenta from the foal's nostrils, opened the animal's mouth and blew his breath into its lungs. After another eternity, the foal began to breathe and they felt the miracle of life in their hands.

But Willow was dead.

Laura named the orphan colt Lone Star.

∞

Shortly after Lone Star was born, Peter had to attend an auction in Austin. Before he left, he made sure Lone Star had been accepted by a "nurse mare." They had disguised the orphan's scent by rubbing its coat with whiskey so the foal's new mother would accept him as her own. He left instructions for Laura to watch the colt's progress carefully and if he should be rejected by the mare, she should try teaching it to drink from a pail of goat milk.

With Peter gone, she tended her garden, cooked and ate her lonely meals, pruned her peach trees, repaired the roof, hauled water from the creek, mended Peter's clothes, and from time to time mounted great hunts with her Remington rifle in the chicken house where snakes often coiled in the hens' nests. She filled her hours and days with work and with dreams of Peter's climb to the governor's mansion, only sometimes mourning the fact that it was Peter's future she was dreaming and not really her own. But of all the things that filled her time while Peter was away, what she enjoyed most, besides Lone Star, was her effort to create the perfect butterfly.

While Peter was seeking to create the perfect horse, Laura was establishing a ranch for butterflies. She had read in Holland's *Butterfly Guide* that there were 127 different varieties of butterflies in Central Texas. Laura had persuaded most of them to come to her garden. She loved having the beautiful creatures near. They were like flowers blooming, little pieces of Eden, a garden in the air. Herman had told her they were messengers from the spirit world. The mourning cloaks were the first to arrive in the spring, followed by the painted lady and the pipevine swallowtail attracted to her yellow daisies. She tempted the white cabbage butterfly to her lantana plants by placing a drop of honey on the blossoms. By midsummer, Laura's garden of pink, rose, purple, and yellow cosmos and towering sunflowers were alive with clouds of delicate winged color.

With Peter gone to the auction at Austin, she decided to mount a butterfly-collecting expedition in her garden. Following the directions in her Holland's guide, she fashioned a collection net from a length of green hickory, one end split and formed into a loop. She covered the loop with green netting. Then, with Lone Star gamboling at her side and her net held high, she moved out toward the river in quest of the wily swallowtail. So numerous were the colorful swallowtails that it took only a moment before she caught one in her net. When she tried to disentangle the butterfly from the netting, one of the red, black, and blue wings came off in her hand. Laura was horrified at what she had done. She threw the butterfly net as far as she could toward the river.

The next morning was an impressionist painting. A haze hovered over the Hill Country and the sun played in the morning moisture, scattering a thousand prisms over the land. Suddenly a mockingbird hurled its wild melody into the morning. Laura looked up into the direction of the song and saw a trail of dust, someone coming from the West. She had often told Peter their mockingbird was a kind of watchbird, warning them of visitors or intruders. Once she had even seen the stouthearted bird torment a rattlesnake and drive it from the yard.

Laura was delighted to see the editor of the *Blanco News* move toward the house. William Wright waved, dismounted, lay his reins over a limb of the peach tree on which the mockingbird sang, then removed and waved his hat. "Wonderful morning," he said as he approached. Then, as he shook Laura's muddy hand, his eyes widened in recognition. "Laura," he said, "the little girl who wanted to be president. Your mama knew Lincoln." William Wright's smile was as bright as the day.

"I'm Laura Woods now. Peter and I were married this past summer."

"That's wonderful news, Mrs. Woods! Is Peter about?"

Laura wiped the Texas soil from Mr. Wright's hand with her apron. "Gone to buy mules." Laura was bathed in the kindness of his eyes.

"I came to see Peter about a pair of matched bays. I've always admired that pair of his. They're so beautifully trained."

"Peter does have a way."

For a while they chatted in the garden, enjoying the gentle air and the sound of their voices and the clear golden light of morning. Laura was flattered by the newspaperman's attention. She remembered how carefully he had listened when she told him about the killing of the Cathertons.

"Are you still interested in politics?"

"Very much, yes."

"There's talk of recruiting Peter to run for office, you know. He'd certainly have my paper's support."

"Peter is a very private person. Sometimes I think he loves the company of his horses more than he does people." As they talked, Laura busied herself with her watering can and shears. Although her butterfly net was empty, pipevine swallowtails now fluttered like windblown leaves about her bonnet.

"What about you, Mrs. Woods?"

"Don't you remember? You're the one who told me Lincoln was wrong. You said a woman could never be elected."

"I didn't say never. First the vote, then the office. It will come. It's already coming. Elizabeth Cady Stanton, Lucretia Mott, Susan B. Anthony, they're changing the world. Women in Wyoming have already won the right to vote. It's just a matter of time before other states follow along."

"Even in Texas?"

"Even in Texas. For twenty years now, the Texas Equal Rights Association has been leading the way. But the women's movement needs writers to interpret how women feel, the problems they face, the discrimination they suffer. Maybe you should give it a try. You're bright. Good with words. And you have an active conscience. I remember how you chided me for not writing that lynching Al Lackey was morally wrong." He paused a moment to watch Laura move along the flowerbed with shears and a basket, cutting bouquets for the table and the mantel. Then he continued. "I've been thinking about a political column from a woman's point of view. Not about cooking or sewing and all that. But a column about the hard issues women face. Suffrage. Temperance. Expectations and the betrayal of expectations."

Laura felt the old excitement stirring. "I don't know if I'd have time, Mr. Wright." She looked around, spread her hands, palms upward, a gesture of futility. "My day is so full."

"Maybe you're filling it with the wrong things. You can plant seeds in a garden. Or you can plant ideas in the minds and hearts of people. Anyway, think about it. Try one column and see how it goes."

"How much will you pay?"

Mr. Wright laughed, apparently taken aback by her question. "Pay? Now, Mrs. Woods, I didn't say anything about pay."

"Then *that* will be the subject of my first column," Laura said. "Exploitation of women. A column about women who work for little or no pay while men are paid well for the same work."

William Wright's smile bloomed again, his eyes bright, his cheeks blushing crimson. "Well, Mrs. Woods, I stand corrected. I'll pay you the same as I'd pay any male reporter. Agreed?"

"Seriously?"

"I am serious. I'm serious about you covering a political rally in town Friday night. James Hogg is the featured speaker. He's running hard for governor. I'd appreciate a column on a woman's view of the rally and of Hogg's speech. Come by the office in the afternoon if you can, and I'll give you some background."

Laura stood, wiped her hands on her apron. "I'll have to ask Peter."

William Wright, who had turned to leave, turned back and looked directly into Laura's eyes. "No you don't," he said. "And that can be your next column." Then he bowed, mounted, tipped his hat, and rode away.

Laura rode Miss Ruth into town on Friday afternoon. She met Peter's sister Jeffie at Pastor Shaw's parsonage, where she had dressed on her wedding day and where she would stay the night after the rally. Then she and Jeffie walked to the offices of the *Blanco News*. The town square was crowded with families often led by gaunt, angry farmers who reminded Laura of her father. Laura and Jeffie pushed through the crowd into the little newspaper office, filled with its clattering machinery.

"I knew you'd come," William Wright said. "I'm very pleased. Have you ever seen such a crowd?"

"They look angry," Laura said.

"They are." Wright surveyed the passing parade. "They've come in search of a leader. A leader who can forge their wrath into the weaponry of economic change. Someone who can right what's wrong with their world. A strong man who can wrestle their demons, real and imagined." Laura did not need much background on hard times from William Wright. She had heard her father's cries of anger and desperation all her life. Her family had known what it meant to be poor and powerless in a harsh and difficult land. The plight of the farmer had grown even more desperate after several recent bitterly cold winters and four years of drought.

On a wooden platform constructed above the courthouse lawn, a politician was sermonizing against the powers that enslaved the workingman and the farmer. William Wright pointed out that the speeches had been going on all afternoon.

"Some people say you measure the worth of a candidate by how long he can speak," Jeffie said. "The really good ones can go on all night."

Children cavorted among large iron pots of barbecue and cowboy stew where people lined up to fill their tin cups with the Hill Country's favorite fare. Men fed branches to the fires near the speaker's platform and sparks swirled dangerously close to the large American flag and patriotic bunting that draped the stand. Behind the speaker fiddlers stood, tuning their instruments, eagerly awaiting intervals in the speeches so they could play "Dixie" again.

Fires cast mysterious patterns of light and shadow on the crowd and the hard faces of the buildings and farmers. The night was filled with music and the heady promise of reform and Laura felt a gathering of almost feverish excitement. It was a feeling not unlike the one she had before a performance of the

Glasscock Brothers Circus. Soon the silver-suited aerialist would soar downward from the heights and the elephants would come trumpeting from behind the courthouse. Even the cadence and passion of the speakers reminded her of the sideshow barker or the proprietor of a medicine show outside the canvas Big Top. As she listened more carefully, she heard a speaker with a flamboyant, florid delivery almost exactly like the Rev. Andrew Jackson Potter, a preacher who could deliver an entire sermon of nothing but verbs. Laura decided there was an amazing similarity between a political rally, the circus and a camp meeting. From the stump and from the pulpit and from the center ring came the promise of holy crusades in which the meek will inherit the earth. "It's wonderful," Laura said to Mr. Wright. "I love it. It's all so familiar. Like I've been here before."

"First-rate theater," the editor said. "It would be second-rate except it's so human. Besides, in a strange, flawed way, the process works. The business of democracy gets done."

The main speaker rose to the platform accompanied by applause and fiddles. Behind the crowd, near the *Blanco News* office, a covey of rockets streaked skyward and exploded in blossoms of gold and green fire. "James Stephen Hogg, James Stephen Hogg, James Stephen Hogg," came the throaty chorus from the crowd.

James Stephen Hogg was a big man with a florid complexion and a shock of black unruly hair. He moved gracefully for a man so large, and he lost no time hurling harsh words at railroads, big business and the "soulless corporations that are guilty as sin of shameful abuses."

"All the best land has been stolen by the monopolies and railroads while Texas farmers are forced to scratch out a living on the rest," Hogg shouted, his large, thick body swaying, his eyes reflecting the firelight. "So we borrow from the same corporations that own the best land and they charge exorbitant and immoral interest rates on the loan we shouldn't have had to take out in the first place. Everywhere the farmer turns he is gouged and cheated and his blood is sucked dry by the middlemen and the capitalists!"

Hogg threw off his coat and tie, rolled up his sleeves and the crowd roared its approval. Each of Hogg's sentences contained a passionate indictment of the New York capitalists. He was interrupted by applause after every sentence. The battle had been joined. The raw recruits could smell the blood of the enemy. The sweating, sunburned farmers in the crowd did not care about detail. They had their leader and they would follow him to hell and back.

Near midnight James Hogg hurled his last accusation and stepped from the platform to be consumed by the crowd of farmers and families. One last salvo of rockets was fired into the night sky. The fiddlers played the evening's last rendition of "America, America, God Shed His Grace on Thee" and Laura knew for certain she had fallen hopelessly in love with Hill Country politics.

"It's all about land," William Wright said, as he prepared to close the newspaper office. "Every issue in this country eventually gets down to a man's relationship to the land. It's a fact whether that man is a red man, a black man or white." *I won't forget to write a column about a woman owning land,* Laura thought. Wright returned to his desk and brought Laura a proof of a story he had written for his paper's next issue.

"Give this to Peter," he said. "It will be big news in a few days. The government's going to sell off its railroad lands. A dollar an acre. Peter could expand his ranch holdings for a song. Tell him he has James Hogg to thank."

"Why James Hogg?"

"It's all here in the story. James Hogg made it happen. The state is offering sections to settlers at a bargain price."

"A dollar an acre?" Laura could not wait for Peter to hear this news. They could double, triple the size of their ranch.

"But there's a small hitch to it. To qualify, you have to agree to build a house on the land you buy and live there for six months of the year."

"Why?"

"To keep land speculators from buying it all up and reselling it at a profit."

William Wright insisted on walking Laura and Jeffie to the

parsonage. Laura folded away the newspaper, and as she waited for the editor to close the office for the night, she listened to the echoes of the rally, the speeches, the music, and the voice of the crowd. She was not sure that the raucous, righteous symphony would ever quite leave her ears. She felt the exhilaration she had felt in the moments after riding the elephant with Herman Lehmann. The power and the promise of that ride was over-poweringly sensual. *Maybe politics is a kind of beast we ride,* she thought, and she toyed with the idea and could almost see the words beneath her byline in the *Blanco News.*

For two days Laura struggled with the story. She filled page after page with words, but when she read the sentences aloud to Lone Star she knew she was failing to capture the excitement she had felt at the rally. She was thankful Peter was not home and she wondered what he would say about her new career as a journalist.

On the third day of her creative struggle, at dusk, she saw her husband riding across their fields leading several horses and mules. Usually when he returned from a trip she could not wait to hear the details of his adventures, of the people he had met, the cities he had seen, and the horses he had purchased. This time, however, it was she who had tales to tell of her adventures in town and her new job writing a political column for the *Blanco News* and their opportunity to purchase public lands for a dollar an acre.

After caring for the new horses and mules, they spent an easy hour admiring little orphan Lone Star as he played with the other colts.

"He's everything I ever wished," Peter said. They talked long into the night, catching up on the news, pouring out their dreams like rich cream to cover the days to come—dreams of horses and land and truth captured forever in words.

Later, in the four-poster, they celebrated the fact that they were together again. Their lovemaking, for the first time, was not gentle. Laura felt a certain ferocity, urgency. When they finally rolled apart, she found she was embarrassed by the violence of their passion. She knew they were both surprised by how aggressive they had been, their lovemaking as contest, Eros in joust. Each seemed to be trying to dominate the other, expressing with their bodies what they were unwilling to express in words. Neither spoke for a long time.

As she lay by his side, listening to the silence swirling between them, Laura revisited the hours following his return, trying to remember what they had said that might have made their lovemaking such a quarreling of the flesh. She had told him of the James Hogg rally and her opportunity to write for the *Blanco News*. She had told Peter what William Wright said about being a voice for female suffrage and how her stories might change the lives of Hill Country women, make it possible for them to vote and hold elective office. With equal enthusiasm they had talked about the new ranchland and calculated how much they could afford to buy. Peter had said they could probably increase their land holdings fourfold and they had marveled at the possibility. They talked about a specific spread of land they knew was available, a beautiful wilderness, unsettled and far away. But it was probably what they did not say that had fueled the hard edge to their passion and that lay between them now in the four-poster. Laura waited for the unspoken words to come from the dark silence by her side. But Peter was silent.

"So you want me to live on the new land." Her voice was light, her heart heavy as stone.

"I don't want you to. But it's the only way we'll ever be able to buy that much land. Somebody has to live on the land. Make a second home out there. It's a chance of a lifetime."

"Why not you?"

"I've got to run this place. I can't be two places at once."

"We could hire someone."

"Every dollar we pay in wages is an acre less we can buy."

"How can we manage two ranches?"

"I stay here with the horses and you take care of the new place."

"I don't know if I can. Not all by myself."

"You can. I know how strong you are. You swam the underwater tunnel at the Narrows."

Laura felt her opportunity at the *Blanco News* slipping away. Writing stories about a new world for women would have to wait. There was no choice. It occurred to her that she was a virtual prisoner of her love for her husband. *How can I be happy,* she thought, *if Peter isn't happy? What would life be like if he were to live with regret for the rest of his days?* He would not blame her, of course, but it would always be there, the opportunity missed, the dream undone, something dark beneath the surface, between the lines of their lives. *So I'll write my stories about a new world for women later. Now I'll have to live in the old one.*

Laura could feel Peter struggling between his dream and his conscience and she felt bad that he felt bad about volunteering her to months of living alone in the wilderness. She sighed and turned into the tension between them and then she pressed it away with her body and her words. "It's all right, Peter. It will be good. It's my dream, too. To be the wife of the man who owns the finest horse ranch in Texas." She kissed him then and this time they touched softly.

Later in the night, Laura left Peter sleeping and went outside to cry.

10 ∞ THE WILDERNESS RANCH

IN 1891, INSTEAD OF WRITING A COLUMN FOR THE *BLANCO NEWS* and covering James Hogg's gubernatorial campaign, Laura Woods moved to the last place on earth. Forever in her mind and conversation these four sections of scrub and stone in the wild empty lands of Central Texas, where the howls of Apache raiders had but recently stilled, would be referred to as the Wilderness Ranch. If the ranch at the headwaters of the Blanco had locked Laura's life away in an outpost on the frontier, the two-room shanty on the primal hills that they had to homestead was more like solitary confinement.

Peter had decided they should continue breeding horses on the Blanco River and that Laura could live in a house they would build on the homestead. It was a difficult decision, but they both knew it was the only way to obtain and hold the land. Laura had become resigned to the idea. Although she would miss the excitement of James Hogg's race for governor and would be so out of touch that writing her column would be impossible, Laura had accepted her fate. *Besides, what could be so bad? I'm mostly alone now,* she thought. She forced herself to see the move not as a sacrifice but as a grand personal adventure. Several months before the move she borrowed Jeffie's copy of Thoreau's *Walden, or Life in the Woods,* hoping to find some pointers on the art of living alone.

As time for moving to the Wilderness Ranch drew near, Laura pored over the pages Thoreau wrote at Walden Pond. "Most of the luxuries and many of the so-called comforts of life," Thoreau wrote, "are not only dispensable, but positive hindrances to the elevation of mankind." He wrote of anticipating the sunrise and the sunset and walking with nature herself and of living a simple life free of the slavery of material possessions. Laura imagined her life at the Wilderness Ranch would be an opportunity to live in harmony with nature and with the beating of her own heart. She decided to keep a journal, like Thoreau. Perhaps her journal would replace the newspaper columns she would be unable to write.

They began their move to the Wilderness Ranch one August morning, hauling their house in the wagon. Peter had purchased the lumber for the house from a mill in Dripping Springs where the boards were precut to the dimensions required by the homestead laws. "I never dreamed I would live in a house designed by legislators," Laura wrote in her journal. She was both troubled and amused that the materials to build their entire house could be carried in a single wagon. The law required the house to have two rooms, at least two windows, and that it be a "permanent" dwelling. *A cave,* Laura thought, *would meet half of the requirements of the Land Alienation Act.*

Laura and Peter's new house was built in a single day. With the help of their friends the Dales, the Eppes, the Stubbs, and the Smiths. Refreshed by a vast table covered with platters and bowls of food and uncovered jars of a fermented beverage called Grandma's Apple Pie, the basic structure was raised in merely two hours. It was a "shotgun" house, two rooms with a porch extending across the front. There was a lean-to shelter in the back for storage of tools and harness. The roof was of tin and the floor of rough-hewn planks. Laura could see the grass through the spaces between the floorboards. The most expensive material used in the building of the little house was nails, wrought by hand from iron bar by Blanco blacksmiths. There was no well, of course, but a small stream wandered nearby and from its banks Laura brought mud to caulk the cracks in the walls. The chimney was made of sticks daubed with the same mud. The only furnishings were a bed, a table, a chest, a cabinet for dishes, and three chairs.

But as the house took shape, there was singing, fellowship, fine food, and the glad good feeling of honest labor. When it was nearly finished, Laura stood back and looked at the house where she would live the next six months. It looked like the old slave shotgun shanties that lined Peter's mother's cotton lands. Even though it was new the cabin seemed like an old toy some giant child had abused. To her surprise, she was proud of this, her private frontier, her foray into the secret world of the wild. Here she would make her statement that a civilized being could live and prosper in a savage land, alone with simplicity and dignity. In years to come, when the main ranch house rose above its gardens and servants hurried through its vast halls bearing cool drinks for their guests, she would remember with fondness this brief interval of minor inconvenience.

In the late afternoon, when the house was finished, they all stood back and viewed what they had done on the rocky hillside. "This is why half of Europe is coming to America," Peter said. "My mother taught us that land is the most important thing in the world. Only if you have land can you be truly free." Laura remembered her friends at the Glasscock Brothers Circus and how they would disagree with Peter's mother. To them, ownership of land was a kind of prison, binding them to one place in a world created for wanderers. But the land she and Peter now walked felt good beneath her feet.

As they watched the sunset, they examined what they had created in the wilderness. Laura sat on an outcropping of stone and read aloud the passage from Thoreau. *"This was an airy and unplastered cabin, fit to entertain a traveling god, and where a goddess might trail her garments. The winds which passed over my dwelling were such as sweep over the ridges of mountains, bearing the broken strains, or celestial parts only, of terrestrial music. The morning wind forever blows, the poem of creation is uninterrupted; but few are the ears that hear it. Olympus is but outside of the earth everywhere."*

That first night, when the house was still and the builders had retired to their tents and fires, Peter and Laura were left alone in their room. "It's like playing house," Laura said. "Tomorrow will come and we'll dismantle the house and play a different game." She came to bed then, trailing her garments like Thoreau's goddess and made love to a traveling god.

∞

Laura was not alone in the house until the final week in August. She and Peter had built a shelter for the horses and stocked provisions to last deep into the winter. They had walked the land and paced off the places where a larger house would rise and where barns and outbuildings and a track for training the horses would be. It was terribly hot and insects waged war on her arms and eyes and the backs of her hands. There was something hard and leathery about the land. The brush tore at her skirt and her clothes were soon gray with dust raised by the wind. The soil looked thin and tired and Laura wondered if she could coax a garden from such bitter earth. She could not imagine butterflies in this hot, heavy air. She looked out at the harsh, empty land, trying to envision how it would look when softened by the barns and vegetable gardens of the farm to be.

Then it was time for Peter to go, and as he vanished into the arroyo to the north, there was a fleeting interval of doubt in Laura's mind. A thin ghost of recrimination, a feeling that she was being used. *An idiot could hold this land,* she thought. *A scarecrow would serve perfectly well. Whatever am I doing out here at the very edge of nowhere. My life is sliding backwards.* Even though Peter would only be a half-day away, and would visit from time to time, it seemed he was on the other side of the earth.

"Peter went back to the ranch," she wrote in her journal that first night. "I have everything I need for the house and tomorrow I will finish the pen for the horses. I practiced for an hour with the Remington. It is late and I can see the moon through the window. Outside is a silence I've never heard before. It seems to ring. There is no wind. I know there are no more wild Indians in these parts. I am not afraid."

∞

The trapper came in early September. He was tall and angular, ugly and curious. Laura noticed him first as he circled the house, scowling, as if investigating the lair of some new and alien animal. He was enormously unkempt, his hair and beard hardly distinguishable from the soiled, turbanlike cap he wore. After he had apparently identified the species of animal living in the lair, he moved to the front of the house and sat down on a flat stone in the shade of an oak, his old Enfield rifle leaning against his shoulder, a sack of dead animals by his side.

At first, Laura was pleased to see another human being. It had been nearly a week since Peter's last visit and she had not spoken aloud since then. She had decided that no matter how lonely she became, she would not talk to herself as she had the previous year whenever Peter was away. As the trapper settled down in front of her house, she began to practice a greeting to make sure her vocal chords still functioned. Then she wondered, *Why had this ragged man not approached the door, why had he waited out front?* Finally, more curious than alarmed, carrying the scissors she had been using to cut a pattern, she moved from the window to the doorway.

She opened the door and he was there, on the porch, cadaverous, smelling of death, the front of his shirt and trousers covered with what she could only imagine was dried blood. He looked down at her with watery eyes.

"You gonna cut me with them scissors?" His voice was a liquid, rumbling whisper forced from somewhere down in his chest. He coughed, causing Laura to close her eyes and turn her head. "Weren't no house here last time I was by. Sure hate folks homesteadin' out here. Pretty soon won't be no critters worth skinnin'." As he spoke, his eyes explored the house and examined Laura as if she was a chair or an ornament. "You here by yourself, little lady?"

"No," Laura said, after a pause just long enough to reveal her lie. He smiled and coughed, his mouth twisting, his lean body contorting, an event so disgusting she turned her head again and held her breath.

"Well, if I gotta have a neighbor, you sure are a pretty one. Name's Gunther. Trap here abouts. Raccoons, skunks, wolves. Some coyotes. Sell the hides. I'll be around. Anything you want, just hang somethin' red in that window and I'll see it and come." Once more he was staggered by the force of a terrible cough and then he turned and almost loped from her sight. He disappeared so fast only his lingering poisonous aroma proved he had been there at all. Laura was stunned. She stood in the doorway, scissors in hand, wondering whether to be afraid or angry that the only human being within miles would be so loathsome and filthy and strange. Surely Thoreau did not have such an awful neighbor. That night she wrote in her journal: "Mr. Gunther came by. He is a fearsome, wild-looking man. There is something familiar about him. I think he has tuberculosis. Living alone in the wild has taken away whatever social graces he might have had. I must be careful not to let myself go like that. It must be terrible making your living killing animals for their skins." Outside, in the night, she heard a distant sound. It was Gunther coughing, a sound like the barking of an animal. She turned back to her journal. "I miss Peter," she wrote. "I must have seen Gunther at the Confederate Reunion. He seems familiar. I am not afraid."

Although she often heard him coughing in the night, Laura did not see the trapper again for weeks. She began to think of him as an animal of the woods. Like the wolf with his slinking, there was a sense of suspended violence about Mr. Gunther. As a hunter and trapper, he was, after all, nature's most effective predator.

Time at the Wilderness Ranch seemed to slide by quickly on its spiral glide. Laura began to make progress on the house and the yard. She felt like she had somehow been dropped into enemy territory and she was slowly widening the territory she controlled, forcing the wilderness back, widening her small island of civilization. She was very careful to flaunt her civilized behavior in the face of the wilderness around her. She would begin the day by brushing her long red hair at least one hundred strokes. Then, after washing in creek water warmed on the iron stove, she would select a clean, fresh dress, recently pressed with a flatiron and fragrant with sunshine from the line. Then she would prepare a breakfast of eggs and cornmeal mush, served as formally as possible, with a white cloth covering the board table and a wildflower in a glass as a centerpiece. With blessings said, she would proceed with the meal. She would linger over coffee and then, with a sigh and enormous resolve, attack the back-breaking chores of the emerging farm.

She dragged stones from the creek to the house to build a foundation as a barrier to the cold air the winter winds would soon seek to force up through the floor. With a shovel she carved a shelf by the creek and lined it with stone so she could get water without muddying her skirts. She built a fence around the chicken house to protect the chicks from the foxes that escaped the wrath of her Remington and Mr. Gunther's traps. She planted a fall garden, and with horses hitched to a grubbing tool she cleared brush from where the yard would be. By the end of the day she was always bone tired, her clothes drenched with perspiration and dust, her body heavy with fatigue and the venom of the great clouds of insects with whom she shared the farm. On some days she was so filthy she would jump into the creek with her clothes on and wash both dress and flesh simultaneously. Then, on other occasions, she would pull herself together, bathe properly and dress as if for croquet. Out would come a white tablecloth and a glass of freshly cut wildflowers and then she would invite herself to dine.

One morning, when she came out onto the porch, she found a pile of skins Gunther had apparently left as a gift. There was no evidence of the trapper, merely the pelts and the smell of rotting flesh. On two other occasions, as the summer waned, Gunther left such presents on her porch. To her dismay, she found herself dreading the morning, afraid she would find another of the trapper's rotting gifts.

Then one morning when she was very sick and depressed and longing for Little Mattie to tell her what was wrong, Gunther came pounding on the door. She was in no mood for company, certainly not the trapper. She picked up her scissors and moved to the door. "What do you want?"

"Friendly talk, missy."

"I'm busy." She grasped for a reason to keep the door between them. "And I'm sick."

"I got cures. Let me in. What kind of neighbor too busy to see a friend?"

Laura felt dizzy and disoriented and the thought of Gunther in her house filled her with nausea. "Go away. I don't want you killing animals on my land!"

Gunther coughed and the muscles in Laura's stomach tightened. "I'll kill what and where I want to. This was my place before it was your'n. *You* go away!"

Laura heard his footsteps move from the door. "I'll be back, little neighbor," Gunther shouted, dislodging a series of terrible sounds from deep in his chest.

As she began to feel better, she finally admitted to herself what she had suspected now for several weeks. She had not kept track of her monthlies and she could not remember the last one. The nights had grown cooler. The chill lingered in the house and she sat at a small table by the stove first admitting, then denying, that she was with child. "I can't believe it! I can't be having a baby!" Then she laughed out loud, covering her mouth with her hand. She stood, anxious to rush out and tell someone, but there was no one to tell. She settled back in the chair, her mood suddenly falling, tumbling down. *What if something goes wrong?* she thought. *Why doesn't Peter come!* It occurred to her to hang a red cloth in the window to summon Gunther who might go find Peter and then she shuddered when she thought of talking with that wild, sick man. She thought of all the women who had terrible things happen, who lost their babies or died in childbirth. Then she thought how wonderful it would be to dress the baby and how fine to feed and bathe a warm living thing. It would be like playing with the corncob dolls Little Mattie had made for her and her sisters. She thought of the company she would have and realized when the baby was born she would never be lonely again.

She wanted to hitch the wagon and drive home to their ranch on the Blanco. She could not bear to keep her secret to herself. But she would not go yet. She would wait until she was absolutely sure or until Peter came.

One autumn morning, as Laura came outside to feel the season change, she found a dead animal on her porch. It was large, like a wolf, but she could not be sure because the skin had been removed. It looked like a great naked child. The next week she found another bloody animal on the porch, its skin stripped away. For the next several weeks, she would often find Gunther had visited in the night. And each time, in the morning, she had to carry the disgusting carrion away from the house.

After she had found the second dead animal, she began to admit to herself that she was terribly afraid. She tried to imagine what kind of sick mind would leave such a "gift." Maybe Gunther was angry that she had refused the gift of his pelts and had carried them away from the house. Probably he was angry that she had told him to get off her place. She thought of the dried blood on his clothes, shivered and resolved to keep the Remington loaded and near at hand.

The worst thing about Gunther lurking about the place was that she found excuses not to go outside. She had to force herself to go to the creek for water and it was difficult carrying the pail in one hand and the rifle in the other. Often she would grow angry that she was being forced to change her habits by a sick old man. He was probably harmless. Just lonely. Then she would remember the sad, naked sinew and tissue heaped by her door and she would know, without doubt, she shared the Wilderness Ranch with a madman. Little by little she neglected chores outside and found herself imprisoned by her fear.

The horrible notion came upon Laura like the kick of a mule. It was night, and as she listened to Gunther coughing beyond the light from the window, she knew with absolute certainty that the trapper was the hanged murderer, Al Lackey. Herman Lehmann admitted that he had cut Lackey down. The whispery voice, as if his vocal chords had been crushed by the rope. He had grown thin because of his sickness. It had to be Lackey—she had seen with her own eyes how he had butchered his victims. The old man outside was the killer Al Lackey. There was no doubt. He had looked into Laura's eyes that night he was hanged and he was in a mood for butchery.

Laura broke apart her only table and used the wood to board up her two small windows.

The next afternoon, the sky to the north grew dark and the

tops of the trees began to dance. Leaves and the wings of birds filled the air. Laura knew a blue norther was on its way, blasting down from the Arctic. The wind began to howl out of the north and the cold came raging into the house through the cracks in the floor and through the sills, around the door and even through the walls. Laura built the season's first fire in the fireplace. It blazed high on the hearth, yet there was something about a Texas norther that defied fire and that crept through blankets and woolens and into the marrow of the bone. No matter how close she sat facing the hearth, she could feel the cold settling down on her back.

Outside in the storm, it grew dark as the eye of evil. Then, as she was growing drowsy by the fire, she heard a cough and then footfalls on the porch and then a pounding at the door. "Little neighbor," Gunther called in his whispery voice. She could barely hear him above the storm. He knocked again, then once more. She heard him cough and whatever he said, whatever sounds he made, were swept away by the rising wind.

Laura sat with her back to the fire, the loaded rifle across her lap, never more awake in her life. She listened for Gunther, but there was no sound save the voice of the storm and the cracking of the fire. She was terrified his awful face might suddenly appear in the spaces between the boards she had nailed to the window; still there was only blackness beyond the glass. She knew the boards would never hold him back. She made sure, for the hundredth time, the rifle was not on safety.

About midnight, the wind began to falter and Laura could see small veins of water running down the windowpane. It was not a driving rain, but more a windblown mist which she knew would soon freeze on the trees. It grew colder as the night passed. Although Gunther had apparently gone away, Laura remained tense and awake with the rifle cradled in her arms.

At first light, Laura moved to the window and it was so beautiful outside she could barely catch her breath. The world had become a universe of diamonds. Every surface—the trees, the grass, the fences—was covered with a glistening coating of ice. The air was still and filled with a sound like the ringing of a thousand temple bells, high and light and holy. As she stood by the window, the rim of the sun rose above the horizon and the light danced on the facets of the ice. Laura imagined this was how the cities of heaven must be in their place above the clouds. She would not have been surprised to see angels playing in the highest maples. The world was so beautiful outside her window that she forgot about the trapper. She put her rifle away so she could run outside to marvel at the frozen wonderland beyond her door.

Laura opened the door and screamed. She slammed the door shut again, her heart pounding. Gunther was out there. She locked and leaned against the door and then realized there had been something wrong with Gunther's face. It had been encased in a thin layer of ice. *Why didn't the ice melt from the heat of his body?*

Then she knew. Gunther had come and left his own dead body sitting on her porch. Whether he had come to do her harm or to seek shelter from the storm she would never know.

It grew warmer during the day. The sun carried the jewels of the ice storm away. Laura dragged Gunther to the shallow grave she had dug through a layer of ice some distance from the house. She was amazed that he was as light as a child. She remembered the great weight bending the hanging tree on the outskirts of Blanco. The man was probably not Lackey after all. Had she caused the death of a sick and innocent man by refusing him shelter from the storm? Then she remembered the disgusting carcasses he had left on her porch, and she kicked the trapper into the hole. It was late afternoon when the grave was covered. Then Laura went back inside to pray and wait for Peter.

A few months after the death of the trapper, Laura's first child was born. He was named Eugene Cavanaugh. A year later came Maxey Charles. Both sons were born in the great white Woods mansion above San Marcos, delivered by the Colonel-Doctor after a fine, glorious, luxurious confinement in a room with elegant furnishings. Laura felt there could have been no greater contrast than between the Woods mansion and the Wilderness Ranch. Here, she was flattered and spoiled and fussed over by Little Mattie, Alice Benny, Miss Ella and the prospective aunts. The considerable Woods sisters seemed at last to accept her, if not into the family, into their regard. Perhaps they admired her role in Peter's life, not only as wife but as partner in the building of the ranch. They were cordial and solicitous and their love for their new nephews was obvious and unrestrained. "If I can come here to have all my babies," Laura told Peter, "I'll give you more sons and daughters than the old woman in the shoe."

Several months after the birth of her second child, Maxey Charles, Laura returned to the Wilderness Ranch. They had fulfilled the requirements of the Homestead Law and were now beginning to build something of real value on the new land. A few horses had been moved to the new ranch, and, of course, someone had to stay on the place, caring for the animals and guarding the property against intruders. Peter spent more time with her now, but Laura was still often alone with the solitude of the land and the infant children. Occasionally, when she would pass by Gunther's unmarked grave, her fear would return and she would remember the storm and the dead face, like a terrible ice sculpture at her door. But usually her thoughts were directed more toward the future and the children and to the next time she would see Peter coming up the arroyo from the north. Sometimes she thought about her lost opportunity to write about politics and the struggle for female suffrage. *What a far cry that scene is from this,* she thought, as she looked out over their vast empty lands.

One late spring morning in 1894, the year Charles Culberson replaced James Hogg in the Texas governor's mansion, it began to rain. At first it seemed to be one of those brief spring showers that visit for awhile and then move on. The air felt fresh and clean and Laura brought the children out on the porch so she could watch them and the rain while she snapped green beans. Eugene was playing with a toy soldier Peter had carved. Laura balanced the bowl of beans in her lap as she rocked Maxey Charles's crib with her foot. Maxey Charles was fretful. He had a cough and a touch of diarrhea and Laura made him some mint tea to soothe his throat and settle his stomach.

It was still raining at the end of the day and the air had grown smoky and close, the light a strange yellow. Overhead, dirty gray clouds wandered this way and that as if lost and in panic against a great looming tongue of black. All at once the sky opened and the deluge began. Inside the little house, Laura and the children listened to the rattling of the rain and watched the distant light show through the window. Now and again lightning flashed and Laura counted until she heard the thunder boom and told the children how far away was the heart of the storm.

Toward evening of the third day it was still raining and the roof began to leak. Laura scurried around with pans and pails to catch the rivulets of water that ran with increasing ease through the cracks in the clapboards. Maxey Charles's cough had grown worse. He was beginning to run a slight fever. The day had been so dark Laura did not know for sure when night fell. When Maxey Charles began to cry, she assumed it must be suppertime and lifted the child to her breast. He was hot to the touch; a nagging ghost of fear crept into the back of her mind.

On the fifth day of the deluge it was growing more and more difficult to find a dry place in the house. Laura had given up shifting the cribs and her bed away from the leaks and the quilts were soaked. When she cooked on the stove, water ran down on the hot iron sending billows of steam into the air. It was what it must be like to live at the bottom of a lake. The thunder grew more frequent now and when its drumming shook the house Eugene would scream in terror. She would try to comfort the child while carrying Maxey Charles in her arms. Every hour or so, Laura boiled a mixture of creosote in water in hopes the steam would help relieve Maxey Charles's cough and congestion. Outside, the water was beginning to pool around the house and the creek had risen into the pens where the horses were growing more and more restive.

During the night, Laura and the two children lay together in her bed. Eugene, his exhaustion eclipsing his fear of thunder, at last slept through the storm. Yet, with all the chaos nature was hurling around them, all Laura could think about was Maxey Charles's cough and its increasing frequency. She held his hot little body on her breast, her fear growing as the hours passed. By morning the coughs came in explosive spasms, five or six in succession and then between the spasms Maxey Charles struggled to catch his breath and the dreaded "whoop" filled the room, louder, it seemed, than the thunder. After the second of these violent episodes, Maxey Charles vomited what little he had been able to eat for supper and a gray mass of mucus appeared on the wet pillow. Holding tight to the infant, Laura rushed from the bed, her mind racing, trying to remember what Little Mattie had told her about whooping cough. She knew belladonna was given, but how much? How much was enough and how much was excessive? What was the line between kill and cure? A bolt of lightning exploded outside and Eugene began to cry. Rain poured in from the roof. Laura put little Maxey Charles in his crib just as another spasm of coughing racked his body. His face grew deep red. She could see the veins beneath his skin as he struggled for breath. Then there was the whooping inhalation and the infant lay back, exhausted, his eyes open and staring.

Tearing herself away from the crib, Laura lighted a lantern and rushed out into the rain. Assailed by the storm and wishing she had never come to this hell of a wilderness and swearing if Maxey Charles survived she would never live in this country again, she somehow managed to calm the horses and hitch the buggy, then rush back into the house for the children. She wrapped them both in quilts and then, one screaming, the other seized by paroxysm, she climbed into the buggy to begin the long uncertain way through the wilderness for help, toward the homestead of a German family some ten miles to the east. But help to the east lay across the creek and the creek was now a river sweeping wildly out of its banks, across the pasture and into the deep arroyo. Laura held Maxey Charles in the cradle of one arm and Eugene on the floorboards between her knees. Then, holding the reins in her free hand and shouting a prayer at the top of her lungs, she guided the terrified horses into the rushing stream. The water reached the hubs of the wheels and the horses struggled to keep from being swept away. Laura had no hand to wield a whip and she could only shout "Please! Please!" as the wagon began to float and slip sideways. The horses began to lose their footing. Then, nearby, on the downstream side of the creek, a column of fire was hurled from the heavens with a blast of sound so loud it would surely wake the poor dead Gunther where he lay. An old oak struck by the lightning bolt literally exploded. The horses, terrified by the blast and struggling to escape the fire, pulled the wagon onto dry land again and raced away through nature's bedlam toward the east.

Old Jacob Luckenbach rode into the little town of Sisterdale and brought a doctor back through the storm to see what he could do for Maxey Charles. Justine, his wife, took charge of the little family. She put all three to bed, covered them with dry down comforters and sang lullabies in a language that soothed like a liniment of melody. Laura was so exhausted and empty that she could only weep small soundless sobs she had no will to control. She was still shaking when the doctor came with his bromide of sodium and antipyrine, his prayers and his kindness.

11 ∞ THE HANGING TREE RANCH

AFTER MAXEY CHARLES HAD RECOVERED FROM WHOOPING cough, the family moved into a lovely stone bungalow where the Little Blanco River began its slide into town. Peter asked Ed Tom, the old man who had been overseer of his mother's properties, to manage the Wilderness Ranch, but he had declined, offering one of his sons instead. "I watched over your mama's lands," he said. "I guess it's only right my boy do the same for you."

In many ways the move to Blanco was like waking from a bad dream. The weight of the wilderness slipped from Laura's shoulders and from her mind. Laura was back among her butterflies, her gardens, her horses, and a growing number of dear friends who lived along the river. After the Wilderness Ranch, the new place seemed like a castle. It was nestled in a grove of giant oaks on a hill by the river, just across the road from the tree where Al Lackey had been hanged. Rarely did Laura pass that tree that it did not bring back memories of Lackey, the Cathertons, and Herman Lehmann, and she would wonder how Herman fared and if he still thought of her. In Peter's presence Laura once referred to the new place as the "Hanging Tree Ranch" and the name stuck.

Laura's new home was spacious, the rooms and halls designed so that Laura could walk from the entry hall to the parlor, then to the dining room, the kitchen, the sitting room, and then back to the entry hall without retracing her steps. Peter had bought a new Epworth piano in San Antonio. When the children played there was now competition for the mockingbirds and cardinals and Inca doves whose symphony was an overture for the day. To the east of the house, beyond the garden, the barn, and the turkey yard was a peach orchard, a patch of sugarcane, and a field of roasting ears. As the first years in the new house passed, basement shelves began to groan under the weight of vegetables canned fresh from the garden, peach preserves, jars of wild plum or crab-apple preserves and dewberry jam. The kitchen was often filled with the warm, fine breath of yeast loaves browning in the iron stove, an earthy bouquet that filled not only the rooms and the house but, according to Peter, the soul. Sometimes Laura would wake in the morning, look at Peter sleeping by her side, then move to her window, where she would look out at the miracle of the day and would feel an almost overwhelming urge to fall to her knees and thank God for His gift of the world and her life.

As the Hill Country people prepared for the coming of the new century, the mood around the Hanging Tree Ranch became increasingly festive. Nearly every Saturday night, sister Lucy and one of her many beaus, and sometimes several simultaneously, would gather around the piano for a singing or to listen to Enrico Caruso or the strange and exhilarating new music called "ragtime" or to the speeches of William Jennings Bryan on the Edison disks Lucy collected. There were dances in the park, lawn parties at the Methodist parsonage, watermelon feasts at the Baptist church, and camp meetings out by the river. Laura's youngest sister, Little Maggie, was often at the center of festivities. Laura was amazed at how she had suddenly grown into a little lady. She seemed abundantly alive and vivacious and possessed a uniquely adventurous spirit. Of all her siblings, Little Maggie was the most graceful and athletic on horseback. Her greatest ambition was to be a bareback rider with the Glasscock Brothers Circus.

Life for the young people of Blanco was a kind of easy ballet, largely choreographed by Laura. She reveled in the flirtations of sister Lucy as she generously distributed smiles and often kisses to Sammy Edwards, the doctor's son, or to Alfred Brodie, or Dr. Walter Kidder, or Cousin Dixie, or to the handsome cowboy Milton Copenhaver. Even though these young men vied for Lucy's attentions, there was a certain fraternal spirit within the group, much as there exists between collectors who love stamps or certain other beautiful or interesting objects. Laura was so fascinated by Lucy's amorous adventures that she could not resist uninvited odysseys into Lucy's diary. It was there that she learned that the reason she broke up with her beau, Milton Copenhaver, was because he had come to her house "sodden with liquor and had used bad language" after a "Dutchman's Dance" and was now living the torment of the loved yet unforgiven.

Laura and Lucy organized their friends from Blanco, Johnson City, and Luckenbach into what would become known as the Narrows Study Group. Their study was centered on a desire to improve the mind and to explore the great mysteries of the universe. Out at the Narrows of the Little Blanco River, pastures of yellow daisies exploded into bloom and Indian Blanket covered the hillsides. The young people lay on sun-warmed quilts, dined on baskets of figs and buckets of peaches, and challenged such long-held positions as the literal truth of the Bible. Alfred Brodie claimed that science, although not disproving the existence of God, certainly made it difficult to believe in such events as the virgin birth and the physical ascension of Jesus into heaven. Although some were scandalized by these assertions, Laura found them intriguing, while Lucy found them titillating and romantic, especially when brought forward by Alfred Brodie or her now-forgiven suitor, Milton Copenhaver.

Each of these weighty discussions was punctuated by a frequent plunge into the cool, clear depths of the Little Blanco. Laura took some pleasure when she realized her younger friends might embark on adventures of the mind, but none, with the possible exception of Little Maggie, would dare swim the dark river passages beneath the Narrows that she and Peter had dared on that summer before they married.

When Laura became pregnant with her third child, she decided that if she were going to spend the rest of her life having babies, she might as well do it in style. She explained it to Peter as she began to grow large. "At this rate I'll surely have one hundred children or more. Why don't we find a really nice place for me to have babies?" Peter's considerable sisters were busy with their own growing families and so the Woods mansion was no longer an option. "Let's find a place that's modern," Laura said.

"Everything in our world is changing. So why do women still have to have babies the same way we've had babies for thousands of years?"

In the *Ladies Home Journal* and the many magazines Laura devoured during the long evenings when Peter was away, she came across some alarming statistics. She discovered that nearly twenty thousand women in the United States died each year in childbirth or from the immediate effects of childbirth. Nearly one-third of the blind people in the world lost their sight because of complications at the time of birth. Laura was not afraid of what the statistics revealed, she was angry. *"Everybody says labor is a natural thing and a woman in labor doesn't need special care,"* Laura wrote in her diary. *"Nature takes care of everything just right. Yet, there are no moments in the lives of families or of nations or of the human species more important than those moments of a child's birth. So why should a woman spend this time in a darkened room, with untrained attendants using makeshift procedures? Peter gives his horses better attention than that. No surgeon would ever think of operating bent over a low bed in a darkened room with little more than kitchen utensils and the goodwill of neighbors."*

And so, as the time for the child's birth drew near, the family packed up and moved en masse from the Hanging Tree Ranch to Fredericksburg where Peter had rented a Sunday house for the laying in and the birth. It was a stout stone house, large and light and roomy, the floors and sills scrubbed clean as a Dresden street. Peter contacted Dr. Albert Brecht of Fredericksburg, a longtime friend of the Colonel-Doctor, to take charge of the event. Trained in Germany, Dr. Brecht was a large, severe man with unrepressed, inflexible opinions. Laura felt he would be more effective commanding a battalion than attending the birth of her third child. After he had completed his initial examination, he ordered Laura to bed.

"But I'm not sick!" Laura insisted.

"Madam, I haff delivered far more babies dan you haff."

"And haff you stayed in bed each time?" In deference to the Colonel-Doctor's friend, Laura did not pursue her sarcasm further and held her tongue. But as soon as he had left, she was up again. *"Does he think I'm an invalid?"* Laura wrote in her diary. *"Ridiculous!"*

It was here, in the Sunday house, attended by Dr. Brecht, Lucy, Maggie, Little Mattie, and platoons of relatives, serenaded by symphonic music from the German opera house next door, that Laura gave birth to her first daughter.

They named the child Winifred, after Winnie Davis, the popular daughter of Confederate president Jefferson Davis. Laura was astonished at the child's beauty. She had always thought newborn babies, if not ugly, were peculiar-looking creatures, not at all like the idealized infants in classic paintings of Madonna and child. They all looked like fat, shrunken old men. But this child, her firstborn daughter, was more beautiful than any artist could imagine. Laura felt she could see the woman lingering there in the child, tall and graceful and mysterious. Laura never tired of looking into Winifred's night-dark eyes, even years later, when the demons came.

Soon after Winifred's birth, the Colonel-Doctor died. His death came quickly, unannounced, yet not unexpected. He had been very frail, a shadow of the man he had been, and Laura had watched Peter mourn his father years before he died. Now they made the hard two-day drive to San Marcos where the Colonel-Doctor would be laid to rest in the City Cemetery.

The day of the funeral dawned bitter cold. The wind was a blade cutting down from the north as it whipped the dark coats and white beards of the old officers who had served with the Colonel-Doctor in the Thirty-Second Texas Cavalry. The Confederate veterans, those who had survived the war and the long years since, had begun gathering in San Marcos at dawn. They were among a great crowd that moved toward the Woods mansion where the casket rested in the front parlor.

An unbroken procession of mourners came to pay their respects. They came up the hill, walking, and in buggies, shoulders hunched against the cold, their faces flushed and burned by the wind. The black crepe streamers atop the carriages and buggies were torn away by the wind and fluttered like crazed ravens through the air until they were caught in the trees. Many of the mourners were former slaves, some carrying children, all dressed in black, climbing the hill to see the man who had been their master before he set them free.

Laura remembered the first time she had been in the Woods mansion, newly married, eager for the acceptance of the Colonel-Doctor and his family. She recalled the dinner table argument with Cherokee and how the Colonel-Doctor had firmly stepped in to prevent an irreparable family rift. She always felt the Colonel-Doctor had been fond of her. Although she had been in his presence infrequently, she always knew he was there, a presence of enormous dignity, sanity, and kindness in a world too often lacking in those qualities. Now she stood in the parlor, looking at his casket, and she knew she would miss him.

She was by Peter's side when old Ed Tom Lawshe came into the room. He seemed to fill the doorway with his presence and with the cold he had brought in from outside. He nodded to Laura and Peter and then moved forward to view the remains. He stood there a long time, looking down, his hat and his hands pressed to his heart, his great wool cape making his huge body seem even larger.

Peter walked forward and Laura followed. They stood with Ed Tom by the casket. The Colonel-Doctor was dressed in black, a black tie and a white stand-up collar. Miss Ella had wanted him buried in his Confederate uniform, but Peter had objected. Laura had rarely seen him so adamant. "My father was not a soldier. He was a doctor. He hated the war. He hated the killing. And he would hate being buried in his uniform." Before they put his uniform away, however, the gold buttons were removed and one was given to each grandchild. And his sword and spurs were enshrined above the mantel. Now he lay in peace, his face like parchment, his head on a tufted pillow of white satin.

"Should be flowers," Ed Tom said, his eyes sad, yet dry. "Too cold. Nothin' to pick."

The lower part of the coffin had been covered with a Texas

flag and greenery Ed Tom had cut from the cedar trees and the blue spruce by the well. It smelled like Christmas.

"I built his house," Ed Tom said. "When he was away fightin' I built this house and watched after Miss Georgia and the children while he was gone. And now I made his coffin just like I done for the first baby he and Miss Georgia had. And I made Miss Georgia's coffin." Ed Tom looked up from the remains and into Peter's eyes. "Master Peter, I sure don't want to make any more coffins. I surely don't. I figure my job is just about done."

Then Ed Tom did a remarkable thing. From his coat he withdrew a small violin. It seemed roughly made, like a toy in his huge hands, but when he drew the bow across the strings a note sobbed into the stillness of the parlor that was beautifully rich and true and clear. Laura did not recognize the melody, but it seemed familiar, and the notes filled the parlor with treble sorrow. Now, at last, the old Negro's eyes filled with tears, flowing in silver rivulets down his cheeks and onto the violin. Except for the notes of the melody, the house was quiet. Mourners outside came into the parlor to hear and stood around the walls, watching and listening. Laura was struck by the fact that the old former slave was mourning his former master in the only way he could. How could it be, she wondered, that these two men, so absolutely different from each other, could have loved each other. As Ed Tom played, Laura realized she was witnessing the passing of an era. The Old South was lying in the coffin. The New South stood at her side. The New South was Peter. The plantation had made way for the ranch and Ed Tom had made his last casket.

Ed Tom lowered the violin, yet it seemed the notes remained in the room like melodic memory, hanging and dancing in the air that smelled like Christmas. Then a new sound filled the parlor. Ed Tom had raised his fingers to his lips and was creating the sound of birds, high, warbling, sliding, gliding, fractional melodies, sweet as ever a mockingbird sang. The parlor where Colonel-Doctor lay was filled with birdsong. And then as suddenly as the singing came, it ended and Ed Tom turned and told them he hoped they did not mind what he had done. "Colonel-

Doctor always liked to hear me do that. So, thought I would one last time."

Then Ed Tom Lawshe shook his head and walked away, out of the Woods house and out of the Old South forever.

One by one the mourners passed by the casket. The governor came, as did William Jennings Bryan, and William Sydney Porter, the Austin writer known as O. Henry. Young Sam Johnson, whose father had brought the severely wounded Colonel-Doctor home at the end of the Civil War, moved by the casket. Miss Ella passed like a spirit in the shadows. She seemed a stranger at her own husband's wake. Laura could feel the presence of her mother-in-law, Georgia Lawshe Woods, once again permeating the parlor.

After a brief service in the parlor, conducted by the aged Rev. Andrew Jackson Potter, who had been chaplain of the Woods regiment during the war, the Colonel-Doctor's body was lifted up by the men of his regiment and carried to a wagon waiting in front of the house. The old soldiers formed into ranks and marched behind the wagon down the hill in ragged formation. The procession of old soldiers, walking mourners, and carriages made their way down the steep lane and out the Wimberley Mill Road to the San Marcos City Cemetery.

Before the body was lowered, Reverend Potter spoke a final word to his old friend. "We have lost our first citizen," he said, hatless, the cold wind tearing at his thin silver hair. "Yours has been a spotless life. You have been an example of all that is noble and good in man. Brave as the bravest, tender as the most tender, you bore yourself in all the trials of life with dignity and fortitude and your memory as a ministering angel in the home of suffering is enshrined in all our hearts. Now your journey has ended, good friend. Sleep well."

12 ∞ THE SISTERDALE DANCE HALL

THROUGH THE OAKS, LAURA SAW THREE LARGE WAGONS STOP before the great house across the river. For a while she watched the unloading of furniture onto the lawn of Lawrence Hall, the gleaming polished hardwood seeming almost grotesque and strangely out of place in the harsh sunlight. She could hardly imagine that the bureaus and chests and secretaries had once been living trees growing in the earth and she tried to determine what kind of people would have furnishings so fine. She wiped her hands on her apron, put Winifred on her hip, and walked across the field to the river. From the bank, the old two-story rock house with its orderly orchards, rock fences, terraced flower beds, and porches framed by clouds of purple climbing wisteria was even more beautiful than Laura remembered. A young girl seemed to be in charge of the unloading. She flitted from wagon to wagon, into the house and out again, bossing the workmen, urging them to take care with the more delicate pieces and to greater effort with the heavier chests, desks, and the piano. She seemed to drift gracefully above the lawn, her skirts like wings, her auburn hair blazing in the sunlight.

Laura hitched up her skirts, hefted Winifred higher on her hip, and began wading across the river. The water was deeper than she had supposed and halfway across she paused and wondered if she should not retrace her steps. But the current gripped her skirts and Winifred, her feet touching the cold stream, began to climb Laura like a tree, one hand hanging onto her hair, the other clamped across her eyes. Then she was down, sliding across the bottom on her backside, Winifred's arms flailing the air, her musical voice raised in both terror and delight. It was a moment Laura would later describe as impossibly embarrassing: to be remembered as a woman drowned by her child in three feet of water. All she could think of as she tried to keep her head above water was how terribly Winifred would suffer for the rest of her life for drowning her mother like this. Out of the confusion came the strong young arms of the girl she had been watching, helping to hold Winifred and arresting their slide along the river toward town. There, with Laura sitting on the river bottom and only her head, shoulders, and Winifred above the rushing water, Rebekah Baines introduced herself to her neighbor and then helped both mother and child toward shore where they collapsed like a pile of wet laundry on the Baines's front lawn.

Soon the warm April sun had dried their clothes, the wagons had rumbled away, and Laura and Rebekah sat on the front porch, each sketching a past for the other. Rebekah had a musical, lyrical way of speaking, the words rolling together softly. Her vocabulary seemed slightly larger than their conversation merited, and Laura made a mental note to look up *dendophilous,* a word Rebekah used in a sentence about Hill Country trees. As the morning eased by, Laura learned that Rebekah was the oldest daughter of Judge Joseph Wilson Baines, a former newspaperman who had been secretary of state under Gov. John Ireland, and a member of the Texas legislature.

"I'm going to be a newspaperwoman," Rebekah said. "Maybe a foreign correspondent or a political writer."

"Me, too!" Laura delighted with the coincidence. "I mean, I want to be a political writer. If I can manage it. I had an opportunity to write a column for the *Blanco News.* But I had to let it go."

"What happened?"

"Children happened. And we moved out from town." She told Rebekah about the Wilderness Ranch.

"Sometimes I think this is the wilderness," Rebekah said. "Here on the river. This is so different from where we lived before. It's beautiful, but it's so quiet."

"You miss Austin?"

Rebekah nodded her head, her auburn hair catching the sunlight and casting it back. "I miss my friends, the life I had. I miss the excitement of my father's political campaigns. All the people coming and going. I miss concerts and lectures and the library. It was like being at the center of things."

"And now you're out on the fringe."

"Oh, Laura, I don't mean to complain. I really don't. I detest complainers. I suppose I'm just lonely." Rebekah's eyes were moist. She laughed away her embarrassment and wiped away her tears before they could fall. "I'm sorry, Laura," she said. "Here I've just met you and I'm boring you with nonsense. Acting like a child."

"Oh, Rebekah, I know what it's like to be alone," Laura said, remembering the solitudes of the Wilderness Ranch. "Loneliness is a demon I know by its first name." She reached out for her new neighbor's hand.

Although Rebekah was eight years younger than Laura, the two became fast friends. Laura could not imagine Rebekah living anywhere else but in that grand home by the river. She and the house were equally graceful, and sometimes Laura felt awkward and plain in their presence. But at other times, Rebekah's beauty seemed to reach out and permeate her surroundings and transform all who were near. It was to Laura like being touched by sunlight on a winter day.

Laura introduced Rebekah to her sisters and their young friends and Rebekah soon became a part of the social life along the Blanco. If she still missed her more cultured life in Austin, she never mentioned it again. As the months passed, a special bond began to grow between Laura and her neighbor. Laura knew Rebekah could confide in her in a way she could not with her mother or her peers. There was no risk of judgment or censure.

Once, while Rebekah was helping Laura gather tomatoes and peas from the garden, Rebekah admitted that she was deeply in love. Laura was certain every boy in the county was in love with Rebekah, but was surprised a girl as sophisticated as Rebekah would find the country boys of Blanco attractive, much less irresistible, and she said so.

"He's not from Blanco and he's not a boy," Rebekah said. "He's from Johnson City. I won't tell you his name. But he'll be famous one day, you'll see."

"So how did you meet this famous man?"

"At a political rally. I was with my father. We were introduced. And I knew at once he loved me."

"Well, what do you think his intentions are?" Laura asked.

"I expect marriage."

"Has he asked for your hand?"

"Not exactly."

"Has he even hinted?"

"No, not exactly either. But he looks at me in a certain way. And it makes me feel strange."

"You want him to kiss you?"

"I really do. Isn't that awful? I guess I should be ashamed."

"It's just natural. If God didn't want us to feel that way He wouldn't have created love. He would have made men and women just alike and had children grow on trees like apples. One time I wanted a boy to kiss me so bad I thought I'd die."

"But that was Peter. You're married."

"It wasn't Peter. It was before."

"Oh." Rebekah was silent for awhile as she helped Laura weed the garden. "The Bible says we should flee youthful lusts."

"That's Paul's letter to Timothy. He was talking to Timothy, not you."

"So what do you think?"

"You mean do I think you should let him kiss you? Or do you mean do I think you should marry him?"

"I guess it's a question of which should come first," Rebekah answered.

"Well," Laura said, "you're a little young to think about marriage."

"But I can't help thinking about it. There's so much to know. I can't talk to my mother about it. Not about what really happens. You know, between a man and a woman."

Laura noticed Rebekah's face was flaming. "You're blushing, Rebekah. You don't have to be embarrassed with me."

"I know. But it's hard to talk about."

"I know. But it shouldn't be. You can ask me anything and I'll try to answer honestly."

After a moment, Rebekah asked, "Did you and Peter, you know, were you together before you were married?"

"Depends on what you mean by together." Laura remembered the time at the Narrows after they had swum through the tunnel and she felt again that strange feeling Rebekah tried to describe. "What do you mean by together?"

"Don't make me say it!"

"If you mean did we love each other physically like man and wife, the answer is no. But I wanted to and would have. Peter wanted to wait. We were very intimate, though."

"I've tried to imagine how it would be. Sometimes I hear my parents. But all I can imagine is how it is with our horses. And, I don't know, it seems so rough. So animal."

"Oh, Rebekah, it can also be so gentle. And tender. To be joined together can be so very nice. It can be like prayer."

"I just don't know what to do. I think about it more than I should. I have pictures in my mind. I know it must be a sin. The Scriptures say . . ."

Laura interrupted. "Rebekah, if you're looking for an answer in the Bible, I think you're looking in the wrong place. Especially in the New Testament. Saint Paul was a bachelor and didn't have a very good attitude about women. I'd look for an answer in Psalms. David was a lot more informed about love than Paul."

"You can't pick and choose advice from the Scriptures."

"That's what Peter says. Between Peter and your father, I'm not sure who's the most devout."

Often Rebekah would invite Laura to tea at the great Baines house overlooking the river. And each of these visits made Laura feel she was at the center of a fairy tale. Rebekah would meet her out front, dressed in crinolines and lace, with a broad-brimmed hat flying ribbons like pendants in the afternoon breeze. In contrast,

Laura felt very ordinary, even homely, in her homemade frock. Tea would be served in thin, fragile cups on crisp linen tablecloths trimmed in delicate lace. Rebekah would discuss Browning or Tennyson, sometimes quoting entire passages, and she would talk of the faraway places she would visit and write about one day when she became a journalist. Laura tried to imagine Rebekah in Paris or Cairo, writing her dispatches on wide porches beneath great fans. But Rebekah, like her tablecloths, seemed too delicate, too pale and thin for such worldly work. Once, very gently, Laura discouraged her friend and warned of the need to come back down to earth again.

Rebekah was mildly offended. "Laura, you don't have a romantic bone in your body!"

The statement shocked Laura and she wondered if it were true. She tried to remember when she last felt romantic and she had to admit it had been some time. Her nights with Peter were still satisfying, sometimes wonderfully exhausting, but she could hardly say it was romance that characterized their nights together. Their lovemaking was more of Earth than heaven, more real than fanciful. Romance, she decided, had something to do with expectation, a sense of looking forward to something rare and unpredictable, whether that expectation was of love or adventure. Maybe she was becoming hardened by life and work and the years. She wondered if romance had passed her by and that she might never again feel the sweet, soft pain of romantic love or the sharp, high-hearted longing for rare experience.

"It's hard to be romantic when you have a lapful of hungry children and a ranch to run."

Rebekah smiled her enigmatic smile and stirred her tea with ancient family silver. "The finer things in life are not things that just happen," Rebekah said. "They are things we seek. If you want to feel like a princess, think like a princess, live your life as a princess lives. You dream your life, then you take a deep breath and you set out and do what you dreamed. It's all a state of mind. And then of gumption."

Laura often came home from Rebekah's teas wondering if she was getting from her life all it offered. Rebekah's romantic notions, and her pursuit of the infinite possibilities beyond the horizon, made Laura feel dowdy and shallow and confused. The feeling made her constantly reevaluate what she wanted for herself and for Peter. She still dreamed of Peter becoming governor of Texas. It was not a cloud-woven dream, as were the dreams of Rebekah; rather, this was a real possibility. She worried that her friend's expectations were too lofty for a mere mortal woman living on a small river in Blanco County, Texas. She was quite certain there had been no princess on the Blanco in recorded history and that there never would be. But there could be a governor. And a governor's wife. Even a president's wife. Or a president's mother.

In 1898, something happened at the Hanging Tree Ranch that made Peter's reputation and prospects for an ascending political future secure. In April of that year, Theodore Roosevelt came to the Hill Country to recruit men and buy horses for his Rough Riders.

"He's coming here? To Hanging Tree Ranch?" The thought of a Republican in the house was more than daunting. Laura imagined a great tumbling sound beneath the ground, like a minor earthquake, as generations of Peter's family rolled over in their graves. Teddy Roosevelt's political views, especially when it came to Populist politics and politicians, was never in doubt. Laura recalled reading that he had accused Populists of plotting revolution and had actually proposed shooting twelve of their leaders dead by firing squad. "I'm not sure I know how to act around a Republican," she told Peter. "And a New Yorker to boot."

"Just be yourself," Peter said. "Or maybe not quite yourself," he added with a smile. "You might want to talk about something other than politics. Let's try to focus on horses. If this works out, our fortune is made. When people discover Roosevelt came here for his horses, the world will beat a pathway to our door."

"But why here?"

"Because he needs horses and Hill Country horses are the

best there are. And then because he's a relative. Buying horses takes a lot of trust. And you trust family. His mother and mine were close all their lives."

To her great surprise, Laura was absolutely taken by Teddy Roosevelt. He was a man of such buoyant and abundant energy that she was swept away by his enthusiasm and youthful spirit. Laura found him to be a joyous man, a man totally in love with life and the possibilities of the future. There was a vigor and intensity to the man that made the very air around him seem to dance and helped make one forget that he was a Republican. When Peter introduced Roosevelt to Laura he said, "Why, Laura, I'm delighted to meet you at last." He pronounced "delighted" as if it had a dozen vowels between the first two consonants.

On the first night of his visit, after spending the day selecting the best horses in the Hill Country for his Rough Riders, Peter asked how Roosevelt's recruiting was going. "Are you finding good men in the Hill Country?"

"Most," he said, "but not all. Fact is, there's never been a more remarkable lot of private soldiers ever gathered. I've got the captain of the Harvard rowing crew and two football players from Princeton. Two polo players from my old team at Oyster Bay, a steeplechase rider from New York and a handful of New York policemen. I've got men from the most fashionable clubs in the East and I've got an ex-marshal from Dodge City, Kansas, whose ear was bitten off in a fight. I've got Cherokee Bill, Happy Jack, Rattlesnake Pete, a bear hunter, buffalo hunters, bronco busters, and bounty hunters. Yesterday I signed up a man that was raised by the Apaches. Best shot with a rifle I've ever seen."

Laura had been half listening and suddenly realized what Roosevelt had said. She felt her pulse drum in her throat. "Herman Lehmann?"

"That's the one. Mean as they come. A real fighter, a warrior."

Laura tried to imagine Herman Lehmann in yet another uniform charging yet another enemy. But all she could see was a golden boy riding an elephant.

Roosevelt proved to be a fine judge of horseflesh. He was very thorough. He insisted on spirit and intelligence as expressed in the eyes. "I'm not looking for the perfect horse," he told Peter. "There is an old Spanish saying. 'The man who would buy a horse without fault, must not buy one at all.' "

Of all Peter's horses, there was one Roosevelt found to be as near perfect as a horse could be. Even the name of the black stallion fascinated the Rough Rider. "Triumph! What commander would not lust to ride such a horse into battle."

Triumph was the son of the orphan Lone Star, the grandson of Sultan and Willow. This was the foundation of the bloodline Peter was establishing, that extraordinary blending of the mustang and the thoroughbred. Peter would not sell. "Any other but Triumph," he told Roosevelt. He would listen to none of Roosevelt's offers, no matter how extravagant. "Everything I know," Peter said, "everything I am has gone into that stallion. Triumph is the future."

On the second and last night of Roosevelt's visit, Laura and Peter were invited to the twenty-fifth wedding anniversary party of a German couple in the little community of Sisterdale. In turn, Peter invited Roosevelt. Laura invited Rebekah, insisting it was about time she met a real-life Republican. Sister Maggie, Lucy, and their friends also attended. The evening began with an enormous supper of sausage, sauerkraut, German potato salad and huge steins of beer served from barrels out beneath the trees behind the cavernous Sisterdale dance hall. When the supper was cleared away and the children were put to bed on pallets beneath the tables, the band began to hurl its strange mixture of Mexican ranchero and German folk music into the hall. The accordion, guitar, tuba, clarinet, and snare drum vied for dominance of the waltzes, two-steps and polkas and they all were equally victorious. The women sat in groups on one side of the hall, the men stood near the doors where they had access to the kegs of beer out back. The floor filled with dancers: old men with their granddaughters, little girls with toddlers, grandmothers with their grandsons. Everyone spun and whirled and rollicked and stomped and scattered laughter into the night. Just when it seemed the dancing had reached its peak, a curious company of strangers, led by Colonel Roosevelt, swept onto the dance floor.

There was Cherokee Bill, Happy Jack, and the ex-marshal from Dodge City whose ear had been bitten off in a fight. Lucy was whirling in the arms of the captain of the Harvard rowing team. Laura found herself dancing the Paul Jones with Rattlesnake Pete. And in the center of the hall, Roosevelt stomped away on the pine floor, his glasses bouncing on the bridge of his nose, his legs churning, his laughter like another instrument of the band.

Near midnight, there was a disturbance at the back of the hall. At first Laura paid little attention, then she grew irritated that anyone would have the poor manners to cause a ruckus at such a joyous occasion. She had expected the drinking, but fighting was simply inexcusable. She noticed Peter and Roosevelt were headed for the disturbance and she followed them to where three of Roosevelt's recruits, including Rattlesnake Pete, were holding a fourth man down, dragging him bodily across the floor toward the door.

"Who is that man?" Roosevelt asked as he approached. Then he reached down and forced the man over in order to see his face. "Lehmann!" Roosevelt looked up at Rattlesnake Pete, his eyes demanding an answer.

"We took a vote, sir. We don't want his likes in the outfit." Rattlesnake Pete rocked from one foot to the other.

"I'm not leading a democracy here. This is a fighting unit. And this man is a fighter."

"There's fighters and there's killers. This man has took white scalps. We don't want no Indians."

Herman Lehmann had quit struggling. He lay still, his face pressed against the rough pine floor. Laura stepped behind Peter, terrified Herman would see her and know she was witnessing his humiliation. She also feared her own reaction and what Peter would think. As Herman's face was pressed to the floor, she could feel the rough boards on her own face, a feeling so real she actually touched her cheek to wipe away the blood. *Dear God,* she thought, *I've brought him to this. I was the one who insisted he give up his Indian ways!* She risked another glance. His yellow hair was long now, unkempt. She had expected his eyes to be filled with hatred. But instead they were empty.

"Let him up!" Roosevelt demanded.

The Rough Riders stood, wiping sawdust from their trousers with loose hands. For a moment Herman remained on the floor, motionless, like a rabbit surrounded by dogs. Rattlesnake Pete pushed at the still body with the toe of his boot. "Get up," he said, kicking him again. Roosevelt held up his hand, a signal to leave the fallen man alone. Slowly, Herman rose, unfolding from the floor, until he stood before Roosevelt, his eyes poorly focused. He held one arm against his stomach where Laura had once kissed a tracery of old scars. He was still slender, still beautiful, but he looked smaller than she remembered as he stood among the Rough Riders. Laura wanted to rush to where he stood and take him into her arms and say how sorry she was to have left him alone in a world where he had no place.

"Is this true, Lehmann? Did you take white scalps?"

"It was another life. Another time."

"Men don't change, Colonel. A rotten apple don't go back."

"What do you say, Lehmann?"

Now Herman looked Roosevelt in the eyes. "There is no better man with a rifle or a knife than me. I should be given a chance to fight for my country."

Roosevelt looked back into Herman's eyes. Except for the children, the hall was silent. All eyes were riveted on the two men, the commander and the white Apache. Then Roosevelt broke the silence.

"It's best that you go, son. I can't risk having dissension in the outfit." Rattlesnake Pete grasped Herman's collar roughly and began to drag him away.

"Pete!" Roosevelt's voice was firm. "Let the man go."

Herman Lehmann turned, and as he began to walk from the room, he tore off his shirt and cast it away. He seemed to become taller and there was the subtle spring in his step that Laura had loved on their walks along the Blanco. She knew he would soon shed his boots and his long trousers. Laura prayed he would leave the white man's nation forever and go back to the brush country where he might find peace.

When Herman had gone and the band again began to play

and the heavy boots of the Rough Riders began to make the saw-dust on the floor dance, she fought to control the impulse to fol-low her warrior into his lost land. *I will never see him again,* she thought. Laura had never felt more like crying, but she had long ago wept all the tears God had given her to weep for Herman Lehmann. Peter touched her arm and asked her to dance. And that was all she could do.

Within a few months, Roosevelt's Rough Riders, many saddled up on Woods and Hill Country horses, defeated the Spaniards at the Battle of San Juan Hill.

Roosevelt's patronage assured the success of Hanging Tree Ranch. More and more buyers from greater distances came to pur-chase the horses that had charged up San Juan Hill, had defeated the Spaniards, and had carried Theodore Roosevelt into the gov-ernor's mansion in Albany and into the White House as William McKinley's vice president.

For Winifred's seventh birthday, Peter gave her a granddaughter of Miss Ruth, the gentle old mare that had been Laura's constant companion as a girl. Like all Laura's children, Winifred had learned to ride almost before she could walk, and now she spent nearly every waking hour riding the little gift filly. Laura remembered the freedom she had felt riding through the long summer afternoons. She envied Winifred's leisurely hours, but she became concerned as her daughter seemed to grow distant from the activities and rhythms of family life. At first, Laura thought it was Winifred's love of the filly, that she had centered all her attention on her horse, and in time, when the novelty had passed, her daughter would return. But Winifred continued to grow more distant. Sometimes when Laura or the others talked to her or called her name, Winifred would not respond. She seemed to be closed away in another world.

One day Laura asked Peter, "Where do you think she goes?"

"Probably the same places you went at her age."

"I mean in her mind. Where does she travel in her mind."

"What do you mean?"

"Oh, nothing," Laura said, knowing Peter had no idea what she was talking about. Winifred was his pride and joy and he would stand for no criticism. "She's just quiet," he told her once when Laura mentioned their daughter's long silences. "She's just not talkative like you and Maxey Charles."

Like so many others who lived through the event, Laura would always remember where she was and what she was doing on September 6, 1901. She was seated on a wooden stool by her garden, aiming a rifle at a rattlesnake that was easing its way through her tomatoes. She had the rattlesnake squarely in her sights when she heard the hoofbeats and Rebekah calling and then saw her leaping from her horse. It was then she learned that the president had been shot.

"He's not dead!" It was more a demand than a question.

"I don't know. Papa said it was bad. They took him to the hospital."

"Teddy!" The thought had substance like a blow.

Laura rushed to the office of the *Blanco News* and joined the growing crowd listening to the staccato conversation of the teletype. Little by little details came clicking from Buffalo, New York, where McKinley had been at a public reception. As the news came in, it was repeated in low monosyllables through the crowd, like waves moving through water.

"He was walking through a crowd."

"He's alive. Two shots in the chest."

"Who?"

"No one knows. He was almost killed by the crowd."

"The president's at the hospital."

Laura listened to the fractional flow of information and supposition with a mixture of horror and fascination. She thought of Roosevelt now as a personal friend and she wondered where he was and if he had been told and what he was thinking. She offered a prayer for the president and then another for Roosevelt who must now have the weight of the world on his shoulders. Then news came that Roosevelt was vacationing in the Adirondack Mountains. He was on his way to Buffalo. As she waited for further word, Laura thought how vulnerable presidents were. First Lincoln. Then Garfield. McKinley was surrounded by Secret Service men and still a single crazed boy could bring him down. Or had he acted alone? The possibility of a conspiracy was heatedly debated by the crowd at the *Blanco News* as President McKinley's life hung in the balance.

Early in the morning, news came that the president's condition was improving. As Roosevelt rushed toward Buffalo, he issued a bulletin that raced over the wire to Blanco. "Like all other people and like the whole civilized world, you will be overjoyed to hear the good news that the president will recover."

Additional bulletins from the hospital indicated that President McKinley was in "hopeful spirits." The crowd burst into cheers. Exhausted, Laura walked her horse home.

On the ninth of September, three days after the shooting, the president had recovered to such an extent that it was thought the danger was past. McKinley joked with his doctors and complained about hunger. He said "it was hard enough to be shot, without being starved to death."

On the fourteenth of September, however, news spread through Blanco that the president had suffered a relapse. Laura rushed to the *Blanco News* where the town waited, shocked, confused by the unexpected turn of fortune, praying for a miracle. At midnight, the clattering voice of the teletype announced President McKinley had fallen into a gentle slumber. Before he lost consciousness his final words were heard by his physicians. "Good-bye all, good-bye. It is God's way. His will be done."

Theodore Roosevelt took the oath of office. *But how awful,* Laura thought, *that it would happen this way.*

In the spring of 1905, Peter and Laura invited all their relatives, friends and neighbors to a barbecue at the Hanging Tree Ranch. It was an idea that grew like a wildflower, welcome but not really planned. Peter said it was to celebrate the success of the ranch and to thank the community for its support. Secretly, Laura thought Peter was eager to show the San Marcos guests, including his sisters, that he was becoming every bit as successful as his father had been. Because Peter had worked so hard, she forgave him his conceit and pretended the barbecue was to celebrate Teddy Roosevelt's first full term in the White House. The previous November, Roosevelt had defeated Democrat Alton B. Parker in a landslide. Laura, of course, was always torn between her affection for Teddy and her Democratic soul, and she had celebrated Teddy's victory in secret. It was Rebekah, however, who provided the announced purpose of the Hanging Tree Ranch celebration.

Rebekah had recently graduated from Baylor College, in Waco. While at school, her father, Judge Baines, had suffered devastating financial losses. The greatest loss of all was the beautiful Baines home on the banks of the Blanco. The family had moved to a small cottage miles away in Fredericksburg where Rebekah taught elocution lessons and worked as a correspondent for the local daily newspaper. Now she had returned to Blanco to visit Laura, brimming with news of the man she hoped to marry.

"His name is Sam Johnson," she told Laura before she had hardly unpacked her bag."

"Not *the* Sam Johnson! The legislator?"

"The very one."

"Is that the secret beau you told me about years ago? The one you wanted to kiss you?"

"The very same."

"And did he?"

"Did he what?"

"Don't be coy, Rebekah. Did he kiss you?"

"Every chance he gets."

"And his intentions?"

"I'm not sure of his. But I certainly know what mine are!" The old friends collapsed with delirious laughter. They embraced and for a moment Laura envied Rebekah's affair with the darkly dashing Sam Johnson. It had been so long since she had been possessed by the joyful lunacy of young love.

"So how did it happen?" Laura asked when they had regained their composure.

"He came to Fredericksburg to make a speech about saving the Alamo. They were going to tear it down. He was sponsoring a bill to have it maintained as a sacred memorial. My editor assigned me to interview Sam. And I fell in love. He was so passionate . . ."

"Rebekah!"

"About the Alamo, silly. Well, Sam won me and kept the Alamo from being torn down all in one fell swoop. His legislation placed the Alamo in the custody of the Daughters of the Republic of Texas. And when he asked my father for the custody of me, Papa said that would be just fine, too."

"What's he like, this Sam Johnson of yours?"

"Tall. He has these dark, piercing eyes. He's quiet, but when he speaks, you're drawn to the sound. He gives the impression of being absolutely sincere and honest. You just know he is. You can feel it. It's like an aura. You'll see. That's how he saved the Alamo."

Sam Johnson was the inspiration for the theme for the Hanging Tree Ranch barbecue. On the invitations, Laura and Rebekah printed: "Come help us celebrate the victory at the Alamo."

The barbecue was an unqualified success. The long balmy April day was filled with laughter and fellowship and huge helpings of barbecued pork, beef, and sausage and discreetly served quantities from twin barrels of cider beside the cellar door. Peter's sisters and their families came down from San Marcos. Among them was the strange little daughter of Peter's distant cousin, a thin, graceless child Winifred's age named Flournoy. Flournoy was named after Capt. W. C. Flournoy, a dashing commander who served under Gen. Stonewall Jackson. The child and Winifred spent much of the day together. Laura would remember the one uncomfortable moment of the entire day was when Winifred insisted to several listeners that Flournoy was a boy. "He's just wearing girl's clothes," Winifred said, before she was admonished and hurried away. Little Mattie, J.C., and little sisters Maggie and Ella, had come in from Hoge Hollow. Sister Lucy, however, was brought to the party by Milton Copenhaver. And, of course, Rebekah was there on the arm of the guest of honor, Rep. Sam Johnson, the man who saved the Alamo.

Maxey Charles and the ranch hands organized a rodeo as a highlight of the festivities. There was steer wrestling, calf roping, wild bronc riding and, to crown the event, a horse race in which all the fastest horses in the county competed, only to lose to Peter's great stallion Triumph.

In the afternoon, Laura organized a family photograph. When all members of the extended family were assembled and posed by the house, there were so many people that they filled the viewfinder of Milton Copenhaver's Kodak to overflowing. He had to back up nearly to the barn to fit everyone in the picture.

At dusk, the guests insisted that Sam Johnson make a speech. He rose and faced the gathering and Laura could see why Rebekah would have fallen in love with this rangy, handsome, intense man. As he told about the importance of the Alamo, his voice hammering out like thunder in the gathering darkness, Laura caught herself comparing Sam to Peter. Both were tall, beautiful men, each with that aura Rebekah had described, each on his way upward in the world. But, unlike Peter, she sensed a fire in Sam that burned white hot, a fire that in Peter merely smoldered. She looked from one man to the other and wondered if it was not the smoldering fire that burned longest while the bright white flame consumed itself and was gone. She shuddered and did not know why.

When Sam finished his speech, a great shout of approval rose from the crowd. Laura hugged Rebekah. "You wrote that, didn't you! All that about the Alamo not being something that happened in history seventy years ago, but a spiritual event happening every day in our own hearts. That's Rebekah Baines prose pure and simple."

Rebekah just smiled.

When the guests had left, Peter took Laura's hand and led her to the barn. His grip on her arm was almost rough. "Why are you taking me out here?" Laura asked. "You'll see."

They stopped in front of Triumph's stall. Only the whites of Triumph's eyes could be seen in the darkness. But Laura could feel the energy emanating from the great stallion, the perfect horse that Peter had created with his skills, his patience, and his love. Peter put his arm around Laura's shoulders and pulled her close.

"I want you to have Triumph," he said. His voice was husky with emotion.

"Peter! Are you sure?"

"I love you more than this. But this is the most I have to give."

Without speaking, together, they moved into the hayloft and Laura smiled as she realized that every bone in her body was energized by her love for this good man. She knew this would be a moment she would remember in absolute detail for the rest of her life. She would forever recall the feel of Peter's hands on her shoulders, the feel of the cool night on her up-turned face, and the sound of Triumph nickering from where he watched in the dark. *How can I possibly ever be happier than this?* she thought. And for the second time in her life, she lay with a man on blanketed bales of hay, but this time, in the fragrant darkness, she gave him the most she had to give.

13 ∞ THE HAWK

(From Laura's unpublished autobiography)

One morning, long years ago, as I was walking along the Blanco I saw a hawk circling above the trees. I watched it for some moments as it rode the wind, signing circles in the air, its wings moving only occasionally, and then turning into the breeze, its tail spread, wide wings beating slowly, gracefully, the hawk rising, then veering into another spiral glide. I was captivated by the sight and I wondered what was the purpose of such circular flight. Was the hawk hunting prey or looking for a place to nest or simply amusing itself, taking in God's world from the point of view God must have. It was glorious, this silent flight of the hawk, an exultation, an affirmation of God's creative power.

The day was cloudless. The sky was as empty and pale as a blind man's eye. The hawk stood out in absolute clarity, alone above the river and the house I will always remember as Rebekah's house, although there are strangers there now. The hawk seemed to fill my vision and my mind. I remembered what Herman had told me about a time when animals and people were the same and could speak to each other and I was composing a salutation for the hawk when it seemed to falter, its feathers blooming in disarray, and then, incredibly, the hawk began to tumble down, softly disheveled, down and down until it disappeared soundlessly into the distant trees.

I was astounded and deeply moved. The hawk had been flying too high to be the victim of a hunter. Was it possible the bird had simply died in flight as old people do in mid-stride, suddenly downed by a failed or broken heart? Surely birds grow old or infirm and die. But it seems inconceivable that death would come in full flight. Or so I thought then. And what of the bird? Did the hawk have any sign, any premonition of disaster as it soared so gracefully and so alive above Rebekah's house and the river?

It took some time to find the hawk. The body was cold by then. I lifted it in my hands and the bird that had been so large and noble in flight was surprisingly light and frail. Its breast was light, almost white, the wings darker brown, the tail the color of a rusted hinge. I examined the body for signs of injury or for evidence it had been shot, but the hawk was entire, unblemished, except for its silent heart. I buried the hawk as I buried the trapper that died on my winter porch and when I tried to pray for the soul of the hawk I failed to find the words.

For days I wondered if I had been responsible for the death of the hawk. I had been concentrating on its flight, seeking to connect our spirits as Laughing Eyes had taught Herman to do, and just as the hawk filled my mind, it died and dropped to the earth. It might not have been an arrow from a bow, but it was something just as lethal from my mind. So certain was I in those distant days that I had somehow caused the hawk's death that it was some time before I could look at a bird in flight without dropping my eyes in fear and confusion.

The Good Book says we should not look for signs, although Moses certainly saw God's signs in the land of Ham when He sent darkness and turned the waters into blood and brought them hail for rain and flaming fire for wind. And as I look back on the full flight of our lives, I wonder if, like the hawk, I should not have known what was coming. Some change in the air, or some tremulous vibration within the inner ear, a gathering of messengers from the dark to be. If I had only known, could I have altered the future, saved Winifred from her demons and

Peter from himself? Or was I the cause, guiding the arrow that dropped them from the full flight of their lives?

Perhaps the death of the hawk was the sign I should have seen. Or the assassination of McKinley. Or Winifred's gloomy silences. Or the war clouds on the border. Or a sky as empty and pale as a blind man's eye. But, now, as I look back, it seems that life is filled to overflowing with abundant signs of peril and disaster. If we were to cower before every storm cloud that gathers, to cover our head when the wolf howls outside our night window, our days would become flight, not life. We would be driven to ground by our fears and our fear of fear. What woman could have a child, what man could live honorably, what child could grow strong if we listened constantly for the hoofbeats of the dark and pale riders of the Apocalypse?

There are those who say the most obvious signs are the absence of signs. When times are good and life is gloriously full that is when we should begin to look over our shoulder. There is some logic to this notion, I admit. When life is best we fail to pray because there is little we need from God that He has not already supplied. Our most fervent prayers, those that must resonate most powerfully in the ear of the Almighty, are those prayers asking deliverance from pain or impoverishment or suffering. We pray passionately for good times and then when they come our prayers of thanksgiving become tepid, uninspired. It must rile the Almighty to work so hard on our deliverance and receive so little thanks in return. I say this knowing that we were created in God's image and therefore He must be the source of guile as well as love and might more readily strike us down when times are good than when they are not.

Like a hawk in full flight.

14 ∞ THE SAN ANTONIO STAMPEDE

THE ROOM WAS FAR TOO CROWDED, ESPECIALLY WITH THE hounds of terror lurking in the hot shadows and with Rebekah and Little Mattie fussing around and pretending everything was fine. The pains had come again. Teeth tearing inside her body and her mind. Laura promised God she would never ever even think of making love again if He would just let her be. Then the pain eased, sliding away downhill, and she began to breathe again, think again, praying that the valley between her pains would be wide and deep. Something was wrong with time, she thought. It is taking too long. It keeps on going. The dark hounds crept out from the shadows and snarled. Could she be dying? None of her other children had been this hard. "I didn't bargain for this," Laura told God, cursing Eve who apparently had. Rebekah was holding her hand, cooling her forehead with water from a basin. Dr. Edwards was looking out the window at the early February ice storm flinging a silver blanket over the ranch. Little Mattie moved about the room like a small bird, old now, diminished by the years. Laura looked for the woman who had saved her children from Carnoviste and Black Cato, but the years had taken her away. "You can do this," Little Mattie said from the foot of the bed. "This will end."

Laura felt the pains rising again. "Wait!" she whispered aloud. "I'm not ready!" Then she felt the teeth once more tearing at her insides. She heard harsh, hard voices and was aware of a cool, sweet fragrance. She began to float and knew she had died and it was not half bad.

She was riding on the wings of a flying machine called the Ezekiel Airship. It had been designed by a preacher Mr. Sam knew. According to Reverend Cannon, the preacher-designer, it was the first flying machine in the world. Now it was high above Fredericksburg, heading east over the limestone hills toward Johnson City where Sam and Rebekah had moved after their wedding.

Laura had first seen the Ezekiel Airship in Reverend Cannon's barn outside Fredericksburg. Sam and Peter had taken her there before her lying-in had begun. Laura thought it looked like an enormous insect, a dragonfly. And like most insects it appeared far too ungainly to fly. Ezekiel was constructed on a square metal frame. Eight wheels with blades, not unlike windmills, were mounted in pairs at each end of the frame. Leather belts led from the windmill devices to an engine powered by kerosene. A chaos of wires and struts held every part of the machine in uneasy balance. With Peter and Sam's help, Reverend Cannon had dragged Ezekiel from the barn into a fenced meadow. The reverend-aviator made some adjustments to the controls, then returned to the front of the machine and somehow had made it start. The little engine had coughed and sputtered to life. Laura remembered the air had smelled like a spilled lantern. Reverend Cannon reentered Ezekiel and the engine labored, the windmills began to turn, faster and faster, whipping the dandelion and bluestem meadow, blowing Sam Johnson's hat away. Then the mechanical dragonfly had trembled and little by little it had seemed to grow lighter and Laura had seen a profound and glorious division between Ezekiel and the meadow, and the machine had lifted into the slate blue of the afternoon heavens.

Now Laura and Reverend Cannon were circling over the Pedernales River. Laura was dizzy. She felt something heavy pressing on her lower body and she heard the deep rumble of voices and there was that sweet thick aroma of new-mown hay. Surely it was the height and the heady exhilaration of flight or the mysterious sensations of death that made her feel so strange.

Laura looked down along the river for Sam and Rebekah's house. Surely these two beautiful people would have a mansion with wide lawns along the shore and porches overlooking pastures and fields of bluebonnets. At Rebekah's wedding, Laura had been enormously happy for her friend, but she had found herself plagued by uncharacteristic episodes of envy. Sam was a promising young politician, a respected member of the legislature, and Rebekah would soon enter that glittering world Laura had longed to enter herself. Laura had felt she was being left behind. She had felt the same way when Rebekah and Lucy had gone off to college and when Rebekah had begun working for the newspaper, a career Laura had been forced to abandon. Ezekiel flew low over the Pedernales, but Laura could not find the mansion of Sam and Rebekah.

Laura tugged on Reverend Cannon's sleeve. "We better go back," she said, shouting above the sound of the engine.

"It's a boy," Little Mattie said. "Go tell Peter that Wilton has made his arrival."

Laura missed her friend Rebekah enormously. Her absence was a small, soft ache she felt daily, and Laura counted the days until she was well enough to ride out to Rebekah's Pedernales home.

One spring morning, Peter hitched a matched pair of mules to the wagon and Lucy, Laura, and baby Wilton rode out early from Blanco on the twenty-mile journey to Stonewall, the nearest town to the Johnson ranch that could be reached by road. At first, it was a familiar way, along the Blanco River, past a thousand childhood memories, across Hines Branch and Cottonwood Creek, Hoge Hollow, and then north across Big Creek and away from the river toward the hills.

They moved high into clusters of maple and live oak trees and then down into the little settlement of Albert on Williams Creek where cypress towered above the shadowed stream. Then up again, along a ridge where they could see the smoky gray hills rising along the horizon behind the valley of the Pedernales.

Laura was shocked when she first saw Sam and Rebekah's house. Its setting along the river was magnificent, yet the little clapboard cabin seemed dwarfed by the immensity of the country. It was roughly made and Spartan and seemed absolutely isolated and alone. It reminded Laura of her long and troubled days and nights at the Wilderness Ranch. She could not imagine her elegant friend in such surroundings and began to fear what she might find in the rude cabin Sam Johnson had built for his bride. A few cattle strayed on fenced pastures, chickens grazed in the swept-dirt yard, the fields were poorly tended.

Country life had not been good to Rebekah Baines Johnson. Her milk-white complexion had been reddened by the sun, and hands that had been more familiar with the ivory of piano keys and crystal had been roughened by her labors in the wood yard and over the kitchen's great iron stove. Again, Laura remembered the burn of lye on her hands, the sound of rats gnawing in the eaves, the cold blast of January winds howling through imperfect walls at Wilderness Ranch. Shortly before her marriage, Rebekah's father had become ill and then died. Rebekah's mother had been forced to sell their home in Fredericksburg. Having no other options, she went to live with her son and his family. Fate had dealt the once prosperous Baines family a crippling blow. Now Rebekah was living in a tiny, ill-furnished, poorly constructed dog-run cabin at Stonewall. Laura's heart wept for her friend's circumstances, a condition made the more poignant by Rebekah's refusal to recognize that she was not still the princess she had once believed herself to be.

"Things change so fast," Rebekah said, as they sat on the front porch watching Wilton sleep. "The world takes a certain shape, then suddenly it becomes something else. I never imagined a world without my father in it. It was inconceivable that the earth could continue to turn and the stars might still travel across the sky. He was my world. Everything I am is his gift. Then he was gone."

"And the stars still shine."

"Differently. Less brightly."

Laura pictured the Baines house standing sentinel above the river. She imagined old Judge Baines still walked its halls and prowled the library where Rebekah had learned her love of Browning and the Bible.

"Don't you get lonely sometimes?" Rebekah asked. The question was almost wistful, as if she did not really expect an

answer. "I mean when Peter's away. Somehow I didn't expect it
to be so lonely. I thought to be married was never to be lonely
again. But when Sam's in Austin, sometimes days go by and I
don't see a soul."

"What about Sam's folks? Aren't they just down the road? I
thought these parts were spilling over with Johnson kinfolks."

"His parents. His brother Tom. There are lots of Johnsons
around. They're there, but not really. They're good people and
good to me. But I feel I'm outside their circle. And I'm sure it's
not their fault. It's mine. They talk to me, but not *with* me. Not
about things I really care about. You know what I mean?"

"I guess you really miss me," Laura laughed. "Somebody to
boss you around and disagree with you all the time."

"I suppose," Rebekah said. "It's not that my life isn't full.
When Sam's home I'm in heaven. He's exciting and loving and
he comes into the house like a whirlwind. Sam didn't run for
reelection after we were married. He said three terms were
enough. But I know he did it for me. Politics is in his blood and
I know he misses it. Bless his heart, he tries to make this place pay.
But there never has been a Johnson who was a very good farmer.
He works out there in the fields. Sometimes on Saturdays he tries
his hand at barbering in Stonewall. But then he comes home and
the whole house lights up." Rebekah paused, lost in her reflection, then her smile faded, slowly, like a lamp turned low. "And I
have visitors sometimes. And my garden. And my books. And I
have Sam. So I don't know why I'm complaining." Rebekah's
smile returned and her shoulders squared, her burdens an invisible cape cast aside. "And besides, I have the future. Promise you
won't say a word to a single soul and I'll tell you a secret.
Promise?"

Laura was amused. "Of course, I promise." She smiled down
at Wilton, thinking surely that Rebekah was pregnant.

"What would you think of your old friend being the wife of
Governor Johnson? The Austin crowd is trying to get Sam to run!"

Laura felt something cold and unpleasant touch her mind.
How dare Sam take away what she had planned for Peter? She
was astonished at the anger she felt and feared revealing her

feelings to her dear friend. Instead, she picked up Wilton and held him to her breast.

"Well, what do you think?" Rebekah asked.

"I think I know one absolutely foolproof antidote for being lonely."

"What's that?" Rebekah asked, without enthusiasm. She was obviously disappointed Laura had not shared her excitement about Sam.

"A child." Laura bent her face to kiss Wilton. "You really need to have a baby."

The Austin crowd showed up in the spring of 1908 in the person of a rather unimposing man named Edward House. When Peter had told Laura that House was coming to the ranch, he had described him as the most powerful man in Texas that nobody knew. "He's a kingmaker," Peter had said. "Every governor since James Hogg has been handpicked by Edward House. He decides who would be best for Texas and then he makes sure his candidate wins."

"And he thinks Sam is right for Texas."

"Sam is bright, young, charismatic. Honest as the day is long."

"So this House has made up his mind and that's it. What about Democracy? What about the people deciding who is best for Texas! What gives one man the right to choose a governor!" Laura heard her voice rising and she blushed when she realized how angry she was becoming.

"I didn't mean to get you all riled up," Peter had said.

"I'm not *getting* riled up," Laura said. "I've been riled up for some while. Ever since I heard about this dictator coming to dinner." Laura knew she was being unreasonable, but as much as she loved Sam, she knew Peter was the better man. There was something wild and unpredictable about Sam—an abandon that was part of his great charm, an attractive, yet troubling quality only a woman would recognize. But she would never be able to speak against Sam, if for no other reason than her loyalty to Rebekah. It simply was not fair. And so she said, "It's just not fair!"

"What's not fair?"

"For one man to have that much power."

Laura was prepared to thoroughly dislike their guest and all through the day of his arrival she worked at convincing herself to be civil. She also worked at designing some strategy to shift the "kingmaker's" attention from Sam to Peter. But each time she fashioned an anecdote highlighting Peter's virtues, she remembered the excitement on Rebekah's face when she had revealed her secret about Sam's future, a future that would free Rebekah from her dog-run house on the Pedernales. Laura remembered the moment years ago when she and Rebekah had met, half submerged in the cool waters of the Blanco. Who would have thought that those two water-soaked girls would one day be in competition for the governor's mansion? Just thinking the unthinkable thought of the life she might lead sent a shiver up her spine. And it made her dislike Edward House all the more.

Laura had expected a much larger man, a man whose presence would fill the doorway and whose voice would set the crystal in the china closet ringing, a man like the flamboyant politician James Hogg, all bombast and zealotry. But she was so astounded by the man who entered the parlor that she was temporarily nonplussed. She stammered a welcome to the little man who stood, hat in hand, looking into her eyes so deeply and with such intensity that it was impossible to look away. And when House spoke her name it was little more than a whisper she heard. Then, mercifully, he released Laura's eyes and turned his attention to Peter who took his hat and led their guest into the parlor.

After a few moments, Laura excused herself and returned to the kitchen where she was roasting a wild turkey she had shot the day before. As she mashed potatoes, she watched the two men through the kitchen door. Although small in stature, Edward House was far from delicate. In fact, his compact body gave Laura the impression of a coiled spring, a wellspring of contained energy and strength. Peter had told her House was the best and fastest pistol shot in Texas and that he had nearly killed a man in a Colorado bar. Yet the man she saw now through the kitchen door was obviously mannered. According to Peter, he was also very, very wealthy. House owned land in more than sixty Texas counties. Laura recalled how their eyes had met in the parlor, a moment that troubled her still. It was almost intimate, that look, a thing that passes between only the closest friends. After that one moment, House had seemed almost shy and self-effacing, never again meeting Laura's eyes with such intensity. Only now was she able to look past those eyes and see the high, intelligent forehead, the short, dark eyebrows, the finely formed nose above a small, sensuous, yet humorless mouth and receding chin. His face was unlined and Laura was sure that he rarely smiled. As she began to prepare the gravy for the potatoes, she remembered those eyes, and wondered if they were not the source of his power.

Edward House did not take long to come to the point of his visit. "Thomas Campbell has two more years as governor. I'm looking down the line to 1911. I want to get a good man established in Austin, and then when we've got everything in shape in Texas, we'll turn our attention to the national scene. I'm tired of the shoddy way government is run. I can count on the fingers of one hand the senators and congressmen who truly stand for anything."

"Maybe it's time you ran for office," Peter said. "Time to put your ideals in action."

"That's not the way. Not my way. The way to good government is to work behind the scenes. Find a good man, build an organization, then strip away the obstacles to his election one by one, whatever or whoever they are."

"And you've found your good man for the presidential election?"

"Governor Woodrow Wilson, of New Jersey. I've never met a man whose thoughts run so identically with mine. The more I see of Governor Wilson the better I like him. I promise you now he will be the next president of these United States."

"And Texas?" Laura asked.

"We're meeting next month in San Antonio to make that

decision. The man we pick at that meeting will be nominated, will be elected, and will serve. We'd like you to be there, Peter. You know this part of the state as well as anybody. And you know Sam Johnson. We'd welcome your counsel."

"I'd be pleased to," Peter said.

"And you, as well, Laura. We need a woman's view."

"I can't even vote. So why does it matter?"

"Because women influence those who do vote." Laura felt the magnetic touch of those eyes, again. "So what do you think of Sam Johnson, Laura?" She glanced at Peter and then back at Edward House, wishing she could avoid endorsing anyone because that would forever destroy the dream she had for her husband. Her thoughts whirled and she felt House had somehow gained control of her mind. She had heard the rumors that Sam drank too much and she was certain Peter would be the better choice. But she would never, ever say these things, partially because she was not sure they were true and partially because House's eyes demanded she say what he wanted to hear.

"Sam is a good man. I'm sure he'll make a very good governor," she said.

In the autumn of 1908, Peter, Laura, and the family set out for San Antonio to meet with Edward House and the Democratic power brokers of Texas. They planned to drive 150 steers from the Wilderness Ranch to the stockyard in San Antonio. Laura's older sons, Maxey Charles and Eugene, both seasoned cowboys, would be among the hands. The youngest rider would be a feisty redheaded barrel of a boy named Butch Neill, whose father had sent the boy to "Old Man Woods" to learn the cowboying trade from a man he considered "the finest cattle and horseman in Central Texas." The only challenger to that title might have been Peter's friend, old Valentine Smith, a lanky, bowlegged giant from a neighboring Blanco ranch, who volunteered to help Peter get the cattle to the Alamo City.

In the days before the drive, the cowhands rounded up,

branded, and dipped the ranch cattle to protect against lice and grubs. It was a time as golden and fine as only Indian summer in Texas can be.

At first, Peter worried that the trip overland would be too rough, too dangerous for Winifred and little Wilton and he suggested they remain home with Little Mattie. Laura pointed out that the days of the "Old West" were gone, and that the most dangerous thing between Blanco and San Antonio was stinging nettle growing along the fences, or maybe rogue prairie dogs. When she saw the hurt in his eyes, she regretted her words. She knew how Peter mourned the closing of the open range and how he yearned for the brotherhood of tough, bold men who celebrated hardship, discomfort, and danger. The idea of a woman among them was bad enough, but a young girl and a toddler was incomprehensible. She knew Peter would enjoy having his entire family along the trail, but he was thinking about the hands and their masculine brotherhood. Finally, Peter agreed after making Laura promise not to infringe on the cowboys' God-given right to curse by keeping the children out of earshot of their storytelling after supper.

The country rolls from Blanco southeast to San Antonio over broken hills and limestone shelves and prairie imprisoned by wire. The coming of the railroad left fenced strips of land stretching across the country in every direction. Now an intricate network of fenced roads and rights of way were beginning to cut the country into even smaller parcels. The way to San Antonio was partly over open country and partly along roadways worn first by the deer hooves, then by wheels.

They set out early on an October morning. Frost silvered the Mexican tea and croton and pastures cropped close by grazing. The air was fragrant and cool, the far distance a smoky blue. The buggy complained woodenly and Laura felt the first sensual warming of the sun rising above the distant horizon. Triumph and Dilcy, Winifred's horse, were loosely tethered alongside. Laura planned to take turns driving the wagon with her daughter as Peter rode with the drovers. Now Winifred drove. There was a rare smile on her face and when she caught her mother's eyes, her smile widened, as if to say, "I'm happy to be with you and riding through Texas on such a beautiful day."

Laura watched Peter move with fluid grace among the cattle and his men. It was no wonder he was so highly respected and that Butch Neill's father would entrust his son to Peter's care and that Valentine Smith would leave his ranch for a week or more to do his friend a favor. As their route moved between two fenced pastures, she could almost feel Peter's sadness, his growing anger at those who would strangle Texas in a web of wire. Yet Laura could not help but notice the ironic difference between the land beyond the right of way and the land within. Beyond the fences the prairie was brown and nearly barren. But along the fences and within, where the cattle could not graze, there were vivid splashes of color, wildflowers braving the first frost, crimson sumac, the greenish-yellow stickleaf, the bluish-purple of the skull cap. She could imagine how the lane must look in springtime when the blue-bonnets were in bloom. In the brush beside the roadway, the cattle occasionally flushed wild turkey, jack rabbits, and armadillo.

It was a two-day ride to San Antonio. The first night they camped on the Guadalupe River east of the little town of Sisterdale where they had danced with Teddy Roosevelt years before. Since the drive was of such short duration, Peter did not bring the chuckwagon. Laura loved the celebrated Woods chuckwagon with its great clattering miscellany of pots, pans, and tubs; its pine cupboards brimming with provisions that would fill a dozen kitchens; its canvas awnings carrying the aroma of dust, beef gravy, and sunlight. On this trip, Fritz Merton, the chuckwagon cook, had brought a scaled-down outfit, including a large iron pot for heating his famous son-of-a-gun stew, and a dutch oven for making biscuits. Laura had brought several lemon pies, covered with a creamy meringue the cowboys called "calf slobber." The cowboys gathered around the campfire, ate their supper in silence, then washed it all down with strong boiled coffee while Fritz Merton washed up the dishes in a tub. The cowhands drifted away, some to a game of cards, some to tell yarns. Maxey Charles and Eugene taught young Butch Neill tricks with the lariat. Fritz Merton leaned against a mesquite tree cleaning dough from beneath his fingernails before rolling a smoke. Laura fed Wilton and sang him to sleep. The evening washed over them and the stars came out one by one.

Laura laid out the bedrolls and, once down, Peter was asleep. The campfire hissed and spit sparks into the darkness. The sound of a fiddle came on the wind from a nearby ranch. A dog voiced his discontent to the night. Then Winifred sat down beside Laura and laid her head on her mother's shoulder. Laura was so thrilled by the rare show of affection that it made her heart beat faster. She longed to throw her arms around Winifred and hold her close, but she was afraid the response would drive her away as it so often did, so she just sat there, looking into the fire, feeling her daughter's presence, wishing the moment would last forever. *If only we could talk,* she thought, *like mothers and daughters do. If I could only know what lingers in the shadows of her mind.* Winifred began to hum a melody. It reminded Laura of the tune Ed Tom had played at the Colonel-Doctor's funeral. It held that kind of sorrow. "What is that song?" Laura asked. And Winifred rose and walked away.

Daybreak promised another cloudless, splendid day. They crossed the river without difficulty and made their way south toward San Antonio. There were more ranches now, and the men had to keep the steers bunched or strung out in a long column where the trail passed between fenced pastures. The ground was trenched with ruts and the grass had been worn away by the iron wheels of wagons. By midmorning, dust began to rise in plumes from the hooves of the leading cattle. The air grew yellow and Laura could feel the dust in her teeth and in the corners of her eyes. It was probably the dust and the diminished visibility that allowed the automobile to come upon them so suddenly.

It emerged from the dust like something from a comic nightmare, a honking, clattering apparition bounding along the rutted way, its engine casting decibels, its metal parts clattering like hail on a tin roof. "Out of the way!" a man in the machine shouted. "Get them damn cows out of the road!"

None of them had ever seen an automobile. It came crashing through the remuda, careening crazily, its horn blowing, scattering cattle, narrowly missing Laura's buggy. The steers snorted and bawled in terror. The cattle nearest the automobile bolted out of the way, the rest began to stampede. Laura could see the riders bowled along by the brown roiling tide. The buggy was nearly lifted off its wheels before it was pushed to the side, out of harm's way, one of its wheels ripped off, the horses somehow torn from the traces now runaway. As the car plowed on down the right of way, the cattle were driven, crashing through the barbed wire and plunging into the surrounding pastures, the leading steers cut by the wire, many down rolling on the ground bellowing and bleeding from awful wounds. The dust closed in like night.

It took several hours for Peter and the hands to round up the steers and establish some kind of order out of the morning's chaos. Half a dozen longhorns were dead. Butch Neill had fallen and was in pain.

"My arm ain't right. If it weren't for Mr. Woods pullin' me out from under them hooves, I'd of been trampled dead."

"Damn automobiles," Peter said, as he bound Butch's forearm to a willow splint.

"It wasn't the automobile," Valentine said. "Was the man in it. Oughta be skinned alive."

"What about them dead cows?" Butch asked. Laura thought he had been very brave when she and Peter had set his arm. He had never complained and now he was more concerned with the cows than with his own troubles.

"I sent Maxey Charles and Eugene out to the ranches hereabouts. Maybe they can use the meat. If not, I guess we leave 'em for the buzzards." Peter looked up into the cloudless sky where vultures had already begun to circle. "Damn automobiles!" It was a sound like spitting.

Laura could feel Peter's anger. It was so powerful, it almost had color, a blood-red aura like the rays of a sunset seen through dust. She wanted to soothe his wrath, to cool the heat she could feel, but no words came, nor would any words do.

"Damn automobiles," Peter said again.

"It's just a machine," Winifred said. "Some iron and wire and a whole lot of noise."

"What it is," Peter said, "is the end of our way of life. Pretty soon there'll be more of those things than horses. Cattle trails will be crawlin' with 'em. What I'd like to do is bust 'em all up and sink 'em deep in the river." And then, as punctuation, Peter cursed for perhaps the fourth time in his life. "Damned automobiles."

"Damn," Winifred said. Laura cut her eyes toward her daughter but decided it was not a time for scolding.

Laura watched Peter's efforts to control his anger. Little by little, as he took stock of the damage the automobile had done, his features loosened, the dark-blue vein in his neck diminished, then disappeared. But Laura knew his anger was deep and that the incident along the road had left a bruise on his spirit.

"Let's move on down a way where there's water. Out of this place. Make camp. Then we'll get Butch to a doctor." Peter looked back down at Butch. "That sorry-no-good-fool could've killed the boy. Or any of us."

It was nearly dark when they heard the automobile coming back. "God Almighty!" Peter said. "Get to your horses!" Peter pulled Laura and Winifred to their feet. "Get mounted and ride out of the way," he said, then he rushed away to join the hands who were watching the approaching automobile with incredulous eyes. "I can't believe this!" Valentine said. "I'm gonna shoot that dag blasted . . ."

"This is my fight," Peter said. "You tend to the cattle."

As before, the automobile came tearing along the roadway, the man honking the horn and shouting for the cowboys to get the cattle off the road. The steers began to fret and bawl and shake their heads from side to side. Then, at some invisible signal, they bolted back the way they had come, away from the metal monster hurtling their way. This time, however, the cattle were not restrained by barbed wire along the roadway, and the stampede spread out into open country.

Winifred raced off to help the cowhands head off the cattle. Laura saw Butch Neill, broken bones and all, mount and catch up with Winifred, obviously to protect her from harm.

Then Peter began chasing the automobile, riding alongside the machine. It was a bizarre image, the automobile and the horseman, riding side by side along the roadway, like an Indian riding a pony in pace with a buffalo, the Indian closing for the kill. It was at that moment the unthinkable crept into Laura's mind. After making sure little Wilton was all right, she flung herself bareback onto Triumph, racing after Peter, calling him, hoping against hope his anger would not consume him.

Peter drew near the automobile and the driver swerved into the horse's path. Peter dodged and drew near again. The automobile bounded grotesquely over the holes and ruts in the roadway. The driver was hurled first to one side and then the other, then so high from his seat Laura thought he might take flight. In contrast, Peter rode with smooth and liquid precision, seeming to anticipate every move the driver made. Laura raced after them, heart pounding, her mind filled with awful possibilities.

Peter drew his revolver and fired at the automobile. Again and again he fired into the engine and the wheels, as if he could destroy the heart of the machine. The automobile slowed, careened off the roadway and onto the prairie. Laura easily caught up and she could see the driver trying to control the machine. He was a big man with a ruddy face and meaty hands. It was a curious ballet, a strange traveling tableau of man and machine.

Peter closed on the automobile and then leaped from his horse onto the careening machine. As the machine lurched over the rough field, Peter climbed up behind the driver and Laura saw a flash of bright steel. The car shuddered to a stop. Its engine coughed and died. Laura had never known the world to be more silent. She approached the car. It was making a hissing sound, a breathy sigh, and steam leaked from the holes Peter's shots had made. Peter was slumped in the backseat. When Laura dismounted she could see there was something terribly wrong with the driver's head. There was a crimson mouth slashed across his throat, his head nearly severed from his body.

"My God," Laura said.

"I didn't mean . . . this. I swear it, Laura." Peter still held the cattle knife. Laura touched his hand and he wiped it clean on the driver's shirt and put it away.

It was dark when Sheriff Gleason came. He called the incident an accident. "You just can't do that to a man's cattle," he said. They loaded the dead man onto a mule and said they would take Butch to see the doctor.

"What was his name?" Winifred asked.

"Name was Quint."

"Who was he," she asked. "I mean why did he . . ."

"Quint was a fool. Born to be kil't. In the old days he'd a been dead long before. But the times got soft."

"But there's got to be a reason," Winifred said.

"I'll be headin' back now," said the sheriff of Bexar County.

"You mean that's all?" Winifred asked so quietly it was almost a whisper. "A person is dead and that's all there is about it?"

"That's the end of it, little lady," the sheriff said. "The no-good fellow tried to take away what belonged to your papa and your papa did what had to be done. You just can't treat a man like Quint done treated your pa. And that's the reason and the end of it. Well, it will be the end of it long as too many tongues don't wag. Some folks might think different about what I should do. But the less folks talk about this, the better." He tipped his hat, turned, mounted, and rode away, followed by the mule and Butch.

Winifred moved to her father and placed her arms around his neck. She hugged him briefly for what Laura was sure was the first time since she had been a little girl. "I'm proud of you, Papa," she said. Laura could see how much Winifred resembled her father. She was smiling now, up into his eyes, and there was a chilling moonlight coldness to her expression. "Can I see the knife?" Winifred asked.

Laura shivered. "For God's sake, why?"

"Well, never mind, then," Winifred said and then walked out into the darkness.

When Peter and Laura were alone, Laura said, "Maybe you better talk to her."

"What would I say? I don't have any words right now. Should I tell her what I did was wrong? Thou shalt not kill?"

"You did what any man would have done. Protected your family and your property from a madman. It was an accident."

The words were true and she believed them to her very soul. But she knew she would never see her husband quite the same again.

∞

Edward House had arranged for three adjoining rooms at the Menger Hotel: one for the boys, one for Winifred and Wilton, and the "King Ranch" suite for Peter and Laura. Laura had never seen a room more magnificently vulgar. It was a room obviously designed for wealthy cattlemen who would spend the night alone or with one of the elegant women of easy virtue Laura had been told frequented the Rough Rider bar and the public spaces below. From the richly paneled walls, the heads of moose and elk stared down at Laura with empty eyes. Long red velvet draperies fell from ceiling to floor. It was a room that made Laura feel absolutely wicked and on their first night in the great canopied bed she pretended she was a woman of the evening who had snared Peter for an interval of profitable debauchery. It was a room like that.

But when she reached for Peter in the darkness, he did not respond. At first she was embarrassed because she had been so bold and wanton. Then she knew.

"It's Quint, isn't it?"

"Of course, it's Quint!" Peter swung his legs off the bed and sat, facing away. "I just feel bad about it. Every time I think about it, it's like a weight drops on me and holds me down. I can't think it away." Peter took a deep breath, then exhaled, and in the uneasy light Laura could see his shoulders loosen. It was the longest expression of any unpleasant feeling he had ever shared. Laura moved beside him and held him, her head against his chest. He seemed so hard, all sinew and bone, difficult to hold. For awhile his hands remained at his side. Then Laura felt a brief, tentative touch, first one hand, then the other, and he turned and she could feel the strength in his encircling arms.

"Talk to me, Peter," Laura whispered. She pulled away and looked up into his face. There were no tears, of course, would never be. "Tell me what hurts." She pushed him lightly down and then they lay on their backs together, side by side, touching, and he told her what he had never revealed before.

"I know it's a sin to kill. It's the most important thing the Lord ever asked. When I was a boy, a little younger than Winifred, I helped my mama kill a man. A Yankee officer. I can't help it. I still hate him. He attacked the women, so we lured him into the stable and we shot him. Now there was plenty good reason. He was laying for us and looking for a chance to kill us down the line. What that man did to my sister, Cherokee, and my mother was something we couldn't let pass. But still it was a killing. Ever since that day I've prayed for forgiveness. So I think about that. Now I think about this."

"About Quint."

"I was beginning to think maybe the Lord had forgiven me the first one. I don't think He's looking to forgive this one." He paused and Laura could hear his heart beating. How familiar the sound, how often over the years she had felt that soft drumming. "This was no accident, Laura," Peter said. "You can't accidentally cut a man's throat. I meant to kill him."

There were silences, but Laura let him talk. She could hear noises in the street below and the distant sound of a guitar and singing.

"The Colonel-Doctor hated killing. The killing my papa did in the war was an agony all his life. He told me once that to kill a person was to kill the whole world. He said when you kill a man, it wasn't just him dying, but the world going out like a pinched candle. So when you kill a man, you kill all of God's creation. No sin could be greater than that."

"Peter, what happened back then? After the war."

"I've never told a soul."

Laura waited.

"It started when my sister, Sweet, shot at the Yankees. She was only fifteen. The war was over. Papa was gone. He was in Austin trying to make some kind of decent peace. The Yankees ordered us to move out of our house and live out back with the Negroes. Troops of the state police and the Army of Occupation officers lived in our home. There was this Prussian mercenary named

Haller. A bachelor fellow. He terrorized the women. He was the conqueror, he told them. My mother. My sisters. He wanted Cherokee and he took her. She was just a girl. Haller said he'd turn Sweet in to the army authorities for shooting at them, and they would hang us all if she didn't come to him in the night. He grabbed my mama once and said he'd do the same to her that he did to Cherokee. We had to do something. You know about those times: no justice, no judges, no juries. Mama was a very strong woman. She did what had to be done. She defended her family herself, with her own hands. He just disappeared."

"What did they do? The Yankees?"

"It was awhile before Haller was missed. But soon they figured out what happened. Haller was that kind of man. When they get killed it doesn't surprise folks much."

"Like Quint."

"They made a house-to-house search. Ransacked houses and questioned people, but no one ever told. They whipped up on the freed people, too. We just knew it was a matter of time before they came to get us. That's when Mama divided up the horses and sent us all away. That's how I got my ranch in the Hill Country."

"You're a good man, Peter. You did what any man would have done. With Haller and with Quint. It just had to be."

"I'm not so sure about Quint. I could have shot at him. Maybe just wing him. I could have knocked him unconscious. Even let the sheriff take him to jail. I didn't have to cut his throat!"

"That's not all that's bothering you, is it?" Laura asked.

"No. There's Winifred."

"Winifred?" A small sense of alarm tugged at Laura's mind.

"You've always said she's just like me. I know that. I've seen it. What if there's this rage, this violent streak, that runs through my family. Through me and on into Winifred."

"You were defending us, nothing more," Laura said. "Peter, that's not even worth thinking about."

"But I do. All the time. Did you see how pleased she was about Quint? She wanted to see the knife!"

"Hush." Laura touched her fingers to Peter's lips.

"First you want me to talk. Now you want me to hush."

"Peter, dear Peter," Laura said, touching her lips to his cheek. "Be still now. I just want to hold you and thank God for giving me such a strong, good man."

They were quiet then, listening to the muted sounds drifting across the river. Laura lay awake all night trying to control the emergence of an unreasonable fear and the impulse to rush to the neighboring room to see if Winifred was asleep and if Wilton was all right.

Sam Johnson was late. He had been scheduled to appear before the kingmakers at 10:00 A.M. and Laura could feel a current of impatience building among the bankers and ranchmen and politicos who controlled the Texas Democratic party. She was seated at a long mahogany table between Peter, representing the Blanco County Democratic party, and Edward House, who was at the head of the table and presiding over the strategy session. Laura was pleased that House was paying her what seemed a disproportionate amount of attention, but she decided his ability to appear keenly and personally interested in others was part of his style and his power.

"Why don't you help us with this campaign, Laura? Help us get Sam elected. We need someone like you. Bright, young, and fearless." His voice was soft, yet intense.

Laura looked up into House's eyes and they seemed to draw her in. "You're serious?"

"Never more serious."

Laura was pleased and flattered. Yet she felt a kind of sadness settle on her mind. "I don't think so," she said. "There's the ranch. The children. How could I do it?"

"Just do it. Peter thinks you'd be a great help. He says you know everyone in three counties and that you have a real gift for making people comfortable and remembering names."

"What would I do?" She spread her hands, palms upward, a gesture of futility. "Where would I start?"

"I'd show you, Laura. We could work together." House explained how he had built a political network based on the strength of loyal friendships. He explained further how he had made a thorough study of the local counties, precincts, voting districts, and the peculiar problems of the people living in those local areas. "We listen to everybody and make friends with both the powerful and the impoverished in order to understand their views. You have to look each voter in the eye to know what's in his soul. People say we're so successful because we have a political machine. Well, it's not a machine, Laura. It's just flesh and blood. Good friends, people who care, working together to make government work for all. Strong friendships like you and I have."

House spoke so softly that Laura found herself leaning toward him to hear his words. It occurred to her it was presumptuous to call their brief acquaintance a strong friendship, but decided it was just his manner.

"You can be my eyes and ears in Blanco County. I've watched you with people, Laura. With the people here. I've seen you walk up to perfect strangers and within a few minutes you've won them over. You did it to me. You made me feel we've known each other all our lives. So you can talk to people about the issues. About what matters to them most. What they dream and fear. What makes them angry. What makes them feel good. Find out what they think. Talk to women. They'll express themselves freely, while men may hold back. Men are often afraid their opinion might be held against them in business. But they'll tell their wives what they think. And with your friendly manner their wives will tell you. Then you tell me."

Laura felt a strange and thrilling bond growing between Edward House and herself. She felt they were about to be involved in something important, something that would make a difference in people's lives. And there was a sense of secrecy. She wondered if this was the way men felt as they embarked on a vital and secret mission.

"Together, we can build an organization for Sam. We've got two years. It shouldn't be difficult to elect the man who saved the Alamo."

At that moment, Mr. Sam entered the room. For a moment, he stared into the cigar and pipe smoke, then he spotted House, Laura, and Peter at the head table. With a few great strides he was at their side, and to Laura's astonishment, he gathered her in his arms, lifted her in the air, and turned a full circle before putting her down again. Then he hugged Peter, then a stiffly reluctant Edward House who seemed hardly more than a child in Sam's lanky embrace, his head coming hardly to Sam's shoulders.

"It's a boy," Sam said, his dark eyes aglow. "Lyndon Baines Johnson. A fine, handsome boy!" Then Sam began to circle the table handing out cigars and shaking hands.

"He's been drinking," House muttered to Peter.

"He's just celebrating. It's natural. He's a new father."

"Does he celebrate often?"

Neither Peter nor Laura answered.

"Do you know what the election of 1911 will be all about?" House asked. "The burning issue, the only issue, will be 'Demon Rum'! The beer trust against the prohibitionist reformers!"

Laura looked toward the foot of the table where Sam was moving unsteadily among the political kingmakers and she knew the man who saved the Alamo would never be governor of Texas.

"It's your decision, Peter," Edward House said. "If you want it, it's yours. As long as you can hold your liquor better than Sam and haven't any skeletons in your closet, I guarantee you'll be the next governor of Texas."

Laura thought of Quint and she turned away as Peter told House what his closet contained. She did not cry, but she longed to be with Rebekah, to hold her dear friend and talk about bitter disappointment and good men who crush the dreams of their women.

15 ∞ THE YEAR THE DOGS WENT MAD

THE YEAR AFTER EDWARD HOUSE AND THE AUSTIN CROWD selected Oscar Branch Colquitt as their candidate for governor, the Rev. Andrew Jackson Potter announced the coming of the end of the world. He said that a milk-white fire would streak across the sky and burn away the world and all its sins. It was the year Halley's comet would again appear and plummet toward Earth from the darkness beyond Neptune. As the predicted arrival grew near, Hill Country philosophers and theologians aimed their spyglasses and telescopes at the heavens and pondered the mysteries of the universe and the meaning of the comet in the lives of men.

On the day before the comet was due to appear, Laura, Rebekah, and Winifred prepared for a family pilgrimage to a place north of Fredericksburg called Enchanted Rock, a huge granite dome towering above the surrounding hills. Peter and Mr. Sam had decided this would be the perfect vantage point from which to view Halley's comet. It would also be the first time both the Woods and Johnson families had all been together since the birth of Lyndon and Wilton.

"Peter says it was Halley's comet that appeared to the Wise Men on the night Jesus was born," Laura told Rebekah some days before the comet was due to make its appearance. "He says it was the Star of Bethlehem."

Winifred disagreed with characteristic certainty. "Every time Halley's comet appears another Messiah is born," she said. "Since Halley's comet first appeared in 1057 B.C., and it comes around every seventy-six years, that means there's been a total of twenty-five Messiahs other than Jesus."

The scientific view concerning the comet, held by Peter and

Sam Johnson, was that the comet would pass harmlessly by, the fear of collision with Earth unfounded. Others, like Rebekah, made cautious by the sermons of Andrew Jackson Potter, wondered if the comet might indeed be a sign of God's wrath and, if not signaling the end of the world, at least would be a harbinger of disaster. It was known the Earth would pass through the tail of the comet and it was suspected that exposure to cyanide gases might cause skin disease or suffocation. In some Texas towns, cynical entrepreneurs sold gas masks and anticomet pills to the fearful. In Blanco, citizens were advised to stay inside and pray.

Laura was especially excited about Halley's comet because its arrival coincided with her sister Maggie's return home from college in California. She arrived driving a machine called an Oldsmobile, a rackety piece of sculpture that impressed everyone in the family except Peter, an acknowledged hater of automobiles. She and two friends had driven all the way across Texas, from El Paso to Blanco, in Mr. Olds's new contraption. It was quite possible, she said, that they were the first to accomplish such a thing.

Laura was amazed at the changes in her little sister. Although she still seemed flighty, there was a certain confidence behind her every move. She was still slim, even tiny, yet she had filled out, become a woman in the few months she had been gone. She seemed to possess endless wellsprings of energy and was adored by her niece and nephews who were drawn to her and followed her around begging for tales of her travels across Texas.

"Sometimes the roads were so bad we sank down in the mud," she told Laura and the children. "The mud would be up over the wheels and the car almost buried. Like a ship sinking at sea."

The boys' eyes would grow round as they tried to imagine such a catastrophe. "How'd you get out?" they asked.

"Mules. Hitched a team to the front of the automobile. We'd pour on the coals and the mules would pull. Having a motor right at your backsides roaring like a lion gave those mules a reason to pull harder. And pretty soon, the mud would let go and we'd have to put on the brakes to keep from running down the team."

Maggie told them about stopping in El Paso where there were rumors of a revolution. She showed them a Mexican newspaper called *Regeneracion* that called for Americans to support the impoverished people of Mexico in their effort to rise up against Porfirio Díaz. She told them of the long stretches of the Butterfield stage trail east of El Paso, and the white, sandy desert and purple mountain ranges where you could see for a hundred miles or more.

"As we got closer to home," she said, "it was like a carpet of grass as far as you can see. Sometimes we just took off across that green ocean, the grass whipping by as high as the fenders, making a sound like a broom on the bottom of the car. Sometimes there'd be this big commotion and we'd flush a prairie hen and some chicks and they'd scoot away quick. There were places filled with wildflowers as far as you could see. And there were times when we were so completely alone out on that wide flower-filled land that I just had to blow the horn to make sure the world wasn't just a painting some artist had made."

"Blow the horn!" Eugene said. "Let's hear it again!"

And Maggie would let them blow the horn. "Oooogah. Oooogah," it would say. It was like music to the Woods boys and to Laura who was being consumed by a desperate need to learn to drive this amazing symbol of freedom and connection to a world beyond her horizon.

"If you had an automobile like this," Laura mused, "you could go anywhere in the world."

"Not over the ocean," Winifred said, then added that oceans accounted for seventy percent of the earth's surface.

"But anywhere in America," Maxey Charles said. "Or Mexico or Canada."

"Or Enchanted Rock," Laura added.

They took Maggie's big Oldsmobile and Peter's ranch wagon drawn by a matched pair of mules. Laura, Rebekah, Mr. Sam, Wilton, and little Lyndon rode with Maggie. Peter, Winifred, and Cousin Flournoy, who was visiting from San Marcos, lumbered along behind in Peter's wagon, which groaned and squealed beneath the weight of the camping gear.

The great dome of Enchanted Rock could be seen from miles away. It seemed out of place, as if God had dropped it accidentally here on the way to the Sierras where He had intended it to be. Laura's first impression was of the top of a skull, a giant buried standing up in a grave too shallow to cover the top of his head. From a distance, the skull-shaped mountain seemed barren, but as they drew closer, they could see a great variety of life growing along its base and even in islands along the approaches to its summit. They passed through stands of gnarled, wind-twisted oaks and junipers, through fields of bellflower and golden coreopsis along the lower slopes. Overhead, literally scores, perhaps even hundreds, of black turkey vultures circled and Laura wondered how much death it would take to amass so many carrion scavengers.

The rising road became dangerously impassable. They stopped about a mile and a half from the rock, parked the automobile and continued on in the wagon and on foot. When they reached the base of Enchanted Rock, there remained a mile-long climb to the summit. They shouldered their quilt bedrolls and other gear and began the climb. They planned to spend the night on the summit of the mountain after watching the sunset and then Halley's comet emerge from its distant darkness. It was a hard climb, steadily upward over wide reaches of gray and pink granite worn smooth by the wind and water of a million years or more. Mr. Sam carried baby Lyndon. And Wilton sometimes struggled along after his father, but was more often carried. Here and there the stone was stained by patches of green or red lichen. It made the mountain seem to be rusting away in the sunlight. They passed small, dry depressions in the stone where seeds had taken root and grasses, herbs, cacti and wildflowers grew, somehow surviving on this barren mountain from one rain to the next. They climbed on, Winifred and Flournoy so far ahead Laura could see only their silhouette against the sky. She and the older climbers stopped now and again to catch their breath and observe behind them how the landscape changed as they climbed higher.

Once they were startled by an explosion of sound and motion

within a hummock of wild Texas persimmon and lavender. First, guttural growling, then the beat of wings and the raucous cry of vultures vying with wild dogs for raw meat. Three gaunt hounds struggled to prevent the vultures from tearing away pieces of what had been a small deer. The explorers hurried on up the mountain.

Laura felt that reaching the summit of Enchanted Rock was what it must be like looking down at the world for the first time from Heaven, or from the wings of the Ezekiel Flying Machine. There was a weary, yet triumphant, sense of having made it so high against all odds, and a view that surely only angels had shared before. "I now have absolute proof the world is round," Laura told Rebekah as she looked out at the green horizons all around. She sank to the stone surface of the mountaintop, breathing heavily, feeling how the sun had warmed the granite. She took a long drink from their water bottle.

The group paused for a long time, looking out at a landscape that was no different now than it had been when the Comanches first came so many years ago. There was no sign, for miles and miles around, that there were any other people in the world at all. To the north, afternoon showers formed a blue-gray curtain undulating before the horizon. Overhead, the sun streamed down through soft white cotton towers. On the crest of the summit huge boulders stood, poised, and Laura felt a finger force could set them rolling. She watched the vultures circle, their great wings sometimes lost in the sun's golden halo, sometimes nearly motionless in the rising thermals.

After being warned about steep drop-offs and stone slides that ended in precipitous cliffs, and urged not to enter the dark caves where rattlesnakes and bottomless pits might be, Winifred and Flournoy went off to explore. Laura worried about the cliffs and the dogs, but then the majesty of the view made her forget her concerns.

Both Peter and Mr. Sam had been to Enchanted Rock before. As the day began to fade and shadows lengthened in the world they had abandoned below, Peter told them about the fear the Comanches had for the mountain. "In some legends, they held it to be sacred," he said. "They would come here once a year to worship. They'd come from all over the West and hold their rites on the summit, right up here where we're sitting. Other legends said they feared this place so much the people wouldn't venture up past the base. They say a tribal chief sacrificed his daughter up here to please the gods. The gods became angry and killed the chief and now the spirits of the chief and his daughter walk the summit forever. They swear you can hear their footsteps at dusk."

"We'll hear them, too," Mr. Sam said. "I've never known a single soul who's been up here who hasn't heard the footsteps."

Laura and Rebekah talked about their children, especially Lyndon and Wilton, who were napping now, exhausted from the climb. "Do you think they'll be good friends?" Laura asked.

"Of course, they will. Like their fathers."

"Do you ever dream of what Lyndon will be? What his life will be like?"

"He'll be a good man, like his father. A strong man who cares for others. A person who explores all the possibilities the world has to offer. Like Sam, but maybe more."

Laura looked over at her friend and was vaguely annoyed that Rebekah would be critical of Mr. Sam, even if in such a small and subtle way. She said, "More than Sam?"

Rebekah lay back on the warm stone, shaded her eyes with her hand. "All my life I've loved to read the stories of Homer. The great epic lives of *The Iliad* and *The Odyssey*. I think what excites me about those lives is that they were heroic, Homer's characters left deep footprints. I think it would be terrible for a man to live a life and leave no footprints."

"Mr. Sam has left footprints."

"I know. I'm not saying he hasn't. But Lyndon's will be deeper and wider. His life will be heroic. I have no doubt he will achieve great things. Deeds that will be remembered forever. Like the characters of Homer."

"How do you know all this?" Laura was amused.

"Because I insist," Rebekah said with a smile. "I demand it. It's the responsibility of mothers to shape the futures of their sons. We are the authors of our sons' lives."

Laura wished she was as confident about Wilton's future. She looked down at her sleeping son, seeking some sign, but all she saw was a small, frail child who came to her at a time in her life when his siblings had nearly depleted her parenting energy, certainly her confidence.

Eventually, as always, the subject of their children came around to Winifred. "How does she enjoy teaching?" Rebekah asked.

Laura looked out to where her oldest daughter was lost in the afternoon sunlight. "I'm afraid she had to stop teaching. It was a fairly brief career."

"Oh, I'm so sorry. She's so bright. I thought she would love teaching school."

"I'm not absolutely certain what happened. They asked us to come get her."

Rebekah was silent. The vultures whirled.

"They said Winifred would assemble the class and then she would refuse to speak. She would just stand there looking at the children, not saying a word. They said we should come get her and take her home."

"Did Winifred explain?"

"She said they lied. That she *was* teaching. She said she was reaching the brighter students with her mind. She was speaking to them with her mind and they were listening and learning."

"I'm so sorry," Rebekah said. "She's such a beautiful girl and she's so sweet to me."

"The hard thing is that she changes so completely. Sometimes she's all right and I think everything will be fine. Then she has one of her spells and it starts all over again. The anger. The fights. Depression. I get so tired of trying to be understanding. Walking on tiptoe around her. Making sure I don't offend her and get her all stirred up again. I just don't know what we'll finally do."

"She and her cousin Flournoy seem close."

Laura watched Winifred and Flournoy in the distance. They were holding hands, both tall and slim. Winifred wore a gingham dress; Flournoy, as usual, wore trousers. "Flournoy is the first friend Winifred ever made. I think they get along because they are both so very bright. And they're both so very lonely. I think they see themselves as two against the world. Poor Flournoy. You know about Flournoy, I suppose."

"Know what?"

"Oh, I don't know how to say it. There's a word for it but I can't say it. I can hardly think it. But once in every million, million lives, God, for some reason beyond our understanding, creates both Adam and Eve in the same person."

"Both Adam and Eve?"

"Oh, Rebekah. Both male and female."

"Oh. Hermes and Aphrodite, like in the myth."

"But real."

"Can you be sure?"

"Yes. It's the scandal of Peter's family. They deny it publicly, but Peter says it's true."

Rebekah looked out to where Flournoy and Winifred were watching the lowering sun. Their heads were very close. They could have been whispering secrets. Laura followed Rebekah's gaze.

"Peter said when Flournoy was little, he always thought she was the most beautiful little girl imaginable. She dressed in frilly gowns. Had long curls. But she was a terribly troublesome child. Always in trouble for some mischief. She preferred to play with boys and was always fighting and being terribly unladylike. At first everyone thought she was simply a tomboy. But when she was about ten years old, she began wearing boys' clothes. At first she was punished and was forced to wear dresses again. But she would rebel and was constantly punished. Peter said everyone thought Flournoy was just naughty or peculiar. Only later, to the consternation of the family, did the truth leak out."

"How very sad," Rebekah said.

"Peter has always been good to Flournoy. He invited her to spend a few weeks last summer, mainly to get her away from Peter's sisters. Flournoy and Winifred became instant kindred spirits."

"Winifred seems to be happy."

"I encouraged their friendship," Laura said. "Now they're inseparable. The only time Winifred does seem happy is when she's with Flournoy. God knows if I've done right or not."

The campers spread their bedrolls on the warm stone as they waited for the sun to set. Peter started a fire for coffee and a dinner of salt pork and dried apricots. Together, the two families watched the featureless golden fire of the sun sink toward the western horizon, lose its heat, constrict like an eagle folding its wings, grow round and red and cut down into the earth, leaving a great sprawling crimson sky behind. Then they heard the footsteps of the Comanches.

It sounded at first like someone was throwing stones. Sharp reports, rock on rock, the sound of Indians making arrowheads. Then the air was buffeted by drumming, deep poundings within the mountain. Alarmed, Laura looked for Winifred. She and Flournoy were two thin dark crosses against the red sunset. They stood at the very highest point of the mountain, facing the abyss. Appalled by a sudden overwhelming dread, Laura thought of the sacrificed daughter whose footsteps made the mountain tremble. Her fear was reflected in her face and Peter hastened to explain the sounds.

"It's just the rock cooling. It contracts as it cools. That's what we hear. That's all."

But Laura could not shake an awful premonition that clung to her mind like a foul shroud. She rose and walked stiffly to where Winifred and Flournoy stood at the edge of the cliff. Her limbs were paralyzed by the fear that they would leap over the edge, bound by some ghastly covenant. "Stay where you are! Don't move!" Her voice broke into a sob and it was only as she drew close that she could see the innocent surprise on her daughter's face. As she joined Winifred and Flournoy looking over the canyon, she heard the dogs and a new fear rose above the old. Sharp barks and growling intermixed with the snapping and booming of the cooling mountain.

Not far across the stone the dark shapes of the wild dogs moved. The sunset reflected red in their eyes. The vultures circled and wheeled, hovering above the dogs. The mongrels clam-

bered forward, moving closer, teeth bared, their hackles like
wire. Laura stood now with Winifred and Flournoy in the near
darkness, cringing as the wild dogs were obviously rushing
toward them. She remembered the sight of the vultures and
dogs fighting for the flesh of the small deer. She heard a howl of
terror heave from her daughter's throat as the buzzards swept
down closer, so close Winifred covered her head with her arms
and Laura could feel the wind of their wings.

As Laura reached for Winifred, she could see Mr. Sam out of
the corner of her eye, wading into the bounding, pouncing
hounds. A sharp vise gripped at Laura's ankle and ripped at her
flesh and she fell, rolling, her arms protecting her face. As the
dogs snapped at her wrists, she fought her way to her feet again,
her mind filled with the savage guttural growling of the dogs. She
no longer felt pain and decided briefly that she might be dreaming. But if it was a dream, she wondered, *then why am I bleeding
so?* Laura did not remember her head hitting the rock. The last
thing she did remember before losing consciousness was Mr.
Sam kicking a howling hound into the air, then shooting another
with his pistol. The wounded dog fell heavily at Laura's feet,
spinning, twisting across the stone trying to bite its pain.

Laura was only partly conscious as Peter and Rebekah washed
her wounds and assured her that Winifred and Flournoy were
not injured by the dogs. Before she could look away, she saw the
ragged, puckered gashes on her wrist and calf, the skin surrounding the wounds the color of cement. Her hands burned and
she could smell the stink of dogs and feel the hounds' hot, heavy
breath; then she heard someone nearby crying and low voices
arguing about an immediate return down the mountain to a
doctor or waiting until morning. She heard words like infection
and the leaving of scars and who would carry the babies in the
dark. Then she felt she had been set on fire as Mr. Sam poured
the Devil's blessed brew out of his secret silver flask into her
wounds.

Mr. Sam made a stretcher of tent poles and canvas and they
began the slow tortuous descent down the mountain. Laura was
only partially aware of their progress. She wandered in and out

from behind heavy hot pillars of cloud, not really losing consciousness again, but losing instead her sense of what was real. She heard the gravelly footfalls and stones set tumbling and harsh whispered calls of her family back and forth. A child, probably Lyndon, bawled out some infant need. Occasionally, Rebekah's face, near and beautiful, smiled down cautious comfort then moved away revealing a night sky filled with diamonds. Soon Laura found herself sinking into dreadful, bottomless dreams of delirium and she became aware that Carnoviste and Quint and Al Lackey were walking beside them in the starlight. Surely they had been appointed by Satan to carry her home to the fires of hell which she could already feel licking at her legs and hands. Within the flames, a bride all in white stood facing away, the groom beside her. As Laura drew near she could see the bride was Winifred. The groom turned toward his bride to place a ring on her finger. It was Flournoy, tall and handsome as a palace guard.

When they reached the base of the mountain, they laid Laura in the backseat of the Oldsmobile. They had already planned to take her to Fredericksburg where the doctor who had delivered Winifred would be awakened. Maggie got in the driver's seat. Peter slipped into the back, carefully raising Laura's head into his lap. The motor ground and coughed gray vapors and then chattered into life. They ground away, wallowing and leaping over the rough road, Carnoviste, Quint, and Al Lackey running alongside.

From the open car, lying on her back, Laura could see all the way to the end of the universe. There seemed to be a strange sheen to the province of night sky north of the constellation of Orion. Then a spectacular shower of stars, a scattering of diamonds in the ordered architecture of the universe. The night was clear and warm. They flew by hills laced with starlight. And then Laura saw what had not been seen in the Hill Country for seventy-six years. Above the bounding Oldsmobile was the white, flowing mane of Halley's comet, easing across the void. *Surely this can't be the end of the world,* she thought. *The night is far too beautiful.* But then she heard the hard breathing of

Carnoviste, Quint and Al Lackey, and as if to outrun them once and for all Maggie pressed for more speed, but it was too late, and Laura was grasped by powerful hands and torn from the car and hurled into the ditch by the side of the road.

Laura heard what seemed like the ticking of a clock. She opened her eyes and saw a wheel turning black against the glowing sky. She wondered what the wheel was, and why Peter was calling out to God so many times in a row, and why she was lying on the earth next to her sister whose eyes were wide and staring through a tracery of blood.

Two months after Maggie's funeral, the scars on Laura's hands and legs had nearly disappeared. But the scar left on her soul would not heal. Laura blamed herself for Maggie's death and sometimes wished her injuries had left horrible scars, like badges, a form of punishment for what she had done. The entire incident on the mountain and on the road to Fredericksburg seemed so tragically unnecessary. At Maggie's funeral, when Laura dressed and ventured out of the house for the first time following the accident, Winifred had said, "Why, you're hardly hurt at all." Winifred had insinuated that there had been no reason for the reckless race through the night to get Laura to the doctor. After all, her wounds were trivial, especially when compared to the mortal ones Maggie had suffered.

In the days after the funeral, Laura rose each morning, prepared breakfast for the family, then lost herself in the tedium of cleaning and tending and doing little more than what the day demanded. She tried to recall every moment that she had spent with Maggie, every word they had spoken together over the years, and realized they had really not known each other at all. Perhaps it was the difference in their ages, but she realized she and Maggie had been little more than strangers, their lives passing, touching, but leaving little on which to hang the portraits of memory. Laura tried to remember her first awareness of Maggie, but the image became confused with the faces of her own children. She was ashamed to admit to herself that most of what she remembered about Maggie was envy. Her little sister had come along at a time when the hardscrabble of family life had softened. Her father had lost the cold hard edge of his bitterness. The Hill Country itself had mellowed. There were no more bears along the creek bottoms or Indians on the rampage or mad trappers lurking in the wilderness. Maggie had gone to college in California, had seen the world, had driven across Texas in an automobile. Her life had been easy, but she had died hard, and Laura knew who was to blame.

As the days passed, Laura realized she had panicked on the mountain. She had been overcome by her fear of what Winifred might do, and the thought of the wild dogs now made her weak and sick. She had been so engulfed with the horror of the moment that she could not remember now if she had even thought of Wilton's safety. She would ask herself: *what could be worse than to be savaged by the mindless, slathering jaws of mad dogs?* Then the answer would come upon a flood of shame. And the answer was *death*.

For several months, Peter was solicitous of Laura's mood. Laura knew he talked more softly in her presence. He filled silences with uncharacteristic chatter about the small forgettable incidents of daily life. There were times when his transparent efforts to bring her back from her malaise annoyed her and she was cross or unresponsive. Soon, Peter found more and more errands outside in the barns or in the fields and took refuge with his horses.

One autumn afternoon, when the first maple leaves were beginning to turn, Laura's brother John Carlton brought Little Mattie to visit. He called from the yard while Winifred and Laura were washing dishes. Laura had just scolded her daughter for dropping a saucer and claiming she half-believed Winifred had broken it on purpose. Winifred's response had been to let a cup slip from her fingers to the floor before turning and traipsing to her room. That was when John Carlton called, and Laura waited at the kitchen door, drying her hands and dreading the thought of facing the mother of her dead sister. She had avoided Little Mattie at the funeral and had not seen her since.

Little Mattie seemed smaller than ever, like a sparrow, wrapped in her dark shawl. As John Carlton tended the mules, Little Mattie moved into the house toward where Laura waited. Looking neither left nor right, she walked directly into Laura's arms and Laura was astounded at how frail her mother had become. Always tiny, she now seemed to be no larger than a starving child. It was like holding a bundle of straw and lavender. Laura wondered that a person could live and survive in such an insubstantial temple of flesh and bone. Laura held tight and they swayed in the kitchen doorway and she could feel a force within her grasp that seemed to grow more and more formidable and comforting. She felt the years falling away. She was a child again in the encircling sanctuary of her mother's arms. She felt tears coming, tears she had not shed since Maggie's death, and they flowed down onto the black tulle netting of her mother's hat. They stood in the kitchen doorway for a long time. Laura reached within the center of her being for the words to tell her mother how badly she felt, how desperately she wished she could bring Maggie back alive again.

"Mama," Laura finally said. "The dogs went mad. I'm so terribly sorry."

Peering around her daughter into the kitchen, Little Mattie patted her daughter on the shoulder. "Don't be silly. It's only a dish. I've broken a thousand of them in my time." Little Mattie then took off her hat and her shawl, rolled her sleeves up one turn and asked where Laura kept the dustpan.

16 ∞ THE DAY OF THE MONARCHS

THE HARD DULL EDGE OF LAURA'S GRIEF LINGERED ON UNTIL the day she would always remember as the day of the monarchs. It was not that her sorrow had fled, but after she and Edward House experienced that magical encounter out on a deserted bend of the Blanco River, thoughts of Maggie's death no longer had the force to drub her nearly to her knees. Her grief altered, softened, even sweetened, and her thoughts of Maggie became quiet conversation, as if Maggie had entered her mind and not the earth.

Peter had returned to the Wilderness Ranch to brand horses. He had taken the boys, even little Wilton, who had been taught to ride before he could walk. It was the first time in five years she had spent an entire day without Wilton at her side. She smiled when she thought of her little man riding with his brothers. She remembered how she and Charles and John Carlton had raced along the river bottom, Miss Ruth's gait smooth and gentle, as if the old horse had been carrying a teacup, not a tomboy. Laura knew Peter and the boys were going to give Wilton his first horse. When she had prepared to accompany them, she could tell from their evasive manner that they did not want her along. It was a rite of passage restricted to the male species, she realized, and was miffed, yet proud, that her little boy was embarking on his journey toward manhood. Finally, it was agreed she would ride out to meet them after several days had passed.

Winifred was visiting Flournoy in San Marcos and Laura had the house to herself. For the first two days that Laura was alone she rattled around the house like a fallen leaf. She felt insubstantial and without purpose, adrift upon the capricious and ungovernable winds that breathed through her life. Once Little Mattie had told her that when hard times came, bringing their inevitable hours of regret and bemoaning, the first thing to do was to write down your blessings on paper. Laura removed a few sheets of writing paper from the secretary, then, feeling that she had been overly optimistic, she put all but one sheet back. She sat at the kitchen table, wrote "BLESSINGS" at the top of the page and then she sat for a long time, writing nothing else, the ink drying on her pen.

Laura was still staring at the page when she heard the buggy. She moved to the window and was surprised and not entirely pleased to see Edward House approaching. When he reached the gate, he paused, seeming puzzled by the uncharacteristic absence of activity around the homestead. For a moment, he appeared uncertain; possibly he considered turning away, and suddenly Laura felt desperate for company and was afraid he would ride away and leave her to her empty list of blessings. She moved quickly to the door and rushed out into the sunlight, hoping that her haste would not be noticed.

As House dismounted, Laura was surprised at his appearance. Before, on his visit to their home, and again when she had seen him in San Antonio, he had been dressed in a suit with starched white collar, silk tie, and a thin gold watch chain across his vest. He had appeared stiff and uncomfortable and the cut of his suit and collar had accentuated the slimness of his neck and the pronounced slope of his shoulders. Now, he was dressed casually, in boots and denim working clothes, and seemed athletic. He moved with an easy grace she had not noticed before. When he took her hand, she immediately recalled the power of his eyes to cast a substance not unlike light ahead of him, as if to prepare a way for the man to come. Standing before her, Laura noticed he was no taller than Herman Lehmann was and blushed, then wondered why.

House explained that he had been visiting his relatives just down the road at the Caldwell place. "I'm sorry I didn't send word I was coming," he said. "But I just couldn't return home without seeing you and Peter."

"Peter's out at the Wilderness Ranch. In fact, everyone is. I've been abandoned by my family."

The lines on House's forehead deepened. "Then I must go. But do give Peter my regards."

Laura realized he was still holding her hand. "You needn't go just yet," she said. She tightened her hand on his for a moment, then turned away. "Come rest a while," she said over her shoulder, looking back to make sure he followed. "You've got a long way to go. I'll fix you a cup of coffee."

At the kitchen table, Edward House asked of each member of the family in turn, seeming to show genuine interest in their exploits and activities. He was especially pleased that Winifred had been teaching. Laura neglected to say that her daughter had been dismissed ignobly from her first teaching position.

"Winifred is a beautiful girl," House said. "I think she and young Rob Caldwell would make an excellent match."

Laura was amused at House's suggestion. "Well, your nephew and Winifred have been neighbors all these years. They've known each other since they were small children. There's been nothing to suggest any special attraction so far."

"That's because they've been too close. Neighbors rarely marry. They know each other too well. Magic requires some distance."

"So you suggest we keep them apart so they'll fall in love? That *would* be magic." Laura laughed at the suggestion, looking closely into House's eyes to see if she were being teased.

"My dear Laura. There's a great deal of similarity between love and politics. It's all a matter of bringing people together. Forming coalitions and alliances. A good politician is essentially a master marriage broker."

Laura loved the idea of the Woods and Caldwell families joined in an alliance. But she still was not sure if House was serious. "Do you seriously propose . . ."

"Oh, no. Rob will have to do that. But what you and I can do is set the stage. With appropriate subtlety, of course."

"Winifred has never found me particularly subtle."

"Then leave it to me. I'll put a bug in Rob's ear. An arrow in his heart. Before you know it we'll be related. Your grandchildren will be my nieces and nephews."

"That will make you and me, what?"

"That will make us," House paused. Laura thought she saw his composure slightly shaken as he searched for a word to define what their relationship would be should Winifred and Rob marry. "That would make us confidants. Or, as Cicero said, we would be each to the other a second self."

Neither spoke for a long moment. Laura listened to the wooden ticking of the clock in the living room. A wagon rattled by on the road toward town. She kept her eyes averted, not wishing to see what House's eyes might contain, nor wanting him to see what hers might reveal. She felt a tremor of excitement and tried to give it a name. Was it possible there was more behind his words than he had expressed? Even though Laura had been in his presence no more than three or four times, House had become a very good friend. He seemed able to reach inside her with his eyes and his mind, to connect in some way, a very personal way that others could not. It was not a physical connection, but it was sensual as well as intellectual. She knew that he admired her, and he cared about her, too. Laura looked down at her hands and was surprised that she held them together tightly at her breast, as if in prayer. The pressure made the scars on her wrists whiten and suddenly she could hear the growling of the dogs and the sound of tearing metal. She began to tremble.

"Oh, my dear!" House rose and came to her side. "What have I said." He stood above her, touched her shoulder, then took his hand away. "If it's something I said, please accept my most profound apology. I only meant . . ."

Laura shook her head, scattering hot tears. She was shocked and deeply embarrassed that she had somehow lost control. "It's not you, Mr. House. Please forgive me. I don't know what's come over me." House offered his handkerchief and she wiped her eyes.

"I think you do know. Tell me. You can tell anything to your second self."

Laura shook her head again, looked out the window, wondered if she could unburden her heart to this most intimate of strangers.

"I know about your sister," House said quietly, his eyes cast down, his hands at his side. "I didn't speak of her before because I couldn't find the words. I should have comforted you but I was a coward." House returned to his chair. "Tell me what you have been telling yourself, Laura. Let your pain come out in the open. It has been hiding too long."

Laura talked for an hour or more. House sat quietly across the kitchen table, listening, saying little. The words tumbled out like living things, scrambling from some dark source. Laura felt she was listening to the anguish of someone else, not her own, and she was able to consider the words, one by one, objectively, turn them over and examine their underside and their overtones. She told him about the mad dogs and the trip down the mountain and how her injuries were not nearly as bad as they had at first seemed. She found the details of the automobile accident were expressed with more clarity out loud than they had been in her dialogue with herself. She spoke of the funeral and her guilt and the dark abyss of dread she felt each time thoughts of Maggie came sprinting into her mind. Then she stopped, astonished that no more words came.

"Poor, dear Laura," House said. "Your guilt feelings are natural and necessary. But it is a masquerade. Guilt is merely sorrow in its prime. It will use itself up, burn itself out, like a dying star and be gone." Now, he patted her arm.

"I'm sorry I went on so," Laura said. She felt weak, not unlike a child whose fever had passed. "You must think I'm pretty silly. Let me get you some more coffee."

"Do you feel better?"

"I do feel different. Lighter. Embarrassed for sure. I suppose it's true about confession being good for the soul."

"You have nothing to confess, Laura. You are innocent of everything but your innocence."

Into the late morning they talked about Peter's horses and the ranch and about House's wife, Loulie, whom he spoke of with a lively and wistful fondness. Laura found herself growing more comfortable in his presence. She tried to call him Edward and each time she called him Mr. House she expected him to invite her to call him by his first name, but he never did. She supposed it was a way to balance the growing intimacy between them. She had emptied her soul to a man, who was now a dear friend, a man whose first name had never passed her lips.

When Laura mentioned that she was riding out to the Wilderness Ranch that afternoon, House asked if he could ride along. "It would give me a chance to find Peter and talk about an idea I have."

After Laura packed a loaf of fresh-baked bread, sausage, cheese, and a wedge of apple pie into a basket, they drove out into the short shadows of noontide. *He handles the bays nearly as well as Peter does,* Laura thought. House had purchased the team from Peter nearly a year before. Within minutes they were out on the river road and the town of Blanco was gone, had disappeared behind them, swallowed by the rugged hillsides.

As the road followed along white canyon walls near the river, Laura asked about House's effort to get Woodrow Wilson into the White House. "We've talked about love and death," she said. "Now, it's only right we talk about politics."

House told how Wilson's candidacy for president was gaining momentum. "All those years I worked on behalf of Texas governors, and never for a moment looked at the national situation. Now I realize that's where I can be of greatest service. And with Wilson, I've found a candidate I can support wholeheartedly."

"I'm not sure very many Texans will support a man from some foreign country like New Jersey." Laura tried to imagine Woodrow Wilson, with his pinched, stuffy, unfriendly visage striding along the Blanco in his tall silk hat.

"They would support him if they knew him. He's a good, decent, immensely intelligent man. Presidential timber of the highest order. And there's a phrase he sometimes uses in his speeches that won't leave my mind. Woodrow speaks of the states as 'the political laboratories of a free people.' He's willing to give the people his full trust and confidence. I think that's very rare. Teddy Roosevelt runs over the people roughshod. He governs the way he charged San Juan Hill."

"And you think Wilson can win Texas?"

"He can. But not without a lot of help. He'll need the help of folks like you and Peter."

"What kind of help?"

"I'm going to bring Woodrow to Texas. Show him that we're not just cowboys and farmers."

"But we are," Laura laughed.

"But we're more. And I want him to know the real Texas and I want Texas to know the real Woodrow Wilson. Not just this picture in the newspaper of a college professor way off in the East, but a flesh-and-blood fellow who cares about people and their problems."

"What can we do?"

"As chairman of the Blanco County Democratic party, Peter can organize a meeting, a supper, or a barbecue. A social gathering of some sort. Social, but all the local leaders would be there. But first, I'd need you to be my eyes and ears again. Find out what folks, mainly womenfolk, are most concerned about. You take the pulse of the community on such issues as women's suffrage. I think you'll find that women will have an ally in Woodrow."

As Edward House talked about his plans for Woodrow Wilson, he became more and more animated. His voice remained soft, and when the horses crossed a shelf of river limestone, his words were lost in hoof sound and the creaking and complaining of the wheels. But there was a passionate timbre enlivening each phrase, a quiet joy, and pleasant, attractive lines appeared at the corners of his eyes.

"Why do you do it?" Laura asked. "Politics? It takes you away from home. From your family."

"I do it because there's a chance we can make this old world a better place. The world is governed by the ideas and actions of a very small group of human beings. A whole planet dances to the choreography of fewer than two dozen dance masters. So it's important that those two dozen men be the right men. I try to find candidates committed to uplifting the human condition.

Folks I know well from this part of the world. Find that good man and give him the power to change what is in error and preserve what is cherished. I think Woodrow Wilson is the one."

"I envy you."

"You shouldn't."

"You'll be in Washington. Doing important work. It would be good to feel that your life mattered to someone beyond your family."

"Your life matters to me."

"You know what I mean. That when you die your life would have made a difference. You had changed things. Made them better."

Soon they came to a two-mile stretch of the Blanco that Laura had always called the Lily Pond. The water was still and the color of quicksilver. Willows grew along the mossy banks and water lilies floated like green stepping stones for wandering elves. The air carried the sweet, subtle fragrance of the white and yellow and blue lily blossoms riding upon the water. Overhead a pair of orchard orioles frolicked in the heights.

House stopped and Laura could tell he was impressed by the scene. "It's beautiful," he said. "I don't think I've ever seen such a peaceful spot."

Laura was pleased and proud. She thought of the Lily Pond as her own possession, given to her by God. "Sometimes deer come down to eat the lily pads. Maybe they'll join us for lunch." She reached for the picnic basket and swung down from the buggy. They moved to a mossy bank shaded by cypress trees whose reflections cast lace patterns on the still, silver pond. Beyond the far bank, the rocky hills were alive with the purple blossoms of blazing star and clusters of goldenrod. Laura spread a cloth in the center of the place she had always known Eden must have been like.

They ate their lunch in silence, listening to a chorus of frogs and cicadas, watching the luminous dragonflies feed and feeling the embrace of a gentle sun filtered by the narrow light green leaves of the cypress trees.

When they had finished, House lay back on a bed of moss

and Laura packed away the remnants of their lunch. As she rose and smoothed her skirt, a great cloud of monarch butterflies descended. It was as if the goldenrod on the distant hill had taken flight and was blooming now on the wind, like flowers on lifted wings. The monarchs settled down on the lily pads, covering the white blossoms with a living orange veil.

"They follow the rivers down from the north," Laura said. "Between the Guadalupe and the Colorado. It's like a funnel narrowing until it reaches the Blanco and this place. Sometimes millions darken the sky. The Indians' myth says the butterfly is a messenger carrying the human spirit between Earth and heaven." She remembered Herman Lehmann said Laughing Eyes told him about the myth of the monarchs. As she spoke, dozens of monarchs and small yellow and white butterflies descended, settling on Laura's shoulders and alighting in her hair.

"It's magical," House said. "There is magic in this place."

Laura reached out her hand, palm downward, and more butterflies settled on her arm and hand. "No one knows why, but some people seem to attract them. I guess I'm one."

"Do you know the story of Psyche? The old Greek myth?"

Laura shook her head, her eyes never leaving the pastures of feeding butterflies. She was remembering Herman Lehmann, a bittersweet memory.

"Psyche was the most beautiful woman in Delphi. She is often pictured holding a butterfly. She was so beautiful that Venus was jealous and she sent her son Cupid to make Psyche fall in love with the ugliest, most frightening creature in the world. But when Cupid found Psyche, he instantly fell in love. Having failed in his mission, he was afraid to return to his mother, so he ran away." House paused and raised up onto his elbow on the moss. "It's a long story and I can't do it justice. But Psyche falls in love with this man she has never seen. And to win his love she has to undergo terrible hardships. After a long wandering she's united with her lover and they become immortal."

The butterflies were rising now, sated on the nectar of the lilies.

"To become a god or to become a butterfly is much the same.

The butterfly escapes from its chrysalis. Psyche was purified by trouble and sorrow." House paused and turned away from the butterflies and looked into Laura's eyes. "Do you know why I'm telling you this myth?"

Laura thought she knew. "Because the monarchs are here? Because of what I told you this morning?"

"You are Psyche, Laura. Brilliant, troubled, strong. And I promise you, your life will open up full and refreshed. You will emerge from your sorrow and be reborn with wings."

17 ∞ THE TRAIN TO FORT BLISS

THE WEEK HOUSE BROUGHT WOODROW WILSON TO TEXAS WAS both the worst time and the best time he could have chosen. Earlier that year, the federal government announced the formation of a postal service that would provide rural mail delivery to remote farms and ranches throughout the country. In order to qualify, however, the local communities had to have good roads, and in 1911 few Texas towns boasted much more than cattle trails. Now, in November, the time proposed for Wilson's visit, the people of Blanco were consumed with work on the roads, digging out rocks and stumps, filling ruts, repairing fords across creeks, improving drainage in town. Peter Woods had been selected as roadmaster, a position responsible for proving to federal inspectors that Blanco was indeed worthy to be included in the new postal system. Personally, Peter did not care if the roads remained impassable forever. The worse the roads, the fewer the automobiles to spew their appalling poisons and noises along the countryside. But it would be fine to have free and frequent mail in town, and his civic spirit eclipsed his hatred of motor vehicles.

At the same time, Peter was also chairman of the Blanco County Democratic party. It was natural that Edward House bring Peter and Wilson together, and what better time to meet a cross section of Blanco County Democrats than at a meeting of the roadmaster's committee.

This particular meeting was held in the far corner of Hoge Hollow where the Lindendale School stood beneath the linden trees. All morning, Laura had been helping her neighbors on the roads. Peter had assigned sections to the various work parties he had recruited. Laura had asked to be assigned to the work on the river road between Flat Rock and Double Horn Creek, a section along the Blanco she had walked with Herman Lehmann in that half-forgotten summer so long ago. Now she waited for the friend who had said he was her second self and the man who would be president of the Republic.

The little schoolhouse was packed and the crowd overflowed out beneath the trees. As House's new Maxwell approached, Laura was pleased that it did not leap and sway as automobiles had before the road was repaired. Perhaps Wilson, if elected, would remember how smoothly he traveled over Blanco County roads and would put in a good word with the head of the postal service. She glanced at Peter, the roadmaster, and it occurred to her that he just might make an ideal candidate for postmaster.

When Woodrow Wilson stepped from the car, Laura thought she would have recognized him anywhere. He was every inch the scholar. Thin, of medium height and wearing wire-rim glasses, he had a rather pinched face and sour expression, as though he smelled something dead by the road. House had said that Wilson was a solitary man and did not make friends easily. Laura could sense the truth of the description. He seemed terribly uncomfortable in his great black coat. He walked rapidly as if eager to get this difficult encounter behind him. Laura began to wonder at the wisdom of House's choice.

In a sense, she could not blame Wilson for being uncomfortable. Here was a man from New Jersey who had probably never ridden a horse or seen a tarantula or a prickly pear cactus, seeking to win the confidence of a rather rough crowd of Texans. When House introduced Wilson to Peter and then to Laura, she was surprised that, up close, he was taller than he had appeared, and his high forehead, firm mouth, and prominent chin suggested both thoughtfulness and strength.

Following informal introductions, Peter called for quiet and Edward House introduced their guest. He positioned his candidate as a progressive, a political reformer who, as governor, had fought against special interests and corruption.

The old schoolhouse became very quiet when Wilson rose to speak. Outside, the people crowded close to the open windows.

"I suppose many of you are wondering if a man from New

Jersey can have an impact on the issues and needs of lives in the South." His voice was clear, the words flawlessly enunciated. Yet Laura noticed there was an absence of the familiar cadences of the Texas stump, that rhythmical echo of the camp meeting that she so loved to hear.

"It may come as a surprise to you that I was born in Virginia and lived much of my life in Atlanta, Georgia. My good wife, Ellen, is a Georgian. Some of my earliest memories are of the church where my father was minister and where, during the War Between the States, he converted the sanctuary into a hospital for wounded Confederate soldiers."

There was a rising murmur from the crowd, a sound like bees. Wilson walked to the old iron woodstove that stood in the center of the schoolroom. "When I went to college in North Carolina, the campus had been nearly destroyed by the war. We had stoves like this in our classrooms and the students carried their own water and firewood. So it just may be that I am not so distant from you as you might think."

Laura was impressed, but she could tell many in the crowd were offended. Wilson had assumed that Texans considered themselves southerners. He had assumed wrong. People from Virginia and Georgia may be southerners, but Texans are something else again. To his credit, Laura saw from Wilson's expression that he realized his mistake.

"Of course, it would be an ideal world," he said, "if a Texan could represent the interests of Texas in the White House. Perhaps a man as able and honorable as your William Jennings Bryan. But this good man has run three times and three times he has been rejected. I am certain, and your Mr. House has assured me, that if nominated I can be victorious. It is my hope you will settle for a Virginian."

After the brief talk, Peter and Edward House took Wilson out to view the work on the roads. Laura walked between Peter and Woodrow Wilson and was thrilled when the governor, as well as Peter, took her arm as they moved over the rougher sections of the road. They passed a woman carrying a bucket of dirt, another carrying drinking water to a crew of men with shovels.

Wilson paused to watch the woman pass with the heavy bucket. He seemed confused, as if uncertain whether he should offer the woman assistance.

"Don't worry," Laura said. "She'll be fine. We've all taken our turn. Maybe that's another difference between Texas and the rest of the South. Peter will take my arm to cross the road in the most chivalrous manner. He'll also let me take my turn in the road with a shovel."

Later, at a barbecue behind Lindendale School, Wilson was asked about women's suffrage. Winifred had joined the group questioning the candidate about the issues of the day. Wilson said he would push for a constitutional amendment once he was elected.

"I'm not sure that's politically wise these days," someone said. "Why take the risk?"

"Because it's right," Wilson said.

"Are you certain you want to remove women from their throne?" Laura was shocked to hear Winifred ask the curious question. Wilson seemed also surprised.

"Are you referring to Balzac?"

"Woman is a slave," Winifred quoted, "whom we must be clever enough to set upon a throne."

"We are wiser than Balzac now," Wilson said. "We are wiser than Dickens and Zola, writers who were unerring in their depiction of social realities, yet had no talent for portraying women."

"And you can?" It was Winifred again.

"I'm not a novelist."

"But if you were?"

"If I were a novelist I would give my women characters the power to vote their leaders either into or out of office. I would give them the freedom to share in the political process. I would write what is right."

Afraid that Winifred might carry the discussion off in some other obscure direction, Laura asked Wilson who he would appoint to lead the new rural delivery mail service.

"I'm not elected yet," he replied. "But if I win the support of the Texas delegation at the Baltimore convention, it's quite likely

I'll select a Texan. Burleson is an excellent man. His grandfather fought in the Texas Revolution with Sam Houston. His grandfather was a general. The grandson would be my choice as the new postmaster general."

"Why Burleson?" Laura asked. "Because it's right?"

"No," Wilson said. "Because it's politically wise." And for the first time since he had arrived in Blanco, he permitted himself laughter. Laura glanced at Edward House. He was beaming. He had his man.

On the last day of Wilson's visit, before he and House proceeded to Austin, House brought his nephew Robert Caldwell to call. He was a tall young man with the body of an athlete, uncomfortable in his stiff, dark, pinstripe suit. Yet, as the afternoon progressed, Laura noticed that he seemed remarkably comfortable with Winifred. The Caldwells had lived adjacent to Hoge Hollow for years and Winifred and Robert had been schoolmates. They had been teachers together at the Valley School before Winifred had been dismissed. Laura agreed with House that Robert and Winifred would be an excellent match. He was handsome, college educated, and his family was one of the most respected in the county. Laura was disappointed, however, when it became apparent Winifred seemed indifferent to Rob Caldwell. She wondered what kind of man might appeal to Winifred and mourned the fact that she had so little knowledge of her daughter's life. Winifred was in many ways a stranger, a beautiful stranger who shared their home and little else. As Laura watched young Caldwell in his obvious pursuit of the girl, she could not help wondering what kind of marriage they would make. The boy would obviously do well in the world. They would have beautiful children. But there was something vaguely troubling about the thought. Perhaps it was the natural blend of sorrow and joy a mother feels when thinking of her daughter's marriage. Perhaps she feared the moment when Winifred would realize she had traded her freedom of choice for a life in which her dreams must become secondary to those of her husband. Laura watched her beautiful daughter listening impassively to the parlor conversation and felt herself grow sad. It occurred to her that she had no idea what Winifred dreamed or if she dreamed at all. Her daughter was comfortable discussing literature with a scholar of Woodrow Wilson's rank, but had no time for even small talk with her mother.

∞

Edward House had selected his candidate well. With the neutrality of William Jennings Bryan, then his support, the help of the Texas delegates and a promise of a Texan as postmaster general, Wilson was able to defeat Champ Clark of Missouri for the 1912 Democratic nomination. It required all of Edward House's wiles and his most creative maneuverings because Wilson did not win the nomination until the forty-sixth ballot. Of course Laura had written letters to each of the Texas delegates pointing out that Clark was supported by the Tammany Hall machine and the evil empire of William Randolph Hearst.

The next challenge was Roosevelt, the candidate chosen by the Bull Moose convention in Chicago to oppose Wilson and Taft. "Looks like you'll have to choose between your old friend and your new one," Peter laughed.

"It doesn't really matter which one I choose," Laura replied angrily. "I can't vote. Why even think about it."

"Because you care," Peter replied.

Laura felt an obligation to back House's candidate, especially since Wilson was solidly behind women's suffrage and Roosevelt was wavering on the issue. But she remembered every detail of Roosevelt's visits as if they were yesterday, and she kept his hat on the very top of the hatrack in the hall.

Roosevelt still had the old fire that had carried him up San Juan Hill. He created whirlpools of excitement everywhere he went. At one point, early in the campaign, the old Rough Rider called out, "We go to Armageddon to battle for the Lord!" It was as if he saw himself as a divinely appointed leader, a man of destiny. But his destiny was to fall victim to a disastrous split in the Republican party, caused, to a large degree, by the strategies of the man now called *Colonel* E. M. House.

One morning, as Laura was watching a deer moving across the

yard, a rider came galloping up to the Woods's house. Laura had first seen the horseman when he was some distance down the road and knew something was wrong. There is something about the carriage of a courier of bad news that clings to him like a shroud. As Laura moved to the porch and awaited what fate had in store, a memory of Maggie swept through her mind, a dread fragment, and she stood on the porch and waited for the dark rider.

The man leaped from the horse. "Where's Peter?" he called. "Roosevelt's been shot!"

"How bad?"

"Don't know. But he's alive."

The news spread quickly throughout the Hill Country. Roosevelt had been shot by a fanatic named John Schrank. Once again, Laura rode to the Blanco newspaper office to learn the details of the shooting as they came in on the telegraph. After McKinley was assassinated, when she had haunted the telegraph for news of his condition, she had decided to teach herself Morse code and had practiced on a little mechanical key at the newspaper office until she could understand the mysterious coded messages of the new age. Now she awaited news of Roosevelt. Soon the clickety keys revealed that the wound was not serious. Roosevelt had been shot as he was on the way to make a speech. The telegraph reported that when he was urged by physicians to go to the hospital, he replied, "You get me to that speech. It may be the last one I deliver, but I'm going to deliver this one." He made the speech, then was taken to the hospital.

When she was satisfied Roosevelt would recover, Laura left the newspaper and walked across town to the Methodist church to offer a prayer of gratitude. *How vulnerable are our leaders,* she thought. *They are like targets in a world filled with assassins. Maybe we're doing our candidates a disservice to vote them into the public eye where they can be shot down by anyone with a bullet.*

The day following the assassination attempt, Laura contacted Colonel House and instructed him to advise Wilson not to make any more speeches until Roosevelt could recover. "It's the only fair thing to do," she said. Wilson did cancel several appearances and Laura was sure it was on her advice. She also believed it was on her advice that Colonel House sent for Texas Rangers to protect Woodrow Wilson from assassins. Two American presidents had been assassinated in her lifetime and she felt the presence of a Texas Ranger would prevent a third. "Prayer is one thing," she told House. "Rangers are another."

Colonel House sent his old friend Capt. Bill McDonald, one of the last great lawmen of the West. Woodrow Wilson's security men were not pleased when Captain Bill arrived with his Colt .45 revolvers slung low on his hips. They said their .38-caliber weapons would kill a man just as dead as Captain Bill's .45s. The old Ranger replied, "Sure, if you give 'em a week to die in."

On November 5, Laura was at the telegraph office when word came that Governor Wilson had received more votes than the total of those cast for his opponents. Colonel E. M. House had made an unknown college professor president of the United States. For the first time in twenty years, the Democratic party had the power in both the House and Senate to enact the reforms Colonel House thought necessary and that Wilson had promised. Laura was both jubilant and a little sad. As she walked home, she tried to imagine Roosevelt in defeat, and she could not. She wondered where he was and what he was thinking and what he would do now that he was a private citizen. Then the excitement of Colonel House's triumph and the Wilson presidency swept over her like a difficult promise kept. She began to hurry along the road and to formulate the programs she would advise Colonel House to advise President Wilson to make the centerpiece of his presidency.

∞

Two years after Woodrow Wilson had defeated Roosevelt in the election of 1912, Colonel House returned to Blanco. When he arrived at the Hanging Tree Ranch, Laura had just shot a rabbit that had been raiding her garden. There was a cloud of cordite in the air. House sat with Laura while she skinned the rabbit and prepared it for a stew. They talked about their families and any possible signs that Rob might be making progress in his pursuit of Winifred, but House wasted little time in getting to the main point of his visit.

"There's something the president would like for you and Peter to do."

Laura looked up from the carcass. "The president?" She shivered, a trickle of excitement lightly walking up the back of her neck. Maybe this is what Colonel House meant when he said her life was about to change.

"Where's Peter?"

"Inside."

"We need to talk then."

"In the kitchen."

Laura gathered up the quartered carcass, washed the pale meat in water from the well, then led Colonel House into the kitchen where Peter was cleaning the rifle Laura had used to shoot the rabbit. Peter rose and the two men shook hands. Laura could hardly contain her curiosity as House told Peter why he had come.

"It's just a matter of time before the United States will have to enter the war against Germany. We're already selling huge amounts of arms to the Allied forces. But now there is another danger. Rumors of an alliance between Germany and Mexico. Now Mexico is in political chaos. The country is overrun with contending bandit armies. Pancho Villa. Emiliano Zapata. Pasqual Orozco."

Laura was well aware of the rise of Villa and Zapata and had heard that the tall, blue-eyed Pasqual Orozco was the most effective, feared, and hated guerrilla leader in Mexico. Villa and Orozco plundered ranchers on both sides of the border. Both were constantly crossing into Texas, raiding homesteads, seeking arms and ammunition. They were reportedly seen as far north as San Antonio and their agents lobbied for support in New York and Washington.

"If an alliance could be forged between Germany and Mexico, the Kaiser would have an ally right on our southern border. An ally that hates Texas. If there is anything that would unite the guerrilla leaders of Mexico, it would be to join forces in a holy war to reclaim Texas. At the very least, it would divert our attention from Europe. We'd have to send troops to Fort Bliss. A massive Mexican movement against the border, armed and financed by Germany, would be a disaster."

"We would have to fight on two fronts," Peter said.

"Or delay our support of the European allies."

"Another war with Mexico."

"Of course, your friend Teddy Roosevelt is spoiling for a fight," Colonel House said.

"Always is," Peter laughed.

"Says he wants to come out of retirement and lead a regiment against Pancho Villa. My own feeling is that our troops on the border are spread too thin. Orozco and Villa seem to have the run of the border as it is. We need more troops."

"And more horses," Laura added, washing the rabbit's blood from her hands. "That's what you're after, isn't it?"

"Exactly."

"How many?" Peter rose and looked out toward the corrals. Laura knew he had just completed his spring sale in San Antonio. He had invested the profits in land, not more horses. He had no more than one hundred of his own.

"Say four hundred. The best you can provide. The same quality you provided Teddy Roosevelt."

Before Colonel House boarded a train for his return to Washington, an informal agreement had been made. Peter would find, purchase, and, when necessary, train four hundred horses and deliver them to the Fort Bliss army post in El Paso.

As Peter began his search for quality horses, the Rio Grande seemed suddenly very close to the Hill Country. It was not unusual for Texans to follow events in Mexico very carefully. History had demonstrated time and time again that what happened in the one country had profound implications for the other. Texas and Mexico were inseparably bound by geography and by the spilling of blood. Laura had heard the stories about Orozco and the blood-red flag carried at the head of his troops. His men were known along the border as Orozco's Colorados. She had been in the newspaper office a few years before when the telegraph wires carried the story of the Paso Malo Canyon massacre. Orozco and his men had derailed a train filled with federal soldiers. One thousand men were killed, one by one, many with machetes. It was reported that blood ran ankle-deep in the railroad cars. Orozco ordered the dead men stripped. He sent the bloody uniforms to President Díaz in Mexico City with a note that read: "Here are the wrappings. Send me more tamales."

As the bloodletting along the border had escalated, life at the Woods place had glided along on its charmed path. Much to her surprise, Laura realized that Peter had grown quite wealthy, not only in land but in cash from the sale of horses. He would have become wealthier if he had not continually reinvested his profits in more horses and land in the attempt to improve the quality of his bloodlines. Quite often he would hear of a blooded German coach horse with the qualities he needed for breeding and would make the long, hard ride to the auction lots in Austin or San Antonio where he would bid for a carload of light harness horses.

Peter Woods catered to the "carriage trade." His reputation, always excellent, had been made secure by his sale of horses to Teddy Roosevelt. And although he had once dealt in mules and horses for heavy draft and for the plow, he now was known primarily for the finest of light horses used for pleasure, even hunters and jumpers. Still, the great majority of Peter's horses were bred, though not specifically for war, with those qualities of courage, speed, and endurance most desired by the cavalry officer. Here were the horses with the blood of Arabia and of the Wild Horse Desert of South Texas and of the Billy Horse of Central Texas.

In order to purchase enough horses for the Fort Bliss contract, Peter had to borrow against his land, including a mortgage on the Wilderness Ranch where Laura had spent so many lonely months when they were first starting out. In addition to those horses with Arabian blood that he had bred on his own ranch, he purchased a herd of fine cow ponies from a ranch near Geronimo, Texas. By midsummer, he had negotiated with ranchers far and near, gathering a remuda of the finest horseflesh in central Texas.

Suddenly, the sleepy little town of Blanco, which rarely had more than three or four visitors at a time, was swarming with cowboys and spectators. The glory days of the Texas cowboy were past and it had been years since the last great cattle drive, yet there were many old drovers from neighboring outfits still around, and these joined Peter's regular hands. Maxey Charles, Eugene, and young Butch Neill, who had comported himself so admirably on the ill-fated San Antonio drive of 1908, spent long days breaking the wiry little Spanish cow ponies. Peter and Laura recruited their friend Valentine Smith to train Peter's quarter horse stock. To Laura, it was like old times. It reminded her of that wonderful summer when she was a girl and Peter hired her to help him on his ranch. Now she was outside again, in the dust and sunlight, wearing her high-neck calico dress, black tooled-leather riding boots, her wide western hat, her hair in a single braid down her back. Side by side with the man she loved, she worked with the horses and prepared for the greatest gamble of their lives.

As time for shipment drew near, Peter, Valentine Smith, and Laura studied maps of the way west long into the night. It was no longer possible to drive a herd to San Antonio. The open country had been locked away by fences. They would drive the horses to nearby Marble Falls and load them on the railroad spur to San Antonio. Then, the long, six-hundred-mile haul from San Antonio to El Paso would be on the tracks of the Galveston, Harrisburg and San Antonio Railroad, a part of the Southern Pacific "Sunset Route" across America.

Peter insisted that only eight horses be carried in each car, and that special stalls be built within the cars for each animal. Since the railroad cattle cars handled more than five times that number of steers, the railroad thought this would be a waste of valuable cargo space and a waste of Peter's money, but Peter was adamant. "It's a long hard ride," he told the officials of the Galveston, Harrisburg and San Antonio Railroad. "Those horses aren't going to do anybody any good unless they get there healthy and ready to ride."

"It's gonna be mighty thirsty out there in July," Valentine

pointed out. "That's dry country. The rail line mostly follows the old San Antonio–San Diego stage line. So there'll be water right along. At least most of the ways. Where there's not, the railroad has water tanks. Some got water, some don't."

"What about rivers?" Laura asked.

"There's the Ataskosa just a little way out. Then the Sabinal and the Nueces before Del Rio. Then we go along the Rio Grande for awhile, down in the canyons to the Devil's River, then the Pecos. From there to Alpine, it's bone dry. And it's dry from there on until we meet the Rio Grande south of the Sierra Blanca Mountains."

"Not even streams? Creeks?"

"Well, there is. But in July there won't be a swaller of water in any of 'em. Not that you can depend on. Just dry arroyos 'cept after a rain. Summer thunderstorms. Then likely as not there'll be so much water the rails'll get washed out."

"We'll have to depend on the railroad water tanks."

"That locomotive's gonna need water just like the horses."

For a while Peter and Valentine seemed to skirt the issue of Orozco and the violence along the border. It was never far from Laura's mind, primarily because she was afraid Peter would not let her make the trip because of the danger. She knew he was putting off a decision. On the Fourth of July, when they had returned from the annual parade in town, Peter, in Laura's presence, asked Valentine about the possibility Orozco might try to stop the train.

"Well, he's done it before," Valentine said as he folded his long frame into an easy chair and began rolling a smoke. "Bad Pass Canyon. But that was in Mexico. I doubt he'd try it in Texas."

"There's no guns. No supplies. No soldiers," Laura said. "There's just horses. And he can steal all those he wants without risking a fight."

"He may not want our horses," Peter said. "But he sure doesn't want soldiers at Fort Bliss to have 'em."

"Or Pancho Villa," Valentine added. "Orozco might scatter the horses just to keep Pancho Villa from stealin' 'em. Those two hate each other about as bad as two men can." Valentine exhaled a blue wreath of smoke. "What about a military escort?"

"That'd make us a target. Soldiers attract soldiers, guns attract guns. Our chances are better if it's just our outfit."

"Gonna be hard to defend a train that long," Valentine said. "I figure with only eight horses per car, it's gonna take fifty cars. Near on a half-mile of rollin' stock."

They followed the route of the tracks on the railroad maps as they cut from San Antonio toward the border. For much of the way it followed the Rio Grande, through remote canyons where the train would be vulnerable to attack. Peter's finger traced the route, then stopped at Pecos. "I sure wish there was a way to get across the Pecos without going over the Pecos River bridge. It's the third highest bridge in the world. A train fallin' down into the river from there sure would make an awesome splash."

That night, after Valentine had gone home, Peter and Laura lay awake, not touching, but each intensely aware of the other. Laura listened to the night and to Peter's thoughts. Then she turned to face him. His eyes reflected the moonlight.

"Peter, it's right that I go, too. It's the right thing for us."

"I don't know."

"It is the crowning moment of our lives together. All we've worked for all these years. It's something we have to do together. I know you're afraid for me. Feel guilt about putting me in danger. But it's what I want, and what I need. The horses are my life, too."

Peter continued to stare into the darkness above the bed. "What if it goes bad? What if . . ."

Laura touched him now. "Peter, it won't go bad! Nothing that can happen can be bad. Not if it happens to us both. Not if we're together."

On July 21, 1915, as Orozco's Colorados were riding toward the little town of Bosque Benito, south of Sierra Blanca, and as the locomotive of Peter's train began to cough its ebony breath onto the crowd of well-wishers in San Antonio, three desperate-looking characters showed up at the railyard. Laura thought they seemed vaguely familiar. The first cowboy handed Peter a folded, dog-eared letter, grimy with sweat and trail dust. Peter read it aloud to Laura and Valentine. "Thought you might need some Rough Riders. Godspeed." It was signed, TR.

Laura looked up at the knot of tough old men and then smiled a welcome to Rattlesnake Pete, Cherokee Bill, and Dexter Slade, the one-eared ex-marshal from Dodge City.

The train moved out over the familiar landscape toward Del Rio and the border. The long serpentine line of cars swayed over the hills, past Hondo, and Laura mourned the diminishing greens of the Hill Country. She had always marveled that nature could paint so many different varieties of green. A whole spectrum could be seen on a single hillside. Now they were moving through a landscape of muted olive and ocher, through country leaning toward desert. Then they were into Uvalde County where they stopped for water at a siding by the Nueces River. They thundered into the canyons where the Devil's River joins the Rio Grande and the train was dwarfed by the great cliffs soaring vertically toward the sun.

Peter had Slade distribute their extra store of lever-action Winchesters, Marlin carbines, bolt-action Mausers and bandoliers of cartridges to the various guard stations throughout the train. When Valentine, Slade, Rattlesnake Pete, and the others were together, Laura felt they were a fearsome, even invincible force. But when they were spread out along a half-mile train, they seemed a woefully inadequate defense, especially against bandits who could fire down from the cliffs above. But the train passed through the canyons without incident and Laura breathed easier.

They also made the breathless crossing of the Pecos without incident. So high was the bridge that Laura imagined how a hawk must feel on its flight above the earth. Then they stopped at the station in Langtry, where Judge Roy Bean had held his deadly court little more than a decade before.

From Langtry the border fell away to the south and the train wound up heavy grades and curves and tunnels through the rock where it seemed all too logical bandits would be. Each time the train was swallowed by a tunnel, Laura wondered if they would see light again, and they always did, the sunlight welcome as the dawn. The train rolled on into the vast reaches of the Chihuahuan Desert.

As the train coiled into the solitudes of the Texas Big Bend Country and Laura watched the silhouettes of Slade, Valentine, and the others scanning the horizon for trouble, she felt as if she were going to war. Once again, some eighty years after the Alamo, Texas was threatened with invasion from the south. Soon, other trains would be racing through the desert with soldiers from Camp Travis and Camp Bowie, Fort Sam Houston and Fort Crockett. Even the names of the camps, names that resonate within the Texas soul, brought back memories of a time when men and events seemed larger than life. Now it seemed to be happening again.

The train climbed up into Alpine, Texas, and the creosote bush, prickly pear, lechuguilla and crimson-tipped ocotillo of the flatlands began to give way to the grasses, juniper and piñon pines of the Del Norte Mountains. How different this Texas was from any she had seen. It was more like pictures she had seen of Switzerland, and the air was fresh and cool after the hard, sharp heat of the desert.

From Alpine they passed through high rolling grasslands to Marfa, then down into the desert again, and into Valentine, a place Valentine Smith claimed for his family on general principles. From Valentine they moved toward Devil's Ridge and Sierra Blanca and the border. The hands grew more alert and tense. Card games ceased.

One night, as the train clattered through the Texas night, the starlight was so bright Laura could see the peaks of the Cuesta Del Burro Mountains where Valentine said the ghosts of Franciscan friars guarded hoards of Aztec gold. She was riding with Peter in the caboose on a bed of saddle blankets. They had just finished a meal of dried fruit and biscuits and the night was pure as youth and filled with mystery. Somewhere, out in the dark, Pascual Orozco was riding toward some murderous rendezvous. Laura began to feel she had never been more alive. As the train swayed, she could feel Peter's warmth beside her and her love for this strong, good man so filled her heart that tears came to her eyes. She felt like a girl again, holding his hand at the Confederate Reunion. Peter had achieved his dream and now the money they would receive for this new shipment would make them as wealthy as the Colonel-Doctor or Georgia Woods had ever been. She felt, as the train moved on through the dark silence, that her life was racing to a new beginning. She was Psyche and her sorrows were behind her and she was as happy as she had ever been in her secret grotto on Eager Mule Creek. The wheels of the train clattered and rumbled the words "tomorrow, tomorrow, tomorrow."

At dawn the train slowed and moved to a siding at a small maintenance shed and water station across the river from a little Mexican village south of the Arroyo Diablo. The train jerked to a stop. The brakes squealed, the engine wheezed, then rumbled and then grew still. A great silence descended. There was only the sound of frogs from the reeds by the river and the dry sigh of the warm wind from the distant mountains. The heat was already fierce and every living thing along the river began searching for shadow. The horses were restless. They smelled the river.

"Frogs say it's gonna rain," Valentine said. "Spadefoots. They dig way down in the mud. Stay there out of the sun. Some say they can hear thunder way off. Thunder we can't hear. So they come up and sing like that. It'll rain soon."

"Not soon enough," Peter said. "The horses need water now."

Cherokee Bill came back from the water tower. "Been shot up," he said, his eyes sweeping the horizon beyond the river. "Somebody must'a done it recent. Tank's empty. Ground's still wet."

Laura stared out into the rising heat, a shimmering veil hiding the distance. "How far's the next tank?"

"This one's shot up, likely the next one will be, too," Valentine observed.

Peter looked toward the river. The water itself was hidden by willow and bulrush and a few salt cedars. Beyond, the mean adobe houses of the town squatted in the dust. "Slade," he said, without taking his eyes from the river, "see what's there. If there's a place for the horses to get to water and we don't have company, give us a wave." Slade motioned to Cherokee Bill and they moved off toward the river.

They waited. Then Slade signaled. Peter turned his eyes from the river to Valentine Smith. "What do you think?"

"Not much choice."

"Let's get it done, then. One car at a time."

"Gonna take most of the day."

"Then it will," Peter said, and the long process of watering the horses in the Rio Grande began.

The day was like walking too close to a fire. Away from the river the ground was cracked like an old plate. Tough bunches of brown grass punched up through the caked earth and clumps of creosote bush grew in orderly patterns, as if planted by intelligent hands. "Them's a regular doctor's office," Valentine said of the creosote bushes. "Boil them down and you can cure snakebite. Good for sore limbs and stomach cramp, too."

By noon, half of the horses had their turn at the shallow Rio Grande. The men working the horses were drenched with sweat. When they could, they rested beneath the willows along the bank. Sentries had been set to guard both river approaches. Another was posted across on the Mexican side to watch the adobe settlement in Chihuahua. At first, Laura waited in the train, but the heat drove her down to the river where she waded in water that was surprisingly cool. As the day wore on, she longed to find a pool and sink down until she was completely submerged, like she had done as a girl in the Eager Mule. She wondered, *How can a person possibly live in such a place?* She looked over at the town and the houses seemed like headstones in a graveyard.

The sentries reported the first riders in midafternoon, eight horsemen, coming from the direction of the town. Even at a distance, Laura could see their tall peaked sombreros with great rolled brims, high leather boots, and the bandoliers slung across their chests and around their waists. They stopped, moved into a ragged line, then watched, waiting, motionless, as if carved against the horizon from stone.

"Just keep on," Peter said. "We're nearly finished."

More riders came. It seemed to Laura they emerged from the earth itself. Peter called the sentries in. "Just keep on," Peter repeated.

By the time the horses were watered and the last were being loaded back on the cars, there were about thirty riders loosely surrounding the train. "It's Orozco," Valentine said. "Only Mexican I ever saw taller than me."

"What's he want?" Laura asked.

"If he wanted the train he'd have taken it," Peter said.

"Maybe not," Valentine said. "Orozco don't cotton to risk. He likes the odds tilted way over his way."

"So," Peter said. For a long moment he scanned the riders, then stared at the tallest, Orozco, as if trying to see into the bandit's mind. Then he asked Valentine to arm the train crew. "See to it that Orozco knows we've got a lot of long guns here. All up and down the train. Let him know he's going to lose some men if he attacks. And tell the crew in the engine to get up steam."

"You aim to light out?"

"Not yet. Just want to be ready. A runnin' fight'll kill horses. Besides this is as good a place as any to be. They're out in the open. No cover. We'll just stick it out here and see what happens."

Night came to the desert slowly, as if reluctant to relinquish the roseate sunset. A coyote barked. The cry of a child was carried on the wind from the village. From the darkness came laughter, the winking of a distant campfire and the faint moving light of cigars. Stars appeared and the night, though moonless, grew lighter. Inside the caboose, Peter, Laura, and Valentine shared sourdough bread and honey. When they had finished, Peter sent for the engineer.

The engineer was a heavy man, middle-aged, with a round face, tanned on only one side from years of looking out the same window in the engine cab. He carried a Winchester, uncomfortably, as if he was a stranger to guns. Peter offered him coffee and asked him about the station at the side of the track.

"Maintenance shed," he said. "Like a cattleman's line shack. There's a bunk, a stove, some supplies."

"What about a telegraph?" Peter asked, and Laura felt a touch of tension somewhere in her rib cage.

"Usually there is," he said. "Sometimes the Mexicans break in and steal things. But if they ain't, there's probably one there."

Peter turned to Valentine. "How far to Fort Bliss?"

"Forty miles, maybe. Maybe less. With luck, could have troopers here tomorrow."

"Laura?"

"We can try." Involuntarily she flexed her fingers like a pianist prior to a concert.

As Laura and Dexter Slade slid down from the train onto the tracks, she wished the night were darker. The starlight gave a pale iridescence to the desert. She could see the outline of the salt cedars by the river and the silhouette of the water tower. But she could not see the bandits and so she imagined they would not see her as she covered the hundred yards from where the train had stopped back to the maintenance shed. But she had never felt more naked. It was as if she were certain every eye in Mexico and every gun along the border were trained on her as she crouched along behind the one-eared ex-marshal. She was so enlivened by nervous energy that the Marlin carbine she carried was light as a feather. She knew she was terribly afraid, but she was also proud that she was in control of their fate. If she could get a message to Fort Bliss, it would be her skills that would save the day and the horses and maybe their lives. It was a curious blend of very basic emotions and she wondered if that was what men felt when going to war.

The door to the shed was locked. The rusted iron padlock was enormous. Slade led the way to a small window on the river side of the shed. It, too, was locked. Slade broke a window with the butt of his .45 and the breaking glass sounded like a thousand chandeliers falling simultaneously. They froze, listening, and then from the train came another sound of glass breaking, a bottle against the train, and Laura knew Peter was covering the sound of their entry. But they waited, for nearly five minutes, then Slade reached through the window, unfastened the latch, and heaved himself through. His guns rattled loudly against the windowsill and they froze again. From the train came the sound of boards cast down upon the track. Slade pulled Laura into the shed.

Inside, it was dark, black dark, at first. As she waited for her eyes to become accustomed to the starlight sifting in through the window, she wondered if the telegraph batteries would be dead or not, how long it had been since the acid had been changed. Then from the gloom beneath the window, she saw the telegraph station and the key and she began to compose a message in her mind. Out in the dark, someone began to play a harmonica. It sounded terribly close by, maybe right outside the shed. Laura wondered, *How far can the sound of the telegraph key travel in the still desert night?*

Laura began to tap out her message. She knew it was like a cry in the dark, unimaginable that someone was listening to this strange staccato conversation. "T-R-A-I-N S-U-R-R-O-U-N-D-E-D. O-R-O-Z-C-O. D-E-S-P-E-R-A-T-E." She was about to tap out their exact location and the size of the bandit force when she heard a sound that sent a spear of ice into her very soul. The harmonica was joined by a silver note of sorrow, a high, howling trumpet call from the past, and Laura knew that Black Cato was alive, a member of Orozco's band, and he was right outside the shed, then at the door, slamming at the padlock, trying to break into the shed. Then came the explosions. The tin building was filled with thunder and lightning as Black Cato shot off the padlock and Dexter Slade returned fire through the door. Then Slade grabbed Laura's arm and literally threw her through the window. She turned to help him through, and his form filled the window as another rapid series of explosions tore through the night and Dexter Slade seemed to stiffen and shudder and then grow shapeless as he fell at her feet. She reached down to help him up and her hand touched bloody meat. "Go," he said. "I'm kilt." He handed her his .45 and then died.

For the second time, Laura ran for her life from Black Cato. She zigzagged as she ran, hoping to dodge the bullets that never came. Hands reached for her and she was pulled onto the train that was already beginning to gather its slow momentum.

"Slade?" Peter asked.

"He's dead." Laura sighed, looking back toward where he lay in the darkness by the river. She wiped his blood from her hand on her skirt. The train pulled away. The riders followed.

Peter passed word through the train not to fire unless fired upon by the bandits. "Once we start exchanging fire," he told Laura, "we'll begin to kill the horses. We've got to avoid that as long as possible."

The train picked up speed and the riders were left behind. "Why didn't they shoot?" Valentine asked. "I can't figure it out." Then, as they rounded a bend and began to cross a low trestle over an arroyo, the answer came.

Laura was in the caboose, watching the desert race by her window, trying to will her heartbeat into its normal rhythm, wondering if Dexter Slade's shots through the door had hit Black Cato, maybe even killed him, when the stars began to spin and she felt as if the train had become airborne, had left the earth for a trip through the heavens. The sounds grew as thunderous and horrible as the rockets Jules Verne had described. She reached for Peter and then she was hurled violently into a dark and quiet cave. For a long time all she could hear was the cry of escaping steam and dying horses.

When Laura awakened, the night was filled with small red fires and twisted steel and the red, raw flesh of horses and men. Her head was in Peter's lap, her mind was filled with pain and her hair was stiff with what she knew must be blood.

"The boys?"

"Shook up, but all right."

"Thank God," Laura managed to say before darkness touched her mind again.

After a time, when Laura opened her eyes again, Peter laid her head down gently on his folded jacket and then stood and looked down at her with haunted eyes. Laura thought he looked like an old soldier defeated in battle, waiting for someone to surrender to. He moved away, his step heavy and uncertain, his rifle hanging at his side. Painfully, Laura raised herself and tried to call him back but the pain took the words away. Then she heard the shots. At first she thought it was Orozco come to kill them all as he had killed the Federales at Paso Malo Canyon. Then, she knew. She listened to the shots, one by one, and she could feel the terrible bite of the bullets in her breast as Peter began to kill his savaged horses. Laura stood, swayed, found a rifle amid the wreckage, then joined Peter on his terrible rounds. As Laura fired into the horses' broken bodies, she could hear Black Cato's horn wail into the night.

18 ∞ THE SCHOOLTEACHER'S FIRE

AFTER THE LOSS OF THE HORSES, LAURA FOUND HERSELF WORKing from dawn until dusk keeping the family together, keeping the house in order, getting the younger children to school, helping Peter deal with the crisis in his life. Most of their assets had been lost in the desert canyon, more than three thousand acres of ranchland, yet they still had the stone house on the Blanco, the gardens and a few cows, pigs, and chickens. By the standards of the day, they were certainly not poor and Laura knew there were thousands of Texas families that had far less than they. She threw herself into the work of the ranch and tried hard to ignore the fact that her husband was becoming an old man before her eyes.

Not long after the train wreck, Laura and Rebekah sat on Laura's porch watching Peter ride in the distance. Laura thought once more how beautifully he rode, as if he and the horse were a single creature from a fable. But the fable was coming undone.

"The hard thing," Laura said, "is watching the light go out in his eyes."

Rebekah reached for Laura's hand. "It's a terrible thing. To lose everything you've worked for."

"Some of the horses were still alive. They were down in the canyon, trapped in the wreckage or they were so badly injured they couldn't rise. It was like something in Peter died that night, as well."

"Hush. Let it go. Peter's strong, Laura. He'll bounce back."

Laura remembered the first day home after the terrible time in the canyon. She and Peter had walked hand-in-hand out on the familiar land by the river. They had walked in silence. The absence of horses was nearly overpowering. "We'll start again," Laura had said and Peter had smiled and then shook his head.

"The world is changing, Laura," he said as they walked through the empty pastures. "The streets are filled with automobiles now. The day of the horse is over. There are tractors to plow the fields. Wars will be fought with aeroplanes and armored trucks. It's too late to start again, Laura."

She had reminded Peter that there would always be a need for fine saddle horses. Peter had agreed and for a while even seemed to regain some of his old enthusiasm. Yet time passed and Peter remained home. He made no more trips to the auction lots of Austin or San Antonio.

Laura poured out her feelings to Rebekah. "All these years Peter had this dream of what life should be. Because I loved him, his dream became mine as well. And so I put my own dreams aside and worked to make his real. Then, all of a sudden, Peter's dream dies in the canyon. And I wonder where that leaves me? I'm stuck here with the wreckage."

"This doesn't sound like you, Laura. Not at all."

"Why should I be the strong one? Maybe I'd like to give up, too!"

"Maybe you should. Why don't you?"

"Because I'm too mad! I'm really angry and I wish I knew who was making me so all-fired mad!"

"Well, don't blame Peter."

"Maybe God. Maybe I'm mad at God." Ever since the Narrows group had argued the truth of the Bible, Laura had become more and more preoccupied with the question, or the answer, of God. The more she wanted to believe, the more she yearned for the spiritual comfort believers claimed to possess, the more convinced she became that the religion of her youth was false. She supposed her doubting nature was due to the persuasive skills of Satan. *So how,* she wondered, *can my doubts be the product of a force in which I don't believe?* There were times when she seemed to feel the presence of God moving through her world, times when she was almost certain of some connection to the divine. When she made love to Peter she was sure God was near. In those moments when she felt reverence toward a power greater than herself, she would luxuriate in that holiness and then realize the moment was characterized not by what she knew to be true but by what she wished to be true. Maybe there was a God, probably was. But she was sure, almost sure, it was a being that could not give a fig for the affairs of individual human beings. He was too concerned with the larger problems of making the universe work. Sometimes she saw God as manager of a great cosmic railroad yard like the ones she would see pictures of in Chicago, God rushing around throwing switches to keep the planets and stars on track.

Then there were times when she would search the Bible or listen to a sermon and the entire structure of the Christian myth would seem so overwhelmingly absurd, so massively unbelievable, that the only possible explanation for its existence was that it was true. Its very implausibility proved its truth. The thing Laura feared most about God was that she would come to believe in Him and then find out at the end of her life that what she had believed was a lie. She would get to heaven and they would say, "God who?" Yet there was this powerful need she had, in spite of what the Scriptures said about looking for signs, to look for signs. And so the greater her doubts, the more urgently she sought to prove her doubts unfounded. *If there was a God who cared for us, for each and every sparrow that falls, how could He have let Pasqual Orozco kill our horses and our future?*

"Peter will be fine," Rebekah said.

"I'm not sure," Laura said. "He's bleeding inside. It's a wound of the spirit. He walks and talks and stands the way he always has. He's still kind and wonderful with the children and we still love each other. Yet it's almost as if he were waiting for something. And he's forgotten what he's waiting for. I ask him what I can do. And he smiles that beautiful smile and says, 'Don't worry about me. Everything's fine.' But I know it's not."

Laura told Rebekah how they had filed suit against the railroad in an attempt to recover their losses. The railroad claimed the wreck was an act of God and in no way due to their negligence. "Maybe it's the railroad tycoons I'm mad at," Laura laughed. She felt her anger melting before her laughter. "God and the railroad."

Winifred was teaching again. Peter had managed to get her a position at Blanco High School. With a troubling sense of maternal disloyalty, Laura suspected her daughter was the most peculiar of teachers and she feared for the education of the children in their Hill Country community. Although people were always saying how brilliant and "deep" Winifred was, Laura found it difficult to make sense of just about anything she said. Once Laura overheard Winifred telling Peter that she had counted the number of times Satan's name appeared in the Bible and compared it with the number of times God's name appeared. The resulting score, overwhelmingly in favor of the Lord, proved the victory of good over evil. Laura felt Winifred's theology, though imaginative, was hogwash and she told her so. Winifred responded with the irrelevant accusation that Laura was to blame for the family's reversal of fortune.

"You should be out working," Winifred said. "If you had some kind of talent or skill, we wouldn't be so poor. You should have stayed in school and gone to college like I did. At least one person in this family is a modern woman with earning power."

As the weeks passed and Peter maintained his strange, passive detachment, Laura found herself becoming less angry and more restless. In a sense, Laura felt she was leading two lives. One was on the ranch with its monotonous and now seemingly meaningless routine, the other in her mind. In the evenings, when her chores were done and Peter had retreated into silence, she would pore over her voluminous and expanding library of newspapers and periodicals, marveling at the turmoil in the country and the world. Again, she had the feeling that life was passing her by. The newspapers were filled with momentous events. Women were locked in a struggle for suffrage and against Demon Rum. The dogs of war were stirring in Europe. In his correspondence with Laura, Colonel House, who continued to be Woodrow Wilson's most trusted adviser, wrote about Wilson's feelings concerning the European war. "If a country and a president ever went to war with clean hands," he wrote, "it was the United

States and Woodrow Wilson. He did everything in his power to prevent our entry into the fight. But civilization itself was in balance. Wilson says the world must be made safe for democracy."

In her midnight sessions, long after Peter had retired to his bed or to that strange, empty province of mind where he wandered alone in the wreckage of his dream, Laura tried to create a plan, some pattern for the years she saw stretching ahead toward a future of uncertain dimension or purpose. Although she loved Peter, it was a love based more on memory and commitment than on any real emotion she felt here and now. He had grown distant. They had not touched physically since the loss of the horses. Sometimes she would lie in bed, by his side, feeling his heat, aware of his heartbeat, and she would pray that he would reach over, even for her hand. She would also pray for the strength to make the first move. It would be so easy to reach across the immense space that separated their bodies and, maybe, with the touch, the space would cease to exist and everything would be good again. But she could not move her hand. It would be a kind of invasion. Somehow Peter must fight out of his morass on his own terms. Peter must have the strength to reach out. But night after night, she could feel his strength slipping away and the distance between them growing.

Laura knew she faced a delicate task. She would have to step up and take the leadership of the family without destroying Peter's sense of self or his dignity, maybe just for a while, until Peter was himself again. But until that time, she viewed a life of painful loneliness, not because Peter was absent but because he was so near.

One night Laura dreamed she was at a glittering ball. A formal affair, held in an immense hall with crystal chandeliers and huge French doors leading onto formal gardens. She was wearing the loveliest gown she had ever worn and knew she was the most beautiful woman at the ball. She walked out into the center of the ballroom and lit a candle. And when she looked around, she saw that she was alone. The music was playing, but no one else was there. It was clear she was either going to have to dance alone or lose this moment in her life. If she were to dance, it would be up to her. Then she was awake again, Peter breathing heavily by her side.

At supper one evening, when Maxey Charles was restless and evasive, Laura knew she and Peter were about to be delivered another blow.

"So when do you leave?" Laura asked. Maxey Charles looked up in surprise.

"How did you know, Mama?"

"It's written all over your face. Have you spoken to your papa?"

"About what?" Peter's face answered her question.

Maxey Charles left a week later to join Black Jack Pershing, who was disengaging from his campaign against Pancho Villa on the Rio Grande in order to lead young Americans against the Kaiser on the Marne. Laura had employed all her persuasive powers to talk Maxey out of volunteering.

"I need you here," she reasoned. "How can I run this place by myself? You know perfectly well that your papa isn't able. He needs you. We all need you here." Even as she said the words, Laura knew her pleading was hypocritical. He was a fine young man. All his life she had taught Maxey Charles to accept his responsibilities as a citizen. To serve his country. Now she was trying to convince him otherwise. But at this moment, the family needed him more than the country. Maxey Charles was sympathetic, but he had made up his mind.

"Mama," he said, tears forming at the corners of his soft blue eyes, "please don't go on about this. I have to go, don't you see!" His voice rose and Laura noticed that it careened between octaves, like a young boy's. "Of course I don't want to leave you, Mama! So just stop about it!" He was quite close to shouting. "Can't you see how hard it is?"

Maxey Charles and his friends left the next afternoon for Austin where their unit was being mustered. Peter watched his son's departure with clouded eyes. Laura felt abandoned by one of the few people in her life on whom she could fully depend.

Long into the nights, with her atlas and her letters from Maxey Charles and Colonel House, Laura followed the writhings of a world at war. Sometimes she could almost hear the weeping, laughing Parisians as they pelted the American soldiers with flowers. Then she imagined she could hear the cries of the wounded and dying as the Americans fought in the Belleau Wood and along the Marne. Words with the lyrical sound of melody and a stench of death crept into her mind and her vocabulary. Chateau Thierry, Verdun, the Argonne Forest, and the rivers Meuse and Moselle. But mostly her mind reached out for Maxey Charles who had the audacity to volunteer against her wishes the moment America entered the war. Perhaps she was not able to dissuade him from joining the army, but she was determined to make his army career as pleasant and as safe as possible by corresponding with his superiors. At one point in the war, in a letter to his brother Wilton, Maxey Charles wrote: "Will you please tell Mama to quit writing to my commanding officer?"

When young Lyndon Johnson was five years old, Rebekah and Mr. Sam moved to a spacious, lovely home in Johnson City, a small town east of Blanco named for Mr. Sam's uncle Ben. It was a thriving little community offering all the "culture" that Rebekah had missed during her years in Stonewall. Laura's visits were more frequent now, for it was only twelve miles between Blanco and Johnson City. The road was better, more frequently traveled than the road to Stonewall, where Rebekah and Sam first wed.

Laura and Wilton would hitch the buggy and drive north over the strange little hills outside of town. They could see a vast distance to the east where clouds cast moving shadows across lush, yet ragged, land littered with limestone outcroppings. They crossed the chalky streambed of Miller Creek and then, quickly, because of Laura's fear of flash floods, they climbed the rise beyond. Occasionally, an automobile would clatter by, bouncing and leaping in the ruts, and Laura would promise herself to campaign harder for a family car.

For Laura these visits were a welcome respite from the tensions of her new leadership role in the family. She was pleased that Rebekah had blossomed with city life and how comfortable she seemed in the rambling white house with its great, cool back porch where Wilton and Lyndon slept, or at least pretended to sleep, at night. She and Rebekah enjoyed watching the two boys leaping and laughing through the days. Lyndon was constantly talking, waving his arms around, Wilton listening, adding a word now and again that almost always brought explosions of laughter from Lyndon, his taller, lanky body so in contrast to the small, lithe Wilton.

In the summer and on weekends and during those times when their schools played baseball against each other, Wilton and Lyndon were friends on opposing teams. Laura was certain they would be lifelong friends. They seemed to be a perfect complement one to the other, the differences in their contrasting personalities blending beautifully, Laura thought.

As the war raged in Europe and Peter and Winifred grew more distant, Laura's attention was drawn more and more to her youngest son. There was a general consensus in the family that Wilton was Laura's favorite. When accused, usually by Winifred, she would deny it, even though she knew there was some truth to the accusation. Perhaps it was not that she loved him more than the others; it was more akin to the feeling one has for a robin with a broken wing. Wilton seemed to bring all her nurturing instincts to the surface. She began to realize that, although he was small and frail, he might become the strongest of them all. He was quiet, fair and universally liked. But the quality Wilton possessed that both troubled and delighted Laura was a kind of natural daring. He was an incurable risk-taker. If her eye caught the silhouette of a child on the roof of the barn, she instinctively knew it was Wilton. If the children embarked on some bold venture down by the river or in the section of the forest where the wildcats were, the leader of the expedition, although smaller and younger than the others, was certain to be Wilton. Only when Lyndon Johnson came to visit did Laura sense Wilton's leadership was challenged. But she also sensed he met the challenge squarely, and although Lyndon's gangly stride might lead them on their wanderings, it was Wilton who decided just where that stride should lead.

Each year, as the nights became chill and the sumac turned the color of blood, the Glasscock Brothers Circus returned to its winter encampment on the Blanco. The day of their return, the sound of the trumpeting elephants and the roar of the remembered beasts hurled Laura back in time until she was the same age as Wilton and Lyndon, and she recognized in their eyes the wonder she had felt when the colorful wagons rolled along the river road and into their lives. She recognized the boys' excitement, how they grew increasingly detached from their everyday world and became alert, listening for voices only a child or a clown or a sorcerer could hear. Laura had heard the voices and could almost hear them now as Wilton and Lyndon watched for the wagons to come into town. When Wilton first came under the spell of the circus, Laura's initial instincts were to forbid him to visit the winter camp. Then she remembered her afternoons with Herman Lehmann and she could almost feel the touch of his hand and his pain. She would almost weep with the joy and the sorrow of the memory. She remembered her own freedom and how much she cherished her wanderings with Miss Ruth. As much as she wanted to keep Wilton safely by her side, away from the dangers of beasts and demons and the terrible temptations she had known, she remembered, and let him go.

Wilton and Lyndon spent entire weekends in the huge Glasscock barn where the acrobats and aerialists practiced their daring skills. When they returned for lunch or supper, they told Laura they were learning to juggle from a clown named Gizzard. In fact, Wilton was an excellent juggler and could keep seven green apples in the air at one time. Lyndon lacked any juggling skill at all, but was an enthusiastic apprentice. Laura soon learned the real reason for the boys' pilgrimages to the Glasscock barn was to learn the mysterious and dangerous arts of the high-wire performers, in particular, the arts of one dark-eyed gypsy girl who had befriended them. When Laura learned that Wilton was walking along the high wire in the upper reaches of the barn, she actually forbade him to visit the camp until he promised on both Old and New Testaments that he would not do his aerial foolishness again. He promised, and within a week he was carried home by Gizzard and Ball Coon and another Glasscock Indian named Running Water. Lyndon trailed along behind with a young girl who wore sequins and little else. Lyndon wore an expression of absolute innocence. Wilton's arm was severely broken.

"It was a juggling accident," Lyndon said.

Even though Wilton was in obvious pain, Laura noticed he often smiled at the little naked girl with long night-black hair and gypsy eyes. *Either he is very, very brave,* she thought, *or he grew up while I wasn't looking.*

As Dr. Edwards, the local dentist and only doctor in town, was setting Wilton's arm, Laura stepped out into the backyard with Ball Coon. He was much older, his long hair streaked with gray, the corners of his eyes veined with thin capillaries of blood. Laura wondered if the years had changed her as much as they had changed Ball Coon.

"I guess you remember me," she said.

"I remember. You and the white Apache."

"I'm married now."

"I can see that." There was a curious glint in Ball Coon's eyes, either mockery or something more kind. She remembered when she and Herman had spent hours with Ball Coon, listening to his stories about Father Sun and Mother Earth and the way of his people. But that was a long time ago. She was appalled that she felt tears welling in her eyes.

"Time goes by," she said, turning away and wiping her eyes on the corner of her apron.

"You were about her age," Ball Coon said, indicating the girl who was comforting her son.

"Who is she?"

"Etta Leon. Born on a circus wagon. Probably die on one."

"Do you hear from . . ." She could not say the name out loud.

"Not much. He came around for awhile. He'd ask about you. Then he went up to the reservation. Maybe still there."

Laura could not think of anything to say. She was embarrassed, yet felt a deep affection for the old Indian who had glimpsed that part of her nature that was wild and daring. But that was another time, another world.

"Don't let my little boy Wilton climb so high," she managed, then turned back to the house.

∞

One night, long after dinner, Laura saw Winifred and a boy named Ralph Edwards slip off into the darkness and down toward the river. They were holding hands, and before they disappeared into the night, Laura had caught a brief glimpse of Winifred's face. For the first time ever, Laura saw a look of pure happiness there. *How could I have been so blind,* she thought. She recalled dozens of times when the two had been together, but she had always thought of Winifred as a person incapable of either expressing or accepting love. Only Flournoy seemed to melt through her glacial defenses. Seeing her daughter apparently opening her heart to someone other than Flournoy was a shock. Although Laura was glad for her daughter's happiness, as she thought any other mother would be, she felt a bitter, unwelcome resentment that Winifred could love a stranger and not love her mother.

As she thought of the two young people down by the river, a curious ache descended on her mind. She remembered the time she and Peter swam through the cave beneath the Narrows and she had been so eager and willing to give herself completely to her man. She wondered if Winifred felt that magic, heavenly pain and if Ralph would be as decently conventional as Peter had been. *How sad,* she thought, *that we can't talk together as my mother and I did back when I attended Little Mattie's Institute for Women.*

Soon Laura learned that Winifred and Ralph were secretly engaged, but she heard it secondhand. Apparently, everyone in town knew about this epic romance. They were a handsome couple. Winifred with her mysterious, distant, melancholy beauty, and the Edwards boy with his outgoing manner and well-known sense of humor.

Meanwhile Laura divided her energies between home, working for the Red Cross, selling liberty bonds door to door, fighting for the passage of a suffrage bill, and raging against that "villainous fool," Texas governor Farmer Jim Ferguson. "He deserves to be hung for treason," Laura insisted, "but I'll settle for impeachment. He's being paid a fortune by the beer trust and his suffrage record is appalling. Even worse than Mr. Sam, who actually believes Texas women *don't want* to vote."

"I'm convinced," Mr. Sam insisted whenever Laura challenged him about his views, "that a majority of my constituents are opposed to national women's suffrage. It's my duty, as their representative, to reflect their will. That's what representatives are for. To represent."

"I always thought the job of a leader was to lead," Laura said. "Buck the tide every once in a while. You're just following along. Taking the easy path."

"I take my stands. My voting record on horse racing, for one. Repeal of prohibition, for another."

"That's because you like to gamble and you like to drink."

"That's simply not true," Mr. Sam said. "Well," he hedged, "it's simply not fair."

Laura loved nothing better than arguing with Mr. Sam. "I wish you liked women as much as you like horses. Then you'd vote for us for sure." She paused to gauge her effect, feeling just a touch ashamed of herself for baiting him so cruelly. "And how can you possibly say your constituents are opposed to suffrage. You've just counted the men. Half your constituents are women, you know. Or at least they soon will be."

In January 1918, at the urging of Colonel House, President Wilson came out in favor of a national suffrage amendment. Laura was elated that her old friend had convinced Wilson of the merits of suffrage. She felt somehow a part of his decision, as if her mind had willed it, her influence making it impossible for the president to take any other position.

Well-known suffragists from around the country were invited to Texas to hold seminars for local women who wanted to become active advocates for the cause. Among these women was lobbyist Jane McCallum, a chief spokeswoman for "the petticoat lobby." Her weekly column in the *Austin Statesman* was seen on the desk of every legislator in Texas.

When Jane McCallum held a seminar in Blanco, Laura invited her to stay as a guest at the Hanging Tree Ranch. In the evening, the kitchen was crowded with neighbor women debating strategy.

"The first step," Jane McCallum explained, "is to pass a bill enabling women to vote in the political party primaries and nominating conventions. To pass this bill, all it takes is a simple majority of legislators. The second step, which we will face much later, will be more difficult. It will be a bill for full woman suffrage and will require a two-thirds majority in the legislature and then approval by the voters in a statewide election."

"So how do we get legislators to pass the primary bill?" Laura asked. "Do you think a majority of them will support it?"

"They will if we organize our efforts and make the irresistible promise," Jane said. "We tell them that if we obtain the right to vote in primaries, we'll use that vote to support those legislators who supported us. Suddenly they will have twice as many supporters as they had before. Half of them women. Lieutenant Governor Hobby wants to be governor. We tell him to get us the right to vote and we'll make it happen."

The suffragists were successful. In March 1918, the legislature passed the bill permitting Texas women to vote in political party primary elections. Laura was jubilant and teased Mr. Sam mercilessly about his woeful misinterpretation of the desires of his constituents.

It was, in general, a victorious year—not only for the women of Texas, but for all women whose sons had been fighting for freedom in Europe. In November, the glorious news reached Blanco that the terrible war against the Kaiser was over. Soon the boys would be coming home.

A few weeks later, a letter came from Maxey Charles. "I am so weary of this army life," he wrote. "I've done my duty and the war is over and I believe it's terribly unfair that they won't let me come home. They've announced that married men with families will come home first. It looks like I'll be away for another Christmas."

Since she had been so successful in her lobbying efforts for a Texas women's suffrage act, Laura immediately began lobbying for Maxey Charles's return home. She wrote a letter to President Wilson demanding his immediate return. In part, her letter read:

> My family has labored for you throughout your political career. We have carried your name and your political philosophy to every ranch and to every citizen in Blanco County. Surely this support of your political career merits special consideration. Maxey Charles Woods has served his country well. Now, I believe it is right that his country, his President, serve him by sending him home for Christmas.

She sent a copy of the letter to Colonel House.

On Christmas Eve, as Wilton was splitting logs for the fireplace, he saw a familiar figure walking up the road. Only his brother Maxey Charles had a dancing, swaying, almost comic walk like that. Wilton ran down the road to welcome Maxey Charles home from the war.

Maxey Charles told the story over and over. "I was just sitting there on my bunk, shining my boots, and my commanding officer came charging in and right up to my bunk. I about broke my neck jumpin' up to attention. He said, 'Woods!' I said, 'Yes, sir!' And I about broke my nose salutin' that fine officer. He was scowlin', lookin' real mean, and I thought, oh boy, I'm in for it now. Then he says, 'Woods! Pack your gear! I'm shipping you home!' And that's what he did. But I never could figure out what he was so mad about."

Laura smiled to herself when she heard the story. She could just imagine how amazed that commanding officer must have been when President Woodrow Wilson ordered him to send the Woods boy home. *It pays,* she thought, *to write letters to friends in elected offices.*

Maxey Charles's safe return punctuated what was the grandest Christmas celebration the Woods family had ever had. By the time Maxey Charles arrived, most of the family had already gathered. Lucy and Milton Copenhaver were there with their little girl, Agatha. Eugene had brought his new bride, Cornelia. Ralph Edwards was home from medical school and he and Winifred were constantly together, holding hands, or playing with the grandchildren. Little Mattie and J. C. Hoge had come from Hoge Hollow. Laura bossed everyone around, to make sure they did Christmas right, and for once nobody seemed to mind. In fact, Winifred gave Laura the best Christmas present she had ever had. On an impulse, risking rejection, Laura put her arms around Winifred and she felt, to her surprise and profound relief, a warm response. Through all the recent years, when she would try to embrace Winifred, the girl's body would stiffen and Laura would feel the pain. As time passed, Laura avoided that pain by avoiding its source, the embrace. But now, Winifred's body softened and for a moment Laura felt something very much like love pass both ways between them. Laura felt tears pooling in her eyes and let them fall for awhile, for all to see, before wiping them away with her sleeve.

Today would be perfect, Laura thought, *if Rebekah and her family could be here, too.* Mr. Sam was back in the legislature where he had once again become embroiled in controversy. A neighbor, the owner of the Little Blanco Inn, had been arrested and jailed for sending money to his widowed mother in Germany. It was a time when bitter feelings were rampant in Hill Country counties where so many German-speaking people lived. The arrest of his constituent, "a good and God-fearing man," enraged Mr. Sam and he made an impassioned speech on the floor of the legislature begging Texans not to persecute their neighbors for "phantom" crimes. Laura missed the old curmudgeon almost as much as she missed Rebekah. Every time she had decided she had lost patience with Mr. Sam for his impossible stance on public issues, he would do something that made her proud. She also missed her old friend Edward House, but he was in Europe negotiating the peace.

After church, the Woods family gathered at Valentine Smith's farm for Christmas dinner. The invitation thrilled Laura because it meant she would not have to prepare a huge meal for company or clean up after it had been consumed. Among the guests were Rob Caldwell and Colonel House's Caldwell relatives. As they enjoyed a beautiful chicken pot pie, perhaps the largest chicken pot pie ever baked in Blanco County, Mary Elizabeth Caldwell talked about her brother's mission for peace in Europe.

"Three times he's sailed to European capitals to negotiate. Then he returns to report privately to the president. All the European statesmen have become House conscious. They consider him the president's alter ego. I suppose he's the most important factor in the American delegation to the Paris conference, the only one who has hourly access to President Wilson."

Laura looked across the table at Maxey Charles. *That makes two of us with President Wilson's ear,* she thought to herself, but did not say so.

After dinner, Winifred played the piano and Laura felt an inexplicable sense of foreboding flood the room. Even though the piano was slightly out of tune, the notes of the old Christmas favorites seemed to have been infused with Winifred's melancholy. The occasion should have been joyous and, to everyone else, all those singing around the piano, it seemed to be. Peter's voice was deep and clear. The familiar melodies filled Laura's mind as she watched Winifred and Rob Caldwell, hoping to discover some sign that they had become more than friends. Rob had graduated from college and was teaching with Winifred at Blanco High School while he waited for a staff position with Colonel House in Washington. *They are both such beautiful people,* Laura thought. *How can they not fall in love?* For a moment she imagined how she would visit the newly married pair in Washington, maybe even stop by the White House to pay her respects to President Wilson. But Winifred only had eyes for Ralph Edwards, the "golden boy" of Blanco County. Soon Ralph would graduate from medical school and Winifred would become a doctor's wife. *She could certainly do worse,* Laura mused, *a physician is nearly as important as a statesman.* She felt a momentary touch of guilt knowing she had purposely not suggested that the Smiths invite Ralph Edwards to Christmas dinner. It was a last wild hope that she could push Rob and Winifred together. *Maybe Ralph Edwards's absence is the cause of Winifred's melancholy. Maybe it's just that.* She watched Winifred's slim, graceful hands moving on the keys. But she could not shake the feeling that something unknowable and ominous was coming.

Looking back, Laura was certain she woke before the ringing of the bells. She was awakened by a dream that was awful in itself—a dream that the ice covering the face of the dead trapper was being melted by fire and his eyes had opened to accuse her of his death. Then she heard the bells' insistent, imperative pealing waking the town. Voices, shouts, Peter thrashing from bed, dressing as he hurried toward where the volunteer firemen were gathering around the new gasoline fire engine that had recently replaced the old "steamer."

Maxey Charles was a leader among the firefighters and had led the effort to replace the old engine that usually arrived at fires too late to do anything but wet down the embers. "Now," he had proudly told Peter, "with our seventy-horsepower gasoline engine we don't have to wait for steam to build up and we can fly to a fire at sixty miles an hour and deliver water when we get there at the rate of seven hundred gallons per minute."

Laura dressed quickly and joined the throng of neighbors rushing to where the night sky itself seemed aflame. Tongues of fire leaped into the dark as if hurled by angry gods beneath the earth. Acrid smoke soiled the air. The night was filled with the sound of barking dogs and male voices and the sharp slapping reports of burning timbers. Laura moved so close she could feel the heat of the fire that was consuming Blanco High School.

The voice of the crowd rose in choral horror when someone

was seen trapped inside the building. A shadowed figure was revealed in the firelight, a woman, standing calmly, waiting, seemingly unafraid, unconcerned, like Joan of Arc upon the pyre. Laura knew it was Winifred long before voices in the crowd began to shout her name. A man broke from the crowd and rushed toward the burning building. The firefighters followed his progress with a stream of water wetting his clothes and the blanket he carried. Laura dropped to her knees and begged God to save her baby. She prayed with her eyes open, unable to look away from the woman in the school and the man who raced the flames.

Rob Caldwell carried Winifred away from the fire and laid the steaming bundle on the ground. When Laura reached her, Winifred was smiling, looking back at the fire. "She's all right," Dr. Edwards said. "It's a miracle."

Laura knelt down beside Winifred and kissed her again and again, then lifted her head into her lap and held her as tightly as she could.

Rob asked Winifred what happened.

"I was standing by the stove and the fire just jumped out. I never saw a fire act that way." Winifred pushed away from Laura's lap, sat up and regarded the crowd around her. "It was like the fire at Master Farryner's bakehouse on Pudding Lane. It started the Great Fire of London, you know." Winifred stood and vainly tried to brush away soot with her hands as she continued. "I would say we were quite fortunate. The London fire destroyed thirteen thousand two hundred houses, St. Paul's Cathedral and eighty-nine other churches. As you can see, our Blanco fire was less destructive. We only lost a little old school."

Within a week of the fire, Winifred announced that she and Rob Caldwell, Colonel House's nephew, were to be married. It was a shock to Laura and everyone else who heard the news because the whole town had assumed Winifred would marry Ralph Edwards. At first, Laura felt it was a joke, then she became concerned because Winifred talked of the marriage in short, hard phrases, as if she were hurling stones. When Laura asked what had become of Ralph, Winifred just stared at her, then turned and walked from the room.

It was Lucy who found the partially burned letter. She noticed it among the ruins of the destroyed schoolhouse. The letter had been blackened or burned, but enough remained to reveal: "I have fallen in love with a girl here at medical school and must break my engagement with you. Forgive me, Ralph."

Laura never did ask Winifred what she was doing in the school that night. She was afraid Winifred might not lie.

19 ∞ THE CAPITAL IN AUSTIN

LAURA LIKED THE EDWARDS BOY, BUT WAS DELIGHTED THAT ROB had proposed and that Winifred had accepted. Colonel House had always spoken highly of both his character and his prospects. Rob had accepted a position as a civil engineer in a faraway place called Indianapolis. Laura could not imagine why anyone would want to live in Indianapolis. "That far north the nights are six months long," she warned Winifred.

Laura had always imagined Winifred's wedding would be the grand affair she had dreamed of for herself. But with the loss of the horses, Peter could afford only a simple wedding in their home. Miss Leila Fulcher played "The Wedding March" on the old Epworth piano and Peter walked with Winifred to the altar where Rev. O. M. Cole performed a brief ceremony. It was the first time Laura had ever seen Peter cry and she knew, for the first time, how very much he loved his tall and mysterious daughter and how terribly he would miss her when she had gone. *Poor Peter,* she thought, *so many things he loves are being taken away.*

Soon after Winifred's wedding, the governor presented a bill permitting full women's suffrage. Texas women had already won the right to vote in primaries; now it was time to win complete and equal participation in the political process. In 1919, the bill passed both houses of the legislature and was presented to the voters in a general election. The problem for the suffragists was obvious: although they had won the right to vote in the primaries, they could not yet vote for their own amendment in a general election and would have to rely on the fairness and good judgment of men.

Wilton was showing Laura his prize tomato plants in the garden when Rebekah brought news that the suffrage amendment had failed by twenty-five thousand votes. "So much for the fairness and good judgment of men," Laura said. She felt as if there had been a death in the family. As Wilton gathered the last ripe tomato and she and Rebekah watched the shadows lengthen and the day depart, Laura began to feel a rage building inside. "Everybody in Texas with the exception of you and me and Wilton's pet pig can vote. Immigrants, Negroes, Republicans, communists, socialists, drunkards, and everybody but lunatics, felons, and women! It's wrong and rotten and I simply won't have it!"

"Where are all the good men?" Laura asked Rebekah. "Where are the men who know what's right? What's fair and decent? It's just a mockery!" Laura stood and threw her metal watering can as far as she could. It clattered on the tin roof of the barn, scattering chickens, turkeys and Wilton's pet pig. "I told you to get rid of that pig!" she shouted at her son, knowing full well she had said no such thing.

"There's still the federal Susan B. Anthony amendment next month," Rebekah said, trying to defuse Laura's anger. "With Wilson's backing there's a good chance it'll pass."

"It better," Laura said. "If it doesn't I really will get mad."

Laura was so angry, in fact, that the next day, over Peter's objections, she bought a car. It was a brand-new 1919 Ford, black as Valentine Smith's mule, with brass lanterns and leather seats. "Maybe I can't vote," she told Sam Johnson. "But I sure as blazes can drive."

A week before the Texas legislature met in special session to consider ratification of the federal women's suffrage bill, Laura received a telegram from Colonel House:

Paris: URGENT YOU ATTEND RATIFICATION SESSION IN AUSTIN STOP LODGING ARRANGED AT STEPHEN F. AUSTIN HOTEL STOP DISCRETION IMPERATIVE STOP FURTHER INSTRUCTIONS AWAIT YOU THERE STOP MY BEST TO PETER STOP RESPECTFULLY. EDWARD.

The remarkable telegram filled Laura with an exquisite and all-consuming curiosity. *What could Colonel House possibly have in mind? Why didn't he just come right out and tell her? Why so secretive?* Not really understanding, Laura hid the telegram for a while and even kept it secret. But she could hardly contain her need to tell someone about the mysterious telegram and the "urgent" mission it demanded. Peter, however, would diminish the excitement of the moment with some logical explanation. Rebekah might mention the secret assignment to Mr. Sam and Laura did not trust his stand on the suffrage amendment. She knew she could rely on her sister Lucy, and in June 1919, after telling Peter she was going to Austin to attend a state meeting of Methodist women, they set out for the state capital and the Stephen F. Austin Hotel. Her reason for the trip seemed to satisfy Peter. And as they drove away, Laura's excitement was tinged with a touch of sorrow. She was about to begin the most exciting and important adventure of her life and Peter was not really that interested where she was going or why.

Austin was alive with passion and energy and confusion. Laura and Lucy could hardly negotiate the press of pedestrians in the streets. Banners demanding equal rights for women crowned the intersections and crowds of women commanded the street corners where speakers shouted their convictions to the heavens and to the top floors of the Driskill Hotel—headquarters of the liquor lobby and other opponents of suffrage. University students milled about, and farmers in from the fields, lawyers, lobbyists, and legislators flowed like lava through the streets, into the hotel lobbies, and onto the capital lawns. Here and there Laura could see the Texas Rangers, their huge white Stetsons towering above the flowered hats of the crusading women.

Laura and Lucy motored through the chaos along Congress Avenue and managed to force their way toward the entrance of the Stephen F. Austin Hotel. Just as she was about to despair, a Texas Ranger approached. He was so tall he had to bend almost double to see into the car.

"Mrs. Woods?" the ranger asked.

"Yes."

"We've been expecting you. Follow me, please."

The ranger strode in front of the Ford and moved forward. The crowd parted before his presence, simply fell away, and Laura drove to a parking space that had been marked off with ribbons. The ranger summoned a bevy of doormen and bellmen who descended on the car and Laura and Lucy followed their luggage into the hotel. They passed the reception desk and moved through the mob in the lobby directly toward the grand stairway.

"Don't we have to check in?" Lucy asked.

"Appears not," Laura said, and started to follow the bellman up the staircase. She had not gone two steps when the ranger stepped forward and blocked their way. "I was asked to give you this," he said, removing his hat and handing her a small white envelope, postmarked Paris, all in one remarkably coordinated movement. "The plan is for me to come here at 7:30 in the morning and escort you from your room to your meeting at the capitol."

"What plan?" Laura asked. "Why? To meet whom?" She looked up into the towering ranger's face, a motion so extreme she was afraid for a moment she would tip over backward. In spite of her excitement, she felt he was being unnecessarily secretive.

"I'm not at liberty to say, ma'am."

Laura took the envelope and slipped it into her purse. "I'll see you in the morning," the ranger said, then inclined his upper body downward in what Laura took to be a bow then moved away through the crowd.

The room was large, modestly furnished, yet somehow luxurious. The walls were covered with a rich pecan paneling. Paintings of bluebonnet vistas adorned the walls. The beds were brass, the bedspreads of red velvet that matched the drapes the bellman now opened upon the Congress Avenue assemblage. The sounds of the crowd came flooding in like an orchestra tuning.

Laura and Lucy stood in the middle of the room waiting for the bellman to leave. Just when she thought he would never complete his errands, Laura realized he was stalling for a tip. She rummaged in her purse for a coin. The moment the bellman had bowed and departed, she grasped the envelope, ripped it open, and with her heart beating like a snare drum, she began to read aloud.

"What does it say?" Lucy asked.

"My dear friend," House's letter began. "I sincerely hope this task I have committed to your capable hands is not too severe an imposition. I would not have called you to this city if it had not been of the utmost importance. It is essential that President Wilson's suffrage amendment be ratified by the Texas legislature so that a better day might dawn for the women of this country. As you must know, it is impossible for me to be there in person to guide the process to a successful conclusion. Our duty is here in Paris with President Wilson. But I have full confidence in your ability to follow through on what must be done."

Laura looked up from the letter, partly to catch her breath. She was torn between her excitement and a growing sense of insecurity. She wondered if she was worthy of House's trust.

"Read on," Lucy pleaded.

"In the closet you will find a suitcase. I suggest that you leave it unopened for the present and wait to review its contents with Speaker Ewing Thomason. A ranger will escort you to the Speaker's office in the morning. Ewing, as you know, is a close friend of mine and he will explain the contents of the case and how you can use it to help President Wilson get the suffrage amendment ratified. I eagerly await a visit in person."

Laura put the letter down and together she and Lucy moved to the closet, and there, as House had suggested, was a heavy leather suitcase. They wrestled it into the middle of the floor and stood looking down at the curious black object, trying to see through the leather, trying to imagine what the contents could be.

"Well?" Laura said. "Should we open it?"

"He said we should wait."

"Just a peek?"

"Laura! If we were supposed to open it, he wouldn't have said not to."

"He didn't say absolutely not to."

"Laura, you know better. Just leave it alone until morning."

After what proved for Laura a long and wakeful night, the

Texas Ranger came to their door at 7:30 sharp. They moved out into the streets and into a very long car and down Congress Avenue through the crowds toward the capitol. Laura could see the dome in the distance towering over the city. It seemed white in the morning sun even though she had heard it was largely built of pink granite from Marble Falls, near Paradise Mountain.

They parked on the green skirts of the capitol grounds and then walked beneath spreading oaks toward the great arched entrance to this place that seemed to Laura almost holy. Although it was early, groups of women were gathering around their placards and banners, planning their day's campaign. Laura could feel an escalation of energy as the gathering crowds and state workers and representatives of the people approached the building. She felt not unlike she always felt when approaching the Big Top of the Glasscock Brothers Circus before a performance.

Then they were inside, the ranger carrying the suitcase and leading their way. He was forced to slow his gait and often paused as Laura and Lucy gazed around the corridors with wonder and delight. Once again, Laura felt a sense of immeasurable awe. Here was the very heart of democracy. Their footsteps echoed on the marble floors and she imagined she could hear the tread of James Bowie and Travis and Austin and old Sam Houston walking beside her. They passed great carved oak doors bearing the names of the people's chosen representatives. As she thought of the men in those rooms, she thought of what Edward House had once said about these same smoke-filled rooms. "The unhappy condition in which the world finds itself today," he said, "has been brought about solely by men. Whether women could have done better may be subject to discussion and opinion, but surely they could not have done worse."

The great rotunda opened out above them, a universe in itself, filled with the spirit of the land and the people. It was a dizzying experience, looking up into the high holy regions the architect had surrounded so beautifully with form. Laura almost stumbled as she tried to take in all the sights and sounds and sensations that assailed her. She hurried on after the ranger, pulling Lucy along by her hand.

The corridor opened into a vast chamber filled with the echoes of many voices. It was like a choir, each member singing a different song. Men hurried on obviously important errands through geometric patterns of wooden desks. Others gathered in small groups, talking quietly, gesturing. At the front of the chamber was a series of risers and the large desk where the Speaker of the House wielded his considerable power over the legislators. Above, and all around, was a gallery, where spectators and lobbyists were already being seated. A vision of the Roman forum she had read about flashed through Laura's mind. Here in the gallery were the people looking down on the gladiators who would soon do battle. They moved on.

Behind the platform was a door leading to the Speaker's chambers. It opened onto a room as grand as any Laura had seen, even more impressive than the Colonel-Doctor's parlor. At an elaborately carved desk at one side of the room, not commanding the center, Laura noticed, was the esteemed Speaker of the House Robert Ewing Thomason. He, along with Governor Hobby and Colonel House, was considered one of the most powerful political figures in Texas.

Ewing Thomason did not look like one of the most powerful men in Texas. There was about him something cherubic, not unlike the illustrations of St. Nicholas in the old German Christmas stories. His manner was courtly, gentle, comfortable. Peter had described him once as "one of the few men in Texas who is both powerful and beloved." Ewing Thomason was also a champion of the cause for equal rights for women. In his first speech as Speaker of the House, he made his position perfectly clear. "If women are good enough to knit socks, cook without sugar, sell liberty bonds and war stamps, work on the farms and in the munitions factories, minister to the sick and dying on the battlefields, and give birth to the knightliest sons that ever fought for freedom, then they are also good enough to vote."

Laura and Lucy were introduced to the Speaker by the ranger, who set the suitcase down on a table, excused himself, and left the three alone in the large room.

After asking after Peter's health, Speaker Thomason wasted

no time explaining the significance of Laura's leather valise. "We are hearing that just about everyone in the House and Senate is in favor of ratification. The people are for it. Almost every preacher in Texas preaches ratification on Sunday. State officials, party organizations, all the newspapers are for ratification. But the fact remains, people were also for the Texas amendment and it failed."

Speaker Thomason looked directly into Laura's eyes as he spoke. She sat motionless, hanging on every word. "Now, since we are good Democrats and on the same side," he continued, "I know I can be candid with you. As Speaker of the House, I have this chamber under control. The House is going to vote for ratification. We've got the votes. It's just that simple. We don't have to spend one whit of our energy on House members. Our problem is in the Senate."

Laura noticed that Lucy seemed awed by the gentle persuasive manner of the powerful Speaker.

"There are key men in the Senate who will vote against ratification. Some of them, the admitted fire-eating 'antis,' wear their votes on their sleeves. But others will say they'll vote for ratification, but won't. They'll vote 'no' or satisfy the 'antis' by being absent with some cooked-up excuse."

Without taking his eyes off Laura and Lucy, he pointed to the leather valise. "Now here's where these records come into play. None of the senators know the records exist. They were uncovered in several major investigations at the federal level. They show which of our state senators have been the favorites of the liquor lobby and why. Colonel House is one of the few men in America who could have obtained these records for us."

Speaker Thomason opened the suitcase and spread the files it contained on the table. "What we have here," he continued, "are records that came from the offices of the liquor lobby. Invoices, memoranda, letters, canceled checks, all of which show that certain Texas senators have accepted gifts from the liquor lobby to influence their votes. What we have here is proof of behavior that's certainly unethical and in many cases illegal.

"As I thumb through these records I see that there are about a dozen senators here who have obligated themselves to vote against ratification or at the very least absent themselves from voting. And that gets me to why Colonel House and I need your help, Mrs. Woods. We need someone who is not a political office holder and who does not have any connection with any particular politician or group. At least no identifiable connection. We need someone who is smart, who's loyal to us, and who is astute enough politically to use these records to persuade senators to vote our way. Colonel House assures me you are that person, Mrs. Woods. And I'm certain you and your sister will make an excellent team."

Laura beamed. Never had she felt so proud and so alive and so important. It was as if all her life had been a preparation for this moment. Lucy smiled proudly.

"What are we to do, specifically?"

"We want you to review these records as quickly as you can. Then we want you to call on each senator, one at a time. Of course you will be polite and tactful, but you will explain to them that unless they vote for ratification, the information in these records will be made public. Once you get this message across, I think we can count on their vote."

Laura and Lucy were assigned seven senators, among them R. M. Johnston of Houston, J. C. McNealus and Tom McClanahan of Fort Worth. The sisters returned to the hotel and for the rest of the morning they pored over the records, memorizing the errors of the senators' ways. Laura was astounded that their behavior was so blatant, especially that of Sen. Tom McClanahan, whose malfeasance was so transparent that only a man of grotesque arrogance could possibly think he could escape accountability.

When Laura moved through the Senate wing of the capitol building, with its high ceilings and great reverberating spaces, she felt a momentary flagging of resolve. But when she stood outside the imposing carved oak door of Senator McClanahan's office, she recalled his violation of the public trust and she realized how small he really was. Her resolve came storming back with abandon.

The secretary was not at all encouraging. "I'm afraid his appointments calendar is full for the next several days, Mrs. Woods."

Laura leaned close to the secretary's ear. Even though there was no one else in the office, with the most sinister whisper she could muster, she assured the secretary of the urgency of her visit. "There is a horrible scandal in his district. Unless he acts quickly it will become public."

The wide-eyed secretary moved to the inner office as if fleeing some minor horror. She returned in less than a minute. "The senator has a moment. He will see you now, Mrs. Woods."

Senator McClanahan was a large, handsome, ruddy man. Laura immediately recognized the personal effects of his long association with the products of the liquor lobby. There was a touch of curiosity in his warm greeting, but no alarm. Laura imagined he was thinking, "After all, what harm could this little woman do." Laura began by telling him exactly what harm she could do.

"Senator McClanahan, some of your enemies have in their possession documents, memos and other things that come from the office of the liquor lobby. I'm afraid they intend to embarrass you if you don't vote for the Suffrage Amendment."

The senator's smile lost a touch of its amiable glow. "My enemies have threatened me before, Mrs. Woods. I'm certain they will threaten me again from time to time. Idle threats are the worthless coin of politics."

"Speaking of worthless, do you know a Mr. Jim Dunnigan? I believe he works for the liquor lobby."

"Austin has many lobbyists, Mrs. Woods."

"But this particular lobbyist kept extensive records on a trip he financed for you to a place called the Chicken Ranch on October 26th and 27th of last year. His records show a payment of $130 to 'the girls for services rendered,' whatever that might mean. There's also an invoice and a canceled check for the purchase of a shotgun, a gift to you, it seems. And there are detailed records regarding the purchase of a lady's bracelet from Tiffany's in New York. According to the invoice, the necklace sold for $649.69. It was delivered to you here in Austin two years ago. The man who purchased the bracelet and delivered it signed his name L. Musconi. And I'm sure you know who he works for."

As Laura recited her litany of wrongdoing, her manner was polite and relaxed, as if she were talking with the senator about the weather. She showed no malice nor censure. She watched Senator McClanahan's face for signs of alarm or defeat, but his expression and manner remained as smilingly civil as her own. Laura had to respect his aplomb, his calm, when it was quite possible she could bring his world down around his shoulders.

When Laura paused, Senator McClanahan thanked her for her visit. He was effusive and seemed quite sincere. "You can certainly count on my vote supporting ratification," he said. Then, for the first time, the smile left the senator's face. He looked Laura squarely in the eye. "I want to be very frank and candid with you, Mrs. Woods. I'm not sure who you are or who sent you, but you seem to be well aware of how political bargains are made. So tell me this. If I keep my end of this deal, can you deliver on your end?"

"Senator, in that regard you have nothing to worry about. The women of Texas will be eternally grateful for the help you give them. You'll find we're tough on our enemies but very loyal to our friends."

While Laura was meeting with Senator McClanahan, Lucy telephoned the Stephen F. Austin and Driskill hotels to determine where each of the other six senators was staying so she could catch them at the hotel if she missed them at their offices. On one of her calls, Lucy learned that the senator in question had just checked out and was apparently leaving town, walking the vote. Lucy and Laura caught him at the train depot. After Laura had a brief chat with him, the gentleman missed his train.

During the next few days, the "anti" forces tried every conceivable method to defer or defeat ratification of the Federal Women's Suffrage Amendment. But like Laura and Lucy, other suffragists were working all over Austin to make sure that the amendment supporters remained true to their cause.

Laura and Lucy corralled all seven of the senators they had been assigned. As Laura confronted each of them with the details of their embarrassing activities, each reluctantly promised support for the amendment.

On the day of the big vote, the lobbyists packed the gallery. Along with the gathered suffragists, they shouted down at the legislators below. Threats were hurled like spears and hecklers became so numerous and disorderly that Texas Rangers had to help the sergeant-at-arms throw the rascals out.

Within the Senate, with very few exceptions, only senators were allowed on the Senate chamber floor. When Laura and Lucy presented their credentials to the sergeant-at-arms guarding the door to the main floor of the Senate, several senators took notice. They obviously wondered how these two unknown women could possibly think they could enter this hallowed domain, especially at such a crucial time. The doorman checked their passes and waved them through. As Laura and Lucy stepped onto the floor, senators turned to stare, open-mouthed, at these improbable intruders who moved with such poised audacity among them. Laura and Lucy paused here and there to greet and shake hands with each of their seven assigned senators. The faces of the targeted senators told the story. If they had any thought of reneging on their pledge to Laura, they quickly abandoned it when they saw the two sisters moving freely in the chamber. Obviously, the two strangers had powerful and intimate friends somewhere close at hand.

Laura chuckled to herself as she pictured how surprised the senators would be if they knew Speaker Thomason had obtained their passes from his hometown friend, Sen. R. M. Dudley of El Paso.

On June 28, 1919, Texas became the ninth state to ratify the Federal Women's Suffrage Amendment. The vote was nineteen to ten, with one absent.

As Laura walked out of the Senate chamber with Lucy, a euphoria swept over her. She felt a wave of energy engulf her body and her mind.

Her thoughts were clear, like a voice within.

You, Laura, have a rare gift—
an ability to persuade people, to influence, to lead.
Call it what you please: politicking,
campaigning, or electioneering.
It is the old-fashioned practice of patriotism.
It is Politics. You love it, you are good at it.
Now you can even vote.

It was what she had always wanted.

"Today was ladies' day in the State Senate," Laura laughed. The day's events had been a glorious victory for Texas women.

As Laura and Lucy emerged from the capitol rotunda into the warm sunshine, she knew for her it had been much more.

"Thank you, God," Laura said.

When Laura returned from Austin, she found a letter from Winifred waiting. Winifred wrote that she and Rob were expecting a child. A flurry of letters and telephone calls passed between Indianapolis and Blanco. Laura pored over her new revised edition of *Obstetrics for Nurses* by Dr. Joseph DeLee, and filled her letters with information she insisted Winifred pass on to her doctor.

"I want you to be sure and watch your diet and get plenty of rest," Laura wrote. "You should expect unusual tooth decay. The baby will use up lime deposits in your body. Tell your doctor to prescribe milk of magnesia. You should take it three times a day. Hold it in your mouth for three minutes so the body can absorb the lime." Laura also advised Winifred to avoid crowds, excitement, and stress.

Winifred's letters seemed to career from joyous anticipation to abject melancholy and Laura answered always with pages as cheerful as a nursery rhyme. Never once did Laura hint at her mistrust of the entire male-dominated birthing process. When Winifred complained about a loss of appetite, Laura quoted a prevailing theory. She wrote that Winifred should "tempt the appetite with light foods served in the daintiest possible manner, using the whitest linen and prettiest dishes." Against her better judgment, she also suggested that a few sips of champagne might well settle her stomach.

Laura was torn between making the long trip to Indianapolis to be at Winifred's side and her duty to Peter, the farm, and the young children. "I should have been twins," she told Rebekah. "There's not enough of me to go around." Little Mattie, whose father had been a physician, assured Laura that Winifred was receiving the best possible care and that Indianapolis was a progressive city with the most modern facilities, even if it was dark six months of the year.

A few months before Winifred's child was due, Little Mattie came to the Hanging Tree Ranch with terrible news. J. C. Hoge had purchased some ranchland in far West Texas that he and Little Mattie planned to homestead. At first, Laura took the news stoically. Then, the true import of her parents' move struck home.

"I'll never see you again," Laura said. "West Texas is farther away than Indianapolis!"

"We'll be back now and again."

Laura measured the tiny woman who had given her life and had nourished that life over the years with gentle strength, and she knew her mother could never survive another pioneer experience, especially in a land as wild and primitive as the Texas panhandle.

"It's not fair," Laura said. "That old man shouldn't be dragging you off to the end of the earth. Why? It's like it's all happened before! Why make you do it all again?"

"Every man should get his chance. Your father's just came a little later than most, that's all. He worked hard all his life to save the money for that land and for some good livestock. He never had much. Now at the end of his life he's got his chance."

"Chance for what? To make me an orphan?"

Little Mattie stiffened, turned away, looked out the kitchen window, then back again. "It seems to me this isn't about you, Little Daughter. This is about me and your father. So why don't you wish us well and say good-bye like a decent person should."

Laura was stung by Little Mattie's words. She tried to recall if her mother had ever spoken harshly to her before and when she did, Little Mattie spoke the memory out loud.

"Remember that time we killed the rattlesnake in the kitchen?" Her voice was calm now, soft, yet brittle with age and disuse. Laura could not imagine conversation between her mother and father and she supposed entire days would go by when Little Mattie would not speak at all. "Seems to me you were all stirred up about running away with the circus. Didn't want to stay put in Hoge Hollow where nothing much ever happened. You were after adventure, you said. Well, it took me a long time to come around to your view, but I did. I'm ready to move on. Leave Hoge Hollow behind and get on with something new. What makes you think it's only your father who wants this chance? Maybe it's me that doesn't want to stay in Hoge Hollow until they lower me into the ground."

Within the week, J. C. Hoge and Little Mattie loaded all their earthly goods onto the wagon on which Laura had made so many passages from the homeplace to town and left Hoge Hollow for good. Laura felt they carried a part of her heart away on that wagon. It left an empty place beneath her breast that nothing on God's earth or in heaven could ever fill.

Laura decided not to go to Indianapolis for the birth of Winifred's child. Instead, she had stayed to help Little Mattie prepare for her grand adventure. Winifred delivered a six-pound baby boy. The infant was born dead.

When she was told her baby had been stillborn, Winifred had refused to believe it and had accused the doctor and her husband of lying. "I want to see my baby!" she screamed. For days she would alternate between angry outbursts and depression. She believed her child was alive and had been taken from her because it was a monster. "Why else won't they show me my baby?" she asked Rob, again and again. "I've given birth to a monster." When she insisted they show her the grave of her child, Rob told her the remains had been incinerated. "You burned my baby! Not even buried in a Christian grave!" Winifred howled until her voice was gone. Then, after a few days, she slipped into a deep melancholia. Peter and Laura brought Winifred home.

Back in her old room in the stone house on the Blanco, Winifred seemed at first unable to remember anything about her pregnancy or delivery. She stayed in her room for days on end, yet she never seemed to sleep. When Winifred would refuse to leave the room, Laura would bring her meals and sit in the old cane-backed rocker listening to her daughter's haunted thoughts. "I suppose the reason they took my little one," Winifred said one day, "is because it had no name. I should have given the baby a name. Now he must wander eternity unknown even to himself. It was a boy, wasn't it, Mother? Or is it a monster? I know Rob is very kind, and if I gave birth to a live monster, he would never allow me to know. He would hide the child in a cage or in a freak show at the carnival." For hours Winifred would speculate about the monstrous deformities she had imposed on her newborn and no amount of reassurance would convince her of the truth.

Laura suffered these sessions with Winifred as if she were enduring a physical beating. Her very soul was bruised by her daughter's gathering madness. She tormented herself with thoughts of how things might have been different if she had helped her daughter through her pregnancy and childbirth. *If I had only been there,* she thought, and felt the guilt and sorrow grow like a dark and poisonous weed. She longed for the counsel of Little Mattie, whose absence only increased the dimensions of her sorrow. *Maybe I should have seen the problem coming. If I had been there, I might have demanded a Caesarean.* But later, when she told Peter about these thoughts, he insisted there was madness enough in the house. He would endure his daughter's delusions as best he could, but he would not tolerate the same in his wife.

For weeks it seemed Winifred was steadily improving. Her tearful outbursts, her insomnia, her depression became less life-consuming. She began to gain weight and lose the haunted look in her eyes. She sometimes dressed and left her room and walked in the yard. When the family engaged her in conversation, she would smile and answer, but she seemed detached and disinterested. There emerged again that quiet and mysterious sweetness that had been so much a part of her personality as a child.

Sometimes when Wilton or one of the other children would speak to her, Winifred would ask, "And you are?" Embarrassed and confused, Wilton would say his name. "How strange," Winifred would respond. "I have a brother named Wilton."

Then one night, Winifred disappeared. When Laura came to tuck her in for the night she was gone. A frantic search ensued and for hours they called and searched the barn and the pastures and the trails along the river.

It was a night in early spring and the Glasscock Circus was still wintering on its grounds nearby, preparing for its new season's tour through Texas and the South. On this night the old barn was alive with activity and excitement as the animals were being prepared for the road and all the circus people were packing their wardrobes and their magical paraphernalia. One of the features of the circus was a side show featuring such characters as the Alligator Man, the World's Largest Woman, the Wolf Child, and other unusual and bizarre attractions.

And it was here they found Winifred. As Ball Coon helped them carry her home, she told them that she had come to reclaim her unknown child from its cage among the freaks before the circus left town.

20 ∞ THE DEVIL'S BACKBONE

(From Laura's unpublished autobiography)

The road from Blanco to San Marcos, Texas, is only forty-five miles as the snake slithers, but it cuts a chasm across my life so deep that it is hard to see across it to the woman I was before we loaded the Ford and the wagons and started out across that wild, beautiful land toward the future. Every mile of that road is littered with little pieces of my soul, with discarded notions of right and wrong, love and duty, and all the dreams and easy pleasures youth sheds on its way toward the setting sun.

That is not to say I was an old woman when we passed, like the children of Israel, across the mountainous road called the Devil's Backbone. I was still on the near side of my fiftieth birthday, young enough to remember precisely what I missed most about my vanished youth, old enough to know why I missed it with such bittersweet clarity. And the journey was not in the direction the sun travels, but toward the south and east, against the sun, against reason, against the grain of all my life had been before.

There is a stream we crossed on that journey called Lone Woman Creek. Although it is larger and in wilder country, its waters proved to contain the same magic as my beloved Eager Mule Creek, where I first found God, or was it Eros, there in that cool canyon of shadow and fern. And the same dragons that left their footprints in the Eager Mule had come this way as well, following me from Blanco to San Marcos, it seems, several hundred thousand years before I was born. Winifred would know precisely when the dinosaurs left their prints. She would also jump at a chance to point out the difference between God and Eros, Eros being the Supreme Being who would have created Eve first and then, on the seventh day, rested with her in the Garden, waiting to create Adam on the ninth or tenth day, if at all.

Sometimes I see that journey as a stranger might have seen us from a distant promontory across the way. Two wagons pulled by mules, furniture and bedding piled high, the sound of pots and pans echoing through the canyons, all the material things one gathers and treasures through the years piled high, some falling, clattering to the ground when the road rose roughly, twisting up onto the ridges. The old Ford similarly loaded, leading the way, grinding up the rises, lurching along, swaying beneath its burden. A camel caravan comes to mind, a family of Bedouins weaving through the dunes of Arabia, or merchants moving along the Silk Road in China, lives on the move, silhouettes cutting across history. We are a migratory animal, a wandering species, ever crossing boundaries and mountains and wild lands in search of peace, or escaping the dark horsemen who ride through the villages of our lives with cruel regularity.

I remember being at the wheel of the Ford, Winifred at my side. Her silent presence was like a stone weight tied to my heart. Even now I can feel the tension I felt filling the Ford. It made a sound like bees. And there was constantly in a near corner of my mind a sense of danger. I gripped the wheel with much of my might, guarding against the possibility that Winifred might try to wrest the wheel from my grasp and hurl us off the higher ridges and into the abyss, not as an attempt to end her life, but mine. So you can imagine what a delight it was, the journey across the Devil's Spine, the high, hard road between Blanco and San Marcos, Texas.

At the time, I was not at all sure where that road would lead. But I knew it led away from sorrows too heavy to bear. I had loved our ranch by the Blanco, even if it was named for the living gallows of a hanged man. And I remember the presence of constant doubt regarding the wisdom of the move, uncertainty that plagued every mile of the journey. Had I done the right thing, uprooting my family, tearing them away from the soil that had nurtured them, and committing their lives to the unknown? But what I felt more than anything else in those days was an all-consuming and numbing aloneness. I suppose I had never been more alone in my life, even more alone than my years at the Wilderness Ranch where the trapper died on my doorstep. Yet to write about those final months on the Hanging Tree Ranch, to attempt to define that aloneness, especially when surrounded by family, is to risk unfolding a tale touching on the comic. Peter was merely a shell of what he had been, growing old in a world he would not or could not understand, unable to earn his way or ours. Little Mattie, at the age of seventy, had gone adventuring out in the Texas panhandle. Winifred, poor Winifred, was locked in an inner world with her demons and the ghost of her dead child. The boys and sister Lucy were away living their own lives, writing their own stories. Even Rebekah was preoccupied with her own private disasters and had little comfort to share. Mr. Sam's monumentally poor business sense had resulted in equally monumental debts. The Johnsons had been forced to leave their fine home in Johnson City and Rebekah, like me, was struggling to keep her little family together.

As a medicine for my ascending melancholy there was only Wilton. But even this sweet, buoyant child was in those days consumed by his dubious adventures in the Glasscock barn and had little time for his mother. Can you see how the true accounting of misfortune contains the seed of comedy? If I were to be more confident of your understanding, perhaps I should omit some of the troubles that pressed me down on the eve of that journey across the Devil's Backbone, an odyssey that changed my life forever, the second half century absolutely sheared away from the first.

With the horses gone and Peter grieving their loss, and with Winifred's teaching career interrupted by the fact that she had burned down the only school nearby where she could teach (comedy rears its head again), the family had no income. Surely, something had to be done. As I was now head of the family, I was the one who would have to do it. Rebekah's example provided an answer. A boarding-house in San Marcos could be purchased at a reasonable cost and the income from rooms rented to students at Southwest Texas State Teachers College could support a family and perhaps earn enough to send Wilton and Lyndon to college when the time came. It was a plan created by Rebekah and me across the kitchen table. But to actually live the plan, make it real, we had to cross the Devil's Backbone. There was no one in the family who would even talk about it, much less help organize the massive logistics of actually leaving.

"Dear Edward." I began the letter using his first name for the first time, knowing Colonel House would be sensitive to this altered decorum. My letter was a plea for comfort, for advice, for understanding from a man who had once claimed to be my second self. "Dear Edward," I wrote, and I think I was closer to him when I wrote those words than I had ever been or would ever be again. I loved him then. If he had been there in my room at that moment, I would have wished for what I'm sure I saw in his eyes when we were both younger. Please understand how lonely I was and how desperate to know what to do.

Edward came. And to my profound horror, he was a lamp burned out. He had broken with President Wilson over some personal issue and he was adrift, his great mission to create a world of peace and justice had come undone. We spent hours together, talking about our lives, but it was apparent I had become the parent and he the child and it was he who was most desperate for comfort.

There was little there to lean on and when he left I felt more lost than ever before.

There are certain actions we take in life that have their own momentum. They are not the results of a decision, but are the response to some inner thought, perhaps dreamed or imagined. We have no way of knowing if this voice speaks truth or folly, but we answer its call because it's the only voice we hear. And so I began to dismantle my family's life and pack it into barrels and boxes and two wagons and a Ford.

Just beyond the Dutch Branch of the Blanco River, the road begins to rise in a series of leaps and lurches onto a thin blade of stone and juniper called the Devil's Backbone. Precipitous cliffs fall away on both sides. At first it would seem strange that such a difficult site would have been selected for the road. But when examining the landscape further, it becomes apparent that this high, windswept way along the crests is the only route the road could have taken through the tortured hills.

Once past Dutch Branch, the ascent onto the Devil's Backbone is a long and difficult climb. I waited at the foot of the climb for the mules and the wagons, one driven by Peter, the other by Wilton. I remember the day was very hot; the wind felt heated and blown by the bellows of a forge and even the vultures had fled the noonday sun, preferring shade to carrion. As the road rose, I shifted into lower and lower gear, partly to ease the strain on the engine and partly to allow the mules to keep pace. We were nearly to the summit, the whole of the Texas Hill Country spread out on both sides of the road, when white smoke began to breathe from the front of the Ford and a sound like a thousand snakes screamed from beneath the car's hood. Not having the understanding of mechanics that I now possess, I at first thought the Ford was on fire. Rather the radiator was boiling over, consuming the water it contained and thereby overheating the engine. I stopped the automobile and its engine and watched in amazement as we were enveloped in a white, moist, wheezing cloud. Winifred and I escaped into the yellow sunlight and waited for Peter and Wilton to do whatever it is men do to heal the wounds of machinery.

Peter looked at the Ford with disdain and said we would have to transfer its load of goods onto the wagons. He had surmised that the Ford was damaged beyond repair and we could only leave its carcass by the side of the road to rust. Wilton agreed. Without water, there was nothing we could do. We had brought only a little for drinking, but what remained was not enough for the intemperate thirst of the engine. The next water would be in Purgatory Creek several miles ahead.

I remember standing in that suffocating sun, on a high harsh vertebrae of the Devil's Backbone, looking down along the ridges and gullies and seeing down far below a silver ribbon, a stream appearing now and again beneath foliage and outcroppings of rock. When I pointed out the water, Wilton volunteered to carry a bucket down and return with nourishment for the Ford. I don't know to this day why I didn't let him go and why, instead, I removed two milk pails from the wagon and began the descent myself. Sometimes I think I climbed down toward Lone Woman Creek as an act of desperation, that I wanted away from this family that I loved so desperately, if only for awhile, to be free of the responsibility of watching over them, maybe to bathe in the crystal water threading its way like a silver chain along the mountain.

The way down was steep. I remember sliding down over loose stone, half-sitting, half-standing, losing one of the two buckets almost immediately. It bounded down the mountainside, clattering, then taking flight, spinning in the sunlight, then clattering down again until it disappeared into the maw of the canyon. Over the years I have sought to construct a metaphor from that wildly undisciplined downward tumble, a mirror image of my own descent, a life I found falling out of my control. Soon I was sliding faster, falling, catching hold, sprawling, the rock handholds tearing loose, then holding, then breaking loose again, as I followed the bounding bucket down. At some point I let my mind and my body go limber and resigned myself to the arms of the avalanche.

There are various phrases used in prose to describe the resumption of consciousness. To "come to" is such a phrase and I made that short journey slowly, thinking first, with shallow pride, that I had not dropped the second bucket, though the knuckles of my hand grasping it were raw and bleeding. My second thought was that my descent had taken me into the shallow creek itself. I could feel its waters flowing over my legs. I remember how cool the water felt and how I was reluctant to move or rise, afraid of what injuries I might discover. I decided to lie there instead, half submerged, watching the pillowed clouds overhead sailing across the sky, maybe forever. At one point, I ran my hand across my hair, felt the knot where my head had encountered stone, and my hand came away soiled with clotted earth, but no blood. I remember thinking that if I stayed where I was I wouldn't have to deal with the terrible uncertainty of the future and the imprisoning tyranny of the past. I wouldn't have to face the dementia of my daughter, the disabling grief of my husband, the absence of my sister and mother, the death of my dreams, the loss of my youth, the injustice of losing my own life to the needs of others. I wouldn't have to mourn the fact that I would probably never again know the comfort of being cared for by a man, of being protected by strong sheltering arms. If I just stayed here on the skirts of the avalanche, covered with mud and limestone dust and the blood of the scrapes and abrasions I had endured on my fall, I wouldn't have to carry two buckets of water back up that impossible hill and deal with that damned broken Ford.

I don't know how long I lay there before the laughter came. I don't believe it started as laughter but as some dreadful cry of anguish, a sound that rose from deep within, an angry, bitter, hopeless wail that startled me, frightened me, when it emerged. I listened to that sound with wonder, feeling it came from someone else, and I was embarrassed for the person who would make such a display of his emotions. I rose to my elbows and looked around for the person in agony, hoping perhaps to comfort them, or scold them for their weakness as Little Mattie would have done. But I was alone, covered with mud, half submerged in some godforsaken creek, in the middle of nowhere, with little prospect that things would get anything but worse. I saw myself as God must have seen me and the sight was wondrously amusing. *Here I gave this woman life,* I imagined God was saying, *and the lives of others to defend, and she can't even fetch two buckets of water to fill the radiator of a Ford. I gave her free will and a strong back and the gumption of the gods, and the power to control her own destiny, and all she can do is lie weeping at the foot of a mountain.* Then I imagined I heard God laughing and the laughter was infectious and soon all the heavenly hosts were consumed by their merry ridicule of this lowly muddied mortal. I couldn't help but laugh along. Tears and laughter are easy neighbors.

I did not long provide amusement for God and his companions. In fact, they had begun to irritate me. After all, I had a mountain to climb and all they had to do was sit up there in the clouds consuming ambrosia. As I struggled to rise from the creek, I discovered I had been half lying in a dinosaur track, one of a series that led along the creek bottom. "Come get stronger," I remembered poor Herman had said nearly a half century ago as we bathed and fell in love in the waters of the Eager Mule. And I thought maybe the two streams were one and they flowed from one end of my life to the other. When standing, I felt for broken bones and, finding none, I began a search for the pail that had preceded me down the mountain. I found it nearby, dented but whole. I filled both buckets with water from the monster's track, hoping that its magic qualities were effective on machinery as well as flesh and spirit and, smiling still at the absurdity of my predicament, I began the ascent toward my family, the automobile and the future.

On that climb I resolved never again to provide laughter for the hosts of heaven. As I lifted the buckets from one ledge to another and pulled myself along over the rough stone, I could feel myself growing stronger. "You can do this," I could hear Little Mattie say from her rough cabin. "Come grow stronger," said my wild boy from the corridors of the past. And I knew, if I could do this, I could do the next thing and the next and the next.

On that climb from Lone Woman Creek I reclaimed my life and self-respect and I reclaimed the pieces of my soul that had been scattered along the road from Blanco. And I knew I could do whatever had to be done to build a new life for my family, even if I had to drag them kicking and screaming all the way. Surely this was the moment Psyche emerged from the chrysalis.

When I reached the summit, wrestling the buckets along, Winifred, her voice filled with sharp irritation, said, "Mama, what took you so long?"

"I've been a long way," I answered.

"Mama, you look terrible!" Winifred added.

"I am not," I said, and began to fill the Ford's radiator with the life-giving waters of Lone Woman Creek.

21 ∞ THE SAN MARCOS ROOMING HOUSE

WITHIN A FEW DIFFICULT MONTHS, LAURA AND HER FAMILY MAN-
aged to settle into their new home in San Marcos. The house,
known locally as the Vogelsang House after the family that built
it, was at 827 Chestnut Street, not far from the Woods mansion
overlooking a great sweep of valley. It had eleven rooms and
seemed huge in comparison to the other homes Laura had
known. It was built on a steep hill, the rooms descending down
several levels, the backyard sloping down to a wooded creek
where Laura planned her garden and a pen for chickens and
Wilton's pig. The area along the creek was called Vogelsang
(German for "birdsong") Hollow and was famous throughout
the town for the colony of Texas swamp rabbits that swam in the
creek, often with all but their eyes and ears submerged. Even
though the house was in town, Laura could sit on the back porch
that overlooked the creek and imagine she was in the country. At
night the eyes of the swamp rabbits glowed like lazy fireflies in
the darkness. "The best of both worlds," she told Wilton. "One
door leads into the country, the other into town."

The sale of the Blanco ranch provided funds not only to buy the
Vogelsang House but to provide a few necessary improvements.
One of the first things Laura did when she moved in was to
install gas heat for cooking and for hot water in the kitchen and
bathroom. It was a splendid luxury. She thought of all the kindling
and wood she had chopped and carried to the fireplaces of her previous homes and smiled to herself every time it came to her that
she would never have to chop wood for a cookstove again.

Because the new house was so large, it was ideal as a rooming
house. Southwest Texas State Teachers College was only a block
and a half away, and several rooms were now occupied by stu-

dents who paid a rent of six dollars each a month. Because of the depressed Hill Country economy, most of the students were very poor and had difficulty paying, or had to choose between paying their tuition or their rent. Students sometimes had to drop out of school to work and Laura never knew from month to month whether or not she could count on the rent. She did not serve meals to her roomers because she did not know where the food would come from. In what spare time she could manage she planted a garden and tended the few fruit trees planted by the Vogelsangs. Frequently, she took rifle in hand and added swamp rabbit to the supper menu. Each time she pursued the rabbits along the creek she was reminded of her response to Teddy Roosevelt's question about hunting: "Sometimes you hunt or not eat." Peter added a few dollars each month by farming a small tract of land out on the edge of town. Each day he rode his old white horse out to the sorrowful remnant of the vast lands that were once under his care.

The family lived on the main floor that opened onto Chestnut Street. The male roomers lived in three rooms downstairs, two to a room, sharing not only the room but the single bed. The boys had their own entrance to the backyard and could come and go as they pleased. The female roomers shared rooms upstairs, a section of the house that could be reached only by walking through Laura's parlor and dining room. When all the rooms were occupied, there were fifteen human beings in the Woods house, all sharing a single bathroom. The student rooms were very spartan. Each contained a bed, a washstand with a tin pitcher and washbowl, and a hot plate for preparing meals. There were no closets nor wardrobes. The roomers hung their clothes on broomsticks suspended across corners or on ropes attached to nails driven into the wall.

The only room in the house that had a touch of elegance was the room where Winifred lived next to the back porch. It was filled with dozens of books and with the china she had received as wedding gifts. At the foot of her bed she kept the cedar chest that had been her wedding hope chest. Often, at night, Winifred would open the lid and remove one by one the baby clothes that had been meant for her infant son had he lived. Winifred would lay the tiny garments out on the bed, refold them and then carefully pack them away again.

Running a rooming house and being the sole support of her family consumed much of Laura's time. Life in San Marcos was every bit as difficult as her life in the country had been. They had purchased the house fully furnished and within hours she was rearranging furniture, climbing up on headboards to hang new curtains, regluing chairs and encountering the hundreds of reasons the previous owners had been so eager to sell. Reasons such as broken pipes, termite conventions beneath the porches and small animals nesting in the eaves. If Laura and her family had been the only residents in the house, she would have ignored the wobbly chairs and leaking windows and dust bunnies that gathered along the baseboards. But there were guests in the house, strangers with a facility for censure, and so Laura felt compelled to straighten and repair and clean and offer her guests the best lodgings to be found in San Marcos. "One day," she was fond of saying, "I'll come home and the house will have fallen to pieces. The whole thing will simply slide down into the creek. There won't be anything left but horsehair plaster and the ghost of the incompetent who built the house in the first place."

Once each week she would build a fire beneath a large black pot in the yard and boil water for the family's washing. On Saturday, she shined Sunday's shoes and lined them up on the back porch. At mealtimes, over Peter's objections, she distributed bibbed aprons to the family so that she would not have to wash their clothes quite so often. She passed out fans from the funeral home to chase away summer's heat and fly swatters to combat the flies that invaded through the tears in the screens. In winter she went out into the freezing cold weather to wrap the water pipes with protective rags, and in summer she tied those same rags to old brooms and soaked them with gasoline to burn out nests of yellow jackets on the porch ceilings.

There was one other duty Laura performed and it filled her heart with a sorrow beyond compare. When her chores were done and the house grew still, it was time for the nightly locking of Winifred's door. Ever since the troubles on Enchanted Rock, Winifred had brooded about the pack of dogs, fearing the terrible needle the doctor had used to inoculate Laura against hydrophobia. The strange pack was never fully explained. People throughout the county reported the animals, some claiming they were mad and describing how they foamed at the mouth and whirled about in circles. Most were eventually hunted down and shot. But Winifred was certain the dogs were somehow connected to the legend of the Comanche chief who sacrificed his daughter. She told Wilton she believed her baby boy had been consumed by the flames of a sacrificial fire. At night she would wander the house and the creek behind the house, listening for the footsteps of her child. Laura had decided to lock her door at night to keep her safely at home.

Each time Laura turned the key to lock Winifred's door, it felt as if the key was cutting into her flesh. She willed the tumblers in the lock to turn silently so God would not hear. But it was becoming increasingly evident that there was something mean living inside Winifred. There were times when Laura could almost feel the violence building up inside her daughter, like steam in a kettle, and it was at those times that Laura urged the other children to stay away.

One morning, as Laura's niece Claydene Hoge was sitting with Laura at the breakfast table, Claydene complained to Laura that Winifred was staring at her and would not stop. When Laura admonished her daughter, Winifred ignored her and her eyes continued to assault Claydene. Then, suddenly, Winifred said, "Why did you kill my baby!" The words were missiles hurled with obvious hatred.

Laura would often discover knives missing from the kitchen and then find them in Winifred's room. She began to hide the knives and to her great sorrow she grew more and more afraid of this child she had brought into the world. Sometimes when she recognized this fear she would become so ashamed she would rush into Winifred's room and gather her sleeping daughter into her arms and hold her and rock her until Winifred would wake, stiffen and push her away.

Early in Winifred's illness, Rob Caldwell had taken her to Menninger Clinic in Topeka, Kansas. After an examination, the doctors said her psychosis brought on by the death of her child was incurable. They characterized her disorder as "periodic insanity" and suggested that the probability of recurrence throughout her life was quite high. They further suggested that Winifred be committed to an asylum. When Rob returned with the news, Laura and Peter spent many nights struggling with a plan for Winifred's life. The most troubling thing about her condition was its periodic nature. If she had been constantly stark-raving mad, it would have seemed a kindness to put her in an institution. But there were wonderful periods of normality, brief seasons when Winifred would return with all her sweetness and innocence, and Laura would begin to think that maybe the demons had been exorcised and all her dreams for Winifred would come rushing back like welcome old friends. But then Winifred would steal a knife and she would cut herself or carve crazed figures on the wall or cut the reed bottoms from the rocking chairs, and Laura would know that her child had gone away again to that dark world no one else could enter.

After one particularly violent episode, brought on apparently by a visit from Rob, whom Winifred now believed to have been responsible for the death of her baby, Peter and Laura approached him with the option of divorce. "We realize how unfair this is," Laura said. "It's only right that you should be free to have your life." Winifred seemed not to care at all and the marriage was dissolved.

One afternoon, the sky grew dark, the air electric, and the wind blew cold from the north. Laura had hung her wash on the line and the sheets began to whip and snap in the rising wind. As Laura rushed outside with a laundry basket to gather in the sheets before the rain, out of the corner of her eye, she saw Winifred step from the back of the house. Laura started at one end of the clothesline, removing the pins, gathering in the sheets, feeling the power of the coming storm and something else powerful in the air. The first few drops fell and the wind tugged at the sheets like sails in a storm at sea. Laura was pleased that Winifred had come to help and she felt a rare closeness to her daughter as they worked and raced the storm. For a moment, Laura lost track of Winifred as she fought the billowing sheets. Finally, there was only one sheet left and Laura rose on tiptoe, her arms high, and suddenly a blade slashed down through the sheet, ripping the cloth, passing inches from Laura's breast. Again she saw the blade swing, tearing a ragged seam in the sheet. Lightning cut into the gloom. Thunder slapped the air and the rain came almost solidly down. Winifred's face was a mask of hatred and anger. Laura stood for a moment, transfixed, thinking maybe she would welcome a lightning bolt to come burn away her dread. Winifred looked up into the storm, dropped the knife and turned away. For a long moment, Laura stood in the rain, her arms wrapped around her middle as protection from the blade. She tried not to think about what had happened, especially that her daughter had come to the clothesline to kill. She pushed the thought away, and away, until it was gone.

When the family moved to San Marcos, Laura had expected Winifred might renew her friendship with Flournoy, who lived only a few blocks away. But Flournoy rarely visited, and when she did, she spent more time with Laura than with Winifred. It was not that Flournoy did not try to reestablish the relationship that had existed before Winifred's engagement to Ralph Edwards and her marriage to Rob Caldwell, but Winifred was as cold and distant with Flournoy as she was with everyone else. Laura, on the other hand, had grown fond of the strange, tall, pale woman who had been Winifred's close friend, and she could tell that Flournoy was hurt by Winifred's coldness.

One day, when Flournoy had come visiting, Laura heard Winifred's door slam shut jarringly and Flournoy came into the kitchen, eyes red-rimmed, the corners of her mouth trembling with emotion. The poor girl had obviously just been subjected to one of Winifred's random cruelties, and Laura opened her arms wide and Flournoy moved awkwardly into their refuge. Laura was a head shorter than Flournoy and for a moment it felt like she might have been holding Peter, except for a breath of rose and the soft, barely perceptible mounds of Flournoy's breasts.

"I'm so sorry," Laura said, patting the younger woman sympathetically. "I had hoped you two would take up again where you left off."

"I wanted that, too," Flournoy said, her voice deep and soft. "I wanted it more than anything in the world." Laura was moved by the passion in Flournoy's voice. She led her to a chair at the kitchen table and offered her tea. They did not speak as the kettle heated, but Laura felt that Flournoy wanted to talk and was searching her mind for what it was exactly that she wanted to say. Even when Laura had poured the hot tea and had taken a chair at the table, Flournoy sat quietly, seeming to look deep into the dark fragrant mists clouding her cup. Laura could not help but wonder about the mystery of this woman who dressed her lean masculine frame with such extravagant femininity.

"It's hard to lose a good friend," Laura said.

"At first I thought it was something I'd done. Or something I am."

Laura reached across the table and touched Flournoy's hand. "It's just Winifred fighting her demons. I suppose it takes all her strength and she hasn't any left for us."

"She understood me. Accepted me. I don't know. I just don't know how things could change so much."

Flournoy sighed and straightened as if in preparation to leave. Then she seemed to change her mind and she settled again in her chair. "We used to talk, Winifred and I, about how we felt about things. And what we should do. I miss that."

"You can talk to me, Flournoy."

"It's just I get so confused, Miss Laura. And I'm always of two minds about things. There are things I want to do with my life, but people say I'm foolish to want such things. Aunt Carrie and Emma. They say even worse than foolish."

"What things do you want to do?"

"You'll laugh."

"I won't laugh, Flournoy."

"It's what I want to be."

"I thought you wanted to be a teacher."

"That's what other people want me to be. But what I want to be is something else."

"If not a teacher, what?"

"A cotton broker."

In spite of herself Laura had to fight back a smile. "A cotton broker?"

"I just love being down at the gin and at the exchange. I love the excitement and the energy of the place. I love how it smells and the waiting to see what the prices will do. And I know I could do well trading. I think there must be a merchant prince back in the family somewhere. I love . . ." Flournoy paused in midsentence, her face clouding and she sighed again. "I don't know. Aunt Carrie and Emma say it's a man's job."

"And what do you say?"

"I say so what. Who's to say what's a man's job and what's a woman's job? Who's to say what's a man and what's a woman?" Flournoy turned her head away and covered her eyes with her hand.

Laura again wondered at the loneliness her neighbor must feel as she struggled daily with the puzzle of her identity. She remembered the painful conversations with poor Herman, who was adrift between two worlds, neither white nor Indian. Now here was poor Flournoy, adrift between male and female, not quite one or the other.

"What's important is where you will be happy. Where you'll feel accepted. And I doubt if you'd be accepted down at the cotton exchange. Neither would I. It's a man's world and that's just the way it is. It has nothing to do with us. It has to do with them. And their blindness."

"So you think I should teach?"

"You have a fine mind. You'd make an excellent teacher."

"And that's a job for a woman," Flournoy added, bitterness in her voice.

"It's where you'll be accepted. Where I'd be accepted if I had been to college."

"I can't imagine the day I'd be accepted anywhere."

"You're accepted here, now. At this table."

"You're a good woman, Miss Laura. Something I guess I'll never be." She rose and moved toward the door.

Laura watched Flournoy walk up the hill toward the old Woods mansion. She had a long stride and seemed terribly uncomfortable in her high heel pumps and yards of floral dimity. Laura decided it was all right that she had offered Flournoy such terrible advice. She had wanted to say, "Go down to the cotton exchange and be the best cotton broker this town ever had!" But she was not sure Flournoy could have endured the pain.

The following Monday, Eugene and Cornelia Woods and their little four-year-old daughter, Betty Claire, came to spend a day. Betty Claire was a lovely child, her strawberry blond hair worn in corkscrew curls like Shirley Temple's. Because she was an only child, Cornelia and Eugene always dressed her in ruffles and lace.

After a while, as Laura and Cornelia busied themselves frying chicken and mashing potatoes in the kitchen, the little girl was missed.

"Do you know where Betty Claire is?" Peter asked from the kitchen doorway. Laura did not know. "Probably playing down by the creek. That's where I'd be on a day like this."

After a while, Peter returned. "I can't find her anywhere."

"Well," Laura said, "she can't be far." But as time passed, and her little granddaughter did not return, a coldness began to settle over Laura's heart. Laura dried her hands and moved to the parlor. "Where's Winifred?" she asked. Peter cut his eyes toward the back hall.

Laura moved quickly to Winifred's room and her heart became ice when she saw the door was closed, locked from the inside. Laura called and there was a muffled answer from Betty Claire, then silence. Laura began pounding on the door, screaming for Peter and Eugene. Now there was only silence. Eugene took a few steps back and hurled his shoulder against the door. It shattered and as it flew back, there was Winifred and

Betty Claire sitting on the pink chenille bedspread among Betty Claire's Betsy McCall paper dolls. Betty Claire had obviously been frightened by the shattering of the door and perhaps something else. Winifred was smiling when Laura lifted the little girl from the bed. Laura looked at Peter and breathed a sigh of relief. Then she saw the large butcher knife half hidden by the paper-doll book.

That night Peter and Laura lay awake not speaking their thoughts for some time. Then Laura asked, "What are we going to do?"

"I don't know."

"Do you *really* think she would have hurt little Betty Claire?"

"I don't know."

"I think she's jealous of Eugene's baby. Maybe she thought 'If I can't have a baby, why should they have one.' "

"Don't say that." Peter closed his eyes against the thought.

"I won't." Laura looked away. She did not want to see Peter's face. "Peter, is it time to think about a place for her?"

"I can't," Peter said. "I don't know if I could. Besides, Laura, maybe it was all innocent. Maybe it was nothing."

They both knew it was not.

Laura continued to cling to the hope that Winifred might be cured. Shortly after the episode with Betty Claire, Laura made an appointment with Dr. Titus Harris, a noted psychiatrist at the Galveston Hospital. A series of interviews was scheduled and on a sweltering August morning, Peter, Eugene, Laura, and Winifred drove to Houston and then down through the sugar and rice fields of South Texas to the island of Galveston. The trip was made largely in silence for Winifred was furious and her anger filled the car like heavy smoke. They passed the grand homes along Broadway and then turned into the complex of buildings surrounding the huge red-brick bulk of the Ashbel Smith Building, or "Big Red" as the University of Texas Medical Department was called.

Dr. Titus Harris held court in a large, beautifully furnished room that could have been one of the lesser drawing rooms of a grand hotel. A Persian rug covered a highly polished floor. The tall windows were heavy with dark red damask and dust floated in the meager streams of sunlight the drapes let pass. The family sat in a circle facing Dr. Harris, a small man with gentle eyes. He studied a file for a full five minutes in silence, a silence Laura hated because she was afraid it might be filled with the cries of the insane who must have been locked away beyond the closed arched doorways of the room. Dr. Harris opened his gold pocket watch and placed it on a table by his chair.

"So," Dr. Harris said. His eyes seemed kind, alert, and active in contrast to his body. "I thought we'd just talk for a while. Get to know each other. Who'd like to begin? Miss Winifred?"

"I'm having a very difficult time with this," Winifred said. Her eyes were cast down where her hands were twisting in her lap. "It's probably the hardest thing I've ever had to do. But the woman is obviously insane."

"Who, darling?" Peter asked.

"Your wife! My mother! Not only is she insane, she is criminally insane. It's only right that we bring her here and have her committed. It's a difficult thing to do but it must be done."

So astonishing was Winifred's accusation, so unbelievable was the moment, that the thought actually flashed through Laura's mind that Winifred was right, and the gates of Bedlam were opening not for the daughter but the mother.

"Tell us why your mother needs treatment?" The doctor's voice was gentle and betrayed no disbelief or bias.

"For one thing, she is trying to starve us to death. Not only does she refuse to do housework, but she burns all the food she puts on the stove. She burns it on purpose. When she goes to the market, she buys spoiled food and cooks it for us and makes us eat it."

"Winifred, you know that isn't so!" Laura said, a bemused vexation beginning to eclipse her incredulity. Dr. Harris held up his hand, as if to quiet Laura's objections and Winifred continued her litany of complaint.

"When my mother milks the cows she never washes the milking pail. She just rinses it with cold water and pours the tainted water out in the backyard. Where she pours, long worms come out of the ground and they crawl into the house. Every night, for two years, I had to pour boiling water on those worms to kill them. But I never could."

Laura could feel her anger rising, like a fever. She was not angry at poor Winifred, but at the fates. She looked up at the ceiling fan flinging itself through the air and for a moment she felt as if she were spinning and the fan was motionless in the heated air above. She knew that Winifred's words were the expressions of a twisted mind. She knew she should feel sympathy or even terrible sorrow, but what she felt was this welling of discomposure, a sense of being unfairly accused.

"You should be ashamed!" Laura said sharply.

"I am ashamed," Winifred said. "I'm ashamed of you! Trying to starve your own husband and daughter!"

"This is ridiculous!" Laura said, pointing her finger at Winifred and rising from her chair.

"See how she threatens me?" Winifred seemed calm in the face of Laura's anger. "She is a dangerous woman. I'm afraid to stay at home alone with her. Sometimes she takes a butcher knife and threatens to kill me!"

Laura sank back into her chair. "Peter," she said, looking back into the cold, dark depths of her daughter's eyes. "Please put one of us away. I really don't care which one right now."

"What do you think, Winifred?" the doctor asked. "Do you want to go back to San Marcos with your parents? Or do you want to stay here for a while. Maybe get some rest."

Winifred didn't hesitate. "I want to stay here. I'm tired of fearing for my life. Being starved to death. Maybe here I'll get enough to eat. I'm tired of her constantly telling me I do everything wrong. I don't do the dishes right. I don't do this to suit her or that to suit her. And then she tries to kill me and I have to lock the door to my room so she can't get to me with her knives."

On the long drive back to San Marcos, Laura replayed the afternoon conference in her mind. As she reviewed Winifred's complaints one by one, she realized much of what her daughter said was nonsense, especially the part about the long worms from the milk pail. But many of Winifred's complaints rose from a seed of truth. It was true that Laura hated housework and she sometimes neglected those chores she disliked most. It was true that she often burned their dinner. After all, there were more important things on her mind. It was true that she was always after Winifred for doing things wrong. But that was because Winifred did do everything wrong. Several times a day, Laura had to simply say, "Oh, never mind, I'll do it myself!" And then there was the story of the butcher knives and the locked doors. Winifred had turned everything backward in her mind. Laura decided that life with Winifred could drive you crazy.

"Peter," she said, as they began to see the lights of San Marcos in the hills ahead, "I don't want Winifred in my house anymore. I just can't live that way."

"We'll see," Peter said from the backseat. "We'll just have to see."

After a few weeks in the hospital, Winifred showed remarkable improvement. The doctors claimed she had gained weight, was sleeping well, was composed and cooperative. In September, Peter and Eugene returned to Galveston and brought Winifred home.

One night, shortly after Winifred had returned, Laura stayed up late reading an article about the experimental work of the Viennese psychiatrist Sigmund Freud. His landmark work, *Introduction to Psychoanalysis,* had been released in 1917 and his theories on manic-depressive psychosis were still being hotly debated. Freud had written that the suppression of guilt or remorseful ideas or anything painful to the conscious mind was the cause of neurosis. It followed, then, that if these suppressed feelings could be released, the neurosis might be eased. As far as Laura could determine, the process was at the heart of what Freud called psychoanalysis. As Laura turned out the lights and headed for bed, she wondered if psychoanalysis would release Winifred's demons.

Laura remembered to lock Winifred's bedroom door. She moved through the darkened hallway, paused at the door, and as carefully as she could, so God could not hear the sound, she placed the key in the lock. Then the door flew inward and Winifred rose on her tiptoes with a butcher knife held high, the sharp iron edge gleaming in the moonlight. Winifred was a coiled spring and Laura knew she was facing the moment of her death. She was totally incapable of motion even though her heart was thrashing and bounding around like a crazed bird in a cage. Laura waited to die. She closed her eyes. She wondered if her heart would tear itself loose before the knife descended.

Then she heard the knife drop to the floor and the rustle of silk and the feel of Winifred's cheek upon her own. "Goodnight, Mother," Winifred said, then slipped into bed.

The next morning, Laura packed Winifred's things for the long trip to the insane asylum in San Antonio. She packed Winifred's favorite outfits, a few books, some writing materials, and almost as a reflex, she opened the trunk and placed a random few of the dead baby's garments in the cardboard suitcase that now contained what little would accompany her daughter into the future. Laura could not bring herself to say good-bye. She watched from a window as Peter climbed in the Ford's backseat with Winifred. Eugene drove and Wilton sat in the passenger seat so that he could observe Winifred in the rearview mirror. Laura watched the Ford rattle away.

Like those of the Woods family, the fortunes of the Johnson family had been steadily declining. Although Mr. Sam had once again been elected to the Texas legislature, his financial affairs were in terrible disarray. Sometimes Laura would look at Rebekah and wonder where the young girl she knew had gone. For years now, Rebekah had been subjected to seasons of grinding poverty, years of raising Lyndon and Josefa, young Rebekah, Lucia, and Sam Houston with Mr. Sam generally away in Austin or campaigning down country roads. Laura had watched her friend, the beautiful, graceful descendant of journalists, justices, physicians, and Scottish kings begin to age before her eyes. Rebekah was the last of a generation of American women who would recite Tennyson and Browning while carrying water in buckets from a stream and scrubbing clothes on a washboard.

Laura could not help but blame Mr. Sam for his family's poverty. Although he was a strong and able legislator, he had for years been fighting a losing battle with "Demon Rum." She could see the pain Mr. Sam's bouts with alcohol caused her gentle, long-suffering friend. Rebekah's father, Judge Baines, had been a towering opponent of alcohol, and all her life the condemnation of drink and its abuse had filled Rebekah's home and her heart. Now, when Rebekah heard the rumors that Mr. Sam would be so unsteady with drink that he had difficulty climbing the stairs of public buildings, or when his friends would bring him home from the Driskill bar, something in her heart must have died a little. "How can you put up with it?" Laura would ask on those occasions. Then she would regret the question because she knew there was nothing that could be done. Rebekah had promised Mr. Sam their union would be "until death do us part," and it was unthinkable that she would break that holy vow.

Mr. Sam was often terribly argumentative. And he was an imposing figure. Well over six feet tall, gaunt, almost cadaverous, with black, fierce eyes, Mr. Sam was one of the last Texas legislators to wear a pistol on his hip. He was equally imposing in his home and Laura was one of the few guests in the Johnson parlor who would not retreat before the force of his opinions. As Mr. Sam's voice and anger rose, Rebekah would intervene. "He's ill," she would say. "Don't argue with him, he's not been well." And she would calm him down with kindness and iced tea. Later, by way of apologizing, Mr. Sam would offer Laura a chocolate or a peppermint stick or some other small candy that he kept on the mantel.

Sam Johnson was one of those rare politicians who could not be bought. He had stood boldly against the Ku Klux Klan at a time when it was dangerous to do so. He publicly called anyone with Klan sympathies, "Kukluxsonsobitches." As a member of the Texas House of Representatives, he voted his conscience on every issue that came before him. He refused to give in to the influence peddlers or to sell out his convictions. Few politicians of the day were more vigorous defenders of the poor or of civil liberties or more committed to the opposition of special interests.

Like the heroes of Shakespeare, Mr. Sam was a great man flawed. And Laura found she could not blame Mr. Sam as much as she blamed the liquor lobby for creating the poisons that were bringing the good man down. It was largely because of Mr. Sam that she fought so passionately for Prohibition.

When Rebekah's plan to purchase a rooming house in San Marcos was delayed by Sam's financial reverses, Lyndon came to live with the sixteen others who occupied the Vogelsang house. Of course Wilton was delighted to have his good friend as a roommate, but Laura felt Lyndon had the impact on her life of ten additional roomers. His energy seemed to fill the house and spill over into the hollow. Everything about Lyndon seemed larger than life, and Laura sensed the rumors of his mischief-making might be more than merely hearsay.

Laura's concern for Lyndon was also due to her awareness that Wilton was generally a part of whatever mischief Lyndon was orchestrating. She knew Lyndon and Wilton would wait until she and Peter were asleep and then would "borrow" the car for late-night rides. She knew that the boys made and consumed bootleg beer from a recipe borrowed from their friend Buster Brown's grandfather, a bootlegger from La Grange. A hundred times she thought about asking Lyndon to move to another rooming house, but she knew it would hurt Rebekah's feelings terribly. And then Lyndon would come striding into her kitchen, all arms and legs and disarming smiles, and would tell her he loved her, give a big kiss on her cheek and she would melt and fall in love with him all over again.

Although Rebekah and Laura had always been able to share their most intimate thoughts, when it came to Lyndon, Laura had learned to be circumspect, certainly to say nothing Rebekah might interpret as criticism. Whenever Rebekah would begin to praise her boy and predict for him the most glorious of futures, Laura learned to simply agree or to hold her tongue. She was amazed that Rebekah could not see or refused to see Lyndon's most glaring flaws. After all, everyone knew that Lyndon was not doing well in school; his inattention and numerous absences were legend. Yet Rebekah could only see what she wanted to see. When Lyndon refused to obey his father or rebelled against authority at school, Rebekah managed to turn the shortcoming into a virtue.

"Some children are born to follow," Rebekah once said. "My children are born to lead."

Once, when a local deputy sheriff accused the boys of burning down a barn, both mothers defended their sons and supported the boys' denial. "Some children lie," Rebekah said. "Lyndon never tells a lie."

"I suppose he also cut down the cherry tree," Laura said, angry at her friend's blind and often misguided faith. "It wasn't George Washington at all. It was Lyndon."

It was one of the few times the two friends parted in anger.

Whenever possible, Laura encouraged the boys to pursue activities at home where she could monitor the acceptability of their mischief. She encouraged their juggling and their practice of circus tricks even though they were dangerous and it was not at all unlikely that Lyndon might try to talk Wilton into running away with the circus, still the ultimate adventure for boys. She felt they spent far too much time going back to the Glasscock place, in Blanco, where the circus people camped. Once, when airing Wilton's bedding, she found beneath the mattress a photograph of the immodestly dressed Etta Leon. She had signed the picture with what Laura thought was an unusually personal expression of regard. Laura was especially relieved each year when the Glasscock Circus left Texas without Wilton or Lyndon or complication.

If there was any bright spot at all in Mr. Sam's bouts with the bottle, it was the impact it had on Lyndon. Mr. Sam's drinking was an embarrassment to Lyndon. As time went by, the rumors of Lyndon's own youthful experiments ceased. Laura was sure the sins of the father had been the salvation of the son.

In 1924, the year Wilton, Lyndon, and Horace Richards created their potato-chip factory in Laura's basement and their "Texas Taters" were becoming popular among the students and faculty at nearby Southwest Texas State Teachers College, Ma Ferguson ran for governor of Texas. She was the first woman for whom Laura could cast her vote. Laura followed the campaign in the newspapers and spoke for Ma Ferguson to all who would listen and to some who would not. When Gov. Farmer Jim Ferguson, the great Populist turned felon, had been impeached and barred from ever again holding office in Texas—an event that Laura felt had happened because she had willed it—Ferguson entered his wife's name instead as Democratic candidate for governor in the 1924 primary. She became the anti-Klan candidate. Laura had detested Farmer Jim, but the anti-Klan theme of his wife's campaign was surely on the side of the angels. The Klan had become terribly powerful in Texas. An avowed Klansman, Earle B. Mayfield, had been elected to the U.S. Senate. In Texas, in the first 1924 gubernatorial Democratic primary, the Klan candidate, Felix D. Robertson, received more votes than anybody else in the race. Ma Ferguson came in second to force a runoff.

The Woods and the Johnson families attended a Ferguson rally in Austin where both Ma and Pa Ferguson made speeches. "The people of Texas," Farmer Jim said, "will have two governors for the price of one."

Then Ma Ferguson asked all true women to rise up and join her holy crusade. "As the first woman governor in our beloved state," she said, "I ask for the goodwill and prayers of the women of Texas. I want to be worthy of the trust and confidence which they have reposed in me."

Laura was surprised that the words of the surrogate candidate would move her so. Ma Ferguson continued, "By the decree of our supreme court we women have been recognized and admitted into all the rights and privileges of citizenship. Many women will be invited to take part in this administration. Let us give the state the best that is in us. Let us render full service, not so much because we are women, but because we now stand side by side with men upon the foundation of equal justice."

Laura had been both excited and saddened by the speech. Ma Ferguson had invited the women of Texas to give the state the best that was in them. Laura thought that was a little like inviting people to a party in a house that had no doors. But it was still good to hear a woman's voice from the stump. And it was exciting to think about a woman governor. Too bad Ma Ferguson could not have the opportunity to run on her own. Even though Laura knew Ma Ferguson was just a front for her worthless husband, a captive woman in the governor's mansion was better than no woman there at all. And then there was the Klan. Maybe Ma Ferguson would have the strength to not only throw out the Klan but Farmer Jim, as well. "It could happen," Laura told Rebekah. "I admit it doesn't happen often. In fact, the reverse is usually true. Power corrupts and all that. But maybe just this once power can enlighten and liberate."

During the campaign, Laura called as many people as she could and asked them to support her candidate. On the morning of the election, she rose before the sun and waited anxiously for the polls to open. She wanted to be the first to vote, to savor this hard-won right, and all day long enjoy the feeling of having done her part. Nearly a million other voters turned out to vote. The majority cast their votes for Ma Ferguson and she became the first woman governor of Texas and only the second woman governor in the nation.

It was a bittersweet victory. Laura was proud that a woman could at last actually become governor, yet ashamed that Ma Ferguson was a pawn of the male establishment. "But sometimes a pawn can take a knight or a bishop, even threaten a king," she wrote Colonel House. She also wrote to Ma Ferguson herself, urging her to be courageous and "stand up to those controlling men." Laura also hinted that she would be open to serve in the administration. But it was not to be. No letter of appointment came from Austin, and Ma Ferguson's administration did nothing to fight the Klan and it achieved little else. It did pardon some two thousand convicts, a policy Laura would claim "gave new meaning to the concept of prison reform."

In the year Ma Ferguson became governor of Texas, the Ford Motor Company produced its ten millionth automobile. To most of her family, it seemed Laura had wrecked most of them. Her driving was the scandal of Central Texas and only the most foolhardy neighbors parked their cars anywhere near the Woods home on the Chestnut Street hill. Continuing his long, bitter resentment against the automobile, Peter refused to drive. He called the Ford "Laura's car." The sight of Laura sitting tall in the driver's seat of her violated and battered automobile while Peter rode in back was a familiar and much remarked San Marcos scene. Wilton said he thought Peter rode in back because it was a safer place to be in a collision.

∞

In January of 1924, two young aviators, Leon Klink and Charles Lindbergh, came barnstorming through Texas on their way across the continent. They stayed for a while in San Marcos taking people for rides at a dollar a ticket. Laura had heard the plane's engines rattling and groaning overhead all day. As she was walking with Rebekah down the Chestnut Street hill, she looked up and saw the aeroplane itself, looping and diving and spinning through the low clouds.

"It's a wonder those wings don't just tear right off," Rebekah observed. "What kind of fools would risk their lives in a contraption like that?"

The tale of Lindbergh's daring was all over town, especially the incident in Utopia, Texas, where he misjudged a maneuver and knocked the roof off a store. A picture of Lindbergh by his damaged plane had appeared in the paper and Laura had decided the young aviator was the handsomest man she had ever seen.

The little plane returned. It seemed to come directly toward them. "I can't believe they'd risk their lives like that," Rebekah repeated. "If I were his mother, I'd . . ." Her words were consumed by the roar of the aeroplane as it came storming directly over town and thundered up Chestnut Street and over the Woods home so low that Laura could see the features of the pilot and the passenger who looked very much like . . . "Wilton!"

Laura was furious. Later, when she analyzed her anger, she knew it was not anger at all. What she felt was envy. Ever since she had watched Reverend Cannon fly the Ezekiel Airship over his Fredericksburg meadow, she had dreamed of flying. As each child and each of life's mounting responsibilities made the possibility that much more remote, her desire to fly grew more intense. More than once, as Laura scrubbed the children's clothes or sat awake with a sick child, she would picture herself in the cockpit of a gallant little aeroplane, her white scarf trailing behind her, the fields and towns turning beneath her as she looped and whirled through the clouds like Marjorie or Katherine Stinson.

On the second day Lindbergh was in town, Laura decided she would learn to fly. She would become an aviatrix and would fly for the Democratic party, taking candidates to rallies throughout the state, maybe the nation. The more she thought about it, the more absolute the logic became.

When she was sure her roomers were at school and Peter was otherwise occupied, Laura drove to the field outside of town where the graceful little Laird Swallow biplane was taxiing to a stop by a persimmon tree. As Lindbergh helped a young passenger down from the front cockpit, Laura approached the plane.

"I want you to teach me to fly," Laura said.

Lindbergh collected a dollar from his passenger and turned to Laura. "I'll take you up, ma'am," he said. "But it takes a while to learn to fly. And I'll only be here a day or two." Laura was impressed with Lindbergh's youth. He seemed just a child with both innocence and daring in his eyes. He reminded her of an aerialist at the Glasscock Brothers Circus, except Lindbergh had found a way to release the trapeze and soar far beyond the confines of the Big Top. "I'd like to take you up, though. Just a dollar."

Laura reached into her purse. "Here's two dollars. I want the full experience. I want to *really* fly!"

Lindbergh smiled and pocketed the money. Laura was relieved that he did not seem amused. In his smile was a warm recognition of her dream, of her need to know this new and rare dimension of our world. It was as if he had felt the same way and he honored the feeling in another, even though Laura must have seemed the most unlikely aviatrix of the new age. So the handsome young man helped the small middle-aged woman into the front open cockpit of the Laird Swallow and he strapped her in behind the 180-horsepower Hisso engine. He asked her to remove her hat and veil, then helped her put on and adjust a canvas cap with goggles. Lindbergh smiled again, then climbed into the rear cockpit and as Laura listened to her racing heartbeat and marveled at the beautifully fashioned wood struts and frames of the plane, the pilot signaled his partner to spin the propeller.

Laura was unprepared for the noise. While the Ezekiel Airship had made a rattle-tap, rattle-tap sound like a soldier's drum, the big Hisso engine was more like thunder unceasing. One thunder clap clamoring atop another and another, and Laura was aware lightning was flashing inside the iron pistons that were very nearly in her lap. Every inch of Laura's body vibrated. Prop wash from the now whirling propeller blew dust back through the struts and into Laura's face, and before she could analyze a new sensation that was beginning to invade her body and her mind, the ground and Laura's insides fell away and she was doing at last what mankind had dreamed ever since Icarus built his wings of wax.

They were aloft. They sped along the San Marcos River, then Lindbergh pointed the plane's nose toward heaven and the sound of the engine changed and grew irregular with its labor. The vibration became an actual shaking and it seemed certain the parts of the plane would fly off in all directions. To Laura's utter surprise, the plane actually stopped in midair, standing on its tail. Then it fell away like a leaf, toppled down, spinning, then caught in another roar of sound and vibration and soared up again above the town. Laura put her hands on the control stick and suddenly an amazing thing happened. All the racket and vibration fell away and it seemed she was sailing soundless on a cloud, drifting, soaring, sliding on stanzas of air. She moved the stick forward and the little plane nosed down toward the hills. She moved the stick back and they eased up into the clouds. She moved the stick to the left and they turned in a magic arc and she knew this was a joy she had been living for all these years. She looked back and Lindbergh was beaming, surely aware of her joy that was holy as prayer. They looped and spun in the cold blue January air. Never before had she felt such freedom. It was like riding on a beam of sunlight and being in absolute control. She thought of her long journey from Hoge Hollow to the Wilderness Ranch to the

Hanging Tree Ranch to Vogelsang Hollow and she knew she had at last become captain of her life and the lives around her. The vow she made on the climb from Lone Woman Creek had been realized. She had risen above the various tragedies of her life that would have left a lesser woman defeated by the wayside. She had suffered the death of her sister, the loss of her husband's strength and will, the madness of a child, the mauling of wild dogs, the bullets of Pasqual Orozco, all the appalling ghosts that had littered her path, grasping at her ankles as she passed, and she had endured, survived, triumphed, with her spirit secure. She thrilled to the knowledge that she had created the rooming house and made it work, had resolved the issue of Winifred, had raised fine children, including one half-done, dear Wilton, whom she would shape into the image of her dreams. She moved the control stick to the right and the little plane turned right. She moved the control stick to the left and the plane flew left. The trick, she thought, once aloft, is to maintain control, whether it's a family or Charles Lindberghs Laird Swallow. They flew down over the San Marcos River and soared up over the college and then low over Vogelsang Hollow and Laura knew she was at last firmly in control of her life and Lindbergh's machine and maybe she would fly them both to the very throne of God.

Soon she felt a pressure on her hand, an insistent counter pressure to her own. She looked back and Lindbergh was pointing toward the ground. Reluctantly she released the stick and the plane sliced off down toward the field.

When they had landed and the thundering engine had stilled, Lindbergh helped Laura remove her helmet. "Can we do it again?" Laura asked.

"Another dollar," he said. It was obvious he was pleased that Laura had loved her flight. "There's still light."

"Let's fly!" Laura said, handing the young aviator another dollar from her purse.

They flew until it was dark. Laura did not tell a soul about her flight with Lindbergh and when Peter asked where she had been so long, she pretended not to hear.

LIFE IN THE HILL COUNTRY HAD ALWAYS BEEN HARD. BY 1926, the Great Depression that would strike the nation a few years later was already devastating the economy of Texas. There had been years of hard drought. Gaunt cows wandered naked pastures and occasionally the dry crack of rifle fire echoed across the fields as farmers shot their diseased and starving cattle. Fields lay barren. Trees were as bare as they were in the worst of winter. When the north wind blew, it carried clouds of red dust from the dead lands of Oklahoma to settle like an alien blanket on the dark Texas earth. In the farming communities there was little money, few jobs, and families struggled just to make it through another day. Most of the families lived on small farms, toiling from dawn until dark, surviving by grit and by faith. Others who lived in town were dependent on the dubious bounty of the countryside.

As the drought deepened, food became scarce. Some, like Laura, who had wells, could water their animals and their gardens. Others could only depend on the kindness of their neighbors. Several days a week, Laura would gather with her United Daughters of the Confederacy group to organize the distribution of food for the needy, especially the elderly who lived on remote farms. "The Tallmans aren't eating well," one of the Daughters commented.

"You mean they're starving to death," Laura said. She had no patience with such delicate words when life itself was at stake.

Among those who were seriously threatened by the hard times were Aunt Emma and Aunt Carrie. The two old women lived alone in the great Woods mansion on the hill. They were rarely seen outside the house. Some said they were victims of their own vanity and had become reclusive so that their neighbors could not tell how low the times had brought them. Several times a week Laura carried a basket of vegetables and sometimes venison or swamp rabbit to the house.

On one such mission to the Woods mansion, she was met at the door by Cousin Flournoy. She was wearing dark trousers, a loose white shirt and tie. Her hair was cut very short. Cousin Flournoy welcomed Laura warmly and then began filling her in on how she had spent the last several years.

"I took your advice," she said when they had settled down in the parlor. "I've been teaching in a little school in Sisterdale."

"How long will you stay?"

"That really depends. I'm afraid Aunt Carrie and Aunt Emma need me here. Some kind of crisis having to do with the house, but I can't quite make out the sense of it. They admit to the crisis but refuse to talk about it. They say it's unseemly to talk about money."

Laura and Flournoy spent the afternoon talking about family and teaching and the hard times that had settled on the Hill Country. Then the conversation came around to the house that had been so important in both their lives.

"It's a mess," Flournoy said. "It makes me sad to see how they've let it go. If nothing else, it needs a good cleaning."

Laura looked at the counterpane of dust that covered the once grand furnishings. "If you really want to clean the house, I'll help. When you run a rooming house you become accomplished at the fine art of cleaning."

"Oh, Laura, I couldn't ask."

"You didn't. I volunteered."

The next day, after Flournoy and Laura had dragged carpets out back and were preparing to attack them with wire rug beaters, they noticed a man parking his car on the Woods Street side of the house. They paused and watched him approach. He was a very large man with a round face.

"Good afternoon," he said, nodding his enormous head. "Are the residents at home?"

"They're inside," Flournoy said. "They're my kinfolks," she added.

Laura noticed how the man looked Flournoy over, apparently trying to decide whether he was speaking to a man or a woman.

"And you are?" Flournoy asked.

"Name's Bleaker. From the tax office. If you're their kin then maybe you know what they plan to do. When they plan to vacate."

Flournoy drew herself up tall. She whipped her trouser leg with the wire rug beater like a riding crop. "Maybe you'd better vacate, Mr. Bleaker."

Bleaker was breathing hard from climbing the hill. He drew a soiled handkerchief from his back pocket and wiped his brow. "Look, folks. I'm just doing my job. I've talked with them nice and I've served all the proper papers and they just ignore it all. But them taxes ain't been paid. And now it's comin' to where I can't be nice anymore. In thirty days we're coming in with the sheriff and we're going to tear the house down. The college needs this land for expansion. You gotta tell those two old ladies to get out now for their own good before the wreckers come."

"Mr. Bleaker," Flournoy said, "one time, a long time ago, some people came up that road to take this house. Just like you. Better than you. And they met with the rifle fire of our cousin. I'll tell you this, Mr. Bleaker. If I ever see you on this property again, I won't vouch for your safety. *Now get off our land!*" Flournoy punctuated the last phrase with a sabre gesture of the rug beater and Mr. Bleaker retreated faster than the Yankees before the wrath of Little Sweet.

In the days following Mr. Bleaker's visit, Laura and Flournoy were able to piece together the substance of the crisis. When the Colonel-Doctor's widow, Ella Ogletree Woods, died a few years previously, the aunts had neglected to pay the Texas inheritance tax on the house. Apparently they had ignored repeated notices requesting payment. It seemed everybody in town wanted the two old ladies out: the state tax collector, the local bank and the neighboring college. Aunt Carrie and Aunt Emma had hoped to solve the problem by denying its existence. But the crisis was real and it was desperate and it was immediate. Somehow, Flournoy had to come up with twenty-five hundred dollars to cover the tax debt. And the debt had to be paid within thirty days.

"My salary is eighty dollars a month," Flournoy said. "I've never been able to save a penny. I buy books instead. I suppose they won't take books. I've still got my last month's check."

"I've saved $100," Laura said. "That's $180 between us."

"So we're about $2,320 short," Flournoy sighed. "I guess it's time to say good-bye to the old homeplace."

Several days after Mr. Bleaker's visit, Laura had an idea. It grew slowly in her mind like an improbable flower, beautiful in its symmetry. Brother Charles was a wildcat oil man who was currently exploring the Darst Creek oil field near Seguin. Recently, on a visit, he had tried to persuade Peter to invest in the drilling of a wildcat well. He had admitted the risk was great, but if the well came in, the profits could be enormous. Peter, who had risked all he had in horses and had lost, declined.

Laura and Flournoy, armed with their $180 savings, climbed into Laura's Ford and made the journey to Seguin in what Laura felt must have been record time. Charles Hoge listened to their story, accepted their investment gracefully and, Laura suspected, added a bit of his own money so they could own full shares in the well he had already begun to drill. Laura and Flournoy drove out to the oil field where the air was filled with the shouts of roughnecks and the ringing of pipe and the growling of engines.

It was obvious to Laura that Flournoy loved the excitement and the controlled chaos of the oil field. Her eyes grew large as she watched the roughnecks wrestle with the long lengths of drilling rod, lifting them with tackle high into the wooden derricks that stood in undisciplined formation in the field. "This is what I want to do with my life!" Flournoy shouted above the racket of the engines. "I want to be a wildcatter!"

Back in San Marcos, the waiting was insufferable. Laura found herself ignoring her tenants and her family and each morning she rushed up to the Woods mansion to share the waiting with Flournoy and picture in their minds how the drill bit was cutting slowly through the limestone toward the great black pool that would be their salvation. Then Laura would return home to await word from Charles.

On July 16, 1928, explorer number three in the Darst field, a producer that would always be known in the family as "Flournoy's Gusher," came in. Four days before the sheriff's sale, Laura called Mr. Bleaker to say he could come and get his money. Bleaker came to the edge of the property but, fearing Flournoy's wire rug beater, he would come no farther. Laura had to deliver the envelope containing the twenty-five hundred dollars out to Mr. Bleaker who stood nervously in the street. The old house had been saved and it was unlikely either aunt ever knew it had been imperiled.

In the fall of that year, as the depression deepened further, both Wilton and Lyndon were enrolled in Southwest Texas State Teachers College, their tuition paid by the profits from their mothers' rooming houses. Rebekah and Laura sat on the porch, overlooking Vogelsang Hollow, watching a sunset stained crimson by windborne dust from the north and the west.

"There goes Little Mattie's ranch," Laura said, indicating the dust. "My father's land is headed for Mexico."

"Have you heard anything from them?" Rebekah asked.

"No. But I'm afraid the news can't be good. There's been no rain. The land's gone bad. People are leaving the farms for jobs in town. But there are no jobs. Not in West Texas. Not here. Not just about anywhere in the country, I suppose."

"Thank God we were able to raise the boys' tuition," Rebekah said.

In the diminishing light Laura saw Rebekah was smiling. Laura, too, felt a glow of pride. "It worked out just as we planned."

"Except for this awful depression. I didn't plan on that."

They rocked. From the creek came a symphony of cicadas. The crimson on the horizon turned a red so deep it was almost black, then was. "What will the boys do when they graduate?

What if this depression lasts on and on? What will they do then?"

"Teach school. There's always a need for good teachers."

Laura shifted her position in her rocker. "Don't you wish more for Lyndon, Rebekah? I know teaching is an honorable profession. But it's hard for me to imagine all that energy of Lyndon's cooped up in a classroom."

"There's not much else. There's no work. Not unless they went away and maybe not then."

"There's politics," Laura said.

Rebekah's laughter joined the cicadas. "That's not the steadiest job in the world. Mr. Sam can vouch for that."

"But it could be steady. Mr. Sam is just too stubborn. He doesn't listen to what the people say. That's the secret. That's why Colonel House was so successful. He listened. His candidates listened. And they never lost."

Rebekah sighed. "It *is* a good life, Laura. A wonderfully exciting life. Nothing is quite as thrilling as when Sam runs for reelection. And he does a great deal of good, Laura." She glanced sideways at Laura as if expecting her to disagree. Laura did not.

"He saved the Alamo. He built farm-to-market roads."

"Those were wonderful years," Rebekah said.

"Maybe our boys can take over now. They're smart. They cut their teeth on politics. Why not?"

"Maybe that's not a life they'd choose."

"Then we'll choose it for them," Laura said.

"Laura! We can't do that."

"They're too young to know their own minds. So maybe they just need a little push from their mothers."

"Pushing Lyndon is not a good strategy. Push and he goes the other way every time."

"Then we'll pull them along," Laura said. "The point is, Rebekah, I'm tired of watching chances slip away. First Peter, then Mr. Sam."

"Don't criticize Sam, Laura."

"You know he could have been governor. Everybody knows that. Then Peter, too. But the opportunity passed for both of them. I don't want it to pass for their boys just because they didn't recognize it was there for the taking."

"You make it sound like a foregone conclusion. Like the door to the governor's mansion is hanging open just waiting for them to walk in. Besides there can't be two governors."

"They'll take turns. Lyndon can go first. Besides, there are other offices. President for example."

The two old friends smiled at the thought, then laughed until tears came. They sat quietly, watching the eyes of the swamp rabbits glowing down in the hollow.

"Look around at the young men in college, Rebekah. Have you seen even one as worthy, as personable, as articulate, as either one of our boys? Lyndon campaigned with your father, distributed flyers for Farmer Jim Ferguson. He listened to debate on the floor of the Texas legislature at the knee of Mr. Sam. Wilton has listened to politics discussed at the dinner table all his life. He helped me campaign for Ma Ferguson. It's bound to be in their blood."

"I agree there's no lack of interest."

"We just have to turn that interest into action," Laura said.

"And how do you propose we do that?"

"We do for the boys what Colonel House did for his candidates. The first thing we do is organize. We create an organization. You've heard them talk about Professor Greene?"

"Lyndon thinks he hung the moon."

"Well, that's where we start."

The professors at Southwest Texas State Teachers College were a strange assortment of educators, some brilliant, some struggling for advanced degrees, some on their way up the academic ladder, some on their way down. Among them was Prof. H. M. Greene, a neighbor of Laura's, a history professor who chewed tobacco and had named his last and ninth child Malbone, or Hambone, as he would forever be called. "Prof" Greene's eloquent lectures were constantly interrupted by his use of the spittoon in his desk drawer. A soft-spoken, casual, and dubiously groomed maverick, he was universally loved by his students and instilled in them a passion for politics and a belief that political action could reform society. Although his field was history, Prof. Greene insisted that each student have a constant and continuing awareness of contemporary events. His classes, often held at 7:30 in the morning before the Hill Country sun began to burn away the cool, began with the question: "What is happening this morning that could change our world and our lives?"

Each morning, Professor Greene passed by Laura's garden on his way to his first class. Quite often he would stop to comment on the morning and on Wilton's progress as Laura tended her cosmos. On the morning after her conversation with Rebekah about their sons' futures, she waited eagerly for Prof. Greene to pass. Then, as usual, they chatted across the fence, Laura's yellow cosmos flowers alive with bright butterflies.

"It never ceases to amaze me how intense and intelligent young people are these days," Prof. Greene said. "They take to politics like they were born to it." Laura was relieved it was apparently too early in the morning for Professor Greene's appalling tobacco habit. It was bad enough that he was dressed like a scarecrow. After a while, Laura maneuvered the conversation toward the future Woods and Johnson as candidates.

"How is Wilton doing?"

"Quite well. He might be the best student in my classes."

"And I'm sure Lyndon Johnson is also a good student." Actually Laura had been surprised and pleased at the changes and maturity she had seen in Lyndon over the past year. He was doing quite well in school now, partly, Laura knew, because Rebekah helped write most of his papers and themes.

"Lyndon possesses a quality that's rare these days," Prof. Greene answered. "A hunger for knowledge. Or maybe not so much knowledge in some theoretical sense, but hard information about how and why people vote as they do. How the system can respond to human need. In a sense, he reminds me a great deal of his father. He has his father's values concerning service to the less fortunate. That's rare in a boy his age."

"What if they choose politics as a profession? How would they fare?"

"Wilton is the better student. Yet Lyndon has a more outgoing personality. Wilton is more reserved, as you know, and I'm not certain he would be as comfortable in the public eye."

Laura reminded herself to teach Wilton to be more demonstrative. Then she asked the question she had planned the previous evening, a question to which she possessed a vague and incomplete answer. "Tell me, Professor Greene, are there political parties in student government?"

"Not exactly. There are what I might call fraternities, or secret societies. They're not encouraged, but they do exist. For several years now campus life has been dominated by a group called the Black Stars. They're mostly athletes and town boys."

Laura had heard Wilton and Lyndon complain about the Black Stars, how they were among the most popular boys on campus and held the most important class and student council offices. With control of the student council, Black Stars influenced the assignment of campus jobs and the distribution of student fees. But what really irked Wilton and Lyndon was that the Black Stars seemed to date the prettiest girls in San Marcos.

"So the Black Stars control campus life?"

"Not absolutely."

"But they control who gets the best campus jobs, I hear."

"That's true."

"Sounds like patronage to me," Laura said. "Just like politics in the larger world. Those in office control the jobs." Laura paused as Prof. Greene nodded his head. Then she asked, "Has anyone taken on the Black Stars?"

"Not really. The town boys mostly bloc vote. They stick together so the farm and ranch kids get cut out of the fun things on campus. San Marcos boys all know each other. They're insiders, more sophisticated, you might say."

"Tell, me, Professor Greene, what if two boys, one from Blanco and one from Johnson City, teamed up with some other country boys from around these parts? Boys from Smithville or Staples or Martindale. What if these country boys organized some opposition to the Black Stars? Could they become a force to be reckoned with?"

"Why, Mrs. Woods, you're not suggesting that the out-of-town boys team up with Wilton and Lyndon, are you?" Prof. Greene was beaming, obviously delighted with the idea.

Laura just smiled.

Prof. Greene offered his hand. "Mrs. Woods, it's a wonderful plan. I'll make a few subtle suggestions. If I know those boys, they'll bite. I'm certain they will."

"Don't mention me," Laura said, remembering how Colonel House always remained in the background. "Let them think they came up with the idea themselves."

Several weeks later, fed up with being closed out of campus life, tired of losing the best campus jobs and the prettiest girls to the Black Stars, and emboldened by Prof. Greene's conviction that social progress requires political action, Wilton and several others decided it was time to wrest power from the Black Stars. Late one night they gathered in a room at the Hofheinz Hotel. The old hotel was nearly abandoned in those depression years and a few rooms had been rented out to students who could afford nothing better. The spartan room in the cavernous building was the ideal place to launch a secret society. Wilton, Horace Richards, Walter Grady, all boys from the country, were at that historic meeting. They wrote a constitution, devised a secret handshake, and named their fraternity Alpha Omega. It would become known in the political history of Texas as the White Stars.

One night, Laura watched from the shadows of her back porch as the boys gathered for an especially important secret meeting. They came along the creek bed that coiled behind the college gymnasium and through Vogelsang Hollow into the Woods's backyard. Some moved along Austin Street or up Guadalupe Street, furtively, being careful not to be seen. On this night there were eight or nine conspirators: Wilton, Lyndon, Horace Richards, Walter Grady, and the others. Laura had heard from Prof. Greene that tonight was the night Lyndon would be formally initiated. She watched the boys file into the woods by the creek. They carried lanterns and Laura was unable to control her overpowering need to know what secrets were being shared out there by the creek so late at night. It was the same uncontrollable urge that forced her to read her sister Lucy's diary when she was a girl. And so she slipped out of the house and through the trees to a place where she could observe the initiation.

"Do you solemnly swear as a gentleman, as a student and as a man, to keep this meeting and all its members secret?" Laura had to strain to hear Wilton's voice. Lyndon's hand rested on what Laura was sure was not a Bible, but was a dictionary that had been around the house for years.

Lyndon said he did so swear.

"Do you hereby dismiss all grievances, irrespective of their nature, that you may now hold toward any member of this meeting?"

"I do," Lyndon said. Laura crept closer through the shadows.

"Presently, you are to become a member and a brother of the Alpha and Omega, letters of the Greek alphabet, being significant of the first and the last. And in becoming a member of this fraternity you are to be a brother in every sense of the word, a brother in spirit and in action. Now repeat after me."

The two familiar voices, Wilton's soft, Lyndon's much louder and commanding, seemed to Laura so definitive of the two friends. Laura found herself repeating the oath, a whispered echo, behind the words of Wilton and Lyndon.

"I do solemnly swear upon my honor as a gentleman never in any way to reveal or impart the secrets of Alpha Omega. Furthermore, I agree to abide cheerfully and faithfully by the rules and regulations of the Alpha Omega, such rules and regulations as may be adopted by three-fourths of the members in session. I swear all these things upon my own initiative as a gentleman, with force from no source, so help me God."

"So help me God," Lyndon repeated.

"So help me God," Laura said in her turn. Then she hurried back into the house and upstairs and out of sight.

"The game has grown considerably more interesting," Prof. Greene told Laura one morning as she stood among her butterflies. And as the months passed she learned about the transfer of power on the little campus atop the San Marcos hill.

Little by little, the White Stars did manage to wrest control of the campus and the prettiest girls from the Black Stars. Lyndon had been named assistant to the secretary of the college president. Laura knew that Rebekah, whose father had been admired by President Evans, had helped Lyndon obtain the position, and Lyndon used it to help White Stars get good student jobs, so crucial during these depression years. Soon White Stars had all inside jobs, working in offices and the library, while Black Stars were working outside in the heat or cold, shoveling dirt or pushing wheelbarrows. One job Lyndon was able to get for White Star Vernon Whiteside involved delivering the faculty paychecks. This position enabled White Stars to reward good teachers with rapid check delivery and punish bad teachers by delaying their checks. When Prof. Greene reported White Star control of faculty paychecks to Laura, he was laughing so hard he could scarcely communicate the news.

For a time, several White Stars lived in a small apartment over President Evans's garage. It was there that the White Stars, including Lyndon, earned funds for college by refining the fine art of five-card stud. It was also in President Evans's garage apartment that the White Stars hid their home-brewed beer in the rafters. One particularly hot midnight, as Wilton, Lyndon, and the others were playing poker, the late-night stillness suddenly erupted in what seemed a fusillade of cannon fire. One by one the overheated bottles of home brew began to explode. All eyes peered into the darkness where Prexy Evans, his white nightshirt flying, would surely come to investigate. But apparently President Evans slept through the explosions, and the presence of the product of Buster Brown's grandfather's favorite recipe remained undiscovered.

One of the first major White Star political challenges was to place one of their own in the office of senior class president. The Black Star candidate, however, was an extremely popular athlete, and the chances of a dark-horse candidate seemed slight. Yet with strategies not unlike those of Colonel House when he made pos-

sible the impossible second term of Gov. James Hogg, the White
Stars began to woo away Black Star supporters one vote at a time.
They began to convince other nonathletes that it was ridiculous
to select a class president just because he had muscle. There were
too many important and complex issues on campus to entrust to
a person whose only qualification was brawn and who might
be "deficient in the brain department." For a time, it seemed the
White Star candidate, Bill Deason, would lose. The night before
the election, Wilton and Lyndon canvassed the seniors and they
estimated Deason was about fifteen votes behind.

"How are we ever going to get fifteen votes?" Lyndon wondered, as they sat gloomily at Laura's kitchen table.

"Where is Spinn's support?" Laura asked. Dick Spinn was
the Black Star candidate.

"Football players," Wilton said. "Football players and their
girlfriends."

"Seems to me there's a whole lot more girls in school than
boys. About eight girls to every boy. They can't all be dating football players. Call all the girls who don't have steady boyfriends.
That's where the votes are. If the Black Stars are dating the prettiest girls, call the girls that aren't so pretty."

"Mama, that's awful!"

"That's politics," Laura said as she prepared the breakfast
table for the morrow. "It might work, but you won't know if you
don't try."

Lyndon got on the phone and began calling. The next day,
when the votes were counted, Bill Deason won by eight votes.

After winning the senior class president election, the next
task was to win the other class offices and to place at least a
majority of White Stars on the student council. Laura knew she
should not meddle in White Star affairs, especially since their
meetings were supposed to be secret, but she knew she was more
experienced than the boys and that they needed her advice. She
was excited by the political challenge they faced and her mind
was alive with strategies. Her biggest problem was how to advise
the White Stars without seeming to interfere. Laura wrote
Wilton a note.

"In the registrar's office," she wrote, "there is a record of every student's grades. Find a way to obtain that list. Then make a separate list of everyone with a grade of B or above. These are the students that most likely will resent the athletes controlling the campus. Concentrate on these." She signed the note "Mama." Then she placed the note on his pillow where she knew he would find it.

Not only did the White Stars begin to win support by courting the scholars, they also began courting the Black Stars' girlfriends.

"They're dating the Black Stars' girlfriends, you know," Prof. Greene reported to Laura during one of their morning garden chats. "Amazing what a fella can learn between kisses. Black Star strategies are now an open book."

"So what's next for the White Stars?" Laura asked, wondering what Colonel House would think of kissing and hugging as political strategy.

"Next target is the student activity fund. If they can wrest control of these funds from the Black Stars, they have promised to increase the amount spent on women's activities. That political maneuver would guarantee female voter loyalty to White Star candidates forever." As Prof. Greene leaned on Laura's fence, laughter shook the rebel professor and set Laura's gate dancing on its hinges.

By the close of the 1920s, Southwest Texas State Teachers College was firmly under the White Stars' control. They controlled all student elections and the all-important student activity fund. As a member of the student council, Lyndon campaigned for and won reform of the way the student activity funds were distributed. Instead of a lion's share going to the men's athletic department, the funds now supported such activities as college theater and the debating team, which was captained by none other than Lyndon Johnson and coached by Prof. Greene. Wilton was editor of the *College Star* newspaper. He was also the legendary "El Toro," an anonymous contributor of iconoclastic editorials courageously rooting out Black Star abuses, faculty error, and other campus scandals. Realizing the critical importance of maintaining close ties with the press, Wilton made sure that the stars on the staff of the *College Star* were White Stars, including staffers Horace Richards, Walter Grady, and Hollis Frazier. Lyndon was president of the press club. Albert Harzke was president of the science club. White Star Archie Wiles was president of the library society. Their secret membership included at least three professors, including the redoubtable Prof. Greene, who made a prophetic disclosure in Laura's garden on the last day of Wilton's junior year.

"It was an extraordinary political accomplishment, Mrs. Woods. And I think this might be just the start. The boys are bright, able, humane and convinced they can do great things."

"But what about principle, Professor Greene? Farmer Jim Ferguson did great things. He got to be governor, but he had no principle."

Prof. Greene beamed. "That's the most impressive thing, Mrs. Woods. The boys are on the side of the angels. On every issue. The White Stars are a force to be reckoned with. They took over the campus and they made it a better place. It wouldn't surprise me at all if one day they took over the state."

Prof. Greene moved on up the hill. Butterflies grazed the yellow cosmos. Laura felt enormously proud of her boys and she wondered if she could convince the White Stars to open their membership to women. It would be a test of principle, she thought. Then she hurried across the street to tell Rebekah what Prof. Greene had virtually promised.

∞

At the urging of Prof. Greene, Lyndon and Wilton began organizing chapters of the Young Democrats throughout the Hill Country. "It's time to sew the seeds of Democratic principles among the young," Prof. Greene told their mothers. "Time to use what they learned in campus politics out in the real world."

In the Johnson and Woods homes, political discussion filled the air and the hours. For one thing, it was 1928, there would be a president elected that year, and the Democratic National Convention would be held in nearby Houston. In addition to the election of a president, a number of state offices were being contested. Tom Connally would make a run for the U.S. Senate and a host of state and local hopefuls would be challenging incumbents. Excitement in the Woods and Johnson households reached fever pitch.

Wilton and Lyndon made plans to cover the convention for the college newspaper. The day before the boys were to leave, Laura decided to stop by the Johnson home. When she arrived, she braked, as was her custom, against the large oak tree that grew beside the house and which carried the scars of Laura's many other visits. As she approached the porch, Mr. Sam, Lyndon, and Wilton were talking politics. Mr. Sam acknowledged Laura's presence. "Rebekah and the ladies are inside," he said, and then turned back toward the younger men and their discussion about the possibility that Alfred Emanuel Smith would be nominated as the Democratic candidate for president. Mr. Sam continued with the point he had been making when Laura arrived. "I just don't think America is ready to elect a Catholic president."

Laura walked up the porch stairs and sat heavily in a cane chair. "Well, Mr. Sam," she said, "I'm surprised. I thought you'd be all for Al Smith. After all, he says he'll repeal Prohibition." Laura glanced at the bulge beneath Mr. Sam's coat where he carried his ever-present bottle of whiskey.

Mr. Sam was annoyed, yet courteous. "We're having a conversation here, Laura. I'm sure Rebekah will be glad to visit."

"Think I better stay here, Mr. Sam. I'd hate for you to convince these boys they should vote Republican to avoid a Catholic. Myself, I'd vote for a turbaned Hindu before I'd vote for Hoover."

"Al Smith can't carry Texas," Lyndon insisted. "Every Baptist in the state will turn out to vote against him."

"He'll carry San Marcos," Laura said. "It's the Methodists who run this town and they'll vote for what's right." Then Laura stood and moved toward the door. "Enjoyed our little talk, Mr. Sam," she teased, and then she joined the ladies.

Knowing that Wilton and Lyndon were going to the Houston convention, Laura began an effort to convince Peter that they should go as well. "It's a chance of a lifetime," she said. "The first national political convention in Texas. Who knows when there'll be another. We've been Democrats all our lives and it's our duty to go." Then she went to Rebekah's and began working on Mr. Sam.

"We can all drive down in my car."

"Not on your life," Sam said. "I'll drive."

"Don't want to be driven by a woman?"

"It's not that. I'm just a better driver."

"Mr. Sam," Laura laughed, "have you taken a good look at your car lately? I've never seen so many dents." In San Marcos it was a subject of some debate whether Mr. Sam or Laura Woods was the worse driver, and which automobile, Mr. Sam's Chevrolet or Laura's Ford, was the most bent and battered from encounters with other automobiles and solid, immovable objects. Mr. Sam kept his Chevrolet in a car shed way behind the house and he had to back along a fence and through a gate to get to the street. He had hit every post along that fence and collided with the gate so many times that his fenders were nearly gone.

In the end, Laura won her argument with Mr. Sam, and on a sweltering June day, the four friends set out for Houston where the great drama of democracy was being performed. Laura drove. Rebekah sat beside her. Peter and Mr. Sam took up the rear. Wilton and Lyndon drove down with Prof. Greene.

When Laura's Ford finally rattled into Houston, she felt that she had entered a strange and alien world. The whole city seemed to be in the throes of some kind of disorderly hedonistic rite. The streets were packed with people and automobiles competing for right-of-way. People leaned from hotel windows, waving and watching the passing parade, and the air was filled with the sound of automobile horns and syncopated music. Al Smith's theme song, "The Sidewalks of New York," could be heard on every Texas corner, and the song seemed to belong somehow. It seemed to Laura the entire town was dancing and, in fact, many of the leading citizens of Houston soon would be, on the magical roof of the Rice Hotel. They passed the Kirby Theater where Al Jolson was playing, and Luna Park, where the world's largest roller coaster loomed against the pale shimmering sky. So consumed by the prospect of the great convention was the city that the presence of Will Rogers went unnoticed. He simply could not hold a candle to the great events that would soon take place within the cavernous spaces of Sam Houston Hall. The nation's Democrats had come to select their candidate for president of the United States.

Laura and the others stayed with Mr. Sam's brother George, a bachelor Houston schoolteacher. Uncle George supported his widowed sister and her children and his crowded little bungalow was hardly large enough to accommodate the influx of conventioneers from the Hill Country, especially when Wilton, Lyndon and Prof. Greene arrived with boxes of flyers and posters urging the repeal of Prohibition.

"How a son of mine can come down on the side of the beer trusts and the liquor lobby, I'll never know," Laura said. "I'll just have to design my own flyers to cancel these out."

Houston mayor Oscar Holcomb, chairman of the convention arrangements committee, had estimated that approximately fifty thousand people would attend the convention. Nearly all of these visitors, on the night of June 28, 1928, descended on the convention site, Sam Houston Hall, demanding entry. Unfortunately, Sam Houston Hall was designed to hold only eighteen thousand people.

Laura and Peter were caught in the rush toward the gates, torn away from their friends by the crowd. Fortunately, Mr. Sam, as a member of the Texas legislature, had given them passes, yet Peter had to literally wrestle his way past the embattled gatekeepers, pulling Laura along by the arm. Later they would learn that the gatekeepers became so alarmed by the relentless press of the crowd that they had locked the gates and fled. Fearing the possibility of fire and eighteen thousand people trapped inside, Mayor Holcomb ordered the police to file the locks on fourteen gates, allowing more and more conventioneers into the roiling frenzied crowd within the hall.

Sam Houston Hall was bedlam. The Houston Municipal Band could hardly be heard above the shouting of the crowd. Placards and banners were everywhere, like the shields of conquering armies. Cigar smoke formed dark low clouds in the high hollows of the hall.

"Look!" Laura shouted to Peter above the noise of the crowd. "It's Mrs. Woodrow Wilson!" The presence of the former president's wife drew Laura's eye because Mrs. Wilson was at the center of a commotion. An angry, beleaguered sergeant-at-arms had not recognized her and was trying to throw her out. Mrs. Wilson was furious. The commotion subsided when the sergeant-at-arms realized the disputed visitor was with Mrs. Jesse Jones, wife of one of the richest men in the world, a major financial supporter of the Democratic party, and the Texas Favorite Son Candidate for President. The sergeant-at-arms recognized Mrs. Jones at once, apologized, and let Mrs. Wilson pass.

Ironically, the first riot began when chairman Joseph Robinson, of Arkansas, opened his remarks with a plea for religious toleration. It was an obvious reference to Al Smith's Catholicism, and it motivated a storm of Baptist ire. Suddenly all eighteen thousand conventioneers, including the sixty-four women delegates, were out of their seats and shouting or seeking to shout down the shouters. Laura found the shouting was infectious and she realized she, too, was yelling, but she was not sure why or at whom.

The demonstration that Laura would remember forevermore, however, the one that seemed to encompass all the excitement and glamour and unpredictability of the political process, was touched off when Franklin Roosevelt presented the name of Alfred Emanuel Smith to the convention. Laura remembered how Colonel House had predicted a golden future for FDR. And he was such a dignified and handsome man. She almost wished it was Al Smith placing Roosevelt's name in nomination. But as soon as Smith's name escaped Roosevelt's lips, the hall erupted into what Laura could only describe later as a kind of mass insanity. Half of the conventioneers seemed to be shouting for joy, the other half in anger. In the southern delegations a host of fistfights broke out. Broken chairs from the Mississippi delegation were hurled in the air and across the aisles into other delegations.

Al Smith was nominated as the party's candidate on the first ballot. And shortly after midnight, Franklin Roosevelt closed the convention. As the band played "Till We Meet Again," Laura and Peter followed the crowd out of Sam Houston Hall. Laura thought the building looked as if mighty armies had clashed on the convention floor. They walked through and over confetti, old newspapers, cardboard signs, broken chairs, cigar butts, and mounds of refuse. And, of course, there were the thousands of flyers Wilton, Lyndon and Prof. Greene had distributed to influence a change of heart among the Baptists and Methodists concerning the repeal of Prohibition.

Driving from Sam Houston Hall to Uncle George's house, where they would spend the night before returning to San Marcos, took several hours. The streets were jammed with automobiles filled with celebrating conventioneers. Laura's Ford crept along, and after a time both Peter and Mr. Sam were asleep in the backseat. As she maneuvered the Ford slowly through the melee, Laura pictured Wilton and Lyndon moving through the delegations, passing out flyers. She had seen them as symbols of youth and sincere resolve within the madcap, flawed circus that was Texas politics. She also saw the joy in their eyes and she knew that the excitement of the convention would be a powerful influence on both of them. They were hooked, as she had planned. Now it was just a matter of reeling them in.

"Maybe we're asking too much of the boys," Rebekah said. "They're awfully young. And the party is firmly in the hands of men like Jesse Jones. Men who are rich and powerful. Lyndon and Wilton haven't got a dollar between them."

"Look, Rebekah, if I weren't a woman I could have won that nomination! It's not that hard. It just takes an organization. And we've already got one."

"You mean the White Stars?"

"We just need to put it to work. We'll find an open seat in the legislature and get the White Stars out working on Wilton's campaign."

Out of the corner of her eye, Laura saw Rebekah turn toward her in her seat. She could feel her friend's eyes studying her in the near dark and she knew Rebekah was considering whether or not to let the challenge pass. Rebekah did not.

"Surely you mean Lyndon's campaign."

"We'll see," Laura said softly, her voice nearly drowned out by the sound of traffic and the snoring of Peter and Mr. Sam in back. As she drove on through the crush of automobiles and Democrats, she reminded herself that the trick to anything in life is maintaining control. And she had rarely before felt so powerfully in control. What she had felt flying Lindbergh's airplane had been metaphor. What she was feeling now was real.

23 ∞ THE PROSPERITY RADIO STATION

LAURA'S PLAN TO CATAPULT WILTON INTO THE LEGISLATURE OR even further came undone in the little Hill Country town of Henley, Texas, in the year of our Lord 1930. One early July morning, Laura drove Peter, Rebekah, and Mr. Sam to Henley where a daylong picnic and political rally had been organized by Judge Stubbs of Johnson City. When they arrived at the oak grove outside of town, they found Wilton and Lyndon had arrived before them. They were talking with a number of girls, including Lyndon's sister, Rebekah, whom Laura fervently wished Wilton would marry. *How beautiful it would be,* she thought, *for our two families to be bound by such a union.* The young people were enjoying great mounds of barbecue, sweet tea, and Big Red soda and sharing the shade of the oaks. Children cavorted through the trees, only occasionally scolded by women wearing fine cottons with islet embroidery and leghorn hats. Men stood talking in groups, their hat brims close, those from the country in coveralls, the men from town in seersucker pants and ties.

A speakers platform had been set up on a wagonbed. Throughout the afternoon, as the people ate, they listened to a long procession of local candidates. The candidates for the less important posts spoke in the afternoon heat. As the day cooled, the place on the wagon bed was occupied by the more important candidates, like Pat Neff, a former governor of Texas and a good friend of Mr. Sam. Neff was running for reelection to the railroad commission.

When the cool of evening came and the people had finished their barbecue and Big Red soda, and the children had been quieted and stilled, Judge Stubbs called Pat Neff to the speaking platform. No one answered. When it became obvious Neff wasn't present, the judge asked for someone to step forward and speak on Neff's behalf. Again, there was no response.

Judge Stubbs was about to move on to another candidate, when Laura heard a familiar voice call out from the crowd. "Well, I'll make a speech for Pat Neff." It was Lyndon, and he made his way through the crowd and climbed up on the wagon. It was fully night now, and the coals from the barbecue pits glowed in the darkness.

"It's Sam Johnson's boy," Judge Stubbs called, and a murmur of surprise rippled through the crowd. Lyndon looked out at his friends and neighbors and then began his first political speech, a stinging indictment of Neff's opponent from the city.

"I'm a prairie-dog lawyer from Johnson City, Texas," Lyndon said, his voice loud, yet sliding up and down an octave, as if his voice had only recently changed. His arms were swinging so violently that Laura thought Lyndon might fall from the wagon. "You have heard a man say that Pat Neff doesn't hunt and fish. I want to remind you the way these Austin sportsmen come into your hills and shoot cattle when they're supposed to be shooting deer. I ask if you want a city-slicker hunter, who doesn't know a cow from a deer, to be in charge of your railroad business and your busline business and your oil business. Or do you want a man whose character is unimpeachable?" Lyndon carried on for about ten minutes, his every shouted phrase inciting whistles, cheers, and applause.

Laura was impressed with Lyndon's performance and complimented Rebekah on it. "He did such a grand job he could run for president."

"I know it," Rebekah replied.

"Well," Laura teased, "I wouldn't brag so on my own kids!"

Welly Hopkins, a candidate for the Texas Senate, was so impressed with the Henley speech that he asked Lyndon to run his campaign. Lyndon recruited Wilton and the White Stars. As the election approached, Wilton, Bill Deason, Fenner Roth, and a gaggle of other White Stars packed into Lyndon's Model A Ford and drove to towns and crossroads communities throughout the Hill Country. They carried with them campaign literature printed free on the college mimeograph machine, accessible because a White Star was night watchman in the building that housed the copy machine. The White Stars would arrive in the town where Hopkins was to speak and they would pass out literature and praise the virtues of the candidate. When Hopkins rose to speak, the boys would cheer and work the crowds into a fever pitch.

Just before the election, Lyndon and the White Stars organized a rally in San Marcos. Lyndon had managed to charm and cajole the president of Southwest Texas State Teachers College to host the rally in the school auditorium. Never before had the highly respected President Evans allowed himself to become embroiled in a political campaign. But Lyndon had even managed to persuade President Evans to occupy a place on the speaking platform. Hopkins's speech was greeted with an avalanche of applause. He won the election in a landslide. "Never have I seen better work," Hopkins said of Lyndon and the White Star volunteers.

In the early '30s, as the Texas and national economy plummeted to rock bottom, it became more and more difficult for many of the White Stars to stay in college. There were only so many campus jobs and few jobs in town. But among the White Stars there was great entrepreneurial spirit. Wilton and Horace Richards had a Ping-Pong concession next door to the "Bobcat," an off-campus soda fountain where students met between classes. There were two Ping-Pong tables where customers could play for five cents a game. Another Woods-Richards enterprise was a watermelon concession in a vacant lot. At one time or another, nearly all the White Stars earned extra money working at the watermelon stand. They bought watermelons for ten to fifteen cents apiece, iced them down, and sold six slices from each melon for ten to fifteen cents a slice. A seat at the table, a fork and salt was provided at no extra charge.

One of the most successful moneymaking schemes was hatched by White Star Vernon Whiteside. Whiteside convinced Lyndon that he could make his fortune selling Real Silk

Hosiery. It was the fall of the year and all the college teachers were back at school. The boys theorized each one would buy at least three pairs and the teachers would become the nucleus of a strong and expanding market. The boys went to Austin and purchased a sales kit from the Real Silk Hosiery distributor. Their first call was at Dr. Evans's house and Lyndon's presentation was so captivating that the college president purchased one hundred and forty-four pair. Laura purchased as many pair as she could afford. Although they were nearly twice as expensive as her Lyle hose, they did not run as easily and they lasted much longer. "I'm sure I'll live to be a hundred," she told Rebekah, "if only to wear all of Lyndon's Real Silk Hosiery." Soon most everyone in the Hill Country was wearing Real Silk Hosiery. According to Wilton, one night Lyndon went from boarding-house to boardinghouse, rousing people out of bed, singing the praises of his socks. He'd sell three or four pair per stop. By morning he had sold 422 pair, for a profit of $42.20. That night he and White Star Bill Hormachea, who was working as a taxi driver, removed the identifying sign from the taxi and took off for Nuevo Laredo, Mexico. No one knew at the time and no one has learned since what Lyndon did on this mysterious trip across the border or what became of the Real Silk Hosiery money he had worked so hard to earn.

Few students at Southwest Texas State Teachers College were able to complete their college careers without major interruption. Because of the depression, they were constantly dropping out to earn money enough to drop in again. Wilton and Lyndon were not exceptions. Wilton left college to teach at a school in Fayette County, where the pupils spoke Bohemian as their first language. Likewise, Lyndon arranged for a teaching job in the town of Cotulla, a desert community south of San Antonio, in the brush country near the Mexican border. He taught in a Mexican-American grade school where the children and their families were so impoverished that they lived in shacks without running water or electricity. "They were," he wrote his mother, "mired in the slums, lashed by prejudice, and buried half alive in illiteracy." In one letter he asked his mother to send him twenty tubes of toothpaste for distribution to the children. Laura was certain Lyndon's experience in Cotulla was the origin of his special empathy for the poor and the powerless.

∞

One night, after the boys had returned to San Marcos, Laura retired to her room to search for new evangelists on her radio. It seemed more and more radio preachers were filling the airways with warnings of hellfire, promise of salvation, and offers of holy relics that could be obtained for small or large gifts of the heart. Several of these preachers broadcast from Mexico, on powerful stations that were called "border blasters." As Laura searched the dial, she heard a familiar voice. It was Wilton's friend and White Star strategist Horace Richards. She turned, thinking he was talking to Wilton in her doorway, then realized Horace was speaking from the radio.

"You are in tune to the Prosperity Broadcasting Company radio station with studios in the showroom of the Taylor Thomas Ford Motor Company located in the heart of downtown San Marcos. As we listen to the theme song of Wayne King and his orchestra, 'The Waltz You Saved for Me,' this is your reporter Horace Richards and engineer Wilton Woods signing off for another day. May you have a good night and a prosperous tomorrow."

Laura was waiting at the door when Wilton came home. "You have got a lot of explaining to do, young man."

"About what?"

"Prosperity Radio."

"Oh that. It's just a radio station."

"At Taylor Thomas Ford? You work for them?"

"No, we work for ourselves. We own it. Partners. Bought it with the profits of our Ping-Pong and watermelon concessions."

"My oh my," Laura said, looking at Wilton with new eyes. She remembered that Wilton had built a radio back in 1923. It was one of the first radios in town. But this one was different. You could *talk*, not just listen. "Do you talk on the radio? I only heard Horace."

"I'm the business manager and engineer. Horace is the announcer. Sometimes Gus 'Pee Wee' Barr reads poetry."

"I think you should talk." Laura loved the idea of a radio star in the family. "You've got a fine voice. Better than Horace. Certainly as good as Gus 'Pee Wee' Barr."

"I'd rather not."

Laura thought of Colonel House and his insistence on working behind the scenes, leaving the glory to others. "And you can say anything you want to? Talk about anything?" Laura felt the small soft tread of an exciting idea creeping into the back of her mind.

"Sure. Mostly we play music. Records we get from the record store. Or somebody at the college comes and plays the piano. Sometimes singing groups. Thomas Yoakum and his Schubert Trio. We read the news. Make announcements about what's going on in town."

"But how does it make money?"

"Merchants pay us to talk about their businesses. Sometimes we trade airtime for things. For meals or clothes or anything we might need."

"What about political campaigns? Couldn't you have candidates speak on your station? Seems like you could get your message out to far more people."

As Wilton grew more comfortable with broadcast technology, he began to take his microphone out into the community for remote broadcasts. Occasionally he broadcast organ concerts from the local movie theater. On one occasion, Wilton and Horace decided to do a remote broadcast from a high school football game. It was the biggest game of the year, the annual struggle between the San Marcos Rattlers and the Kerrville Antlers. Laura insisted that Peter take her to the game, not because she liked football, but because it would be an opportunity to see Wilton and Prosperity Radio in action.

When Laura arrived, the stands were packed with students and with the two high school marching bands and majorettes and platoons of drill-team girls, in outfits as skimpy as Etta Leon's, waving colorful crepe paper pompoms. Wilton, Horace and Lyndon had already begun to set up their exotic broadcast equipment and had become a major center of attention. Students clustered around their microphone and as the Rattlers and Antlers took the field, their pregame calisthenics and muscular posturing went almost unnoticed. "Show business" was introducing itself into Texas high school football, which, until Prosperity Broadcasting, had been the predominant Hill Country entertainment medium. The crowd around the broadcast booth grew, the concession stands were abandoned, even the cheerleaders gathered around to hear Gus "Pee Wee" Barr read the rosters, many members of which had also abandoned the benches to hear. There was not a quorum among the bands to play the national anthem.

Soon the combined coaching staffs and the San Marcos high school principal descended upon the broadcast booth and asked them to leave. There was a near riot as the broadcasters were led away. But Wilton refused to give up on his broadcast. He set up his equipment in a grove of trees by the cafeteria and employed runners to bring word of the progress of the game. Lyndon, Wilton and the other White Stars moved in relays from the stadium to the cafeteria, bringing breathless news of the action and the mounting score. Gus "Pee Wee" Barr used his lively imagination to fill in the spaces and provide color and continuity. The success of the broadcast confirmed the potential of the idea Laura had been nurturing.

Laura timed her announcement carefully. She invited Prof. Greene for fried chicken and made sure Lyndon and Wilton had no other plans and would join them at the table. Realizing the boys would give more credence to her idea if it was proposed by Prof. Greene, she nodded to him over pie, the cue they had previously planned.

"Wilton," Prof. Greene said, leaning far back in Laura's dining room chair until she winced, "the White Stars did themselves proud getting Welly Hopkins elected to the state legislature. Have you thought about getting one of your own elected? A White Star."

Laura noticed Prof. Greene had the boys' attention. "To the state legislature?" Wilton and Lyndon exchanged glances.

"The Eighty-first District. Run against Henry Kyle, the incumbent. I think you boys could pull it off," Prof. Greene said. "You did it for Welly. Why not for one of your own?"

"We'd need a candidate," Lyndon said.

"How about Tom Dunlap. Former class president, member of the student council. Besides Lyndon the best debater I know."

"His family background would be a good advantage," Laura added. "He's the grandson of pioneers who settled this country. Both his grandfathers fought for the Confederacy. He's perfect."

"I'd love to whip Henry Kyle," Wilton said.

"It won't be easy," Prof. Greene said.

"But you've got a huge advantage," Laura added.

"What's that?" Lyndon wanted to know.

"Prosperity Radio," Laura answered and her scheme for the first use of the broadcast media in political campaigning had been hatched. "If radio can draw attention away from Texas high school football, it can surely draw attention away from Henry Kyle."

The White Stars organized for Dunlap's campaign in much the same way they had for college elections and for Welly Hopkins. They put signs up all through the district, passed out literature at rallies and box suppers that Laura organized among her friends. Volunteers went door to door talking about Tom Dunlap's qualifications and his conviction that the state had been ignoring one of its most valuable resources, the ideas and energy of its young people. From platforms White Stars built in town squares throughout the Hill Country, Tom's strong, clear voice stressed the need for new ideas. "The old guard politicians got us into this depression," he would announce, "now it's time for the young guard to get us out."

Laura was certain the "young guard" theme was her idea. When it came time for the White Stars to write speeches and radio announcements for Tom Dunlap, they turned to the same two resources they had used when they needed help writing their themes. Rebekah and Laura spent long evenings struggling to find just the right message for the difficult times. "We need to combine the ideas of tradition and destiny," Rebekah insisted. "Continuity. Here is a candidate whose ancestors set-tled this land. But he brings fresh, new ideas."

"The old guard makes way for the new guard," Laura said.

"Exactly. It's important that his grandfathers fought for the Confederacy. Now the grandson fights for Texas."

It was a compelling message. And the new technology of radio gave it strength and reach. Radio spread Dunlap's message over a three-county area. The radio announcements featured White Star Paul Carter and his sister singing and playing the guitar. The issues of the day were set to music. Among the announcements Rebekah and Laura wrote was the one they called "The New Guard."

> *If you are tired of what things cost*
> *Brother, you need some clout.*
> *The Old Guard got us in this mess,*
> *Let Tom Dunlap get us out.*

Even though Henry Kyle was only a few years older than Dunlap, he was painted by the White Stars to be a representative of the bankrupt past. As an incumbent, however, he was a strong candidate and the contest ended in a runoff between the old guard and the new. But eventually, the new guard won handily.

A few weeks after Tom Dunlap's victory, Prof. Greene stopped by for his early morning chat at Laura's gate. He was obviously in great good spirits. "I've never seen anything like it, Mrs. Woods! Those boys sure haven't wasted any time. First thing Tom Dunlap did when he got in office was to get jobs for White Stars in the capital. Edwin Smith, for one. And Ernest Morgan and Charles Hancock. They're up there in Austin learning the ropes while they go to law school."

Prof. Greene seemed as proud of his boys as a new father handing out cigars. Laura felt no less proud, and when she looked up from her gardening and caught the professor's eye, they both began to chuckle like pranksters. "Looks like we started something," she said, and then they both surrendered to laughter for a while.

"Looks like Slats Frazier will win in Franklin County."

"Then they'll have two White Star state representatives to contend with in Austin."

"I'll tell you what beats all," Prof. Greene said, leaning forward, conspiratorially. "Tom Dunlap got himself appointed to the appropriations and education committees. And you know one of the appropriations that committee controls?" Before waiting for an answer, Prof. Greene continued. "Teacher salaries, that's what. There's rumors that when the state budget hearings come along, our boys are going to cut the salaries of those wrong-minded college professors that didn't back White Stars. The good ones get raises and the bad ones get cuts. And they've singled out Dean Speck as one of the bad ones. Fortunately," he added, turning away so that Laura could not see him spit into his ubiquitous cup, "I am one of the better professors at this august institution."

"And a White Star to boot."

"What I'd call this, Mrs. Woods, is a movement to promote excellence in education." As Prof. Greene moved up the hill toward the college, Laura could see his shoulders shaking and she knew laughter would pursue him all the way to his morning class.

One Sunday after church, Peter's cousin Will Donalson and his wife joined the Woods for dinner at Laura's table. The discussion turned to the problem of educating the children who lived in the Mexican-American settlement south of San Marcos on the Seguin Road.

Will Donalson outlined the problem. "The school is in a predominantly Anglo section of the northwest side of town. So the children from the Mexican-American settlement have to walk about three miles to school, up some steep hills and across rocky creeks and through some pretty rough country."

"That's not fair," Laura said.

"Some good people on the school board agree with you,"

Donalson said. "They want to build a new school more cen-
trally located. But the trustees are divided. And there's another
problem. The trustee whose election is coming up doesn't want to
build a school for Mexican-American children in the community.
He wants to spend the money on remodeling the present site. He's
the swing vote. If he wins the election, the issue is closed."

"Will he win?" Wilton asked.

"He's running unopposed."

"You mean that just one trustee could change the balance of
power on the Westover school board?"

"Why don't we get someone to run against him?" Laura
asked.

Donalson shook his head. "He'd win for sure. The election's
just a few days away. There just isn't time to announce a candidate and mount an effective campaign."

"We need Lyndon," Laura said. "You've seen how that boy
can sway a crowd. A campaign on Prosperity Radio. White Stars
working the streets. It wouldn't take long."

Donalson shook his head again. "But Lyndon's not a resident
here."

"Peter? Why don't you run?" Laura asked. Her heart leaped
at the thought of Peter taking an active role in civic affairs again.

"I've had enough of school boards," Peter said.

"Maybe the key is an unannounced candidate," Wilton said.
"Since the current board member is running unopposed, there'll
probably be a pretty light turnout. His supporters will be saying,
'If he's certain to win, why bother to vote?' What if we propose a
write-in candidate. But we keep it secret. And we organize supporters to show up at the polls just before they close. Then we
flood the polling place with our supporters at the last minute,
cast our write-in votes and the election is ours."

"It just might work," Will Donalson said. "But there's just
one problem. We need a candidate."

Suddenly everyone at the table was looking at Wilton.

"Not me."

"It's your plan, Wilton. Besides, it's time we had some young
people on the school board. What do you say?"

"I'm thinking," Wilton said. "I wouldn't want to run to lose. How many votes do you think we'd need?"

"I'd say twenty-five. No more."

"We can get Prof. Greene and Horace Richards to round up teachers and eligible students."

"I can get that many supporters myself," Laura said.

"But it's got to be hush-hush. If they find out what we're doing, they might alert the incumbent in time to roust out his friends. Just be low key."

"Well," Laura said, as she began to clear away the dishes, "it looks like Westover is going to get a new school."

On the evening of the Westover school board election, at 6:00 P.M., one hour before the polls closed, Laura Woods arrived at the polling place with a carload of voters. Within minutes Prof. Greene arrived with a caravan of supporters. One by one, other cars arrived and Wilton's secret supporters filed in to cast their write-in votes. At 7:00 P.M. the election judges closed the polls and it was apparent from the low turnout for the incumbent and the high number of supporters for the challenger that Wilton had finessed the election.

"My son, the politician. Looks like Wilton is following in my footsteps," Laura said with genuine pride, as they headed back to the Woods house for postelection peach ice cream. She was also secretly pleased. *And to think it was my son who got elected first!*

24 ∞ THE BACHELOR CAR

IN THE EARLY '30S, BOTH WILTON AND LYNDON WERE SERVING their apprenticeship in the real world of state and national politics. Wilton was working in San Antonio with the powerful Oil and Gas Division of the Texas Railroad Commission. He had been appointed by Pat Neff, the former Texas governor for whom Lyndon had made his first speech in Henley, some years before, and, of course, the White Stars supported Neff when he ran for the railroad commission. Wilton's agency at the railroad commission was responsible for regulating oil and gas production. It was during a time when the East Texas Field, the biggest oil discovery in the state's history, was coming into production, and each day decisions were made in the railroad commission that created millions of dollars for individuals and companies in the oil industry. With his soft-spoken, easy manner and his intuitive understanding of the political process, Wilton was establishing contacts that would prove essential to his generation of Democratic candidates in the years to come.

While Wilton worked quietly in San Antonio, Lyndon was swept into the heady world of Washington politics. On the advice of Welly Hopkins, whom the White Stars had supported in his congressional election, newly elected congressman Richard Kleberg, heir to the great King Ranch fortune, had appointed Lyndon as his secretary. Kleberg was essentially an apolitical congressman, preferring to occupy his time with horses, golf, and high-stakes poker. The work of the office was left to Lyndon, labors that began long before dawn and lasted long into the night.

However, serving as secretary to a congressman was not absolutely all work and no play for Lyndon, as Rebekah learned in the autumn of 1934.

I can't exactly say why, but there is something vaguely familiar about this, Rebekah thought. She stopped setting china plates on the supper table to look across at the beautiful young woman who braced herself by clasping the sides of a dining chair.

"It just happened so quickly," the girl said. She seemed shy, but her dark eyes were direct and steady. "Lyndon borrowed that big yellow Buick Wilton and his friends own. He picked me up at my home in Karnack early in the morning and the car door was hardly closed before he started demanding that I marry him. He badgered me every inch of those four hundred miles between Texarkana and San Antonio. I kept saying I wasn't ready or I tried to change the subject, and he kept insisting. It wasn't an argument. And I really did want to marry him, but everything was happening much too fast. By midmorning, he pulled off the road and called his friend Dan Quill in San Antonio and told him to get a preacher, a church, and then he hung up the phone."

"He didn't ask your opinion?"

Lady Bird Taylor, now Johnson, laughed. "Well, you know how Lyndon is."

I thought I did, Rebekah said to herself. *And the Lyndon I thought I knew would have never run off and married without even inviting his mother to the wedding.*

"So we arrived at the Plaza Hotel at six o'clock in the evening. Lyndon announced the wedding would be in two hours. It was now or never, he said. He had to get back to Washington."

"We could have had a nice ceremony here at the house," Rebekah said. "We could have invited kinfolks and friends."

"There just wasn't time. I didn't agree to marry him until two hours before the ceremony. Dan Quill had to impersonate Lyndon to get the marriage license."

Rebekah remembered telling her own mother about her courthouse wedding so many years ago. Sam also had been in a hurry. He had to get to Austin for the legislative session. He, too, had said it was now or never, and they had been married on their way out of Fredericksburg.

Lady Bird laughed nervously as she twisted her new wedding

band. "We didn't even have a ring. So Dan went to Sears and Roebuck and bought a half dozen for $2.50 apiece."

"One ring will usually suffice."

"He didn't know my ring size. So he bought six different sizes, hoping that one would fit."

Rebekah managed to smile. *How familiar this all sounds.* She remembered the dark traveling suit she had worn to the courthouse ceremony. "What did you wear?"

"This," Lady Bird said, smoothing her hands over the purple dress she was wearing. "I wanted a nice go-to-church attire so I bought this. But now that we're married, Lyndon says purple is to wear to funerals."

The room was silent except for the ticking of Grandpa Baines's clock.

"I just want to make him happy and be part of his dreams," Lady Bird blurted into the silence.

"I only wish Sam and I could have been there," Rebekah said, trying not to sound angry.

"I know it seems awfully hasty," Lady Bird said. "But I loved him too much to lose him."

"Oh, my yes," Rebekah said. "Me, too. I loved him too much to lose him."

Shortly after Lady Bird and Lyndon left, Rebekah called on her old friend Laura for comfort.

"Don't be sad, Rebekah. It's time to celebrate. And here you are grieving like somebody died," Laura said.

"Well, it happened so quickly." The girl brushed her hair back from her forehead. Her hands fluttered with excitement. "We were at the Driskill Hotel, in Austin, for the White Star Reunion. Out of the blue, Lyndon stood up and rapped on his glass with a spoon. The band stopped playing. The dancers all stood still and Lyndon shouted out, 'Wilton and Virginia are going to run away and get married!' The fellows rushed up and pounded Wilton on the back. The girls hugged me. Slats Frazier grabbed the microphone and sang to us. He sang 'To the End of the World with You.' "

Virginia Bergfeld, now Woods, was justifying, even defending herself.

Laura remembered her introduction to Peter's considerable sisters at the Woods mansion so many years before.

Virginia continued her wedding story: "We borrowed the big yellow Buick and drove out to West Texas, to Marfa. We were married by the same preacher who married my parents and grandparents. It was a sentimental idea I had to please my mother in Seguin."

But what about me? Laura thought. *What kind of son would run off to get married and not even invite his own mother to the wedding?*

Laura remembered her own wedding to Peter nearly fifty years before when the Woods family chose not to attend. "We are not women who panic," Little Mattie had said. "We are not women who cry." Laura bit her lip to keep from crying now.

Virginia laughed nervously. "Brother Dodson is quite elderly. More than ninety years old. When he got to the part about I now pronounce you man and wife, he forgot his place. So he started all over again and we pledged our vows twice."

"So you were married not once, but twice." Laura managed a smile. She remembered her own homemade wedding dress. "What did you wear?"

"This," Virginia said, smoothing her hands over her summer frock. "I wanted a nice go-to-church dress and a big navy-blue picture hat. Wilton's favorite color is bluebonnet blue."

The room was silent. Laura wondered why she did not know that Wilton's favorite color was bluebonnet blue.

"I just want to make Wilton happy," Virginia said now. "I just want to be a part of his dreams."

"I only wish Peter and I could have been there," Laura said, trying not to sound angry.

"But, he said you couldn't!" Virginia said. "Wilton said that his family couldn't come because of his sister's illness. When he proposed to me, he told me, 'I love you, Virginia, and I want to marry you but, before you answer, there is something you need to know. I have a sister who suffers mental problems and is prone to violent outbursts.' "

"Oh," Laura said. Her heart reached out to the young couple like a hand.

When Virginia and Wilton had gone, Laura turned to her old friend, Rebekah, for comfort.

"Don't be sad, Laura," Rebekah said, imitating Laura's tone of voice. "It's a time to celebrate. And here you are grieving like somebody died."

The women had to laugh.

25 ∞ THE LOYAL FRIEND

(From Laura's unpublished autobiography)

There seems to be around certain people an aura that demands attention, that draws the eye and the mind as a blossom lures the butterfly. This phenomenon is especially evident when I browse through the photographs taken of our lives over the years. Several boxes and as many albums leak these black-and-white memories of former times from my bureau and a blessed plurality of them are of Lyndon Johnson, a lamentable excess, to my mind. If it is a portraiture of the Johnson family, there is Lyndon squarely in front, posturing as if taking a third encore upon the stage. If it is a group of children, the light seems to fall more firmly upon Lyndon, his undisciplined arms and legs all akimbo, his smile wide and engaging as a summer day. As a child, even as a man, Lyndon wears only two basic expressions, each with several subtle variations. One is unbridled joy and its various cousins, the other is a dark and troubled sorrow. Lyndon has always had a capacity for greater joy and deeper sorrow than any soul I know.

There is a photograph among my collection that haunts me and must haunt Lyndon, as well, especially now that the dogs of war have been unleashed. It is a small postal card, one of thousands I addressed and sent out to encourage voters to support Lyndon for this office and that office, from the Senate to the White House, where he now resides. Most of these cards show Lyndon with Rebekah, perhaps to demonstrate to the world how much the candidate loved his mother, a qualification for American office more imperative than any other. This particular card was mailed out when Lyndon was campaigning for the Senate and it contained a brief quote from his opening campaign speech which promised: "If the day ever comes when my vote must be cast to send your boy to the trenches, that day Lyndon Johnson will leave his seat in the U.S. Senate to go with him."

Ah, Lyndon, what sorrow I sometimes see in your eyes. What torment you have earned with your goodness and your bright, caring mind. How dear is the memory of the days when you were free to sow the seeds of your compassion in the parched soil of your beloved Texas. Where in the room filled with generals and Mr. McNamara and the old sorrowful Commander and Chief is the loving boy I knew? Perhaps, dear Lyndon, your life has erred only because you loved too well and you possessed the noble gift of seeing too much in everything.

There is a letter I have that Rebekah wrote to Lyndon when he was first elected to Congress. How it came into my possession, I don't recall, but perhaps, I admit, I copied it down, hoping to incorporate some of Rebekah's gifts of language into my own correspondence. Rarely did a week go by that Lyndon didn't write his mother, and her responses would fill a heavy volume. But when I think of the terrible war in Vietnam and Lyndon's awful responsibilities, this letter comes to mind because it was at the beginning of his career when so much seemed possible, not, as now, when so much seems to be ending.

"My darling Boy," she began. "Beyond Congratulations Congressman, what can I say to my dear son in this hour of triumphal success? In this as in all the many letters I have written you there is the same theme: I love you; I believe in you; I expect great things of you.

"To me your election not only gratifies my pride as a mother in a splendid and satisfying son and delights me with the realization of the joy you must feel in your success, but it in a measure compensates for the heartache and disappointment I experienced as a child when my dear father lost the race you have just won. The confidence in the good judgment of the people was sadly shattered then by their choice of another man. Today, my faith is restored.

"How happy it would have made my precious noble father that my firstborn of his firstborn would achieve the position he desired! It makes me happy to have you carry on the ideals and principles so cherished by that great and good man. I gave you his name. I commend to you his example. You have always justified my expectations, my hopes, my dreams. How dear to me you are you cannot know, my darling boy, my devoted son, my strength, my comfort.

"Take care of yourself darling. Write to me. Always remember that I love you and am behind you in all that comes to you. Kiss my dear children in Washington for me." Then she closes: "My dearest love, Mother."

I have often marveled at the love expressed between those two, the mother and the son. How much that letter would mean to Lyndon now as with deep reluctance he sends other mothers' sons to the trenches.

I have always envied Rebekah her ability to make her love so real, so vivid, on the flat, white surface of the page. I am certain I have always loved Wilton equally well, but I regret my inability to tell him so as eloquently as Rebekah has in her letters to her son. But if, in a letter to Wilton I would write, *"You have always justified my expectations, my hopes, my dreams. How dear to me you are you cannot know, my darling boy, my devoted son,"* I imagine it would be cause for confusion, if not for merriment. Between Wilton and me, love has been a reality not requiring poetic expression. It is just there, real as air, as earth, as abiding as faith itself. Our love was such that elegant sentiments were not required, or so I think now. Could I have been mistaken all these years, and Wilton might have hungered to be called "my darling boy, my dearest love"? I mourn the lost opportunities to express my pride and my love for my son in writing. Especially when his little Janice, my beautiful grandbaby, was born.

It was Rebekah's love, more than anything else, that inspired and drove Lyndon to greatness. I have always known he has been in desperate need of reassurance, whether in the form of the people's votes or Rebekah's adoration. Maybe if I had told Wilton more often that I loved him (and now I try to recall, with horror, that I may never have done so, not spontaneously), he might have conquered the reserve and humility that held him out of the public eye.

So I study the images of the Kodak and think about love, and about Rebekah and Lyndon and Wilton, and how our lives and loves were so intricately interwoven. There is a snapshot among the many of Lyndon with his arm around Wilton in a comic, crushing, carefree headlock. Both are beaming at the camera, Lyndon is wearing his joyous visage, Wilton is smiling, but seems, as always, to be acting the foil for his old friend, letting him be the focus of the picture. There was love expressed in that photograph, too. I know Wilton admires and adores Lyndon, but I don't believe I really knew the extent of that love until Rebekah told me about the time Wilton risked everything, including his own future, to save Lyndon's political career.

It was in all the papers, but not the truth of it, as Rebekah told me that long ago day. All his life, Lyndon told Rebekah everything, and that's how she knew about the suitcase full of money Wilton took to Washington and what he did to protect Lyndon and Franklin Roosevelt. You'd have thought he robbed a bank to hear how people talked.

I admit I was not privy to this clandestine episode at the time. If the truth be known, when I asked Wilton why he was going to Washington in such a hurry, and he was evasive about it, I thought he and Virginia had quarreled and he was moving to a hotel. In fact, I scolded Virginia for her misbehavior, assuming she would know full well what it was, even if I didn't.

It was in the year 1940, the November elections were looming and a number of Democratic congressmen were in trouble and there was a possibility that the Democrats would lose control of the House. President Roosevelt called in Lyndon and asked him to do whatever had to be done to help the Congressional Campaign Committee raise funds to help put the beleaguered Democrats over the top. Well, Lyndon came back to Texas and he raised the money from Clint Murchison and Sid Richardson and a number of other oil barons. The problem then was how to get that money to Washington and distribute it to the Democratic candidates. It had to be done secretly, because Lyndon had raised money from rich Texans to finance the campaigns of liberal Eastern candidates. If the Republicans found out, or even if conservative Texas Democrats discovered what he had done, it might have cost Lyndon his next election. So Lyndon called on his old friend Wilton, the only man he knew who was sufficiently discreet and in whom he had absolute trust. Wilton picked up the suitcase full of money in Houston, took it to Washington, and made sure it was distributed to the liberal candidates who needed it most. Because of Wilton's mission, the Democrats kept control of Congress and Roosevelt was able to complete his New Deal for America.

But the reason Rebekah told me the story was something that happened several years later. News of the clandestine campaign funds leaked out. Republicans were enraged. They organized a witch hunt by suggesting to the Internal Revenue Service that there were criminal campaign financing irregularities involved. An IRS hearing was held and Wilton was brought to Austin to testify under oath.

There were two things Wilton could have done. He could have answered all the questions of the IRS agents and attorneys. After all, nothing they had done was illegal. They had broken no laws. But the complex story, the whole truth, would have been terribly embarrassing to President Roosevelt and detrimental to the New Deal and Lyndon's political future. The second thing Wilton could have done was to take the Fifth, his right to refuse to answer questions on the grounds that his answers might incriminate him of wrongdoing. Wilton chose to do what was right rather than tell what was true. Even though it made Wilton appear to be covering up his own misdeeds, he took the Fifth, and protected both Lyndon and President Roosevelt from censure. Any chance Wilton might have had for a political career was gone forever.

When Rebekah told me this story, she tearfully expressed how thankful she was that Wilton had protected Lyndon's career. I suppose I must have known at the time how lonely Wilton must have felt testifying before the IRS hearing. And now I wish fervently I had written him a letter saying: *"You have always justified my expectations, my hopes, my dreams. How dear to me you are you cannot know, my darling boy."* What a comfort that would have been, I'm certain. And I suppose that was the first time I understood the depth of Wilton's loyalty to his friend. It was also the first time I really accepted the fact that Wilton would not occupy an important government position in Washington and why, years later, I would not become the mother of a member of the president's cabinet.

I look at the Kodaks and I see the years flying by, each frozen still by some trick of light and chemistry. Here is Wilton on a date with Little Rebekah, Lyndon's sister. Here is a photograph of Lyndon and Lady Bird shortly after their wedding, an event to which, for some absolutely unfathomable reason, Rebekah was not invited. Although she became very fond of Lady Bird, I believe it was a scar she bore for the rest of her life. My own feeling is that Lyndon knew it was important to prove that there was a new woman at the center of his life. He could have invited Rebekah to the wedding, but withholding the invitation was a means of cutting the golden cord.

I remember the letter Rebekah wrote to welcome Lady Bird into the family. She had recovered from the hurt and grief she felt and she knew it was important to set the tone for a relationship that now included a stranger. She worked on the letter a long time, and it survives as perhaps the most eloquent love song ever a mother sang to her son and his bride. Lyndon was so proud of his mother's letter that he sent it to the San Marcos newspaper where it was published and the clipping remains among the photographs in my bureau. Listen to the love song of a wise and elegant soul.

"Dear Lyndon," she began. "Thinking of you, loving you, dreaming of a radiant future for you, I someway find it difficult to express my feelings. Often I have felt the utter futility of words, never more than now when I wish my boy and his bride the highest and truest happiness together. That I love you and that my fondest hopes are centered in you, I do not need to assure you, my own dear children.

"My dear Bird, I earnestly hope that you will love me as I do you. Lyndon has always held a very special place in my heart. Will you not share that place with him, my child? It would make me very happy to have you for my very own, to have you turn to me with love and confidence, to let me mother you as I do my precious boy. My heart is full of earnest wishes for your happiness. From a mother's standpoint, however, I can scarcely say more than this. I hope, and hope you know it is composed of desire and expectation, that Lyndon will prove to be as tender, as true, as loyal, as loving, and as faithful a husband as he has been a son. May life's richest blessings be yours, dear little girl.

"My darling boy, I rejoice in your happiness, the happiness you so richly deserve, the fruition of the hopes of early manhood, the foundation of a completely rounded life. I have always decreed the best in life for you. Now that you have the love and companionship of the one and only girl, I am sure you will go far. You are fortunate in finding and winning the girl you love, and I'm sure your love for each other will be an incentive to you to do all the great things of which you are capable. Sweet son, I am loving you and counting on you as never before.

"Now, my beloved children, I shall be longing to see you soon. Write me. Enjoy your honeymoon in that ideal setting then hurry home to see us. My dearest love to you both. Mama."

How I wish I could have written such a letter to Wilton and Virginia when they were married. Since Wilton, like Lyndon, neglected, for some absolutely unfathomable reason, to invite me to his wedding, I'm not sure I could have disguised my pique quite as well as Rebekah did. But I did manage to write a word or two about ingratitude and bitter disappointment, a letter which was not published and does not survive, but I'm certain expressed clearly how I felt at the time.

But of all the images and sentiments filling the albums, the boxes, the cluttered miscellany in my bureau drawers, the dominant presence is Lyndon. He was the center of our lives and his life defines who we were and are. Or is it possible we in the Hill Country shaped Lyndon as a sculptor shapes clay, and the chisel we used was love. Here he is now, one photograph after another, his face alive with joy or sorrow and their various cousins, images of a life larger than life and nourished by more love than he was ever able to return or express, except when he began his letters: "My dearest Mother."

26 ∞ THE JOHNSON CITY PORCH

ON FEBRUARY 22, 1937, REBEKAH CALLED LAURA TO REPORT that Congressman James "Buck" Buchanan, of Brenham, Texas, had died of a heart attack.

"Is this the time?" Laura asked.

"I think so. There's going to be a meeting here at our house. Lyndon wants Wilton there. And Peter. Mr. Sam. And of course Bill Deason and as many White Stars as can get away."

Laura was so excited she had to sit down in the cane chair by the telephone. "He'll do it, won't he?"

"I don't know. My father ran for Congress and lost. It was an awful experience. I just don't know."

"This is different."

"Probably. But I'm afraid. Come with Peter, Laura. I need you with me."

When Laura hung up the phone she remained in the cane chair for a moment, thinking about possibilities. Lyndon had told Wilton there were three things he wanted in life: a seat in the U.S. House of Representatives, a seat in the Senate, and the third thing, the last challenge, was never spoken of by name. Now, with the death of Buck Buchanan, his tenth congressional seat was empty, and Lyndon just might try for the first of the three things that would define the progress of his life.

They drove to Johnson City in Laura's car, through a cold rain threatening to freeze on the windshield. The Johnsons had moved back into their comfortable old frame house when the boys had finished college and Laura looked forward to a gathering before the fire in the parlor, a lovely room that Rebekah used only for special occasions. And surely this was a special occasion. They would design a campaign, assess the chances of victory, judge the mettle of the competition, develop a strategy, and assign responsibilities. In spite of the cold, she could feel her blood warming to the incomparable challenges of Hill Country politics.

There was a fire warming the parlor, and the room was filled with Rebekah's lovely antique furniture and Lyndon's most valued advisers. Lady Bird was there, and Uncle George and Bill Deason and Sam Fore, the editor of the Floresville newspaper. Also at the meeting was Dr. Bob Montgomery, the grandson of Little Sweet Woods, Peter's sister who fired on the Yankees. As a relative, a Texan, and a member of Roosevelt's brain trust, he was a welcome adviser. There had been a rumor Dr. Bob would run for Buck Buchanan's seat himself and Lyndon had delayed his plans until he was sure Dr. Bob was not running. Laura had just settled down on a fainting couch when Mr. Sam made it abundantly clear that the women were to leave the room. "We've work to do here," he said. "Rebekah, will you see to the ladies?"

"I hate this," Laura said, rolling her eyes, as she and the other women retired to the kitchen where they began to prepare the evening meal. At that time, a young girl named Louise Wiedebusch lived at the Johnson house. In return for room and board, she served as a housekeeper. As the menfolk discussed whether Lyndon should run for Congress, Louise moved in and out of the parlor, pouring hot tea and coffee, listening carefully to the discussion, and then reporting back to the women what was said.

"Lyndon said he won't run to get beaten," she reported. "Said he'd only run if he was sure he'd win."

Lady Bird and Wilton's Virginia were sitting on the porch swing, hands in pockets, collars raised against the cold. Virginia had been an absolute surprise. Somehow, Laura had imagined Wilton would marry little Rebekah Johnson or someone close to the family. But Laura was beginning to warm to this bright young woman with her engaging smile and manner.

Soon Laura grew impatient with Louise Wiedebusch's spying, and she stationed herself behind the kitchen door where she could hear the conversation directly, without the error of translation.

Uncle George was expressing his doubts. "Gotta face the

facts, Lyndon. Your chances are pretty slim. Nobody knows you in the tenth district. Voters there don't know what you've done or what you can do. Political leaders will support people like Avery or Harris or Brownlee. They're familiar, trusted faces. And another problem is you're only twenty-eight. That's a drawback."

Laura listened to all the reasons why Lyndon could not win. Then Sam Fore offered the one great advantage Lyndon would have over any other potential candidate.

"Franklin Delano Roosevelt," Sam Fore said. "People in the Hill Country love Roosevelt. If you're gonna win, you've got to be Roosevelt's man."

"But everybody who might run is pro-Roosevelt," Wilton argued.

"But the real Roosevelt man is the one who says he is first!" Fore countered. "Lyndon's gotta beat the others to the punch. Get in there first. Might make some good potential competition back down."

"What about Buchanan's widow?" Wilton asked. "There'll be a lot of sentiment for a widow lady. She might get a lot of support."

"Maybe we ought to wait and see what she does," Lyndon said.

"Dammit Lyndon," Mr. Sam snarled. "You never learn anything about politics! She's an old woman. Too old to fight. If she knows she has a fight coming on, she won't run. Announce now before she announces. If you do, she won't run."

"What about money," Sam Fore wondered.

"We haven't got any."

"I've got some," Uncle George said. "About a thousand dollars. You can have all I've got."

"You can have my car," Bill Deason offered. "It's worth another thousand."

"And there's Senator Wirtz," Lyndon said. "He said he'd support me if I ran. And he's got his fingers on cash. Oil money."

"How much do we need?"

"Ten thousand to get started."

Then Laura had to move away from the door because her legs were cramping up from crouching in one position so long.

In midafternoon, as the meeting continued, the women went for a drive around Johnson City. Laura knew the men would be deep into strategy now. Would Sam Fore be able to get endorsements from the newspaper editors in San Marcos, Blanco, and Bastrop? Who would make contact with the district's many preachers whose influence on their congregations could be critical? Who was going to sponsor the barbecues and arrange for Lyndon to speak at country schools? Who was going to do the legwork? Would we have enough people to cover the territory? Who would write and print postcards and what should they say? How were we going to get people without cars to the polls on election day? And, of course, would we have enough money to run an effective campaign? All these questions, Laura knew, would have to be answered before Lyndon's decision could be made.

In late afternoon, the women returned to the Johnson home. The men were in the yard, and Laura saw that the die had been cast. Their faces were animated by the most boyish of grins, and they walked loose and stood tall and they were fruitlessly trying to hide a bottle of whiskey Mr. Sam had been saving for special occasions. "Here's to Texas and a roll of the dice," Laura heard Uncle George say. Although she hated liquor and even the idea of liquor, for the first time in her life, Laura longed to offer a toast to the great adventure they were all beginning.

The weeks of Lyndon's campaign for Congress were enormously fulfilling for Laura. At last she was able to throw herself foursquare into the center of the political fray. She would drive herself to the local rallies and to the fish fries she could reach by car in one day. Peter would sit tall in the backseat as they careened down country roads in search of prodigal voters and crowds. When she would spot a gathering, Laura would park her Ford against a tree or occasionally against a Chevrolet, then burst forth to attack the potential supporters on foot, passing out cards filled with praise of Lyndon's accomplishments on one side and a photograph of Lyndon with Rebekah on the other.

"Now here is the one you should vote for," she would say to even perfect strangers, as she passed out the cards.

Wilton drove the car Bill Deason had contributed to the campaign with Lyndon in the front seat and Sam Fore in the back. When they arrived in a town, Wilton would park the dusty used car on the gravel country roads and they would all pile into a clean car prearranged for use in town. While Lyndon was speaking, Wilton would move around the crowd, listening carefully to the reactions of the people. Then he would report back to Lyndon so that new ideas could be incorporated into the speeches or phrasing could be changed to more adequately capture the sentiments of voters in the next town.

Perhaps Laura's most effective campaigning took place after the meetings of the Lone Star Chapter of the United Daughters of the Confederacy. The memorial drinking fountain on the courthouse lawn had been erected by this chapter in memory of Peter's father, Col. P. C. Woods, "Doctor, Soldier and Man of God." Laura had been an active and enthusiastic member of the United Daughters of the Confederacy since 1930. It was against the rules of the UDC for anyone to conduct open political debate at the meetings, yet after the singing of "Just Before the Battle, Mother" and "Tenting Tonight on the Old Camp Grounds," when the eyes of the members were moist with memory of the gallant soldiers and noble deeds of the Confederacy, Laura would serve equal measures of refreshments and advice. "Now, don't forget to vote for our boy, Lyndon," she would say over her teacup. "He's a hometown boy with our interests at heart. He grew up here and he knows what we need." Although each of Lyndon's opponents lived within a day's drive of San Marcos, Laura's praise of Lyndon was liberally spiced with the suggestion that Lyndon alone was worthy of Confederate support and the others were somehow alien, if not out-and-out Yankee.

Lyndon's strategy was to capitalize on Roosevelt's popularity in Texas. People were beginning to feel the economic chains of the depression falling away. New Deal reforms and such programs as the Civil Works Administration and the Works Progress Administration had begun to put people back to work and to give the people of the South some measure of economic control. After serving as secretary for Congressman Kleberg, Lyndon had been appointed by Roosevelt to the post of director of the Texas National Youth Administration. As a Roosevelt appointee, Lyndon had been a part of New Deal reforms.

"Our plan," Wilton told Laura, "is to keep hammering away on Lyndon's connection to Roosevelt and his programs. We keep him constantly out among the people, shaking hands, talking about the promise of the future. I drive while Sam Fore drills Lyndon on the issues and how people feel about the issues. Then, when we see a farmer plowing in the field, I pull off the road and Lyndon walks over and talks with the farmer about his crops and his plans for his family. In town, there's always a café where people gather. When we find it, we stop and Lyndon goes in and talks with the people. He not only talks to the owner and the customers, but he goes back in the kitchen to talk with the dishwashers and cooks."

As Laura heard about this one-on-one campaigning, she recalled the strategies of Colonel House. It was not as if Lyndon was merely going through the motions, playing the obligatory role of a Texas politician. Laura could sense that he truly believed in the people and in his power to help them to a better life. Laura once told Lyndon that he should be careful not to spend all his time with the big shots. "Lyndon," she said, "remember the little people vote, too. Be sure you make them know their vote counts." As the weeks went by, she was pleased to see he had taken her advice.

Lyndon won the election handily.

Congressman Lyndon Johnson and Lady Bird left for Washington. Soon Wilton joined them in the capital, where he trained for his new appointment as a regional director of the U.S. census bureau. Virginia and little Janice remained in San Antonio to close the house and store the furnishings until they could relocate with Wilton in Waco, where the regional office was located.

∞

Laura's house was quiet. It was as if a storm had passed and swept everyone away. Soon Laura received word that Colonel House, who had written Laura that he did not wish to live too long, was dead. For the first time in her long life, Laura felt empty. Try as she might, she could feel no enthusiasm concerning anything or anybody. Each morning she would wake and say out loud, "This is the day the Lord hath made, rejoice and be glad in it." But the old mantra did not work as it once had, and each time she determined to make a list of blessings, she would be unable to find a pen or her glasses, and she felt the tyranny of the years. She was now sixty-five years of age, and her eyes were failing. It was difficult for her to read and she turned instead to the radio for company.

During the depression, when farms continued to fail and the wind carried away both soil and hope, the people of America had reached out toward a company of messengers who promised a better life in the world to come. The depression was gone, but the messengers remained. The voices were familiar; they were the voices heard in arbors, along southern rivers, and in the white frame churches of rural America. Several times each day, when she was not listening to Roosevelt's fireside chat or Pappy O'Daniel and his "Pass the Biscuits, Pappy" show of gospel music and sermons praising mothers' virtues and Hillbilly flour, Laura listened to the radio evangelists who were trying to bring a demoralized nation back to God. When her hearing began to fail, she could no longer easily hear the services in church. But at home, by her radio, she could turn the volume up at will and the gospel came in loud and clear.

Laura loved to listen to the evangelists. It was like being washed in the grace of a brush arbor sermon without worrying about the dirt daubers, the spiders that sometimes crept down from the branches, or the moths that gathered in the lantern light and would fly sometimes right into your mouth when you took a breath between lines of a hymn. Each night she listened to a preacher from Houston, two from San Antonio and one from Tennessee. She also listened to the Rev. Herbert J. Armstrong of Eugene, Oregon, a former Quaker who called himself

Chairman of the Worldwide Church of God. "If you're going to name a church something grand," Laura told Peter, "you could do no better than name it the Worldwide Church of God." Most of the radio sermons were the same old fire and brimstone she had heard all her life from barnstorming preachers such as the Rev. Andrew Jackson Potter. What intrigued her about Herbert J. Armstrong was his strangely skewed interpretation of certain scriptures. He preached, for instance, that Christ was not crucified on Friday, but on Wednesday. Jesus was not resurrected on Easter Sunday but late Saturday afternoon. Laura loved this kind of irreverent iconoclasm, especially because she could challenge Rebekah's conservatism with these shocking new facts about the Crucifixion and the Resurrection. Because Laura was nearly deaf now, she would have to shout Reverend Armstrong's thesis about Good Wednesday and Easter Saturday into Rebekah's ear, revelations which more than once raised the eyebrows of neighbors passing by.

Since Roosevelt and Lyndon were hard at work on social programs, Laura began to feel less compelled to align herself with ministers who preached the social gospel. In truth, almost all the radio evangelists of the period were far more concerned with matters of heaven and hell than they were concerned with the human condition on earth. As the decade of the thirties passed, Laura began to rediscover Aimee Semple McPherson, primarily because Herbert J. Armstrong hinted she was not the queen of heaven her followers claimed her to be. "The people who enter Angelus Temple," he wrote, "are simply thrill-seekers looking for sensual pleasure and excitement." Laura felt his remarks were high praise. Surely there was nothing more thrilling or exciting than a life lived close to God. And surely the God who gave us five senses would not deny us the pleasure they afforded. So Laura turned her dial from the evangelists who threatened hell to those who promised glory and of all these it was Aimee Semple McPherson who made life seem most abundantly glorious. Laura identified with Aimee Semple McPherson's childhood dream of becoming a great actress. In Laura's mind, few actresses could ever match the charisma and magic that this amazing woman possessed. Everything she did, every word she uttered, was the stuff of legend. She was beautiful, glamorous, and she had this marvelous capacity to make things happen in the world around her.

When Aimee Semple McPherson had disappeared in the twenties and had claimed she had been kidnapped and held for $500,000 ransom, most people in America felt she had orchestrated the event herself. "The Queen of Heaven is a sham," the headlines howled. Yet Laura stood by the controversial evangelist all through her ordeal, her trial for obstructing justice, and through her nervous breakdown that followed the trial. And later, in 1944, when Aimee Semple McPherson was found dead, an empty bottle of sleeping pills by her side, Laura grieved as deeply as she had when Colonel House died. Aimee Semple McPherson's death convinced Laura that she should make every effort to live forever.

As Laura approached her seventh decade, her eyesight deteriorated further. Peter believed this was another reason she turned so completely to the radio for news of the here and the hereafter. It had become too difficult for her to read her many books and magazines that she swore were being printed with smaller letters to save paper. For a while Peter was afraid she was retreating into a world fashioned from the one-dimensional offerings of the radio. Yet several years before Aimee Semple McPherson died, something happened in Texas that brought Laura out from her room and away from her radio and, to the horror of her neighbors, back into her old battered Ford. Lyndon Johnson was running for the Senate. Everybody was coming home to make the good fight against impossible odds.

On the day Lyndon announced for the Senate, Laura was ticketed for reckless parking. She had always been known for driving down the very center of the road and her logic for straddling lanes was beyond reproach. "If I don't know whether my next turn is to the right or to the left," she told Peter, "the safest place to be is in the middle." When she could not find a parking place, she simply turned off the engine and left her car in the middle of the road and walked away on her errand. The Ford by this time had been in so many collisions, small and large, it looked as if it had been attacked by maniacs wielding ball-peen hammers. The investigating highway patrolman ticketed Laura and suspended her driver's license because of her poor vision. She told the officer, "License or no license I will drive if and when and where I want to." No power on earth was going to keep her from working Lyndon's campaign, and to do that she needed a car. She was totally unrepentant and so forceful that she was issued a special limited license with a warning not to straddle lanes or park in the middle of the road.

When Lyndon ran for the Senate in 1941, he had the political backing of Franklin Roosevelt and the financial support of Brown & Root, the giant Texas engineering firm. There were twenty-seven candidates in what one national magazine called the "Screwball Election in Texas."

"He can't lose," Laura promised Rebekah. "He's running against a Baptist preacher with a drunken press agent urging prohibition, two other preachers who list the power of prophesy as their only qualification for office, an ex-bootlegger, a fool who sells goat gland medicine, and a laxative manufacturer."

"But Laura," Rebekah warned. "There's Pappy. And he's probably the most popular man in Texas."

Laura did not dispute Rebekah's warning because she often turned her dial to Pappy's radio show.

Lyndon's chief opponent was the redoubtable Pappy O'Daniel, a showman who sold flour on the radio, and the race finally narrowed down not so much to which of these men could best serve the state but which could provide the most entertaining campaign. Pappy O'Daniel's radio show reached millions of Texans. He had proved in his successful governor's race that he was a wonderful entertainer and could win voters with his blending of old-time religion and salesmanship. He announced he was running on a platform that promised one hundred percent approval of the Lord God Jehovah. He was for widows, orphans, low taxes, the Ten Commandments and the Golden Rule. On the other hand, Lyndon was well known only in Central Texas and was not a particularly entertaining public speaker.

The polls showed he had fourteen percent of the vote and had little chance of winning.

Pappy O'Daniel traveled the state on a bus with a hillbilly band. If he was not inspiring the people with his patriotic songs and his down-home philosophy, he was telling them they did not need some New Deal Socialist to represent them in Washington. His campaign was part traveling circus, part medicine show, part revival. Lyndon's campaign committee decided to fight fire with fire. "The Senate seat is going to the candidate who can put on the best show," Wilton said. So, Lyndon got a twenty-three-piece jazz band and a chorus of vocalists who came out on stage performing such crowd-pleasers as "Hail Columbia" and "The Eyes of Texas Are Upon You" and "San Antonio Rose." Then Lyndon would come on stage and swing his arms and make his heartfelt promises, and the band and everybody would stand and sing "God Bless America." There would not be a dry eye in the crowd and Lyndon's ratings in the polls began to climb.

Early in the campaign, after Laura had been issued her ticket for reckless parking and had been issued a license for limited driving, Wilton organized a Corpus Christi for Lyndon Johnson Committee. The key element of the campaign was a huge motorcade of cars, bearing LBJ signs and banners, which would move noisily from Corpus Christi to Sinton to Beeville to Stockdale to Seguin. At each town, additional cars joined the motorcade so that it grew larger and more demonstrative as it progressed northward. When the motorcade reached San Marcos and began circling the square with horns blaring and banners unfurled, there was Laura at the wheel of her old Ford emblazoned with LBJ signage. She was ready to join the motorcade, which was now on its way to a rally in Waco. When Wilton spotted his mother, he jumped from his car and rushed to where Laura was bluffing her way into the parade by racing the engine and moving forward in violent little fits and starts. "Mother, you don't see well enough to drive to Waco. It's a long way. You can't go. You can't drive at night. You can just ride with us."

Laura merely glared. "Well, I certainly am going," she said.

"I'm going in my car. Don't worry about me. Anybody can drive in a motorcade, it's just like a funeral procession. You just stay behind the car in front." It was not difficult for Laura to find a position in the line of cars. When other motorists saw her coming, they gave her all the room in the world.

On election night, Laura and Peter joined the crowd at the courthouse, where huge blackboards displayed the election returns. As each precinct reported, the results were posted. Laura rejoiced as box after box revealed Lyndon was ahead. Before midnight they returned home, confident that they had done their part in getting a good man into the Senate. Late in the night, as Laura was searching the radio dial for an evangelist, she heard the news instead, and it was so inconceivable, it would haunt her nights for months to come.

Several years later, when Laura was trying to explain to her granddaughter Janice why Lyndon lost the election, she said it was because Pappy O'Daniel stuffed the ballot box. "Well, Sweetie Pie, some of the people who voted for Pappy O'Daniel were dead people. We didn't know we were supposed to have dead people vote for Lyndon. Every once in a while," she told Janice, "an innocent man gets sent up to Washington. But this wasn't one of those times."

During the Second World War, a conflict that Laura was certain followed the First World War by only a matter of moments, Laura and Peter moved to a big house on Hutchinson Street where they rented rooms and apartments to war brides, students, and widows. These were hard times in San Marcos and food was severely rationed. Many people in town ran out of meat stamps before the Sunday meal. Although the Vogelsang Hollow swamp rabbits did not survive depression poachers, Laura was able to grow much of the family's food in her garden. With the orchard and chicken pens, she generally had stamps left over which she gave to her renters and neighbors in need. Her old Ford, that had somehow survived all these years, used so little gasoline that she had extra gas ration stamps to give to her children. Every two weeks she would climb into the Ford to carry vegetables and fresh dressed chickens to Austin to share with Wilton's family. She was especially concerned for Janice and her new baby brother, Wilton, whom Laura called Little Son. She worried they would not have nourishing food and would not grow up strong because of wartime food rationing.

In 1945, President Roosevelt died. Two years later, Little Mattie passed away. Little Mattie's large family came home for the funeral, including Laura's youngest brother, Lee, who had been born after her marriage, and who had been living in California. She saw him so infrequently he seemed like a stranger come to mourn. Laura found her mind returning again and again to death; too many people around her were dying. She wondered if the little girl her mother had been so many years ago had still been there at the end. Poor Mama, she thought. She was so tiny and eternity is so large. How will she ever find her way? Sometimes when it was quiet in the house, Laura could push her mind out into the air and look back at the person she had become, and what she saw was a girl masquerading as an eccentric old woman. In these moments of clarity she knew she was considered "odd" and that her behavior was a source of amusement to both neighbors and family. She knew they sometimes laughed at her peculiarities and that her grandchildren told stories of her antics to their friends. This awareness saddened her, yet reminded her that she still retained the power to impact the lives around her. She was still a person and she felt it was more and more important that those she loved remember her as more than a source of amusing anecdotes in years to come.

When her granddaughter was six, Laura wrote her a poem. She never knew for sure if it had been delivered or found, or was lost amid her avalanches of papers, notes, and letters. Laura could rarely remember anything she had written, the words seemed to disappear from her mind as if written with invisible ink. But this poem to her granddaughter she would remember until the hour of her death. It was headed by the words, "To Janice."

Inside us all there is a fire
That burns hot as a star.
We change, grow old in time;
But the fire is who we are.

27 ∞ THE SUMMER IN SEGUIN

LAURA HAD BEEN THINKING ABOUT WINIFRED. ALTHOUGH HER daughter was well beyond middle age, the image Laura carried in her mind was a tall, slender mystery of barely twenty. The eyes were very dark, shrouded by what Laura imagined was a foreshadowing of her tragedy. Over the years, Peter and the children would often visit Winifred at the state hospital. Laura's visits were far less frequent, and even on those rare occasions, Laura's mind refused to see anything but the dark-eyed girl Winifred had been before her madness.

Peter wrote his daughter faithfully, letters alive with news and affection. Laura wrote only when her conscience grew too painful not to write, and she was now able to admit to herself that she hated the terrible trips to the asylum. A few years ago, Winifred had begun writing a diary. It was written in the third person and was as gentle and sweet as a needlepoint rhyme. On the scented pages, Winifred recalled how she "was a sophomore when Lyndon Baines Johnson was a senior at Southwest Texas State Teachers College" and how Lyndon was "a tall, handsome young man with dark-brown eyes, brown hair and big ears and was making quite a name for himself as a debater." When she wrote about Lyndon's mother, Rebekah, she described her as "sweet, good humored, and so pleasant you couldn't help but like her." Of Mr. Sam she wrote, "Often Winifred said of Mr. Sam, 'He was an alert, kind neighbor and he was always helping the sick.' " Her chapters were filled with descriptions of an idyllic world of perfect order. Her people were kind, the landscape a sylvan delight of meadow and houses with window boxes spilling flowers and even her own portrait seemed as if it had been plucked from a Norman Rockwell cover. *Where, then,*

Laura wondered, *was the violence, the death, the awful melancholy?*

In 1948, when Lyndon again made a race for the Senate, Laura had thought about writing a book. Perhaps it was Winifred's journal that inspired her. Over a period of several weeks, she made a detailed outline. But when she read the chapter headings aloud she realized her book was more about Lyndon Johnson's life than her own and she grew quite angry. For days the fate of her life story hung in the balance. *"Isn't it just like Lyndon to dominate everything around him,"* she laughed to herself. *"But I will not have him dominate me."* That very night, with ceremonial flair, she tore her outline into small pieces, being careful, of course, not to tear them so small they could not be pieced together again.

The suspended life story was one of the reasons Laura purchased the small blue Olivetti. Her failing eyesight and what her family called her "galloping penmanship" made writing by hand both difficult and indecipherable. The reason she bought that particular brand of typewriter was because it was the most attractive typewriter in the store. "If our lives are going to be cluttered with machines," she said, "we might as well try to avoid the ugly ones." Another reason she bought the Olivetti was to write letters to Texas newspaper editors urging them to support Lyndon in his effort to win a seat in the U.S. Senate.

In August of 1948, Laura became deeply involved in what she always believed was the most important and pivotal event in the political career of Lyndon Baines Johnson. In the Democratic primary, Coke Stevenson claimed a majority of votes in the race for the U.S. Senate. A runoff between Johnson and Stevenson was set for August 28. Lyndon had won only 17 counties compared to the 168 counties won by Stevenson. "We were overwhelmingly, vastly, horribly behind," Laura later wrote in her autobiography. "It looked hopeless."

Wilton was asked to organize Lyndon's campaign in Hays and Guadalupe counties. All over the state of Texas the White Stars went to work, organizing county campaigners, and reestablishing the precinct networks that had served Lyndon so well in the past. In Hays County, headquarters were set up in San Marcos by the Donalsons and other family friends of the Woodses. In Guadalupe County, the campaign was centered in Seguin.

The Johnson-for-Senate Committee asked Virginia Woods to have a tea at which Lady Bird would be introduced to the women of Seguin. Lady Bird was known as a gracious and effective campaigner, and whenever she appeared she generated enthusiasm and support for her husband. The tea would be held at Virginia and Wilton's home on election eve. Surely, Lady Bird's presence would generate critically needed support and help close the gap between Lyndon and Coke Stevenson in Guadalupe County, which was a Stevenson stronghold.

The strategy to hold a tea was, however, rife with perils. Even though women had long ago won the vote, to discuss or even mention politics at a social gathering was considered unladylike and in poor taste.

"It's a risky idea, might backfire, and some people will criticize," Virginia said. "But, in a close political race like this one, it's a chance you have to take." Even though everyone would *know* the tea was a political event, it had to be handled as if it was merely an opportunity for the ladies of Seguin to meet Virginia's good friend Lady Bird Johnson, whose husband *just happened* to be running for the Senate and whose election would be decided the next day.

"Your biggest problem will be Mrs. Weinert, because she's for Coke," Wilton told the committee. Hilda Weinert, the formidable national Democratic committeewoman from Texas, was the wife of a wealthy Seguin banker and oilman.

"She's a tough opponent who works hard for her candidates and pours money into their campaigns. I wish we could get her on our side," Wilton said.

Mrs. Weinert was a large and buxom woman, her eyes as flashing as the diamonds she wore. Rumors went around town that she was shocked and indignant that "a nobody like Virginia Woods" would enter her domain of Democratic party politics.

Perhaps the most sensitive task facing the tea organizers was the selection of hostesses. For a woman to agree to be hostess might well put her husband's career or social position in jeopardy. Some who accepted later called back to decline rather than risk the wrath of Miss Hilda. Zella Buerger, a woman of voluptuous proportion, had the most creative reason for declining. "Virginia, honey," she said, "I'd love to come to the tea, but I've been in terrible pain ever since I closed my left breast in the store safe."

At the same time, the hostesses had to be carefully chosen to represent different segments of Seguin society. The friends of Hettie Donegan, wife of Henry Donegan, chairman of the board of directors of the First National Bank of Seguin, were all from prominent families and members of the Federated Women's Clubs. Arlene MyCue, whose husband, Roger, was president of the volunteer fire department, was active and well-liked among the women of the Fire Department Ladies' Auxiliary. The hostesses joked about the necessity of carefully timing the invitations so that women who were compatible would be together at the same time. "We have our cliques," Hettie Donegan laughed, "best not mix the Baptists with the Catholics or women from town with folks from the country."

While formulating the party plans, Hettie Donegan suggested it would be rude not to invite Miss Hilda to the tea. Virginia volunteered to deliver the invitation in person and when she appeared before the redoubtable Miss Hilda, the woman opened the interview by saying, "Whatever you have to sell, I don't want any." Then she not only declined the invitation, she criticized Virginia for forcing politics down the throats of her guests. "You must give Lyndon my apologies," she said, "and tell Lady Bird I'm sorry, but I have another engagement."

It had been drizzling rain all morning the day of the tea and by early afternoon, when the guests began to appear, it was raining still. Yet the women of Seguin came in their finery, a milliner's delight, veiled to the eyebrows and gloved to the elbow. A hostess greeted the guests at the front door where they removed their right glove to shake hands with the hostess and sign the guest book. Then, carrying the glove in their left hand, they were introduced to the women they had known all their lives. Each was ushered into the dining room where they were served pineapple and strawberry punch at one end of the lace-covered table or coffee and tea at the opposite. Laura served as hostess-at-large and moved from room to room making polite conversation to camouflage the fact that Lady Bird was late. The corsage of red roses and the matching centerpiece on the dining room table were beginning to wilt.

Ruthie Boyd Wright answered the telephone and Laura could tell from her expression that something was wrong.

"Mrs. Woods, come quick! Something awful has happened," she yelled, handing the phone to Virginia. "There's been an accident!"

A few minutes later Laura watched in horror as Lady Bird moved from the car to the house. She appeared to be half drowned. Her clothes were plastered with mud and a random green and rose pattern of grass stains and blood. Maxine Halm, Virginia's sister, and Laura rushed outside and grasped Lady Bird's arm to help her across the backyard.

"You'll get all muddy," Lady Bird warned.

"But are you all right?" Laura asked, certain she was not.

"Just a few bumps and scratches. I'll be fine once I have a quick bath and borrow a few things from Virginia to wear."

Lady Bird was slipped through the backdoor and into a bedroom. A few of the guests saw her pass and word spread quickly that Lyndon's bride had been horribly injured and her assistant was hospitalized. A hush settled through the house and guests spoke in whispers, fearing the worst.

Lady Bird nervously related what had happened as Laura and Virginia and Virginia's sister Maxine helped her take off her muddy shoes.

"We were on that hill just beyond Zorn. Rain was coming down in sheets. I was looking at my notes, preparing for my radio speech tonight. I really don't know what happened.

"All of a sudden I felt like I was in a Mixmaster—twisting and turning upside down all at the same time.

"The car must have turned over two or three times—maybe even end over end—I just don't know. Then everything stopped. Total quiet, dead silence all in a split second.

"'I'm all right' was my first thought. Then I realized the car was upside down. I asked Marietta if she was all right. She didn't answer, only moaned. Then I crawled out my car window without too much trouble, but I couldn't get to Marietta. I knew I had to hurry and get help.

"It took me a moment to figure out where the highway was because the car landed in a field. I started to climb up the slope to the road, but it was steep and mud was so slick I couldn't crawl up without sliding back. I walked along the ditch till I could climb up, and we were really lucky because here came a farmer in his pickup truck.

"The old gentleman tried to help me get Marietta out, but we could see if we pulled on her it might injure her worse. I stayed. He left to call an ambulance. Marietta came to and said only her leg hurt. When they put her on the stretcher, she insisted it was only a hurt leg, that I should come on because she would be fine and would catch up with me later."

"You should rest," Virginia said. "After your bath, you should climb in bed and rest for a few minutes."

"Are you sure you should go through with this?" Maxine asked.

"I'm sure," Lady Bird said, squaring her shoulders and then standing unsteadily by the bed. "Do you have some alcohol? Maybe Maxine can just touch up the cuts and scratches where it won't show."

Laura was amazed at the transformation in Lady Bird's appearance. From someone who had looked like a cross between a tar baby and a rain-soaked scarecrow, a beautiful, stylish young woman emerged. Within an hour, Lady Bird had moved from a shattering near-death experience to a woman of calm and gracious confidence.

Wearing the bright yellow dress she had pulled from a garment bag in the backseat of the wrecked car, Lady Bird walked gracefully into the dining room toward the gathered guests. She stood in the receiving line, poised and collected, as if nothing at all had happened. All who were there were charmed by her courage, grace, and wit. But of course, she never uttered a word of politics. She did mention, "Tomorrow is Lyndon's birthday and I'm pretty sure I know what he'd like everyone to give him for a birthday present."

The Texas newspapers had widely bantered that candidate Johnson's wife, Lady Bird, was to make a statewide address that evening in San Antonio on radio at 7:30. Afterward, she would attend a birthday barbecue and rally with entertainment by cowboy singer Gene Autry. Wilton, who had returned from the hospital, timed her departure from the tea so they would arrive in time for the live broadcast. Lady Bird said her good-byes to the last of the guests and hostesses. When she was leaving to join Wilton at the car, she was confronted by the formidable presence of Miss Hilda, who had arrived in her chauffeured black limousine. Laura was aghast when Mrs. Weinert planted her imposing self between Lady Bird and Wilton's car. Everyone knew there was barely time for Lady Bird to get to San Antonio in time for her well-publicized radio broadcast.

"Oh, Lady Bird, my precious friend," Miss Hilda said, her words sodden with syrup, "I'm so very sorry I couldn't be here with these ladies to tell them what a charming person you are."

Laura tugged Lady Bird's sleeve, trying to guide her around Miss Hilda toward Wilton's car, but each time Lady Bird went right, Miss Hilda stepped left, and when Lady Bird stepped left, Miss Hilda moved right. It was a strange country dance of two-step and western swing right in the middle of the yard. Finally, with Laura tugging on her sleeve, Lady Bird was able to sidestep the Texas national Democratic committeewoman and escape into Wilton's car. "Well, my, my, my," Laura said as Wilton's car rushed away. "And they say only men play dirty politics."

Lyndon won the election by eighty-seven votes. Several newspaper editors around the state criticized him for "stealing" the election. Laura was furious. She immediately began another letter-writing campaign to the critical editors. "So he only won by eighty-seven votes," she wrote, the little Olivetti a very slow and unsteady metronome. "A miss is as good as a mile, and thank God for it. Coke Stevenson is a racist, an isolationist, and a crook." She then quoted J. Frank Dobie's remark that Stevenson "knew as much about foreign affairs as a hog knows about Sunday."

Several days later, when Virginia, Wilton and Laura were reliving the most glorious moments of the tea, Wilton asked how many invitations had been sent.

"About two hundred," Virginia said.

"How many came?"

"I'd say at least eighty-seven," Laura smiled.

Laura continued to write to her elected officials in Washington offering ideas to men like Maury Maverick and Sam Rayburn and, of course, Lyndon. In 1951, she wrote Lyndon with advice on how the Korean War should be handled. "Dear Lyndon," she wrote. "Thank you for answering my letters. I'm sure you're very busy and that you get many letters. I'll make mine short. Lyndon, I have read carefully what the Assistant Secretary replied to you in regard to Nationalist China assisting in the fighting. He speaks of the expense to arm the Nationalists, who are already trained. I don't think we should sacrifice another drop of American blood in Korea fighting Communist Chinese when the Nationalist Chinese just sit around watching. I wish we had more Texas men at the head of international affairs and that our military directors were Texas men. Our family thinks of you."

It was during this period that Laura also began to write to General MacArthur. Lyndon had met the general in the Pacific during World War II and had written Laura that if America was dead set on a general for president, MacArthur would be a far sight better than Eisenhower. Unfortunately, he added, there don't seem to be too many Democrat generals. When Laura heard Walter Winchell announce on her radio that Truman fired MacArthur for challenging his conduct of the Korean War, she was so disturbed she asked to be alone and went out onto the front porch to swing away her indignation. After a few hours, she realized that Truman had done the right thing. "We can't have our military people running the country," she decided. That afternoon Laura took little Janice aside. "I don't care if your entire sixth-grade class sides with General MacArthur," she said, "you go right back to class and volunteer to debate on the side of President Harry Truman."

Yet there was something about MacArthur that reminded her of the days when war was pageantry, when the warriors were cloaked in armor and honor, chivalry, banners and steel. MacArthur seemed the reincarnation of Alexander the Great or Charlemagne. Of course, she detested war and killing, but didn't MacArthur look fine standing on the broad steps of the capitol in Austin, every bit the great leader?

After the death of Aimee Semple McPherson, Laura could find no evangelist who inspired her to correspond. She continued to listen to the radio preachers and she sent them money to keep them on the air. But there was one young man whose voice came into her room from Oklahoma who offered something she had begun to secretly crave. Oral Roberts offered her healing. In his broadcasts he had revealed his own body had been healed by the grace of God. He had been a stutterer, had been diagnosed with tuberculosis, and he had been healed of both in a revival tent filled with miracles and the holy ghost. When Oral Roberts would lay on his hands and ask God to heal, and the crowd would moan, plead and pray, Laura felt all the passion, wonder, and mystery come into her room and she knew that God was there by the radio.

Laura wanted Oral Roberts to heal her eyes. She felt the hearing-aid salesman could cure her hearing, but only Oral Roberts could make her see again. She wanted to see the world with the clarity and color she remembered from youth. She wanted to throw away her spectacles and the dozen or so spares she kept in conspicuous places around the house. But she knew at the heart of her prayer for sight was a need to defeat the process of aging. It was not vanity that fueled this need, it was a sense that she had too much left to do. There was the story of her life to write and surely Lyndon would need her when he ran for president and Janice would need her to guide a safe course through her adolescence. She must come to terms with Winifred and her ghost and she needed more time to tell Peter how dear he was and how pleased she had been to share his life. In a way, she was ashamed that she would ask such selfish things of the Oklahoma healer. But if he could make the lame walk again, he could give the blind sight. There was a precedent for it in the Bible. Many times Oral Roberts asked his listeners to place both hands on the radio and pray to be cured and she would grasp that little box in both her hands, squeeze and pray that the clouds in her eyes would part. When the cure did not happen, rather than doubt the powers of Oral Roberts, she told Peter the radio was in need of repair. She began to write Oral Roberts, enclosing generous checks and asking for a private audience. After all, it would be unseemly to be healed in front of all those perspiring faithful.

Laura tried to remember how the world looked when she could see it clearly. What precisely were the colors of a sunset or of a rose? How did the blue of Peter's eyes reflect the light? She was sitting with Peter in their parlor when she decided to tell him about her planned trip to Oklahoma and how, once healed, she would be able to read the nuances that flecked the iris of his eye. For a long time she talked quietly to the tall figure in his comfortable chair by the cherrywood table and then she realized he was not responding. When had she last heard Peter speak? She was rocked by the realization that she did not know. Their lives together had become so comfortable and harmonic that they moved like a cloud through each other's days. "Peter?" Then she spoke his name again. "Peter?" For a moment, the specter of death passed before her eyes, but then she felt his hand was warm and his face moist and when she touched his eyes she could feel the feathery touch of his eyelids sweeping her fingers. Peter was alive, but he was not responding to her words or her touch.

Peter had suffered a mild stroke.

Laura was sick with fear. Although Peter was in his ninetieth year and his mind often made pilgrimages to worlds where Laura could not follow, there was a certain steadfast allegiance to routine that kept him in motion through space and time. Each day he walked from the house to the post office when he thought another train had come in and the mail had been put in the boxes. Laura would hand Peter his cane, pull his collar together against the chill, then send him on his way. It was always difficult for her to hold back the tears as the tall, erect figure moved toward the post office, his progress painfully slow and a bit unsteady, as if he were being blown off course by a powerful wind. Yet he somehow maintained the dignity that had accompanied him through all the years. It never occurred to Laura to keep Peter at home. Instinctively, she knew he must stay in motion, and she prayed the phone would not ring. Then it did, and she knew what she feared most had happened. Peter had been injured by the thing he had hated most all his life. He had been hit by a car.

Peter spent much of the day in bed, Laura at his side, rubbing his arms, patting his hand, combing and brushing his hair. She would leave his side only to bring him his food and to find sugar and cream for his coffee. Each time Dr. Sowell would come by to see Peter, Laura would demand that he get Peter out of bed. "Now you are going to get my husband up!" she insisted. "He must not just lie there. If you let him just lie, he'll just get weaker and die!" Often the children would come into the room and visit for awhile. But as soon as they were gone, Laura moved to his bedside to hold his hand. They spoke not a word that others might hear, but in his eyes Laura could see the reflection of the fire glowing in the one-room house where each of them had first explored the intimate corners of the other's mind and body. In his eyes she could see the shadows they cast on the wall as they made love. They listened together to the mockingbirds and the cardinals that sang them awake in the mornings and they heard the hoofbeats of the horses that had filled Peter's dream. Laura looked down at her husband and saw a man strong and hard as an oak and, for the first time in a long time, she saw with clarity the blue of his Hawkins eyes. She held him and told him how dear he was to her and how pleased she was to have shared his life.

Then one evening Peter died. Laura chose to tell the others in the morning and sit alone with Peter this one last night. She closed her eyes and dreamed she was a girl, watching a tall, mysterious rider in the distance. At dawn, she decided to tell John Pennington, the undertaker, to not let anyone, under any circumstance, play that tear-jerking hymn "Nearer My God to Thee."

The funeral was in the First Methodist Church. It reminded Laura strangely of their wedding, for none of Peter's family had come. For a moment, she felt a tug of resentment, then realized, of course, most were gone now. Georgia Lawshe Woods, the Colonel-Doctor, Little Sweet, Cherokee, Pinckney were all dead. Whatever their secrets, they were now buried with Peter.

On April 10, 1956, at 9:30 in the evening, Laura turned her hearing aid to the high setting, her radio to the point on her dial marked in red and she waited, not so patiently, through a series of commercials, for Lyndon's speech.

Everyone in San Marcos was talking about the speech and the movement within the party to have Lyndon lead the Texas delegation at the National Democratic Convention in Chicago as a favorite son candidate for president. Soon, Lyndon's familiar voice began to emerge through the electronics separating the candidate from his most passionate supporter.

"On May 5, the neighborhood precinct conventions will be held throughout the state. They are the first step in the process that ultimately selects our delegation to the national convention. These precinct conventions are the instruments through which your voices are heard. They give you the opportunity to exercise the American right which is most envied by the people of the world—the right of free choice.

"We must all turn out to the precinct, county, and state conventions. Turn out with our wives and our sons and our daughters. Turn out so that for all time to come you can look your fellowman in the eye and tell him that you thought enough of your American heritage to exercise your rights where and when they counted—at the precinct convention.

"I am appealing to all Democrats without prefixes or suffixes. May 5 is indeed the day of decision. It is the day upon which the voice of Texas can be heard. And whatever your decision may be, you know I will abide by it in good faith. This is Lyndon Johnson, your senator. Goodnight, good-bye, and God bless you."

When Lyndon's voice had stilled, Laura could actually hear her heart beating through her hearing aid. May 5 was the neighborhood Democratic precinct conventions, the day of decision. And she, Laura Woods, had been chosen to play a key role in how that decision would be made.

Lyndon Johnson had asked for the support of Democrats without prefix or suffix. Unfortunately, as the party maneuvered toward the 1956 presidential elections, there was really no such thing. Control of the Texas delegation was being contested by the three factions of the party Laura called the Shivercrats, the Uglycrats, and the Yellow Dogs.

The Shivercrats supported Gov. Allen Shiver's efforts to be chairman of the Texas delegation. Laura detested the ideals of the Shivercrats because they had voted for Eisenhower and Richard Nixon in the last election and were, in her words, "Democrats in the springtime and Republicans in the fall." The Shivercrats had bolted the party primarily on the issue of tidelands oil. They favored state control of offshore minerals while Adlai Stevenson had called for federal ownership of these resources. Laura also sensed a certain arrogance among the Shivercrats. Among their leaders was the formidable Hilda Weinert, who felt she owned the party lock, stock and barrel. In Laura's precinct, the top Shivercrat was the local banker Henry Kyle, the same Henry Kyle the White Stars had defeated when he ran for the state legislature against Tom Dunlap. For ten years running he had been selected Democratic precinct chairman and it seemed to most observers he would be selected chairman once again. Laura was actually fond of Kyle, even though he was a bitter political foe.

The Uglycrats were a group of vulgar racists centered around a local truck driver named Ross Carlton. Among his leading supporters were his wife, a cook at a local truck stop, and his wife's brother, who worked at the slaughterhouse outside of town. The Uglycrats wanted the Democratic party of Texas to convince the legislature to call a special election to amend the

Texas constitution. They supported an amendment that would prohibit school integration and outlaw interracial marriage.

The third force contesting for control of the Texas delegation was Laura's Yellow Dog Democrats. The Yellow Dogs were so named because they were absolutely loyal to the Democratic party and would vote for a Democrat no matter what, even if the only Democratic candidate offered was an old yellow dog. Laura's group was comprised of moderates. Among them was a librarian, a few schoolteachers, the owner of the taxi company and the confectionery, a history teacher from college, and her very close friend and fellow activist Daisy Posey. Daisy was barely five feet tall, had soft brown eyes and hair white as cotton. Although she was eight years younger than Laura, at age seventy-eight she was a veteran of the precinct wars and she, too, had been selected to play an important role in the Yellow Dogs' battle against the Uglycrats and the Shivercrats.

Laura dearly loved the amazing phenomenon that was the Texas Democratic Precinct Convention. It was here, at the grass-roots, in knock-down-drag-out fights among neighbors, that the president of the United States was selected. Here, the glorious process began. Yet in Laura's precinct, no more than twenty people would attend the convention, some abstaining out of choice, others because they found the doors locked. So passionate was debate, so vulnerable were the participants to ridicule or censure, that the great majority of people in the community stayed at a distance as interested observers. Others stayed out of the process because they were unwilling to fight with neighbors. "Henry Kyle and I are the best of neighbors on every day but election day," Laura told Rebekah. "Sometimes I think we are better neighbors because we do have this chance to air out differences and yell at each other this one time every year or so."

When election day dawned, Laura felt she awakened in someone else's body. She felt young and strong and the moment she opened her eyes she was eager to do battle with the day. No other day had quite the same texture, quite the same potential of drama. It was like opening night at the theater and Laura had rehearsed her lines to perfection. This particular election day held a special magic for Laura. For at age eighty-six, Laura Woods contended for public office.

All week, Wilton, Daisy Posey, Prof. Greene, and Laura had refined their strategy for taking control of the precinct convention. It was a strategy based on the apparent inevitability that Henry Kyle would once again be elected precinct chairman, as he had each election day for a decade. The second part of their strategy was simply getting out among the people and talking up Lyndon as a favorite son. All week, Laura had walked her neighborhood and had visited door to door just as Wilton had advised. She followed his instructions for taking control of a precinct convention carefully. "Politics is no longer taboo in social gatherings," Wilton taught his volunteers. "But talking politics requires facts with tact. You can feel comfortable about it nowadays because two out of every three Americans generally favor the Democratic party. Just ask a person directly and sincerely to help you with the vote. Know your facts and know the local impact of Democratic party proposals. If the other person wants to argue, change the subject and save your energy."

The polling place was at the San Marcos library. As was her custom, Laura voted early, then returned home to make a telephone survey of her friends and neighbors who had committed to be in the Yellow Dog delegation. Because of her poor hearing, a telephone conversation with Laura Woods was relatively one-sided. One by one she dialed the telephone numbers, and because she could not hear the phone ring, she counted to herself slowly, all the way to twenty. By then, she could only assume there was someone on the other end of the line and she began her instructions. She reminded them of their promise to attend the neighborhood convention to be held immediately after the polls closed at 7:00 P.M. at the library. "Seven o'clock sharp!" she insisted. "You must be inside the building by seven o'clock. And don't forget to bring your stamped poll tax receipt. And be sure you're there by seven o'clock. You never can tell what kind of shenanigans the Shivercrats might pull." At this point in her instructions, Laura paused for a second or two, then she added, "Well, good-bye." Never once, in the entire conversation, had she heard a single word of response. But she never doubted for a moment that her friends had answered their phones, had heard her instructions, and would be at the library at the appointed time.

Immediately after the polls closed, at precisely seven o'clock, the Shivercrat, Uglycrat, and Yellow Dog delegates began to flow into the little San Marcos library. Each faction was resplendent with political buttons, bunting, banners, and hats, each a variation of the colors of the flag, both stars and stripes and stars and bars. The delegates settled at library tables and among the stacks and some sat high on the card catalog cabinet where they could be seen and recognized easily from the chair. Laura climbed a library ladder so she could count heads. She worried that little Daisy Posey would be lost in the crowd and she told someone to lift Daisy onto the librarian's desk where she, too, could be more easily seen. At precisely 7:15, Laura slammed the library door and locked it with the key provided by Mr. Devenshire, the librarian and longtime Yellow Dog collaborator. The room was filled with the sound of voices and library chairs scraping on the floor and the furious shouts of late-arriving Uglycrats pounding on the door and yelling to be let in or else. Then, Henry Kyle, who had been elected temporary chairman on ballots cast earlier in the day and who was eager to get started before Laura could pull any more tricks, called the meeting to order.

"I declare this convention open." He pounded his gavel and shouted to be heard above the noise of the Uglycrats outside who were trying to force open the windows. "The chair will now entertain motions for permanent precinct convention chairman." This was the point where, in previous conventions, Kyle's name was presented and he was almost automatically named chairman. But in the convention of 1956, as he waited for his name to be placed in nomination, the Shivercrats waited an instant too long, for Daisy Posey, standing tall and proud on the librarian's desk shouted, "I nominate Laura Woods for permanent chairman!"

The Yellow Dogs howled their approval and a strangely sobered Henry Kyle pounded his gavel again. Only then did one of the Shivercrats stand and nominate Kyle.

Laura wondered if so much sound had ever been heard in this library where signs calling for silence were on the end of every stack and above the drinking fountains. It was not so much sound heard, but sound felt, and Laura could feel it in the nerve endings leading to the center of her heart.

Someone from the Yellow Dog delegation called for a vote. "All right, listen to me now," Henry Kyle shouted, his composure now somewhat ruffled. "We're gonna have a voice vote. First, everybody for Henry Kyle for permanent precinct chairman." Again the room was filled with sound. The Shivercrats were in fine voice and it was not uncommon for delegates to be selected for the strength of their lungs as much as for the power of their convictions. "Now, everybody for Mrs. Laura Woods!" Another outburst of shouts and whistles, hardly different in quality or intensity from the first one.

Henry Kyle broke his gavel on the rack containing the *Reader's Guide to Periodic Literature*. "Here's what we're gonna do," he shouted. "I want everybody who's for me to get over there." He pointed the gavel toward his left. "And I want everybody who's for Mrs. Woods to get over by the windows."

Immediately, the delegates began to migrate from one side of the room to the other, shifting patterns of neighbors noisily voting their convictions. Laura moved to the window side of the room and then watched the milling delegates assume a new pattern at the two sides of the room. She was shocked to realize how equal in number the two groups had split and she was horrified the outcome would depend on the Uglycrats. Ross Carlton and his lieutenant from the slaughterhouse moved to join the Shivercrats.

Laura's quick head count revealed the two sides were exactly even. Then she saw Gladys O'Mally Carlton hesitate. She was alone, now, in the center of the room. As she looked from one side of the room to the other, she seemed almost beautiful to Laura, who had only seen her as the blowsy fry cook with desperate eyes, an anonymous presence seen only through the veil of vapors rising from the truck stop grill. Now, before Laura's eyes, Gladys Carlton assumed a glorious metamorphosis. She took one last look at her husband, whose face was beginning to change horribly, and she turned and proudly walked directly toward where Laura stood by the windows.

"It's time, don't you think," Gladys said with a smile and a toss of her head and then turned to face the now very impermanent chair. The Yellow Dogs had won control by a single vote, and Laura was permanent chairman of the precinct convention. She took the broken gavel from a stunned Henry Kyle and began pounding it to silence Ross Carlton, who was shouting that his wife had made a stupid mistake and did not mean it and if they would recess for just five minutes he would set her straight. Finally, the Yellow Dogs shouted Carlton down and the business of the convention proceeded.

The next order of business was to vote on resolutions, among them the Uglycrats' referendum to prohibit school integration and mixed marriages. But their forces were so demoralized by the defection of Gladys O'Mally Carlton that their resolution died without a second. The business of the Republic whirled by in a carousel of noisy conviction and confusion. Yet, like a carousel, the sound and fury was fully under control and the most cherished activity of a democracy was consummated. Within an hour, the Shivercrats' grip on the Texas Democratic party had been loosened, the Uglycrats had been driven from the field in disarray, Gladys O'Mally Carlton had found new meaning for her life, Lyndon Baines Johnson had been selected to head the Texas delegation as a favorite son candidate for president of the United States, and Laura Hoge Woods had been elected to be a delegate to the state convention to convene the following month in Fort Worth.

At the state convention, Laura was a member of the resolutions committee. As speeches and high school bands and shouts from the floor rocked the hall, Laura heard the resolution naming Lyndon Johnson as the party's favorite son candidate for president and she moved that it be accepted by acclamation. When the Yellow Dogs were again victorious, the empress of Texas Democrats, Mrs. Hilda Weinert, rolled up to Wilton, shook her finger in his face and said, "Wilton Woods, I'll never forgive you or your mother for this if it takes the rest of my life!"

At the end of this week of political triumphs, Laura lay in bed so elated and alive that sleep was out of the question. After all these years of dreaming and working, she had run for political office and had won. She had taken action which might well directly influence who would become president of the United States. *There was a time when I couldn't even vote. And now I've actually been elected to public office and I helped nominate Rebekah's boy.* She began to consider the next step in her political career, but was interrupted by the memory of Peter, who seemed to come and lie by her side. She could feel him there, and when he touched her she felt young and languid and in love. "Oh, Peter, you would have been so proud," she said and then she remembered a time before they were married when she asked Peter if men and women whinnied and neighed like horses when they made love. "Oh, Peter! You should have seen your face!" Laura's laughter turned and danced above the bed as she remembered. "You were so good, Peter," she said aloud. "We were so good." After a moment, Laura fell asleep, her body wrapped around Peter, her dreams of horses and immortality.

28 ∞ THE PEDERNALES OAKS

(From Laura's unpublished autobiography)

I watched them lower Rebekah's body into the ground in the little shaded cemetery by the Pedernales River, but I knew she was not there. Rebekah is alive. She is alive as God's breath in the wind or the turning of time or the tides. It is an absolute certainty, even now, as I write these words and curse this infernal typing machine, that Rebekah is a presence in this world still. I watched her strength wane as she lay in the hospital, but I know she was not dying. She was, by some miraculous, mysterious process, passing her strength on to her son.

I have tried to find in nature something parallel to this transference of power from one living thing to another. Winifred would know. She might suggest that a planet is born from the death of a star, or point out that the young of nearly all forms of life take nourishment from the bodies of their parents and in the process the parents are diminished. It is the natural order of things, the everlasting ballet between parent and child. But what happened between Lyndon and Rebekah was more than natural. It was magical, even terrifying, and it changed the lives of millions of Americans forever.

It is no secret that Lyndon and his mother have always been close. Their letters were love songs. Rebekah gloried in her son and Lyndon was devoted to his mother. Their love for each other was abundantly apparent and much remarked. When he was young, Lyndon was known as a "mama's boy." But he made no effort to reduce the ridicule by hiding its cause. All his life he had been motivated by a need to please his mother so he could delight in the sweet pleasure of her approval. And one must know Rebekah and the treasury of her spirit to know how compelling her approval could be. If Lyndon was secretive, and he has been very secretive, it was generally caused by his need not to inspire Rebekah's disapproval, a punishment far more terrible than the switch or the brush.

Rebekah created Lyndon from an image she had of how the world should be. And since she had never seen the world, he was a product of the world she found in her bookshelf. His values were inspired by the classics, toughened by the Hill Country, softened by the books of the Gospel. She led him along a path that was blazed by the great men Rebekah had met in her library, men of high ideals and extraordinary souls, spiritual acquaintances who strode confidently through the pages of her biographies. But Rebekah's task was made difficult in that Lyndon was of more flesh than spirit, more Earth than heaven. His father had been the last American politician to wear his six-shooter strapped to his side on the floor of the Texas House of Representatives. Even today, as Lyndon struggles to disengage from Vietnam, he still wears that revolver his father wore. "I will not be the first American president to lose a war," Lyndon says. That's vintage Mr. Sam, God rest his soul, not Rebekah at all.

But the extraordinary thing that happened between Lyndon and Rebekah happened not when he was president, but years earlier when he was in the Senate. Rebekah was in the hospital dying of cancer, they said, when I came to visit her and read to her letters from Lyndon. As Rebekah became weaker and weaker, Lyndon became stronger, stronger than he had ever been before. And for that brief season, before Rebekah's casket was lowered into the Pedernales soil, Lyndon was a giant. He risked everything for a cause that was just and right and good.

No one would have thought Lyndon could have done

what he did. I must admit he rarely did anything unless it promised some measure of political advantage. Even I, who love him dearly, know that he still wears Mr. Sam's revolver on his hip. Oh, there is goodness in Lyndon, as there was in his father. For one thing, there has never been a single ounce of racial, ethnic, or religious prejudice in his heart. Rebekah has seen to that. But that essential goodness is often buried deep beneath the trappings of his ambition. So I've looked into his eyes and into his past to find clues as to why that goodness emerged so beautifully and unexpectedly that season in 1957 when he was Senate Majority Leader.

I recall the time he spent teaching in the little Mexican-American school where the children were so terribly poor. His compassion for those children was reflected in his letters to his mother. He had lived with Negroes and Mexicans and he knew they had no chance for a decent life. There were those years in college when he and the other boys from the country had suffered indignities and injustice at the hands of the Black Star city boys. He must have remembered the hurt of being closed out, ridiculed, denied opportunity. But there is no one moment or incident that I can remember, before 1957, when Lyndon performed a truly selfless public act. And so, when he led the fight for Civil Rights in the Senate and risked the hatred and rejection of his beloved Texans and any possibility of a political future, including the presidency, the nation, the world was astonished. But I wasn't. I had been with Rebekah during those days and I had seen her pass her strength and her absolute awareness of what was right across the miles.

Lyndon insisted he had nothing to do with the passage of the Civil Rights law. "I am strongly and irrevocably opposed to forced integration of the races," he declared, after the White House introduced the bill. To be considered in the Civil Rights camp by his fellow Texans could easily have ended his political career. He might have been rejected as a delegate to the 1960 national convention, even passed over as a candidate for reelection to the Senate. But behind the scenes, Lyndon maneuvered to get the bill passed. This was pure Rebekah. *Tell them what they want to hear and then do what must be done.* He shaped coalitions between liberals in the North and southern moderates, he pulled strings, twisted arms, convinced southerners that they should drop their usual "corn and pot liquor" positions on civil rights and then he convinced them it had been their idea in the first place. And so, against great odds, a Hill Country boy engineered the passage of the first civil rights legislation in three-quarters of a century. It was a great triumph for democratic justice, the beginning of a new chapter in the American experience. And it was Lyndon's finest hour.

But was it Lyndon who fought so hard and so effectively for the violated rights of his Negro neighbors? Would Lyndon have taken the risk? Dear as he is to me, I'm not at all certain. Or should not the credit go to my lifelong friend Rebekah, the bright, good and beautiful descendant of scholars and theologians who had never been more than a few miles from her home in the Hill Country, whose mighty will had triumphed over the confines of distance and the hospital walls. And it was Rebekah twisting arms on the Senate floor and making promises in smoke-filled rooms. They had always been close, these two. But I am certain at that moment they became one, probably still are, and Rebekah does not dwell in the Pedernales soil, but in the Oval Office of the White House where she always knew she would be.

29 ∞ THE GLORY DAYS

EARLY IN 1959, WHILE LYNDON WAS ACTIVELY DENYING HE would be a candidate for president in 1960, Laura's brother Lee and his third wife, Frankie, came to San Marcos for a visit. They stayed at Laura's house and the announced weeklong visit stretched into months. Lee was a handsome, broad-shouldered man with a shock of pure white hair and a voice so deep and powerful it could make the window frames rattle. He could speak eloquently and at some length on any subject, particularly the subtle shades of meaning to be found in the Revelations of Paul of Patmos. Lee was not exactly a preacher or an evangelist, yet was somehow deeply involved in a mission to save souls in the town of Paradise, California. When pressed, Lee claimed he was a consultant for the most successful evangelists in California, an advisory position not unlike that of Colonel House to Woodrow Wilson or Harry Hopkins to Harry Truman.

Lee's wife, Frankie, was as glamorous as Aimee Semple McPherson had been. She was a gifted seamstress. She could take an old hat, an old dress, and transform them into stunning outfits that might easily have graced the pages of *Vogue* magazine. For the children she would make flowers and other elaborate creations out of seashells and clothespins. Rarely had a couple as fashionable as Lee and Frankie been seen by the grandchildren of Laura and Peter Woods. It was whispered that Frankie was rich, which did not surprise Laura because Lee's first two wives had been rich; rather, they had been rich for a while, then poor, then gone.

Laura was not completely comfortable with Lee, which was a troubling thing for a sister to say about her brother. She was certain she did not want him interfering in her relationship with the Almighty. Yet she loved to hear his stories of the great temples being built in California on a foundation of saved souls and spent savings.

During her brother's visit, Laura invited the entire family for dinner. She also invited Lyndon, Lady Bird, and Dr. Bob Montgomery, who had just returned from a Washington convention on nuclear energy. Laura had rarely been more excited about a dinner party. She would be surrounded by her family and a U.S. senator and a man who talked regularly with presidents and another who talked regularly with God. Unfortunately, Lyndon and Lady Bird had to decline because the Eighty-sixth Congress was still in session, but Laura refused to let it spoil her party or diminish her spirit.

Although all the other guests were seated at the table, Laura spent her time standing, moving from one guest's side to another, making comments on what she thought they might be talking about and taking tiny bites from the tiny saucer on which she had served her tiny meal. Saucer in hand, hearing aid turned up to the maximum, she roamed 'round and 'round her dining room table as her guests discussed the possibility that Lyndon would challenge Kennedy for the Democratic nomination, the rise of Christian Dior's influence on Paris *haute couture,* the dreadful Communists, and the haunting possible consequences of the explosion of the first hydrogen bomb on the Isle of Eniwetok. Dr. Bob Montgomery assured Wilton that Russia and America possessed the power to make the earth completely uninhabitable within fifteen minutes. Lee's wife, Frankie, said she certainly would not want to live in a world that was uninhabitable, or at least that seemed to be the sense of her comment when translated electronically through Laura's hearing aid.

Dr. Bob had a great shock of white hair that stood on end as if he had literally been shocked by electricity. Laura thought it remarkable that Dr. Bob and Albert Einstein, both acknowledged experts on nuclear energy, had similar hairstyles. Maybe it has something to do with nuclear power, she thought. A kind of occupational hazard. In the closing phases of World War II, Dr. Bob had been called to Washington to help decide which

Japanese cities should be targeted for the atomic bomb. In years past, Laura had talked with him about that terrible responsibility and Truman's decision. Dr. Bob told her it was the most agonizing time of his life. He had tried not to think of the schools and homes and people that were a part of the equations he was analyzing. His sleep had been filled with nightmares. But he had told Laura there had been no other possible choice but to use the bomb. Thousands of American lives were spared. A war that might have savaged both sides for years was brought to a close in an instant. Laura was one of the few to whom Dr. Bob revealed the emotional pain of his work with Truman. It was no wonder, she thought, that he now worked so hard for responsible nuclear policy.

After dinner, Lee characterized the age in which they lived as the Last Great Awakening. "The first three Great Awakenings," he said, "were led by Congregationalists, Presbyterians, Methodists, Baptists and Pentecostals. They were really just revival preachers with the power to make people fear death. Now we're in the hands of men and women who possess the power to transcend death."

Lee then told of witnessing an Oral Roberts revival in which he saw a lame man throw away his crutches and hundreds of others freed from a long roster of afflictions. "Once I saw Oral Roberts lay his hands upon the wounds of a man whose fingers had been mangled in a threshing machine. The wounds disappeared. The fingers became whole. It was as if the cells themselves had been altered by prayer."

Wilton was skeptical. "How do you explain it? Maybe it was your perception that was altered."

"It's the power of belief," Lee answered. "The person believed so thoroughly in Oral Roberts's power of healing that the mind actually intensified and channeled the healing power inherent in nature."

With her hearing aid turned to its maximum level, Laura listened to the conversation with growing fascination. While dessert was being served Laura decided she would meet with Oral Roberts and ask him to heal the various systems of her body which were so desperately in need of repair, not only her sight and hearing, but the infirmities resulting from her bitter and constant combat with gravity.

Over the years, the physical weight of the world seemed to press down on Laura's slim shoulders, curving her spine, driving her closer and closer to the earth. Laura decided the greatest enemy of mankind was not pestilence or famine or any of the other horsemen of the Apocalypse. The greatest enemy of the species was gravity. It was gravity that pulled us to the ground when we stumbled or when falling from trees or from ladders, causing broken limbs. It was gravity that caused airplanes to crash and that caused the alarming curvature of her spine. She was terribly embarrassed by her osteoporosis and she suffered this awful fantasy that they might have to bend her straight and tie her down in her casket at her funeral when she died. Her greatest fear, which she expressed to Frankie, was that during a particularly emotional passage of her eulogy, the rope would break and she would spring suddenly to a sitting position, as if come alive. "I'd never live it down," she said. "And it's all because of gravity. I wish that apple would have missed Newton's head entirely."

In Lee's silver Lincoln Continental, Laura and Lee glided through the beautiful Arbuckle Mountains between Texas and Tulsa. Lee had promised to take her to see Oral Roberts if she would consider selling her house and come to live with him in California. Laura decided she would think about California later, after she had been healed. As Lee's Continental consumed the miles, Laura tried to justify her pilgrimage. Was it right, she wondered, to embark on this selfish mission when all the world seemed to be turning upside down? There was revolution in Cuba. The Russians were rattling their sabers. Sputnik was soaring above their heads carrying Lord knows what kinds of horrors. But if Oral could make her a new woman, if he could clear her eyes, there was so much more she could do in this world. Yet her body was failing and falling apart, leaving her mind, her soul, naked and unprotected. If she were to live and to fight, she had to believe. As Oklahoma boomed by, she prayed for the gift of belief. When soon she would come face-to-face with Oral Roberts and he laid his hands on her eyes, it would be imperative that her belief be as sound and sure as the Rock of Ages. All the way to Tulsa, Laura prayed. In her less ecclesiastical moments, she felt somewhat shielded by the fact that over the years she had tucked in the folds of her letters to Oral Roberts a sum of something greater than two thousand dollars.

When they arrived at the Howard Johnson Motel in Tulsa, Laura was exhausted from the trip. She sent Lee to make arrangements for her private session with the evangelist. "Tell him I've arrived," she said. "Ask him what time I should meet with him at his chapel." Then she lay down. She dreamed of angels floating in the sunlight above the Howard Johnson, their wings God's very best idea in the eternal warfare between good and gravity.

For three days, Laura waited for word from Oral Roberts. None came. "He is a very busy man," Lee said, and he reminded Laura that he had hundreds and thousands of people to heal each week. Laura was furious. On the fourth day she confronted the gray platoon of functionaries who managed his revivals. Laura thought they looked like bankers and they seemed to possess that same arrogance bankers have because they know they have the key to the vault and you don't. When she demanded to see Oral Roberts, they told her a private audience would be impossible. She could see him at the Assembly Center Arena that evening where he would conduct a revival. Obviously, there had been some mistake. The bankers had neglected to let Reverend Roberts know she had arrived. They were probably the same incompetent bankers who sent her the form letters to thank her for her contributions.

The arena seemed more suitable for a rodeo than for matters of the soul. She imagined in the blur beyond her eyes that there were rows of horses carrying banners and clowns in barrels, and cowboys limping around rubbing their injured bottoms. She could tell the arena was filled with thousands of people. She could feel their presence, the beating of all those hearts, the power of all the prayers that trembled, yet to tumble from their lips. She turned her hearing aid high and could hear what sounded like a million birds, a mindless murmuring and thrashing of wings. Then she heard the choir, its voice riding the great organ to higher and higher praise. Laura felt it must be like this at Lourdes when the lepers come to bathe in the healing waters of the grotto spring where the peasant girl Bernadette saw the Virgin Mary. How different the rodeo arena from the grotto of Lourdes, yet each is filled with pilgrims wishing for a miracle. Laura began to feel unclean, oppressed by the miasma of this crowd and by the odor of sin. She wished miracles could be less proletarian, less vulgar. She wondered if these were some of the people who mailed in five dollars to the radio station in Del Rio for their genuine auto-graphed photograph of Jesus Christ.

She recognized Oral Roberts's voice right away. It was the same voice she had heard so many times before on her radio. But now the actual words were falling on her mind. There was no cur-tain of distance and electronics between the utterance and the ear. The passion of the voice, the tremulous pleading seemed com-mon, even grotesque. Surely it was rude to be so demanding of God, ordering Him around like some altar boy late to arrive for his chores. When Oral Roberts's voiced reached a crescendo of volume and emotion, she could hear the sound of the crowd boil up from its gaping mouth in a great plural litany of need. Lee told her now that people had fallen to the ground and were writhing and rolling and Oral Roberts was holding them and shouting for a mir-acle. Laura tried to pray that she, too, would be healed and that a miracle would come light on her shoulder like a dove. But as the moments passed, rather than pray, she felt an overpowering need to apologize, to distance herself from the rude pilgrims who were so offensive to the God she and Peter knew when they had listened to the mockingbirds and the cardinals along the Blanco. She could not see clearly. Beyond her eyes was a tangled tapestry of color, motion, and shadow. All she heard now was the rodeo crowd, cheering the horses and the courage of the clowns in bar-rels and the endurance of the limping cowboys.

"*Dear Lord,*" she whispered as the pilgrims writhed and pleaded, "*I'm sorry about the rodeo. Thank you for my life. Maybe we can get together another time under more favorable circum-stances. Amen.*"

In the morning, they left Tulsa for Texas.

∞

In 1960, John F. Kennedy was elected president with Lyndon Johnson as vice president. Laura's first thought was how unfair it was that Rebekah did not live to see the day. Her second thought was a furious regret that Lyndon had not won the nomination himself.

"I'm going to Washington," Laura announced. "To the inauguration. Lyndon needs our support."

"He seems to be doing pretty well on his own," Wilton said.

"Oh, Poppycock! If it wasn't for Hill Country folks, Lyndon wouldn't be anywhere. It's time we shared the glory." She could tell Wilton was not paying attention and moved to where he was standing and stood absolutely in front of him, both hands clutching his sleeves, a posture making inattention impossible. "And it's an outrage that Prof. Greene isn't going to be there. Prof. Greene taught Lyndon everything he knows. I'm going to Washington and Prof. Greene is going, too. And that's all there is to it."

The train thundered across a winter landscape. Small clouds of condensation formed where Laura pressed her face to the window. Occasionally, she wiped the glass with her sleeve in order to see the world go by, but it was a blur beyond the window, a vast mystery brushed by a thin powdering of snow. Prof. Greene had gone to the observation car to spit and talk politics and brag on Lyndon. He tried to persuade Laura to come with him, yet when she encountered the terrible roar and rush of air between cars, and the wildly shifting, vibrating platform between the doors, she hurried back to her seat, justifying her fear by recalling the train wreck that had killed poor Peter's dreams.

The train was filled with Texans going to the inauguration, a joyous, boisterous gathering of political pilgrims, part of eight thousand expected to descend on the nation's capital to celebrate the finest hour of their favorite son. "You'd think it was Lyndon's inauguration, not JFK's at all," Prof. Greene had said several times to several listeners.

Laura was surrounded by what seemed a Democratic political

convention set in motion. Bankers, lawyers, lobbyists, visiting firemen, a sheriff's posse from West Texas, entire high school marching bands, including the San Marcos Rattler Marching Band, all moving like lava in the aisles, talking across the backs of their seats, claiming their little piece of history, sharing Lyndon's glory. Some had been invited; others were making the trip because Lyndon was theirs, a part of them, a part of all they could be. Once again, Laura checked her purse to make sure she had not misplaced the engraved invitation she had received as a Democratic precinct chairman. It was there, but she would check again and again because every time she touched those raised letters she felt a flutter of thrill above her heart.

When Prof. Greene returned to his seat, he told Laura that most of the people in the observation car were surprised when he told them about some of Lyndon's antics.

"I'm sure you gave them an earful."

"They see him up on a pedestal. I don't know why it is when a man becomes president, people think he quits being a man. Like presidents don't have red blood and put on their pants like everybody else."

"You mean vice president. Lyndon will be vice president."

"Details. I'm a big-picture man. Never been good at details."

"So you talked about Lyndon, the man. The human side."

"And the boy. About playing baseball and how he threw overhand like a girl. How he could eat a whole fried chicken at a single sitting. About how he and Mr. Sam didn't gee and haw too well. About how he'd lay down his life for his mama."

"That's quite an earful. I didn't know you were gone so long."

"I told them how Lyndon looked walking into my classroom, his mind spinning with ideas, swinging his long arms, just walking like his britches was on fire."

Laura felt a stirring of nostalgia. "Remember the Houston convention? It had the same excitement as this."

"I remember Lyndon and Wilton took those two girls."

"What two girls?"

"You were there. Surely you knew they were with those two

girls. Stayed with them the whole time. But, then, I suppose the mother is the last to know."

Laura searched her memory for the girls.

"I knew a long time ago that Lyndon would go this far," Prof. Greene continued. "At college he was always on top of that hill trying to promote something. He always wanted to be in the front row and usually was. I doubt few students started so low and climbed so high. When he first came to San Marcos, Lyndon had thirteen dollars and it took fifteen to register. Vernon Whiteside lent him one dollar and I lent him the other. Before long, he and Wilton and the others were running the place."

Laura wiped the window with her sleeve. In the glass she caught the reflection of Prof. Greene bent over his awful cup.

"Did I ever tell you about the first election Lyndon ever stole? It was president of the junior class."

"I remember."

"But I don't suppose you remember that he was elected president of the junior class by a senior. Horace Richards. Horace was taking both junior and senior classes, so he voted in one room with his junior classmates, then hurried across the hall and voted again as a senior. They counted the votes right then. Lyndon won. Guess by how many votes?"

The train pulled into Washington at the height of one of the most spectacular snowstorms in the city's history. The train moved slowly through great steaming drifts. It was nearly dark, yet the world was white. Streetlights burned blue against the snow. Outside her fogged window dark figures moved, breathing clouds of vapor, struggling, leaning against the cold.

Laura was exhausted, not so much from the long trip, but from the constant barrage of Prof. Greene's memories. Yet, as the train slowed, iron wheels grinding, brakes squealing, a sense of electric excitement filled the railroad car and Laura's weary mind. She felt again for her engraved invitation.

The freezing wind whipped through Laura's heaviest coat, and she found herself clinging to Prof. Greene, feeling lost and wishing she had been more attentive when Wilton explained how to get to the hotel. Prof. Greene's arm seemed very thin, far less substantial than his vocal chords, and she could feel him shaking with the cold. The snowflakes, seeming as large as dinner plates, settled on her eyelashes. They followed the crowd into Union Station and for a long while stood in the center of the massive building, rivers of travelers moving in swirls and eddies around them. Everyone seemed to know exactly where to go. Some were met with people holding signs bearing names. Others embraced and gathered into warm, close groups. Voices filled the great space like a chorus of bees.

"What now?" Prof. Greene asked.

"I thought you knew," Laura said, more alarmed than she had been by the lurching space between railcars. "I think we call Lyndon."

"You have his number? Maybe it's listed." They moved toward the phone booth.

Then Laura recalled that Lyndon's home number was in her address book. She had called it many times to warn him about the dangers posed by Castro's Cuba. She dug in her purse and handed the number to Prof. Greene. Neither of them could read the small numbers in the low light and they were forced to ask someone passing by to dial the number. It rang and rang.

"He wouldn't be home on a night like this! Biggest week of his life!"

"It's early. He should be home getting ready."

Prof. Greene's face lit up with relief. "Lyndon. It's me. Prof. Greene from San Marcos. I'm with Laura Woods. We've ridden a train all day and night to get up here. What are you going to do with us now?"

There was a long pause as Prof. Greene listened to the phone. Laura thought it was a miracle that Lyndon actually answered the phone himself. But then she decided that Lyndon had been worried about them and had stayed home to await their call. Suddenly, she was overcome with love and with pride for Lyndon and she reached for the phone, hoping to tell him so. Prof. Greene pushed her hand away, and there was a brief struggle before he hung up the phone.

"He said wait right here. He's sending Cliff Carter to get us. All the hotels are full, but they're going to find us a room. He's got tickets to all kinds of events for us and some spending money." Laura remembered that the White Stars had collected money to tide Prof. Greene over while he was in Washington.

They waited a very long time. It was not as cold inside the station, and they found a bench where they could wait. Laura felt small and tired and ashamed that she had not planned better for their arrival.

Cliff Carter and Liz Carpenter, Lyndon's press secretary, swept into the station. After a warm welcome, they led them through the milling throng to a large black limousine waiting outside in a place Laura knew only the cars of very important people could park.

The streets were packed with cars. The once wide avenues were invaded on each side by snow drifts, some so deep they nearly covered parked cars. On some side streets, people had abandoned their cars and were vainly trying to hail taxis. Laura saw Washington as a city totally devoid of color, the snow somehow sucking color away. Occasionally they would pass something, some building or monument or tomb, that she had seen in a picture and she yearned to ask what it was but did not because she thought she should know. It was warm in the car. And quiet, a sort of hush. Prof. Greene was bragging on Lyndon to Cliff Carter and the driver, telling about how he stole his first election. Laura drifted away.

They arrived at the Raleigh Hotel and the bellman carried their luggage into the lobby. Cliff Carter checked them in and gave their keys to the bellman.

"Why don't you rest for a while, freshen up, and we'll be back in an hour to pick you up and take you out to Lyndon's Texas gala. Mr. Johnson's eager to see you at the party."

"You're not taking me anywhere," Prof. Greene said. "I've been riding for thirty-six hours on that train and I'm nearly frozen to death and I'm going to take a hot bath and go to bed."

"Mrs. Woods?" Carter asked. "Shall I come back for you?"

Laura heard herself say, "Surely we can get together with Lyndon tomorrow."

As Laura moved toward the elevator, she saw the black limousine pull away. She could still feel the clacking of the iron wheels on the track and the lurching of the cars and even though the hotel was warm and bright, the cold she had felt before had settled into her bones. It was all she could do to stay upright and awake until the bellman had performed his various errands in her room, pausing for some reason she did not understand before he moved to the door and left. She undressed, wondering at the mystery of growing old. *While others are getting dressed for the greatest party this city has ever seen, here I am getting undressed for bed.* She decided it was the only thing she could have done to avoid embarrassing Lyndon's old professor.

In the morning, the nation's capital was a white wonderland. Laura felt wonderfully refreshed, the pain in her joints eclipsed by the excitement in her heart. The day unfolded like a dream, full of strange and unlikely associations and transitions. Laura felt she was being pulled by the mind and hand through a setting and events larger than life: the city held captive by the snow; the countless limousines, long, black and in stark contrast to the surrounding drifts; a team of ten Huskies pulling a sled. Among the traffic jams and down alleyways hundreds of horses and mules stood in the snow. Everywhere she looked were undisciplined formations of uniformed men, some carrying rifles, some carrying flags, others bearing gleaming silver or gold tubas, all apparently waiting to form into the inaugural parade. Thousands of people looked on. Dressed in heavy woolens, they stamped their feet against the cold and maneuvered for better positions along the curb.

After breakfast, Laura and Prof. Greene were taken to a coffee held at the National Gallery of Art. The rotunda was filled with blooming azaleas and the music was provided by the Marine band, background music that Laura could hear quite well even with her hearing aid turned low. There was a stirring in the crowd and Laura was told Mrs. Auchincloss, the president's mother-in-law, had entered. A bit later, Mrs. Truman and Mrs. Hubert Humphrey joined the celebration and the visitors crowded around to catch a glimpse of the celebrities. "I once got so close to President Roosevelt that I could have reached out and touched him with a broom handle," Prof. Greene shouted into Laura's ear.

It was still cold and snowing when members of the Senate and the House, the justices of the Supreme Court, the president's cabinet, top military commanders, the governors of the various states and ambassadors from foreign countries were escorted to the Presidential Platform in Capital Plaza. Although Lyndon's staff had arranged a preferred spot for Laura and Prof. Greene, the massive crowd pressed around them and even on tiptoe she was able to see only fleeting moments of the ceremony. Thankfully, the body heat of the crowd chased much of the chill. Cardinal Cushing prayed. It occurred to Laura that the selection of Cardinal Cushing for the invocation was the first act of a Catholic president. Lyndon probably would have preferred Billy Graham, or Rev. Andrew Jackson Potter, had he still been alive. Marian Anderson sang the national anthem. Then Sam Rayburn administered the oath of office to Lyndon. His voice seemed strong and clear, a beloved sound, filled with the texture and soul of the Hill Country. Laura found herself crying, standing on tiptoe in a foreign city, tears mingling with falling snow. "I love you, Lyndon," she whispered, and for a moment she was certain Lyndon looked her way and grinned. It was as if he were acknowledging the fact that she had received an invitation to the Inaugural Ball and he would save a dance for her.

Finally, to Laura's relief, a Protestant said a prayer. He was also a Texan. And when the minister from Austin was finished, the poet Robert Frost came to the podium to read a poem he had written. At the age of eighty-six, he had been invited by Kennedy to participate in the ceremonies and for the occasion he had written a special preface to his poem "The Gift Outright." Like a thin, small reed, his hair white as the falling snow, he moved to the lectern. The wind riffled his hair and tugged at the sheets of paper he held close before his eyes. There was a long pause, and then he began.

"Summoning artists to participate in the august . . ." Then he stopped. Laura longed for him to continue and she felt her heart

going out to this man that was so near her own age and who suffered the same maladies the passing years had brought her way.
The silence continued. All the greatest men in the nation—the
Senate, the House, the members of the Supreme Court—waited
for the ancient bard to continue.

Then, not in a poet's voice, but in the complaining cadences
of an old man, Frost called, "I am not having a good light here at
all!" Apparently the glare off the snow had made it impossible to
read his text.

Laura was horrified when the crowd erupted into laughter.
Even the heads of the military and the foreign ambassadors
smiled. Then Lyndon came forward and offered his top hat to
shade the poet's eyes from the glare and he held down the windblown pages with his free hand. But the poet had regained his
composure and he put the pages away and recited from memory.

Laura could not remember much of the ceremony after the
poem, not Kennedy's inaugural address nor the triumphant
parade back to the White House. What stayed in her mind was
the image of Lyndon and the old poet and how it was Lyndon,
not Kennedy nor the members of the Supreme Court nor Cardinal Cushing nor the honored ambassadors who cared and came
to an old man's aid. It was Lyndon.

Liz Carpenter had arranged a place by a high window overlooking Constitution Avenue for Laura and Prof. Greene to
watch the inaugural parade. "Who's defending the country?"
Prof. Greene said when he saw the thousands of soldiers and
sailors marching and playing their horns, waving their battle
flags and beating their drums. There were units from the army
and the navy, the U.S. Military Academy, the Air Force Academy, the coast guard, the merchant marines, the reserves and
even the ROTC.

"Bands don't fight," Laura said. But she was worried about
Castro just the same.

It took nearly three hours for all the bands and flags to pass.
But what Laura would remember for the rest of her life was the
moment when Lyndon and Lady Bird and Speaker Sam Rayburn passed below their window in their long black car. The fact

that President and Mrs. Kennedy had been in the car just ahead of Lyndon's did not matter at all. She had eyes only for the vice presidential car and its escort and color guard. Of course, Laura could not really see any of the cars. They were too distant for her failing sight, yet she saw them perfectly in her mind's eye.

When Laura returned to the hotel, she sat in a chair by the window tracing the letters of her invitation to the Inaugural Ball with the tips of her fingers. Although there would be five balls in all, her invitation was to a dance at the Mayflower Hotel. She stood and looked out into the snow. Then she turned and began to prepare for the ball.

Once again Cliff Carter came in his long black Cadillac. Wearing a navy blue velvet gown with a shawl of white lace and a pearl-covered pillbox hat, Laura felt small and alone in the huge limousine, but not necessarily lonely. As she twisted her wedding band, she felt almost certain Peter was in the dark beside her, sharing the magic of the night.

The Mayflower was alive with light and laughter and music. As Cliff Carter ushered Laura and Prof. Greene into the ball-room, she caught sight of three men who looked remarkably like Peter Lawford, Frank Sinatra, and Chet Huntley. Then, Lyndon was there, familiar as her own soul, that dear grin curving from ear to ear. He embraced Laura and Prof. Greene simultaneously as he said, "If it weren't for folks like you, we wouldn't be here tonight."

"May I have the honor, Mrs. Woods?" Lyndon asked. He seemed as tall as a tower standing there beneath the chandeliers. As he led her out among the whirling couples on the great wide floor, she recalled a time many years ago when she and Rebekah had tried to teach their boys to dance. Now, once again, it was Wilton she thought about. Laura imagined it was her son who held her in his arms as they waltzed.

"This time, Mama, let me lead," she remembered him saying.

Then she and Lyndon danced and danced. Laura felt proud as a queen and light as a moth.

30 ∞ THE RANCH WHITE HOUSE

FOR LAURA, LIKE SO MANY OTHER AMERICANS, THE DAY JOHN Kennedy was assassinated seemed frozen, like a memory cut loose from the flow of time. Laura had been struggling with a magnifying glass to read the volume of Alexis de Tocqueville that Colonel House had given her so many years before. She would even remember the very sentence she had been reading. "The health of a democratic society," de Tocqueville had written, "may be measured by the quality of the functions performed by private citizens." It was the moment Laura read this line that she heard a lone killer had shot down John Kennedy. After a moment of shock and mourning it came to her mind that she had lived to see Lyndon Johnson become president. Within hours, Wilton received a telephone call from Washington. "Get yourself to Washington as fast as you can. Lyndon's going to need all his friends to help."

Laura experienced a sorrowful sense of déjà vu, remembering the exact moment she heard that McKinley had been shot and the hours of waiting in the office of the *Blanco News,* listening for the telegraph to reveal his fate. She recalled the moment she heard that Teddy Roosevelt had been shot. Now John Kennedy. *Is there some violent strain in the American character,* she wondered, *some murderous instinct, that leads us to kill our presidents?* She read the line from de Tocqueville again. "The health of a democratic society may be measured by the quality of the functions performed by private citizens." Laura felt that the health of society was in serious peril and she prayed for Lyndon and for the country.

Now it was 1964, and Lyndon was planning his first presidential campaign. He was running against Barry Morris Goldwater, the angry storekeep from Arizona. Laura was astonished such a man would have somehow risen to the top of what she called the "Republican Heap." Where were all the great king-makers of the Eastern establishment? Where were the financial sovereigns of Wall Street and Fifth and Madison Avenues who had ruled and financed the Republican party for generations? Laura actually longed for the Old Guard because they were so pre-dictable, arrogant, stiff, and vulnerable to the frontier politics of a man like Lyndon. Why wasn't Lyndon running against Rocke-feller or Henry Cabot Lodge or George Romney or William Scranton? These were the kind of candidates Lyndon could have for breakfast. But Goldwater was something else again. Laura was concerned with what appeared to be his smoldering rage. "There is no joy in that man," she wrote to Lyndon. She advised Lyndon to choose Hubert Humphrey as a running mate for that very rea-son. "That will give you in abundance what Goldwater lacks most. And that's generosity of spirit."

Laura recognized Goldwater as a man of courage and con-science and she held him in a kind of restrained respect for his triumph over the Eastern establishment, the elite power brokers Laura had detested all her life. Yet she was troubled by the fury he carried inside. There was about him something of the mad prophet wandering the wilderness, and his primitive outrage and passion seemed to attract the psychotic fringe of the Ameri-can electorate. Dr. Bob felt Goldwater represented one of the greatest perils to humanity since Genghis Khan. "I know a lot of what he says is just posturing for his followers," he told Laura. "But the man is actually dangerous. Here's a man who says the solution to our problems with Russia is to lob an atomic bomb into the men's room of the Kremlin. His foreign policy has all the sophistication of a schoolyard brawl.

"Just think of the agonies other presidents have gone through before they committed this country to war," Dr. Bob went on. "Think of Woodrow Wilson. And Roosevelt. But here's a man who sees war as a kind of moral necessity. Something every man must do to be a man. A holy crusade against the infidel Com-munists. What's really frightening is the support he has."

"Then we'll have to work that much harder and send him

back to his haberdashery," Laura replied, thinking of the wars that had come and gone in her life. Each had been so terrible, the human cost so high, and it seemed unthinkable that anyone who had been alive in those years would even consider another war as within the realm of possibility.

On election eve, Laura drove with the family to Austin to meet Lyndon. He was coming home to watch the election returns and he spoke briefly on the steps of the state capitol. It was a lovely night and the University of Texas band was playing, and there was a soft and easy optimism in the air. Laura turned her hearing aid to maximum and felt Lyndon's words flow through her, and if her old eyes had not been so dry, she would have spent that hour wiping tears away. Lyndon had never been more eloquent, more sincere, more humane.

"It was here," he said, "as a barefoot boy around my daddy's desk in that great hall in the House of Representatives, where he served for six terms, where my grandfather served ahead of him, that I first learned government is not an enemy of the people. It is the people. The only attacks that I have resented in this campaign are the charges based on the idea that the presidency is something apart from the people, opposed to them, against them. I learned here when I was the National Youth Administrator that poverty and ignorance are the only basic weaknesses of a free society. Both of them are only bad habits and can be stopped."

When Lyndon finished speaking, Laura felt a deep and satisfying sense of accomplishment. She had done her best. In her mind she knew she had shaped the character and guided the philosophy of three American presidents and had influenced the actions of at least eight others. She felt sure she had coined the phrase "League of Nations" for Woodrow Wilson, had suggested the concept of the "New Deal" for Roosevelt and had inspired "The Great Society" for Lyndon Johnson. Along the way, she had also had some major impact on Teddy Roosevelt, Taft, Harding, Coolidge, Hoover, Truman, Eisenhower and Kennedy. As the family made its way to the Driskill Hotel to watch the returns, Laura remembered how she had dreamed of being president of the United States. She could almost hear the bands playing and the banners and the electric excitement and applause. She felt what Lyndon was feeling, and sensed the joy of the moment. She calculated Lyndon would run again in 1968 and when his term was up in 1972, the party would be looking for a candidate, perhaps a woman of intelligence and political experience. *Why not,* she thought. *In 1972 I'll only be ninety-nine.*

The next morning, Laura learned Lyndon had been elected in a landslide. Feeling victorious and abundantly alive, she moved slowly and painfully to her old blue Olivetti and began formulating her platform for 1972. *There are some very difficult issues to resolve. It is as good a day as any to begin.*

On the evening of her ninety-second birthday, Laura looked long and carefully in the mirror and saw an ancient clown looking back. She was horrified. She had dressed and applied her makeup, and now, in one of her rare and usually depressing moments of clarity, she had seen herself as she must appear to others. Her large powder puff had left saucer-size patches of pink on her forehead. Circular stains of Pond's rouge covered her cheeks. There was a slash of Tangee natural lipstick across her lips. Applied with an unsteady hand and failing eyes, her makeup created a grotesque mask. She could feel currents of shame and embarrassment flowing down her spine. For a long moment she closed her eyes and wondered how long the clown had dwelled here in her rooms.

In recent months Laura had found herself victim to alternating moods of excitement and despair. In moments of despair, she found herself somehow irrelevant to the lives of those around her. They were polite and kind, yet she sensed a kind of silent ridicule. She became guarded in her opinions, and reluctant to discuss such matters as her 1972 presidential campaign and the life story she had been writing. Her book increasingly occupied her thoughts, especially the troubling matter of the last chapter. Until she was visited by her recent mood swings, she had always imagined she would live forever, and there would be plenty of time to create an appropriate ending for her book. But now, in her moments of clarity, she became almost desperately aware of the passing of time and of the beating of her heart and the nearness of the dark. She was not afraid of death, but she was afraid of leaving something important undone. *There should be something in this last chapter,* she thought, *that gives meaning to everything preceding.*

It was during these seasons of despair that she realized she must provide some kind of closure to her relationship with her daughter Winifred. She must once again venture into that awful realm of madness and regret. *Perhaps if I see Winifred, she will tell me what I need to say to explain what my life has meant.*

Over her birthday cake and ice cream, Laura announced she would take the Greyhound bus to the state hospital where Winifred had been committed for more than half a century. Wilton offered to drive her there in the car. On a hazy bright morning in late April, they drove through the rolling pastures of bluebonnets to the Hill Country town of Kerrville. And there, on a hill of stone and living green, were the red brick buildings of the Kerrville Hospital for the Mentally Ill.

On previous visits, Winifred had been waiting in the parlor reserved for family guests, but this time the room was empty. It was simply furnished, with a wide window looking out over the grounds and the treetops. Beyond the trees, the Guadalupe River wandered through the hills. For a while, Laura stood with her back to the room, watching the wind walk through the yellow constellations of spirea blooming beneath the window. She listened to her heartbeat, to the footsteps and voices of the doctors, and to the patients in the rooms beyond the parlor. She had the oppressive feeling something was about to go wrong. It was like watching the approach of a storm with no way to get out of the rain. Then, she turned and was shocked to see an old woman observing her with eyes as calm as a millpond. Obviously, Winifred did not have trouble with gravity. She was tall, and Laura could see Peter's dignity there, and beneath the veil of the years was the thin, dark girl she once rocked in the chair made by Georgia Lawshe's slaves. They embraced in a cloud of lavender.

Winifred paraded her guests through the rooms and halls, introducing them to the doctors, nurses, and especially her friends, the thin, gray citizens of this world of illusion and shadow. Here were the friends who shared her world for all these years, the few chosen by pain and fate to live their lives behind walls. Winifred displayed her friends with a sense of pride and decorum and it was obvious they were fond of her. It was as if there were some secret they shared and once all the guests had left the grounds, they would smile and nod their heads knowingly to acknowledge their fraternal bond.

Winifred took them to her room. It was small but bright and tidy as a display in a museum. Light from the window leaned down on a bed, a chair, a small trunk and the desk where Winifred had written her pleasant narratives about her childhood. On the windowsill and on an easel in the corner were two canvasses Winifred had done in oil. One was a vase of roses, the other a vase of poinsettias. Laura was astounded, not at the quality of the paintings—there were hundreds of like quality in county fairs throughout the South—but at their astonishing tranquillity. Never had still-life paintings seemed so still. It was as if Winifred had found the stillness within the center of things and had brought that quiescence into her room. Then Winifred opened the trunk to reveal tatting as perfect as a snowflake, lovely graceful lace lining the collars and sleeves of dozens of tiny garments for a newborn child.

In that small room, as Winifred worked on her tatting, they talked of home and family and how Lyndon had done them all proud. Winifred said she was content and her greatest joy was to walk along the Guadalupe to sketch the wildflowers blooming by its bank. She said she prayed often for Laura and for Peter and she no longer asked God to let her come home. Laura listened and watched the old woman sew lace on a tiny blouse and she wondered where was the great truth she had come to find. She talked of tatting, the roses, and the Guadalupe, all the while yearning to ask Winifred's forgiveness. If only she could be released from her guilt. She wanted to take her daughter in her arms, rock her and tell her how she should have been with her when the baby was born and how terribly sorry she was and how she would do anything in the world if she could change how life had been. But Winifred was an old woman sewing clothes for a child dead more than fifty years. Laura could only say good-bye.

They drove back to San Marcos in silence. As they moved through the harsh, low hills Laura was surprised to feel her mood lightening. She searched the hills and the passing trucks and the back of Wilton's head for the reason she was beginning to feel so free. Then she recalled the stillness of Winifred's paintings, the smiles of her friends, and the aura of peace that permeated her daughter's small room. In a strange way, Winifred's world reminded Laura of some Eastern sanctuary not unlike the world of the Maharishi, the Indian mystic who was making such a stir among the young. People spent their lives seeking that kind of peace. Then Laura began to feel the presence of the great truth her visit with Winifred had provided. She realized the pain and turmoil and guilt she felt were only proof of her humanity, even her sanity. She knew now that motion, suffering, and the terrors of feeling the approach of the dark were essential to life. *To truly live,* she thought, *one has to kick a fuss, shout and shake your fist*. Madness lay in stillness. Maybe she had not found truth in Winifred's room, but she had discovered peace was the last thing she wished to find, and she would never again need to fear for her sanity.

Laura's enlightenment, her discovery that the meaning of life was to kick a fuss, was the primary motivation for her migration to California. "I could stay here in San Marcos," she said, "or I can seek my fortune in California." She was ninety-three years old when she and her youngest brother, Lee, loaded up his silver Lincoln Continental and headed out Highway 10 toward Ozona, Fort Stockton, Van Horn, El Paso, and the City of Angels by the Pacific Sea.

It was the second time Laura had traveled westward through the Chihuahua Desert. She could hardly believe nearly sixty-five years had passed since she and Peter rode the train this way bringing horses for the fight against Pancho Villa and the other desperadoes of the border. She remembered the night Black

Cato came and she could hear the silver wailing of his horn and the thunder of gunfire and the screaming of dying horses. Then she remembered flying with Lindbergh and the sound the old biplane made as it rose above the hills. Now there were enormous jet airplanes that carried hundreds of people faster than sound and John Glenn had orbited the Earth in an iron beach ball and there were plans to send a man to the moon. *How completely the world has changed since Peter and I passed this way, our hopes so high, our lives so new.* As she looked out at the desert and the distant mountains, she realized that she and the world had changed enormously, yet the land, the Earth, seemed eternal.

Laura had never felt so free. When Lee had invited her to come live with him in California and meet the famous evangelists she had heard for years on her radio, she almost immediately accepted. *What an enormous change,* she thought. *If I can get to California where the air is always soft and fragrant and the hills are green and smooth as corduroy, it just might be I'll live forever, after all.* California is that magic province at the end of the rainbow and she longed to go there and bathe in a shower of color. But most of all, Laura yearned to see the Pacific Ocean. She had been to Galveston, with its melancholy gray horizons, yet she longed to see the Pacific, a sea that reached all the way to China and Mandalay.

In a small corner of her mind she felt uneasy about having run away from home without telling a soul she was leaving. She had not planned to keep her move to California a secret, it had just turned out that way. It was so much trouble to explain her reasons. She remembered how she had felt when Little Mattie had announced her plan to go adventuring in West Texas. And that's the major reason she did not tell Wilton or Eugene or Maxie or anybody else she was going to California, because she hadn't understood Little Mattie's motives, and it was certain they would not understand hers. In a way, it served them right. They rarely consulted her any more and turnabout is fair play. Besides, they would have argued endlessly about the move. She could tell they did not trust Lee, especially when he advised her to sell her house and all her things, and they did not trust her to make a reasonable decision. They should know by now, she thought, that she had a will of her own and would do what she pleased with her life. She sold her house for five thousand dollars cash down to the same Mrs. Parker who purchased her Hutchinson Street house, the balance to be paid into her account in quarterly installments. Lee had insisted he guard the cash for her on the trip. He would invest it for her when they got to California.

Now she was flying through the Sierra Nevada Mountains, through gardens fine and alive as Eden. Like Jack Kerouac, she was on the open road, her belongings tied in a red bandanna on a staff, her mind and spirit open to the adventures of a new life in a new land.

The town of Paradise, California, lies northeast of San Francisco in the foothills above the Sacramento Valley. In the early days it was mining country. The largest nugget of gold ever found in California was discovered in the Willard Mine below Sawmill Peak. It was called the Dogtown Nugget and weighed nearly fifty pounds. In the literature from the Paradise Chamber of Commerce, Laura learned the town had once been called the Apple Center of California. Of all fruits, Laura supposed the least likely to be found in California would be the apple. She had been looking forward to more exotic species, like guava or papaya or mango or some other tropical delight one might have found in Gauguin's salad. In fact, Laura discovered to her dismay, it was very cold in Paradise. The town was some thousand feet above the Pacific and at night the wind came howling down from the Sierras bringing a tenacious chill that settled deep into Laura's bones. The Chamber of Commerce brochure did not say what the town was famous for now. It took Laura a day or two to realize it was a mecca for those who wished to escape all those things Laura wished to experience. Paradise was as bland as tapioca.

When Laura asked about Frankie, Lee said she had lost her faith and left. Laura suspected she had lost her money, which in some people amounts to about the same thing. On her third day, she began to pressure Lee to take her to the "real" California. She would love to see the temple of Aimee Semple McPherson and the Mission of Capistrano, the endless fields of flowers, the stately palms and the fountains of bougainvillea spilling down the coastal range. She wanted to see the blue Pacific reaching west-ward toward Cathay and maybe fill a small bottle with its water to keep on her shelf.

But all she saw was Paradise, the town once called Poverty Ridge, where the Elks Club holds a picnic every July and there is a horse show on Labor Day and each October a celebration hon-oring Johnny Appleseed.

There were nineteen mobile home parks in Paradise, Califor-nia. Lee lived in one of them. It was called the Cape Cod Mobile Park. To Laura, nothing seemed farther from Cape Cod, or from California, for that matter. It did not take Laura long to realize that Lee was not nearly as well situated as she had imagined. His work as consultant to the evangelists of California seemed little more than a shabby effort to raise money for a struggling ministry called Adventures in Paradise. The church building itself was quite impressive, a kind of Nordic chalet set on a hillside over-looking Dogtown, the former stagecoach stop where the great nugget was found in 1859. The church was a confusion of angu-lar hardwoods and stained glass where each evening Lee preached about the Last Great Awakening. Then one or more associates would come forward to give moving testimony involv-ing miraculous cures from nosebleed and other dread diseases. At least that seemed the general sense of their testimony as translated through the static in Laura's hearing aid. The Sunday wor-shipers were primarily locals, a few lost tourists, and workers in the apple orchards. Most of the weeknight pilgrims arrived in the two Adventures in Paradise buses from Sacramento and Lake Tahoe. Lee told Laura everything would be fine if he could enlarge his fleet of buses so more tourists could be brought from Lake Tahoe to the Lord. He said the breakthrough would come when he could afford billboards to attract sinners from Reno.

In the brochure from the tourist bureau, Laura learned the road from Reno and Tahoe to Paradise climbed Donner Pass, a way so rugged that thirty-five people died in the winter of 1847 attempting to negotiate the pass. The trail was so steep wagons and oxen had to be hauled over the cliffs with ropes and chains.

The survivors were said to have eaten their dead companions. Laura felt it would be no less difficult luring worshipers across that pass to the Adventures in Paradise revivals. In fact, by the second week, Laura was thoroughly disgusted with her brother Lee, who spent all of his time with his ridiculous church. At first, he took her with him to Adventures in Paradise, but Laura hated every minute of it and she let him know it whenever she could. Then, as the days passed, he left her at home in the Cape Cod Mobile Park, where she paced in her room at the back of the trailer, growing more and more angry each hour.

Laura admitted to herself that her brother Lee planned to cheat her out of everything she owned. One afternoon Lee brought Laura her checkbook and asked her to write a check for a thousand dollars.

"I already gave you five thousand," Laura said. She was astounded that he would have such gall.

"That's all gone," he said. "It cost that much to bring you out here and to take care of you." But when Laura saw the two new Adventures in Paradise buses, she knew where the money had gone—to the ludicrous attempt to transport sinners from the casinos of Reno to Paradise. The next day, Lee asked her again for money. Laura refused. Then, as if she were dreaming, she saw her brother grasp her upper arms, and lift her, and shake her. "I've got to have that money," he growled. Then, realizing what he was doing, he quickly put her down again. He was trembling and sweating heavily and he wiped his brow with his arm. "I'm sorry," he said, avoiding her eyes. "But I'm your brother and it's important to me." It was the last time he shook her, but in the days ahead he tried threatening, coaxing, flattering, and starving her, yet Laura held firm. "I don't care what you do or say. I wouldn't give you a penny more, even if you killed me."

On the morning Laura decided to go home, she found she had been locked in her room. When she turned the door handle and realized her predicament, it was like a physical blow. She actually grew dizzy and had to hurry to the safety of her bed. She closed her eyes and tried to will the room to stop spinning. Her heart was beating wildly, and she had to press her hand to her chest to keep it from escaping and bounding around the room on its own. *How is it possible,* she thought, *that I could be locked in a house trailer in Paradise, California? Life is a circle,* she thought, as she remembered locking Winifred in her room so long ago.

It was not difficult to escape. All she had to do was lie. Laura promised Lee she would not run away. She apologized for her behavior, and even wrote him a small check for cash. Then, when he relaxed his guard, she called a taxi. At the age of ninety-three, Laura Woods wrote a check for her busfare, and began the long, lonely journey across America toward Texas and home. This time she did not feel like Kerouac. She had no cash for food, no clothes, only her thin cotton house dress and a purse. She felt empty, old and betrayed.

The Greyhound bus thundered across the Sierra Nevadas and through the long, lonely reaches of the Navajo, Papago and Apache. One night, at a rest stop in Las Cruces, the driver walked back to where Laura was gazing out her window at the lights. He asked if there was anything he could do for her. "Could I get you anything to eat?" he asked.

Laura thanked him for his courtesy and said everything was fine. "I'm going home, you know."

When Laura arrived in San Marcos, she moved slowly from the bus to a seat in Younger's bus terminal. She sat there as she had seen the others sit, first for an hour, then another. *I must move,* she thought. *In stillness there is death. I'll just have to start again. California was just another bump in the road.* But she was so tired, and she remembered she had sold her home to someone and she was not quite sure where she was. But it was not cold. Out the window she could see the night was clear. She decided she would sleep just for a moment and closed her eyes. She dreamed of the broad Pacific she had never seen. She awakened when Mr. Kornegay, a Hutchinson Street neighbor who ran the taxi stand next to the bus station, recognized his old friend and took her home. Then, she seemed to dream again and in the dream Wilton came and carried her to the car. She remembered thinking how amazing it was that Wilton had grown so strong.

And then she was at Maxey Charles's house and the dreams went away. She settled into a deep and untroubled sleep.

Laura willed her body to rise from the bed. She opened her eyes, but she could not see. She listened for footsteps or voices and all she could hear was the singing of silence. Then, in an instant, she knew exactly where she was because the room was filled with the aroma of freshly baked corn bread, made from a recipe she had learned from her mother and had taught her children to prepare. She thought of molasses and how, long ago, she had placed a drop of honey on blossoms to lure butterflies to her garden. She remembered about the great monarch butterflies and how they migrated thousands of miles from one coast to another in a single season. *Surely,* she thought, *if those fragile wings can carry a butterfly all the way across America, this old body can get up from bed.* As she rose, she was angry at the pain she felt in her body and she wondered what purpose it served in God's plan. Surely to be nearly blind, deaf, and bent like a Comanche's bow was punishment enough for her sins, although at the moment she could not recall a single one. She made her way toward the kitchen. She would have just a bit of warm corn bread, and then find where Maxey Charles kept the garden tools. She was digging a flowerbed by the side of the house when she fell.

One morning, Laura woke from a terrible dream that she had been taken to a home filled with very old people. They sat in the halls with alabaster faces and desperate eyes. Many lay in their beds staring at the ceiling or watching the blue illusion of television. Nurses in soiled white uniforms wheeled these very old people here and there and then left them scattered about like antique dolls. Laura called for Maxey Charles. A large woman all in white came and held her hand as she read her pulse. Laura tried to rise, and the woman held her down. "Now, now, sweetheart, lie back for me. Lie back and rest."

Laura had never been more furious and never more elated. She was furious that her dream was real, that someone had kidnapped her while she slept and had taken her to a nursing home. Her elation was due to her conviction that she could get out of this fix just as she had managed to overcome so many other obstacles in her life. *I survived the Wilderness Ranch, the mad trapper and the ragin flood. I survived the train wreck and Pascual Orozco. I survived brother Lee and Paradise, California. I raised a family of fine children. I started over in life more times than I can count. So there's no reason in the world I can't put this place behind me.* "Sweetheart, my left foot," she whispered to the haze before her eyes. *Maybe if I was old like these others I'd lie back and rest. But I've got things to do.*

For the next few days, Laura fumed and absolutely refused to accommodate herself to the schedule of the Lutheran Home for the Elderly. Most days she took her meals in her room, avoiding for as long as she could social encounters with the other guests who were so much older than she. Laura did insist on regular appointments at the home beauty parlor and the almost constant attention of a nurse named Milly, a black woman of immense kindness and understanding. She confided to Milly her plans to complete the final chapters of her life story and together they schemed to rescue the blue Olivetti from storage.

At night, when everyone in the Lutheran Home for the Elderly was asleep, Laura sat on the edge of her bed and performed isometric exercises. She took long walks in her room, and little by little the pain and disorientation she had suffered from her fall in the garden began to subside. Although she continued to insist Milly attend her hand and foot, do this and that, fluff the pillow, find her magnifying glass, discover where the staff had hidden her slippers or her hearing aid, she was indignant when each errand was accomplished. "I can take care of myself," Laura would insist. Then she would ask Milly to go see why her supper was late.

One day she noticed a difference in the atmosphere in the institution whose name she refused to let pass her lips. There was a kind of lightness in the air, a gentle expectancy, a wash of color she had not seen before. Christmas music played constantly, including "The Little Drummer Boy," a piece she had always detested. Soon it would be Christmas and then the beginning of the New Year 1966, and she was almost ready to put her plan into action.

One afternoon, as Laura was talking with Milly in the recreation room where carolers were entertaining the people who were really old, an attendant came rushing to their side. "Miss Laura, come quick to the telephone. It's long distance."

Milly helped Laura to the telephone, listened for a moment, then held the telephone sideways away from her ear so that Laura could hear as well. Laura struggled with the control on her hearing aid, then asked, "Who is it? I can't hear."

What Milly heard was this: "Mrs. Woods, this is the Johnson City White House calling for you."

Milly's eyes grew bright. "Oh, Miss Laura. It's the president. It's President Johnson."

"Hello, Lyndon?"

"He says Wilton said you weren't well."

"Tell him I'm just fine," Laura said.

"She's just fine," Milly said. She listened again, holding the phone away from her ear. "He says he's calling all his old friends and he wanted to wish you a Merry Christmas. He says he misses hearing from you."

"Tell him I miss him."

"She misses you, too, sir." Then Milly turned to Laura. "He wants to know if you have any ideas on how to end the war."

Laura grabbed the phone from Milly's hands and she spoke so loudly the carolers glanced her way. "What you need to do, Lyndon, is get more Texans in your cabinet!" Laura listened for a moment, then passed the phone back to Milly. "What's he say?"

"He says he loves you."

"Tell him I love him, too. Always have."

The next morning, just before dawn when the halls were still, Laura got up from bed, dressed and carefully applied her makeup. After looking in her purse to make sure she had her checkbook and her hearing-aid batteries, she squared her shoulders and walked down the empty hall, past the Christmas tree, to the telephone. She called a taxi. She drew herself up as tall as she could and then walked out of the building into the sunlight. The new day was unseasonably warm for December and there was a scent of cedar in the air.

As the taxi driver held the door open and Laura slipped into the backseat, she heard, or perhaps felt, a sound. *Whoopity, whoopity,* the sound seemed to say. Like the sound of thunder in a distant county. *Whoopity, whoopity.* Laura fumbled with her hearing aid. "What's that?" she asked the driver. He was looking up into the golden light of the dawn sky.

"Helicopters. Those big Hueys like they use in Vietnam." The driver closed the door, walked around the taxi, got in and started the engine. "Probably flyin' wounded soldiers to the military hospital in San Antonio." He peered out the window, searching for the source of the sound. "Hey, wait. I bet that's LBJ's chopper! Takin' folks out to the ranch for Christmas. I betcha old Lyndon's spendin' Christmas at the ranch."

"He is."

"Is what?"

"Lyndon is at the ranch for Christmas!" Laura said casually.

"Could be," he said. They were driving now. The *whoopity, whoopity* was merely an echo.

"Not could be. He is for sure at the ranch," she said politely but firmly.

"How do you know that?"

"Because I talked with him last night."

"Oh, you did, didja."

"He telephoned me from the ranch."

"Wait a second. Let me see if I've got this straight. Are you telling me that the president of the United States, Lyndon Baines Johnson, called you last night?"

"Yes, that's right."

"Well, tell me, little lady, what did you and the president of the United States talk about last night when he phoned ya?"

Laura could see the driver's face reflected in the rearview mirror. He was grinning like a Cheshire Cat, obviously making fun of her. She started to turn off her hearing aid and ignore him, but then she decided to answer him honestly and convincingly.

"He asked me what I thought we should do to end the Vietnam War."

She saw the silly grin disappear from the driver's face as he said, "To be honest with you, lady, I have a hard time believing that the president of the United States telephoned you last night and asked you how to end the war. But you sure don't sound like you're making it up. So if you say it's true, I guess it's true."

"Oh, it's true all right! There are lots of things about me— lots of things I've done—that you would find hard to believe, but they are all true. Matter of fact, I'm writing a book about my life. I'm going to call it *Hill Country*."

Then Laura spoke slowly and softly, more to herself than to the driver. "Some day I'm going to get that book finished—one way or another."

As the taxi moved on through the Hill Country, Laura noticed a cloud of monarch butterflies migrating toward the south, and she wondered again, *How beautiful is that place— where all the monarchs gather at the end of their long, long journey?*

AFTERWORD

SEVERAL DAYS AFTER THE DEATH OF MY GRANDMOTHER, MY father and I began to sort through her possessions, which had been moved from San Marcos to my parents' home in Seguin.

One of the first things I found was an old cardboard box labeled, "For my Janice when I'm gone."

In the box were her wedding ring, her old Olivetti typewriter, and all of her notes for the *Hill Country* manuscript.

IDENTIFICATION OF CHARACTERS

Judge Joseph Wilson Baines, grandfather of Lyndon Johnson; secretary of state of Texas.

Max (Buck) Bergfeld, great-uncle of author Janice Woods Windle; city marshal of Seguin, Texas.

Alice Benny Lawshe Brady, daughter of former slaves, Martha Benny Hawkins and Ed Tom Lawshe.

Dr. Albert Brecht, delivered Laura's daughter, Winifred, in Fredericksburg, Texas.

James Robert (Rob) Caldwell, husband of Winifred.

Winifred Woods Caldwell, Janice's aunt, daughter of Laura and Peter Woods (born 1895, died 1995).

Carnoviste, Apache Indian.

Liz Carpenter, personal friend and press secretary to the Johnsons.

Clifton Carter, assistant to Vice President Lyndon B. Johnson.

Judd and Nancy Catherton (at the request of the descendants of the murder victims, the real names were not used; Catherton is a pseudonym), murder victims who were ranch neighbors of the Hoges.

Black Cato, former slave who joined a tribe of Apaches.

Ball Coon, Indian elephant trainer for the Glasscock Circus in Blanco, Texas.

Lucy Hoge Copenhaver, Laura's sister.

Milton Copenhaver, Laura's brother-in-law; Lucy's husband.

Willard (Bill) Deason, White Star, appointed U.S. interstate commerce commissioner by President Johnson.

Thomas (Tom) Dunlap, first White Star to be elected to public office (1934) through efforts of the fraternity.

Ralph Edwards, first boyfriend of Winifred.

Jim (Farmer Jim) Ferguson, colorful and controversial governor of Texas, took office in 1915, impeached 1917.

Mariam (Ma) Ferguson, first woman governor of Texas.

Flournoy (a pseudonym), Woods family cousin.

Sam Fore, publisher of the Floresville, Texas, newspaper.

Gizzard, juggler in Glasscock Circus.

Sheriff Gleason, sheriff of Bexar County, Texas.

Professor H. M. Greene (Prof. Greene), teacher at Southwest Texas State Teachers College, San Marcos, Texas.

Gunther, the name used by the trapper at Wilderness Ranch.

Maxine Halm, sister of Virginia Woods; Janice's aunt.

Dr. Titus Harris, psychiatrist in Galveston who treated Winifred.

Charles Hoge, Laura's brother, founder of Hoge Oil Field.

John Campbell (J.C.) Hoge, Laura's father; husband of Little Mattie Hoge.

John Carlton Hoge, Laura's brother.

Lee Hoge, Laura's youngest brother.

Maggie Hoge, Laura's sister.

Martha Adeline (Little Mattie) Hoge, Laura's mother; wife of J. C. Hoge; great-grandmother of Janice.

James Steven Hogg, flamboyant governor of Texas (elected 1892).

Oscar Holcomb, Mayor of Houston.

Edward Mandell House (Col. E. M. House), Peter and Laura's friend who, as adviser to Woodrow Wilson, was considered one of the most powerful advisors to any U.S. president.

Loulie Hunter House, wife of Edward M. House.

John Ireland, Texas governor from Seguin, Texas.

Lady Bird Taylor Johnson, married Lyndon Johnson, became one of the nation's most beloved and successful First Ladies.

Lyndon Baines Johnson, thirty-sixth president of the United States (1963–1969).

Rebekah Baines Johnson, mother of Lyndon; wife of Sam Johnson; friend of Laura.

Sam Ealy Johnson, Jr., father of Lyndon; husband of Rebekah Baines Johnson.

Dr. Walter Kidder, Laura's neighbor at Wilderness Ranch.

Jeffersonia (Jeffie) Woods King, Peter's sister; Laura's school teacher.

Leon Klink, aviator who barnstormed in Texas with Charles Lindbergh.

Henry Kyle, prominent attorney in San Marcos, Texas.

Herman Lehmann, kidnapped by Apache Indians as a youngster.

Charles Lindbergh, aviator who barnstormed in Texas; made first nonstop solo flight from New York to Paris (1927).

Jacob and Justine Luckenbach, Laura's neighbors at Wilderness Ranch near Luckenbach, Texas.

Jane McCallum, suffrage movement leader.

Senator Tom McClanahan (a pseudonym), one of the state senators Laura persuades to vote for women's suffrage.

Sarah Cherokee Woods McGehee, Peter's sister.

Phil Medlin, "Singing Sheriff" of Guadalupe County.

Fritz Merton, chuck wagon cook for Peter on roundup.

Charles Montgomery, Peter's brother-in-law; husband of Sweet Woods.

Dr. Robert Montgomery, economist active in Roosevelt's World War II military planning.

Sweet Woods Montgomery (Little Sweet), Peter's sister.

Roger Moore, mayor of Seguin, Texas.

Butch Neill, young cowboy for Peter who later became prominent Hill Country rancher, storyteller and historian.

Pascual Orozco, Mexican revolutionary leader, active along United States–Mexico border.

Rattlesnake Pete, Rough Rider for Teddy Roosevelt; accompanied Peter and Laura on train to Fort Bliss in El Paso, Texas, along with Cherokee Bill.

Rev. Andrew Jackson Potter, Central Texas Methodist preacher; friend of Woods and Hoge families.

Daniel Quill, deputy county clerk, Bexar County, 1932; friend who made arrangements for Johnson wedding in San Antonio, later appointed postmaster.

Quint (a pseudonym), driver of automobile that stampeded Peter's cattle.

Horace Richards, first White Star; editor of school newspaper (1930).

Theodore Roosevelt, Rough Rider who became twenty-sixth president of the United States (1901–1909).

Fenner Roth, president of sophomore class (1930), Southwest Texas State Teachers College; later founded Roth and Richards Refrigeration Company in Corpus Christi.

Dexter Slade, ex-marshal from Dodge City, Kansas.

Valentine Smith, prominent Hill Country rancher and personal friend of Woods and Hoge families.

Claydene Hoge Steakley, Laura's niece.

Carrie Woods Stone (Aunt Carrie), Peter's sister.

Robert Ewing Thomason, Texas House speaker, who later became U.S. congressman and U.S. district judge from El Paso, Texas.

Emma Woods Thorpe (Aunt Emma), Peter's half-sister.

Hilda Weinert, national Democratic committeewoman from Seguin, Texas.

Woodrow Wilson, twenty-eighth president of the United States (1913–1921).

Janice Woods Windle, author; granddaughter of Laura Woods.

Cornelia Redd Woods, married to Eugene; mother of Betty Claire.

Ella Ogletree Woods, Peter's stepmother; second wife of Colonel-Doctor Woods; mother of Emma Woods.

Eugene Cavanaugh Woods, Laura and Peter's son; father of Betty Claire.

Georgia Lawshe Woods, Peter's mother.

Laura Matilda Hoge Woods, wife of Peter Woods, Jr.; grandmother of Janice.

Maxey Charles Woods, son of Laura and Peter.

Colonel-Doctor Peter Cavanaugh Woods, Thirty-second Texas Cavalry; Hays County physician; Peter's father.

Peter Cavanaugh Woods, Jr., husband of Laura; grandfather of Janice.

Pinckney Woods, brother of Peter.

Virginia Bergfeld Woods, mother of Janice; wife of Wilton Woods.

Wilton Eugene (Woody) Woods, grandson of Laura and Peter; son of Virginia and Wilton; brother of Janice.

Wilton George Woods, son of Laura and Peter; father of Janice.

William Wright, editor of *Blanco News.*

Acknowledgments

Hill Country is the joyous accomplishment of my family and many friends who helped me by providing interviews, research, access to letters, photographs, and personal papers.

Thank you to my wonderful, loving family: my husband, Wayne Windle; my mother, Virginia Woods; my son, Wayne Wilton Windle and his wife, Mary Jane; my grandsons, William Wayne, John Wilton, and Benjamin Emmett Windle; my daughter, Virginia Laura, and her husband, Randy Shapiro; my son, Charles Kendrick Windle; and my brother, Wilton Eugene Woods.

I am particularly grateful to Mrs. Lyndon Johnson and her daughter Luci Baines Johnson; to Shirley James, assistant to Mrs. Johnson; and to Harry Middleton, director, and to the staff of the Lyndon B. Johnson Library in Austin.

A special thank-you to Mittie Kirk Caldwell (Mrs. James Robert Caldwell), who celebrated her ninety-seventh birthday on July 11, 1998. Mrs. Caldwell not only telephoned me with information, she gave me a long interview. She is the second wife of Rob Caldwell, and provided detailed stories about Rob and Winifred.

And thanks to the superb Blanco historians and storytellers: Foster Carroll Smith, Roy Byars, Roy Finch, Tom and Louise Koch—you were fantastic!

The following are people who have helped me develop *Hill Country* (a few listed are now deceased). Many thanks to: Agatha Hoge Anderson, Phyllis Hoge Anderson, Sally Anderson, Jean Angelone, Joyce Armke, Leroy Armke, Howard Balenscifen, Cathleen Coats Barker, Gus "Pee Wee" and DeeDee Barr, Anne Bell, Bessie Bingham, Bea Bragg, Johnnie Buckner, Larry Budner, Liz Carpenter, Fred and Marian "Cookie" Clarke, Bill Cole-

man, Rogers and Mary Lou Coleman, Willie King Coleman,
Theora W. Crosby, Clay Dalton, Patty Dalton, Willard "Bill"
and Jeanne Deason, Isabell Thomason Deckert, Frank Donalson,
Raymond Dwigans, Marylyn Elwell, Georgia Mae Erickson,
Louise Weidebusch Felps, Lulynn Lawshe Foster, Michael L.
Gillette, Bonnie Glasscock, Suzanne Glasscock, Pete Greene,
Otha Grisham, Joe P. Harle, Mary Elizabeth Harle, Bessie Her-
ron, Bill and Garlyn Hoge, Doyle and Billie Ruth Hoge, Bonnie
House, Bessie Mae Johnson, Beanford and Ethel Kidder, Rick
and Michele Kinsey, Maggie Lambeth, Francis Lawshe Latham,
Lynn Lawshe, William H. Lawshe, Jr., Jeffie Carolyn Lemons,
Graham Little, Shirley Joe Little, Al Lowman, Mary Mont-
gomery Mauldin, Vonnie McCormick, Chester McLaughlin,
Daddy Jack Montgomery, L. C. Montgomery, Dr. Robert Mont-
gomery, Dr. Henry Moore, Jr., Maxine Montgomery Morgan,
Rebecca Garrett Patterson, Dan and Harriett Peavy, Janestine
Coats Pedigo, Dan Quill, Rose Hoge Reynolds, Edward Richards,
Horace Richards, Sen. Walter Richter, Fenner Roth, J. Lewis
Rutledge, Paul Rutledge, Gloria Woods Schlender, Dorothy and
Gene Schwartz, Jane Smith, Azalee Snow, Mary Nell Spak, Dr.
Claydene Hoge Steakley, Charles and Bess Stone, Melvin P.
Straus, Janice Woods Stroh, Roy Swift, George Woods Taylor,
Robert W. Tessing, Jr., Sharon Tippets, Beverly King Vansickland,
Del Ward, A. O. Webber, Bette Woods Wehner and Sterling
Wehner, Bernice West, Vernon Whiteside, Elizabeth Whitlow,
Dianne Wilcox, Roy Willbern, Libby Willis, Joe Wimberley, Dol-
lie Dale Woods, Gladys Woods, the people of Seguin who con-
duct *True Women* tours to historical sites, the McClure Braches
House committee in Gonzales, the board of directors and staff of
El Paso Community Foundation, Longstreet Publishers—John
Yow, Ph.D., senior editor, and Scott Bard, Director of Market-
ing—Leann Phenix, publicist, of Phenix and Phenix Literary
Publicists, and my agent, Robert B. Barnett. Special thanks to
Marah Stets, associate editor at Simon & Schuster, the publisher
of the trade paperback edition of this book.

In a multigeneration saga based upon the families of Woods,
Hoge, and Johnson, it is, unfortunately, not possible to use all

family members as characters in a historical novel. Many wonderful lives of relatives and friends that I knew and loved could not be biographed in *Hill Country*. However, it is important for the reader to know the names of all the children of the main characters.

Georgia Lawshe Woods and Colonel-Doctor Woods had eight children: William Pinckney, Sarah Cherokee, Carolina Davidson (Carrie), Georgia Virginia (Little Sweet), Peter Cavanaugh, Jeffersonia Ellen, Frank Lawshe, and Mary Lois. Colonel-Doctor Woods and his second wife, Ella Ogletree Woods, had five children: Emma Fischer, Lenora Ogletree, Ella Moore, George Sidney, and Wilton Davis.

Martha King Hoge and John Campbell Hoge were blessed with ten children: Charles Hugh, John Carlton, William Henry, Laura Matilda, Lucy Sarah, Marguerite Jane, James Monroe, Ella Cyrene, Sidney Lee, and Clay. (The Hoge family name, by the way, is pronounced to rhyme with *vogue*.)

Laura Hoge Woods and Peter Woods, Jr., had seven children: Eugene Cavanaugh, Maxey Charles, Winifred Davis, Leonora (Nona), Mattie King, Wilton George, and Peter Clifford.

Rebekah Baines Johnson and Sam Johnson had five children: Lyndon Baines, Rebekah Luruth, Josepha Hermine, Sam Houston, and Lucia Hoffman.

They were all good people, many of whom told me stories which now enrich this book.

AUTHOR'S NOTE

For information on the life of Herman Lehmann, I am indebted to two sources: *The Autobiography of Herman Lehmann* (Texas History Center), and A. C. Greene's *The Last Captive* (The Encino Press, 1972).

JANICE WOODS WINDLE is the author of the best-selling *True Women,* which was made into the enormously popular miniseries of the same name. A lifelong Texan, Mrs. Windle grew up in Seguin and now lives in El Paso, where she is president of the El Paso Community Foundation. In 1964, she was cochairperson on the El Paso County presidential campaign of Lyndon B. Johnson. She is married to attorney Wayne Windle and they have three children.

HILL COUNTRY

DISCUSSION POINTS

1. Why do you think Windle chose to tell her grandmother's story as fiction rather than writing a memoir or biography? Why does she include actual excerpts from Laura's own diaries? How do they shape your impressions of Laura?

2. *Hill Country* features incidents common to many tales of the Old West—including the attack on Laura's home by renegade Indians and the lynching of a suspected murderer. Discuss how Laura's reactions to these events offer insights into her character.

3. Why was Laura so attracted to Herman Lehmann? What does he teach her that changes her outlook on the world? Was Laura justified in keeping their relationship a secret? Should she have responded more forcefully to her father's attacks on him? Do you think Herman could have overcome his background and made a place for himself in Laura's world with her support? Why or why not?

4. Inspired by her mother's story of meeting Abe Lincoln, Laura dreams of becoming president one day. But Maggie also tells Laura "God . . . gave women the privilege of bearing and raising children. He gave men the responsibility of providing. Maybe you think that sounds unequal. But I don't think so. It's just the way it is" (p. 115). How does Laura incorporate these two lessons in her own life? Which do you think has a stronger influence on her?

5. Does the dinner at Peter's family home (pp. 144–47) change Laura's feelings about her husband and the world he comes from? Why does she leap to her father's defense when his political views are attacked by Peter's sister? Is she only trying to protect her father?

6. Laura gives up the chance to write a political column for the local newspaper when Peter asks her to live on the new ranch land they buy. Was Peter's request a fair one? In the end, is Laura's time on the land more than a sacrifice she makes because of her love for Peter? In what ways does it strengthen her confidence in herself?

7. Do you agree with Rebekah Johnson's statement that "The finer things in life are not things that just happen, [t]hey are things we seek. . . . It's all a state of mind. And then of gumption" (p. 191)? What events in Rebekah's own life contradict this?

8. Do Laura's political activities interfere too much with her responsibilities as a mother? Do you think she should have recognized her daughter Winifred's problems earlier? Why is Winifred more comfortable with Flournoy than with her own parents and siblings? Discuss the difference between Peter's and Laura's reactions to Winifred's deteriorating mental state and her eventual institutionalization. Whose behavior do you sympathize with more and why?

9. Laura treasures her friendship with Rebekah, yet she is overcome by jealousy and anger when Rebekah announces that her husband, Sam, is likely to be the Democratic candidate for governor. Are her feelings normal? Based on your own impressions of Peter, how realistic is Laura's hope that he might one day be elected to office?

10. Is Laura right to forgive Peter's acts of violence—from the killing of a Yankee soldier when he was a child to his murderous outburst against the driver who runs into his cattle—or is she blinded by her love and political ambitions for him? Do his own dark impulses make it easier for Peter to empathize with and understand Winifred's behavior?

11. Discuss Laura's role in persuading the Texas legislators to ratify the suffrage amendment by threatening to reveal secret records. Is this politics as usual? Do you believe that the end—granting women the right to vote—justifies the scheme devised by Wilson's trusted adviser, Edward House, and Laura's complicity in it?

12. After their horses are destroyed by Mexican revolutionaries and Peter retreats into a world of his own, Laura transfers her hopes to her youngest son, Wilton. How did she apply the lessons she learned from House to further both her son's and Lyndon Johnson's political careers?

13. This is a book about profound loyalty and friendship—especially between Rebekah and Laura, and Lyndon and Wilton. Years after helping Lyndon and President Roosevelt, by ensuring that donations for congressional Democrats made it safely to Washington, Wilton took the Fifth Amendment during an investigative hearing, refusing to answer questions about the transactions on the grounds that his answers might incriminate him (pp. 385–87). Why did he effectively destroy any possibility for his own political

career by invoking the Fifth? Do you agree with his actions? What do you think of the use of the Fifth Amendment today?

14. In her diary, Laura writes "Lyndon wears only two basic expressions, each with several subtle variations. One is unbridled joy and its various cousins, the other is a dark and troubled sorrow. Lyndon has always had a capacity for greater joy and deeper sorrow than any soul I know" (p. 382). Does this description support what you know about Johnson, whether from your personal memories of his political career or from books and articles you have read about him? Did learning more about him, his family, and background in *Hill Country* change your feelings about Johnson as a man and as a president?

15. Laura Woods wielded tremendous influence on local politicians, congressmen, senators, and several presidents during a period when women were just emerging as a political force. She was finally elected to public office at the age of ninety. In your opinion, were the personal sacrifices she made in order to achieve her political goals justified? How do the choices Laura faced compare to the choices available to politically ambitious women today?

Author's Note on *Hill Country*

Readers frequently quiz me about whether the characters in *Hill Country* are real. I tell them that all of the characters in my books are actual people, and the *Hill Country* brood was made up of red-blooded, living, breathing individuals who were human in every way. They were the leading actors on the stage of my own life.

During the first few months of writing *Hill Country* I was inexplicably tearful and depressed, which is not at all my nature. One evening, in a fit of frustration, I told my husband, Wayne, that I was going to abandon the story and move on to something else. Surprised that I would do such a thing—also quite contrary to my nature—he asked wryly, "Why don't you talk it over with a shrink? Maybe the two of you can analyze why this book bothers you so much." The mere suggestion that there was something more profound going on than ordinary writer's block made me feel as though he had turned on the light in a darkened room. All at once, I realized that I was actually grieving for the people that I was trying to write about. And, in those first months of writing, I had been almost paralyzed by the thought that though I was trying to capture their lives on the page, they were no longer with me.

I had to ask myself a hard question: Who would tell the story of their lives if not me?